Seasons
OF
Destiny

Also by Lee Dunne

Poolbeg Fiction

Barleycorn Blues
Dancers of Fortune
Goodbye to the Hill

Other Fiction

A Bed in the Sticks
Paddy Maguire is Dead
Does Your Mother?
Ringleader
Ringmaster
Requiem for Reagan
Hell is Filling Up
Trials of Tommy Tracey
The Corpse Wore Grey

Midnight Cabbie
Day of the Cabbie
Cabbie Who Came In From
the Cold
Virgin Cabbies
The Cabfather
Maggie's Story
Big Al
Harbour Hotel

Non Fiction

Sober Thoughts on Alcoholism

Stage Plays

Goodbye to the Hill
Return to the Hill
Does Your Mother?
Busy Bodies
One Man's Meat
Only the Earth
The Full Shilling
Tough Love
Bless Them All (One Man Show)

Co Adapter/Director – Plato's Dialogues

Television

Only the Earth
No Hiding Place
Callan
Vendetta
Troubleshooters
Wednesday Play
Weavers Green

Radio Plays

Whatever happened to you
Mick O'Neill?
Tough Love
Aunty Kay
No Hiding Place
The Pot Wallopers
Only the Earth
Kennedys of Castleross
Harbour Hotel
Konvenience Korner
(2,000 scripts in all)

Film

The Pale Faced Girl
Paddy
Wedding Night
Goodbye To The Hill
Do You Remember Bray?
Riley's Bonfire

MA Honours Screen. IADT.
June 2004

Seasons OF Destiny

LEE DUNNE

POOLBEG

Published 2006
by Poolbeg Press Ltd
123 Grange Hill, Baldoyle
Dublin 13, Ireland
E-mail: poolbeg@poolbeg.com

1 3 5 7 9 10 8 6 4 2

A catalogue record for this book is available from the British Library.

ISBN 1-84223-229 0

Typeset in Palatino 10/13.5 by
Patricia Hope, Skerries, Co. Dublin
Printed by Litografia Rosés S.A. Spain

www.poolbeg.com

About the Author

Lee Dunne burst into fame in 1965 with his novels *Goodbye to the Hill* and *A Bed in the Sticks* before the final part of the trilogy, *Paddy Maguire is Dead*, was banned by the Irish censor in 1972. By that time he had escaped from a poverty-stricken background to work as clerk, actor, singer and cocktail bartender in Jersey, before deciding to become a London cabbie to have more time to write.

Lee has written twenty novels and ten plays. Of his three movies, two were Hollywood productions, including *Paddy*, adapted by him for the screen from *Goodbye to the Hill* and banned by the Irish film censor in 1970. He has written plays for television and radio and has contributed 2,000 episodes of radio serials to RTE. He is currently a book critic for the *Sunday Independent*.

In 2004 he graduated with an MA Honours Degree in Screenwriting from IADT and in 2005 *Goodbye to the Hill* was launched on its 40th birthday by the Lord Mayor of Dublin in the Mansion House.

He lives in Greystones with his wife Maura, walks the coastline daily and at the age of 71 declares he is "looking forward to middle age".

His most recent novels are *Barleycorn Blues* and *Dancers of Fortune*, both published by Poolbeg Press.

Acknowledgements

I want to shout thanks to Gaye Shortland for the devotion she showed in editing this book. And to thank Jason O'Toole for his friendship and encouragement.

For Maura,
my unique missus who is my best friend.

Part One

1

Wicklow, Ireland

August 22nd, 1922

Sam glanced sideways at Deirdre and saw that she was equally bewildered. Father O'Keeffe had come back – as silently as he had left a minute before – to stand before them in front of the altar of the tiny church at Clara Vale, close by the village of Rathdrum, deep in the southern hills of County Wicklow.

The cleric seemed to have recovered from whatever had caused him to abandon the congregation waiting to witness a ceremony 'The Church' had wanted to avoid at all costs.

Sam flicked his powerful eyebrows at Dee, causing her to grimace as she killed the scream of laughter that almost exploded from her throat.

The priest gave a tiny cough behind his slender hand, a gentle call to the couple to take their eyes from each other and attend to the ceremony.

Sam had earlier complimented Dee as they arrived separately – their first night apart in ages – at the church. "Patient beyond imagining!" he had said with feeling. She had demurred but silently – truly she had never been frustrated or angry about their situation during the time the bishops had tried to deny them the right to be married in 'The Church'. And now she felt simply grateful that it was finally happening.

The priest had indicated he was ready to perform the ceremony just minutes after her brother Paddy had walked her down the aisle, 'giving her away' to Sam who was waiting with a smile, like a man who had all the time in the world.

As they moved to stand closely side by side, Sam whispered: "I'm finally beginning to believe I'm a very special fella!"

"About time, too," Dee said in a hushed tone. "You suddenly come to know what everybody else has known for years."

But then, as Mary Doyle, sister and bridesmaid to Dee, took up her position, Father O'Keeffe had chosen to disappear in the direction of the vestry.

When he reappeared he looked pale, this alteration to his appearance being the cause of the amusement landing on Sam and Dee as they waited to become man and wife. It's face powder, Sam thought, catching Dee's eye again in time to see her mouth the single word 'powder'. To add to their silent hilarity, the organist arrived at that point and began to play "Here Comes the Bride", clearly unaware that the lady in question was already standing beside her husband-to-be.

Before the ceremony, it had been explained to the congregation that the resident curate had been taken ill, Father O'Keeffe being ferried in at short notice to avoid postponement of the wedding.

Right up to the last minute, Sam had been half expecting another excuse from the clerics who were a law unto themselves in Catholic Ireland. They had all the power, this being applied particularly in the event of the marriage of a Roman Catholic to a Protestant. That one of their own might consider marrying a Jew hardly seemed to have entered the equation.

The slender, softly spoken cleric wasted no time in running through the wording provided for the occasion – he spoke hurriedly, like a man wishing he was somewhere else, and yet there was something touching about the care in him when he asked of Sam: "Do you, Samuel, take this woman to your lawful wedded wife?" His voice faded since Sam felt Dee's emotional response to the moment and found himself with joyous tears hovering on his eyelids, until a nudge from the woman he had loved for so many long years encouraged him to do the right thing by saying yes in answer to the question.

For her part, Dee could barely take her eyes from Sam's face as the wedding ring slid along the third finger of her left hand. For all the years of their loving, she felt she was coming to him for the first time, in consummation of a relationship come upon them over many years of being the best friend of the other.

Sam looked at her then and Dee was powerless to stop her tears. "I love you," she said quietly, somehow

3

holding back the laughter that almost broke free when Sam replied: "And why wouldn't you!"

The kiss stunned them both for several moments after they finally pulled away from each other in the back of the wedding car.

"Good God!" Dee gasped before she began to chuckle and shake her head in disbelief.

Meanwhile Sam blew tubes of air through the circle of his lips while he moved in a deliberate way to adjust his dress pants.

Dee feigned disapproval before her act crumbled to a gentle, throaty laugh. "You're very wicked, Sam Sweet, very wicked." She leaned closer and kissed his lips for a second: "And I love you for it. I love you for all you are, all you have always been to me."

Sam moved back, his hands on her upper arms, his deep dark eyes like oil shining in the sheer joy of the moment. Taking a deep breath as though he was drawing her into himself, he said: "Let me take a gander at you, Missus Sweet." Moved by the words acclaiming Deirdre's new title, her brand new fifty-three-year-old husband chuckled to cover the tears riding on his voice. "Missus Sweet," he repeated. "It sounds good on you, Dee."

"All I need is a child to go with it, Mister Sweet." Her emerald eyes twinkled as she cocked her head at him, a bold twist to her mouth. "I'm thirty-six so I'm in a bit of a hurry. Would there be a possibility you could rise to that for me?"

"D'you think you can manage to hang on till after the reception?"

His new kiss charged through her and she turned quickly passionate, pulling back in moments to look at him again in further surprise. "What have you done to me, husband?" She was quite breathless. "I was half alive until you scooped me up, rendered me helpless with all that you are, sent me soaring with all that you do to me!"

He kissed her forehead, wrapped her up in his arms then, attempting to ignore a nagging attack of the 'why me's'. How could any man touch for such luck in a short lifetime? Did any man deserve to feel as he did right now?

Sensing his disquiet, Dee pulled her head back. His facial expression caused her to touch his face. "What? What is it, Sam?

"It's – well – I thought I'd reached the limit of feeling." He sounded more than surprised, shook his head for a few moments. "You draw me out, make me better; you help me find new things in me, new levels of feeling even. It's something to gape at, I can tell you."

"You don't know the half of it," Dee said with a rasping chuckle. "From the first realisation that you were the love of my life, I was, as the poor girl said, undone." She embraced him, nuzzling into his neck, glowing in gratitude for her blessed life, even more so now that they had finally become man and wife. "And it's a real bonus now that you finally accept that you're a very special man."

"That you could love me makes me feel very special

indeed. I've even got to the stage where I don't worry I might wake up and find it was all just a beautiful dream!"

But Sam was trying to ignore the nagging mind that continued chastising him for feeling guilty because he was happy. 'You Jews are all the same,' said the voice that spoke its mind. 'You feel you have to be miserable, unhappy, not entitled to much more than your basic needs. Ridiculous is what you are. If you were asked why this should be so, you would not be able to render a sensible answer.'

Dee kissed him, he came back to the present, and they remained wrapped up in each other – the line of cars behind forgotten – their lips gentle this time, loving care replacing the earlier shaft of lust.

As the Rolls drove through Rathdrum, on the way to the reception at Dunbla House, which lay just north of Killiney, Sam remembered he was but a stone's throw from Avondale, the ancestral home of Charles Stuart Parnell, who alongside Michael Collins was his heart's hero. A great man burned at the stake of public opinion whipped up by his enemies and those who feared him for being a man of his time and, arguably, *the* man of his time. Until his love for Kitty O'Shea led him to the Divorce Courts of London and the front pages of the papers of that city, and damnation and ruin and an early death.

Remembering Parnell with love, Sam was soon caught by a fervent wish that Collins would survive the trip to County Cork. Moments later he found himself sighing before a drawn-out yawn stretched his face, while without moving he tried to see if Dee had drifted into a nap.

The morning was yet early, no time for a middle-aged man to be getting hitched, Sam thought. But, when the visiting priest – sent down from Dublin to perform the ceremony – had telephoned days earlier, Sam had given in. "I have a midday meeting in the city, Mister Sweet, so if you and your bride-to-be would agree to a nine o'clock ceremony, I would be forever grateful to you both."

Sam had acquiesced simply because he didn't want to risk another postponement, give 'The Church' another opportunity to block the wedding they had shuffled laterally from the first day Deirdre and he had applied for permission to marry, in the hope that it would simply go away.

Convert or not – Sam smiled grimly on the thought, as he heard Dee release the tiny sigh that signalled a nap was in progress – they don't want people to get the idea that a Jew, any kind of Jew, is welcome in the Holy Roman Catholic Church.

Collins drove back into Sam's thinking so that he could not shift his concern for the Big Fella's safety. There had been no end to the warnings that the Commander-in-Chief of the Free State Army should not, at this time, take on the hazardous visit to the county of his birth.

Sam shifted on the car seat and got a cigarette going with one hand. Instantly he felt a quick prick of discomfort in his chest. Moving away from Dee who napped contentedly, he lowered the car window.

Offering his face to the morning, he was more than surprised by the startlingly crisp mountain air as August moved closer to September.

He felt the pain in his heart area as surely as if he had been stabbed. He was not thinking in terms of a heart attack and he was not superstitious, so he was discommoded by the nagging notion – as though he was receiving some kind of sign that things had gone badly for Collins, who was making anything but a social visit to Cork.

Sam could not have known that in the moment of his fierce discomfort, his beloved Collins – facing the gunfire of the Anti-Treaty volunteers – had been killed by a bullet from a sniper's rifle. Not that the gunman had found his target – the deadly bullet had entered the back of his head, above the right ear, having apparently ricocheted off the nearest armoured car.

Dee moved closer to him on the car seat, sighing as though she missed him. He felt aroused with an urgency that caused him to chuckle – lust always arose when he was insecure – the idea of Collins being ambushed had encircled his mind for a few seconds. He let it go. Dee snuggled more deeply into the cushion of his shoulder. The familiar cheep sound she made confirmed that the quality of her nap had been restored. He smiled, forgiving himself for his dart of lust, welcoming his mood change, not dwelling on what might have happened in Cork.

Michael Collins could look after himself – besides, he would be protected by men willing to die in order to keep him alive. Like Sam, those men had walked through danger and the death of many comrades, in the absolute belief that they did so for the benefit of a country still finding its feet, a nation divided yet by the Civil War that had erupted back in June.

Dee whispered in her sleep and he caught the words "I love you" before another cheep assured him she was in the arms of Morpheus. Laughing quietly at the ease of her demeanour, on this day of all days, he said softly: "You're great, just great!" She had been easy throughout the time they had been forced to wait to get married – this was how she was about most things in life. So why would she be any different just because 'The Church' had finally decided to fold its hand?

"It was all right, love, I knew we'd win out in the end," had been Dee's smiling verdict on that period.

Sam moved to give Dee more support as the car lurched and swayed on the twisting mountain road. His reverie turned critical as he wondered if the powers that be in 'The Church' had deliberately sent a priest who was half-jarred, and surely homosexual, to baptise him.

Sam had converted, having passed an oral examination on the Catechism and the Precepts of Roman Catholicism. He had been baptised at a ceremony deep in the Wicklow hills – the venue had been imposed on the couple – the demigods in dark suits begrudgingly accepting at last that Sam was not going to fade away.

He didn't care that the priest was outrageously effeminate – the man was presumably celibate so it hardly mattered where his sexual predilections lay – not that Sam gave a damn one way or the other.

A wedding blessed by 'The Church' had been important to Dee – ergo, it mattered to Sam.

Dee had always been a free thinker but she wanted a church wedding for her father's sake. This came as no surprise to Sam who had been party to her first marriage to his late friend, Arthur Brewer. That time he had been the matchmaker – ultimately becoming the architect of the idea that demolished Pat Doyle's resistance to the notion of Deirdre being wed to Arthur.

This was an apparently irresolvable situation. Pat Doyle was well known as a man who would frame a ha'penny – he was also known as a very religious Roman Catholic. The fact that he was willing to eschew a man of untold wealth because he was a Protestant said it all.

Sam smiled, remembering how Pat had ordered Deirdre never to see Arthur Brewer again, or leave his house immediately. Deirdre had stood her ground in the room her father used as an office, her emerald eyes wary, her father's flaming with intent as he towered over her.

"I want you to tell me here and now, Deirdre, here and now in front of Sam Sweet, that you will dismiss immediately any notion you might have been holding that you are going to marry Arthur Brewer!"

Sam could still taste his reaction to the vehemence with which Pat had unleashed this demand. He remembered being all too aware that the tall, powerful ex-hackney driver was not above using every inch of his height to try and dominate his daughter.

Deirdre stood tall, her shoulders straight, and Sam

10

could only admire her quiet, respectful attitude. This cut no ice with her father. Pat's face was puce to the hairline while Sam wondered was he about to have a seizure of some kind.

She had spoken with quiet conviction: "I have never disobeyed you, Father, when I felt you were entitled to order me about, tell me how I should live my life. In my opinion, that situation no longer exists, and though I mean no disrespect to you, I can't possibly give you the assurance you want from me."

The big man's eyes had widened in disbelief – Sam saw his fists clench, hoped that his old friend wasn't about to physically attack Deirdre. He moved on his seat, prepared to spring between them, should that be necessary.

Finally, Pat, breathing down his nose like a confused bull, said in the flat adenoidal tones of his native city: "Hear me now, young woman, and hear me real good. I'm telling you now, just this once, that unless you promise, promise me here and now, that you will do as I say, I want you out of this house this very minute."

Sam was shocked to hear Pat talk in this way, standing like a large rock that had been dumped in the middle of his office.

No arguing with that, Sam thought.

Deirdre looked at Sam. "Will you wait and take me with you?"

He nodded his head. "Of course, I will."

She left the room and Pat turned to face Sam. "That you, of all people brought the Brewers into our lives! You're a Jew, part of a race that disowns them that marry out. Could you not have put the boot into this madness, before I even heard about it?"

"Times are changing, Pat." Sam recalled his sense of sorrow for the big man he had known for twenty-five years. "None of us has the right to tell another how to live their life, including a son or a daughter." He pressed on though he knew full well his words were falling on ears of stone. "Deirdre is the finest of the fine, and whether you believe it or not, Arthur Brewer is worthy of her. Besides that, he needs her and he loves her, Pat, and he is as decent a skin as you'll meet in this lifetime. I give you my word on that as an old friend. I'm only sorry you feel so strongly against it."

"He's a bloody Protestant, Sam. She is a Roman Catholic. The two do not go together, especially since he belongs to the Ascendancy. Can't you help me here?"

"We're talking about a young woman of twenty-one years of age, Pat."

At the same time Deirdre was in the kitchen embracing her mother, Elizabeth, grateful for her whispered support: "Between now and Easter, girl, I'll try getting him down off his high horse. If he'd met Arthur, if he knew him even as little as I do, he mightn't be so set. But, set he is, like cement at the minute, so it's best to let him be. Meet me for a cup of tea tomorrow, and we'll talk without whispering."

2

Dunbla House, County Dublin,

August 22, 1922

The newly weds had no problem admitting to each other that they would sooner have retired to bed for the day but, with Deirdre's family all present and correct in their best bib and tucker, Sam had no problem in accepting that this delightful, wild notion was simply not on.

Allowing this, he acknowledged that one member of the Doyle clan was missing. As Sam was all too aware – now that he had come back to earth again after the somewhat bizarre wedding – Cormac Doyle was alongside Michael Collins in Cork. One more reason, Sam felt, why his idol should return to Dublin unscathed – his brother-in-law was more than willing to die in the protection of the Big Fella.

In relation to the wedding reception, Sam had simply placed the whole affair in the reliable hands of Séamus Byrne and his companion Angela. The couple were getting on a bit, but Séamus still had his wits and his drive about him – once he kept the whiskey manageable – while his life companion could, for Sam's money, still create in the weariest palate the desire to dance at life's table.

They lived a semi-retired life in a cottage on the estate, their only official duty being the welfare of Kelly, the old woman of the roads adopted by Dee, who lived alongside them.

Séamus was showing wear and tear – the patina of self-abuse evident in his goat-like countenance – the dashes of red thrown across the whites of his eyes, above the twin puce patches like a mask that had slipped to his cheeks and across his nose.

Yet he looked and acted in a sparkling manner today, his butler's attire cleaned and pressed by his lady-love, serving drinks with the help of local girls hired for the day.

Angela, who had cooked all the food, was a handsome woman yet as she neared the age of sixty. She remained blessed with energy to burn, bustling about as she had always done.

When all food was ready and prepared for the table, she removed her overall apron and within minutes was acting as maître d' in the dining room.

She served a soup of home-grown vegetables, the accompanying croûtons wrapped in slivers of transparent ham dipped in flour and cooked in olive oil – this causing a ripple of delight among the guests.

Angela preened somewhat as she observed the entrée of braised beefsteak being ladled carefully and gently onto the plates with the kind of care she had drummed into the serving girls.

Deirdre gathered Angela to her for a hushed moment or two as the entrée plates were being taken away.

"That was the most delicious dish I've ever tasted," she whispered: "How did you manage it at all? Sam says the same thing."

"Absolutely, Angela," Sam leaned close. "You added a whole new dimension to the taste of braised steak – delicious, no other word for it."

"Ah thanks, Mister Sam, my own recipe." She turned to Deirdre, whispering now, protecting her precious secrets. "I tenderised the meat under the mallet, brushed both sides with a coat of liquid mustard, the pie crust is me usual, and today it did come out well."

Angela departed to supervise the arrival of the main course – great joints of beef, each guest offered rare, medium rare or well done, served with a Yorkshire pudding and vegetables grown in the walled-in garden attached to the property.

A dessert of fresh strawberries and cream was complemented by being served alongside some of Angela's shortbread biscuits and her own bread and butter pudding for the seriously hardy appetite.

As the guests filled the veranda overlooking the Dunbla shoreline, some were quietly in need of a nap after a full midday dinner washed down with a light Chablis and a well-rounded Burgundy. As liqueurs and cognacs were offered alongside coffee and tea, Dee was grateful for her own short sleep in the car coming from the church.

A group of professional musicians provided a fairly general musical entertainment, their programme of tunes taken from the operettas of Franz Lehar with some popular melodies from the Victorian music hall. Included here was a well-sung rendition of "Goodbye, Dolly" a song – synonymous with the Boer War – which was still popular more than twenty years later.

Deirdre arrived in the kitchen with a bottle of champagne. "A gesture of thanks, Angela, for your contribution to my wedding day – I won't ever forget your generosity of spirit." Dee was remembering how gracious Angela had always been, right from the moment she had first set foot in the house as Arthur's wife, all those years ago.

Angela sniffed back her own tears as she was captured by rapture over Deirdre's wedding gown. "Oh, Miss Deirdre, you're only beautiful, and your dress! Pale tangerine, lovely!"

Dee nodded, saying behind a smile of sheer happiness: "I could hardly wear white now, could I, Angela!"

This quip sent the earthy mistress of Séamus Byrne into a gale of laughter which ceased only when Dee kissed her face and thanked her again before returning to her guests.

By nine o'clock Sam and Deirdre were silent as they undressed in the master bedroom. Dee was quickly down to the red pantaloons she had made to give Sam a laugh on their wedding night. And laugh he did until she lowered the cotton pants, to reveal the full-length white stockings supported by wide red garters of her own design. Sam hurried up the undoing of his trouser belt, his eyes on her slender long legs, making no bones about wanting to make love to his wife. Not that Dee needed any further confirmation here – the evidence was in plain sight as he stepped out of the striped trousers he had worn under his frock coat.

"I knew you wouldn't keep your wife waiting on her wedding night, Sam Sweet." Laughter gurgled in her throat as she threw herself onto the great bed. She rolled around, tossing the bedclothes this way and that, chuckling in delight at their newly granted freedom, stopped now by the sight of Sam as he came to her grinning like a satyr, his tumescence allowing her to see that he continued ready and able to consummate their marriage.

Sam stood for a moment gazing down at her as though he could never see her enough. "You are an essential part of every day."

"I know what that means," Dee could barely hear her own voice. "Come to me now and come into me. Don't keep me waiting."

Sam knelt by the bed and began to roll down her cashmere stockings. She gasped as his hands touched her thighs and he, grinning wickedly, did a little finger dance to deliberately drive her to a level of distraction that made her want to reach out and pull him on top of her.

"You devil, Sam Sweet!" Short of breath and needing to laugh at her own discomfort, but unable to do so since his lips on her thighs had made a prisoner of her.

"Oh, I suppose I'd better do what you want," he said, his own breathing under some strain, as he drew the second stocking quickly from her leg. He ran his hands hungrily along her thighs and moved to lie with her, his mouth kissing her with all the fervour and passion she had known from him in their first lovemaking in the long grass of a field in New Jersey.

On that never-to-be-forgotten day – again they were using the married couple mask that had served the Cause so well – with their mission completed, they finally surrendered to the irresistible pull of love they had denied for longer than either wanted to remember.

Dee's legs were trembling as she moved to wrap him up, his entrance as thrilling and exciting and as new as that first time – even more so because of the trust and the confidence that devoted lovers grow into in the glow of giving and giving and giving.

Deirdre responded to his every move and sound, her mind playing its own symphony, while Sam groaned voluptuously as she held the length and the girth of him even tighter as his movement mounted in intensity.

In the moments of recovery that followed their tumble from the heat and the heights of their shared sensation, he found he was free of the muted anger he had tried to hide from Dee down the years of their waiting. He was here now, married, so how stupid was it to be beating a drum for an idea that had passed into history? He moved, and in a moment took his wife in his arms and settled down for a cuddle which would take them both to sleep.

As he felt Dee gently slide away into sleep's warm embrace, he said quietly: "Can we make a bargain never to go to sleep with a huff in the wind?"

Dee turned back to him, kissing his neck, touching his face with feather fingers: "That's the nicest wedding gift you could have given me."

She was gone then – sleep claiming her, taking her to the place of the good death after another day, another blessing from some god gone laughing at the joy his creation could inspire in people. This thought energised Sam as he lay gazing at this woman who filled him like life's energy coursing through his veins.

He got out of bed and sat on the balcony overlooking the sea below, bathing in the silence of the oncoming night. It was ten o'clock but there was light yet in the sky above the horizon where the two became one like an inspired abstract wall hanging.

The August day had been bliss-filled for him and he felt replete after the lovemaking with Dee. He began to feel guilty that he had been free of concern about Michael Collins since the dart of heart pain as he was coming away from the early morning church at Clara Vale.

In that moment the telephone rang and he reached quickly for the extension on the balcony table, not wanting Deirdre to be woken up.

As Brendan O'Connor's voice reached Sam, his eyes were riding the Killiney coastline on its way to Bray. The twilight was now swallowing the waning sun as it splashed a gold wash over the sand where the white beard of the ocean threw itself onto the shore.

Brendan, his right-hand man for some years now, came straight to the reason for his telephone call.

"Mick Collins was shot dead in Cork today. A bullet, a ricochet so they say, killed him instantly."

Sam fell forward onto his knees, his cry of rejection an elongated moan of the word *nooooo!* It was a hell-bent, fear-driven plea to turn back every clock in the world – a cry so pitiable that it brought Dee back to awareness in the instant, so that she was there to help him up off his knees.

"Is it Michael Collins?" Her eyes showed the despair they now shared, her intuition knowing the cause of the heart-torn cry that had left him so desperately wounded.

Sam nodded, falling back into the chair as the night closed in about the great snail of Bray Head in the distance, Killiney Strand slipping into the embrace of the landed darkness.

She set the telephone back on its cradle, then her arms were enveloping him, pressing him to her breasts, as he sat there – too numb to do or say anything, his tears falling – while he groped for the hope that Michael Collins was at peace in a just world somewhere.

Dee got him into bed and used the telephone to call their ageing doctor friend, Paddy Lote. She found herself shocked by the change in Sam's appearance. He seemed to have aged ten years in a matter of minutes.

Satisfied he was now resting, Dee took a bird-bath and donned a dressing-gown. Her head was filled with images of Michael Collins – a man she had never met, Sam and herself being of more use to the movement if nobody knew they were involved in the ongoing struggle.

She paused to take a series of deep breaths – a clear head was a priority – Sam needed all of her. She had to stay balanced, to fend off the price they would have to pay for this early death – Collins was just thirty-two years old – in Cork.

When she had left Sam he was sleeping deeply, but she could see that the weariness of his spirit had turned his beautiful face into a map labelled pathos. This image of him added to her sadness, but this was no time for tears or projections as to what might happen.

Knowing how resilient Sam was, she had left him to the recovery that deep sleep would surely bring. In her drawing room, she telephoned her closest associate in the Lying-in Clinic, Joan Ryan.

"I won't be with you tomorrow, Joan –"

Dee got no further as her Number Two chortled and said: "I wouldn't be expecting you and you on honeymoon, Dee!"

"Sam's not well this evening, Joan." Dee kept her impatience at bay. Joan was a wonderful woman who shared Deirdre's lust to help the needy and was also involved in a passionate affair with a man who was as married as she was – she meant no harm, her energy and her earthiness being at times a boon to the convalescence of many a patient who had come through a difficult birth.

"Oh love, you take all the time you need! And fret not, Dee – between us here we will manage until you can come back to us. And don't be miffed with me for being bawdy, will you?"

"I cherish the bawd in you. Now I have to go, see if

21

my husband needs anything." Dee chuckled. "I'm practising those two words: *my husband.*"

The telephone call ended and she went to her drawing room, astonished that she and Joan had talked about Sam's health and the clinic, and had a chortle about 'my husband', without so much as a mention of Michael Collins passing between them. Such is the world, she thought, so much going on at such a pace even great men can be forgotten in no time flat. She took out the book in which she had, like her mother before her, begun to record the things that mattered in her life but in minutes she was dozing by the fire although it was only just past eleven o'clock.

At twelve, Sam woke up and went to the bathroom. Dee came awake in the instant she heard the tap running upstairs and went to find him. She watched silently as he rinsed his face over and over in cold water. Going to the bedroom, she picked out a dressing-gown and took it to him as he was drying himself. He kissed her gently on the lips, nodding his head, allowing her to tie the cord for him. Then he took her by the arm and brought her back to the bed.

"I'm all right now, Dee. You go back to sleep. I promise you, I'm fine."

Knowing that tone and ready for sleep, Deirdre kissed him and by the time he had walked out of the room onto the veranda, she was already snoozing.

He stood smoking a cigarette – he had to try coming to terms with the news of the tragedy in Cork. He didn't have to remember the man – there was simply no forgetting him.

Even now, standing above the night shore invisible but alive to him through its sound as the sea found the sand, he was still shaking his head a little in denial. He had done this many a time, shaken his head in sheer disbelief over Michael's ability to be out and about on the streets of Ireland, despite the price on his head in the past. He remained in awe of such raw courage, grateful that Collins had it in abundance as he faced continual stiff resistance to many of the positions he had taken.

Sam had been staggered by the tolerance Collins had shown in the face of accusations of perfidy on his part. This related to his agreement to work with his old Republican comrades – conflicting loyalties apart, it was a case of too many loyalties – unwisely he sought to solve the country's problems by exploring any avenue offered by those who were seeking to force their separate solutions. Sam let go of a sigh that voiced the words of Othello as they applied in this instance to Collins, though not in a romantic context: *"One that loved not wisely but too well."*

Sipping a brandy, Sam lit a cigarette, allowing his mind to segue to the mission set up by Collins back in 1920, when he unleashed his team of trained assassins against the elite of England's killers.

Sam had become involved, more by accident than design. Cormac Doyle had been one of the gunmen – his role turning to a disastrous farce that had cost the lives of Arthur Brewer and Lisa O'Brien who had been, half a lifetime before, Arthur's 'belowstairs' mother – while his birth-parent had eschewed him – and mistress to his father.

Placing Arthur on the back seat of his car, Sam had

covered him with a tartan rug, and closed the door. As he opened the boot, Cormac arrived with Lisa's corpse wrapped in a sheet. Sam helped him shove the body in and slammed the boot shut. A few moments later, they drove away from the hotel, Sam keen to get out of the city as fast as possible but driving easily to avoid attracting attention.

As they reached the township of Blackrock, Sam had things worked out sufficiently to be able to tell Cormac what they had to do.

"The way it happened, nobody needs to know about that," Sam said, nudging Cormac with his elbow. "Do you hear? Nobody needs to know."

"I shot Arthur."

"Arthur was in the wrong place at the wrong time, and Lisa. We have the bodies, so nobody need ever know what happened. Now stop looking like you want to kill yourself, and tell me you're with me on this, tell me you can understand what I'm saying to you."

"But I didn't get the officer – you had to do it."

Sam gave him a severe dunt with his elbow and Cormac winced in pain. "He's very dead, Cormac, so you got him, right? Only you and I know how it happened. A lot of these very special English spies are gone for their tea this morning, along with your man. Mission completed." He got a cigarette going, took a deep drag from it and passed it over. "Jesus knows the extent of the retribution that'll come down on our heads." He lit one for himself. "So, you shot him, Cormac. Tell me, say it." He inhaled deeply as he waited for confirmation from Dee's brother.

Cormac nodded but Sam needed more.

"Let me hear you say it. You have to say it, believe it, come to feel it, whatever it takes. We have to get our story straight and stick to it."

The young man exhaled a wall of smoke and then he said quietly: "I shot him."

Sam glanced sideways at him a few times, saw him begin to shrug off his melancholia, but not yet free of concern.

"Arthur was Dee's husband," said the boy. "What are we going to tell her?"

"Arthur got hit in a shooting on the street," Sam said firmly. "We only found him because we were looking for him all night. The pair of us spent hours looking for him, have you got that?"

Cormac looked at him, no longer shaking in terror. "You're a cool customer."

"We found him on Sackville Street. That's close enough to Monto for Dee to buy it. Oh shit! I forgot about Faires, his driver. Where the hell was he?"

"He's one of us," Cormac said. "He had a mission just like I had. He knew Arthur wouldn't need him before breakfast. He'll be over at Lisa's house now, looking for him."

"We tell Dee we found Arthur on Sackville Street, between Nelson's pillar and the bridge on the east side. You OK with that?"

"Yeh." Cormac was subdued but he was back in control. "What about the body in the boot?"

"It's something I won't be showing around. We'll have to dump my old friend into some wet concrete.

You and Brendan, get something fixed for tonight. I'll drive by when it's dark, and we'll give Lisa a midnight burial. The job the bullet did on her – she wouldn't want anybody to see her like that. And she knows I'm doing the best I can in the circumstances. She was a good girl, and I always loved her like a real pal should."

As they turned into the drive of Dunbla House, Cormac said, "You're probably right about reprisals. Lloyd George's piles could explode when he hears about this operation."

Despite all that had happened, Sam chuckled and punched Cormac in the arm. "You hold onto the sense of humour." Cormac nodded, Sam hoping the lad would be all right now. "You're right there, about the Welsh Wizard's piles. But no matter how heavily they come down on us, the world is watching, and this will bring the Brits to the table. They'll sit down with Dev and Collins after this."

He turned to look as he heard Dee come out of the house. "But do you know what? I don't honestly know if we'll ever really be a republic, like we dream about when we're in our cups."

He took Dee in his arms as she turned from the sight of Arthur's body on the back seat of the car. "We brought him home, Dee. We might be grateful he never knew what hit him."

She was weeping but she knew he was right. "God love him," she said, her tears touching Sam's neck.

"Paddy Lote will sign the death certificate and we can bury him here at Dunbla," Sam said quietly as he took her towards the house. "He's home for good, Dee."

"He loved the Pets' Cemetery," she said weeping. "We'll lay him to rest there; it's so peaceful and still. Can we do that, Sam?"

"We can do anything you want, Dee. You're the boss around here now."

3

August 1922

The week following the death of Michael Collins was a brutally sad time for Sam Sweet, the big man stalking his mind – flashes of him falling down dead in his home county of Cork, where he had been born just thirty-two years earlier.

Sam's inability to accept what he called the madness of this murder was choking his will to be reasonable. What other name could you give it, he asked himself, knowing his friend had been trying to pull the country and its warring factions together.

Such culpable stupidity seemed to stultify his ability to accept the death as a fact of the uncivil war. The pain and soreness of his mind and heart between them kidnapped his reason – he could not consider the hows, the whys, and the wherefores of the tragedy. He was fit for little else but walking the land and the seashore at Dunbla.

In the middle of their honeymoon week, Deirdre,

about to leave for the Lying-in Hospital in Dublin, stood for a while on the headland above the ocean watching Sam as he forced his legs along the water's edge. As day followed day, she had left him to his private grief, knowing that no words could help him through this time. Sam, one of nature's listeners, had turned deaf to well-meant words and acts of kindness.

Deirdre understood this all too well – this private time of his walking and weeping – it was like a silent retreat to get in touch with his inner self, the part of man that helps him release the need to understand.

At the start of the week she had sent the children – Eddie, Alfie and Sam's daughter Sarah – to stay at the house at Merrion Square, to allow Sam the space to mourn his loss in peace. In any case, school was about to resume after the long summer holidays and, during the school term, the children would spend five nights at Merrion Square each week, coming down to Dunbla each Friday evening and returning on Sunday night.

So Deirdre left Sam alone, knowing that his suffering, this intimacy with his grief, would lead him to new discoveries within himself. This belief allowed her go in comfort to work with the poor of Dublin, women in childbirth, some of whom had never slept between a clean pair of linen sheets before arriving at the clinic.

On the eighth day Sam took off his shoes and socks and paddled in surf rough enough to wet his pants to the knee. The water was very cold and he began to weep as a need for revenge rose in his chest and throat. Somebody should pay for the death of Collins – but who?

A hell-bent sound tore across his mind as he heard

his accusing voice spit out the words: "What if it was one of ours shot Mick in the head? A ricochet is very bloody handy. And if we're good at anything it's producing bloody turncoats!"

Sam was staggered by the notion, appalled for a few moments that he could even give houseroom to such an idea. Relieved that he had not articulated the words to another, he was willing to back off but, when he thought about the numbers of men who had gone over to the Republican side after the Treaty had been signed, he felt no shame in allowing that his outrageous consideration was not totally far-fetched.

He fell to his knees as the words 'Help Me!' slipped from his heart – this prayer to a god unknown, a plea and an admission that he felt incapable of going it alone. The water washed about his waist now and he knew that he had lost faith in men he had been willing to die for. Volunteers whom he knew – men he was on first-name terms with, many of them who had used the arms he purchased for the cause – some of those had deserted Collins. Men who shared his beliefs had deserted him to join the de Valera faction, refusing to settle for the Twenty-Six County Treaty that Collins and Griffith had signed in London.

Those men, along with the rest of the country, knew by now that Lloyd George had outmanoeuvred Collins and his team – the British Prime Minister had warned the Irish revolutionaries and Collins in particular, that unless they accepted the offer that was on the table he would unleash upon Ireland the greatest fighting force the world had ever seen.

Sam stood up in the surf and began to undress, flinging his clothes onto the sand. When he was naked he threw himself into the waves and swam along the shoreline until he was out of breath. Coming to his knees on the sand and stones of the beach he knew that he had lost trust in those who would soon be running the country. Allowing that he could be wrong, he continued to believe that Dev had won the day, won everything. This included the prize of staying alive, his reward for refusing to go to London as part of the Treaty Team, while he left his arch-enemy Michael Collins to carry the can.

Sam picked up his sodden clothes and got dressed, aware of his fingers on his skin now, like someone coming awake after a deep sleep. 'How could you have forgotten, Sam?' He felt a sliver of amusement as he asked himself the question. 'How could you have so forgotten the sense of touch? After all the peace and space it helped you find. My God! You really were shattered by the news from Cork.'

He had discovered this simple device – or, as he would say down the years to come he "came to his senses" – one day while driving his motor car. Of course he was in a hurry, otherwise the horse-drawn dray loaded with straw bales would not have annoyed him so. The glorified single slip of laneway led to the main Wicklow-Dublin road and he was deeply resentful that some farmer was holding him up when he had an important meeting in town. He grabbed the steering wheel in exasperation, and found that his resentful feeling towards the farmer had been taken away in the instant. Letting go of the contact between his fingers and the steering wheel, he found that he was looking at his watch again, immediately caught up in the day-to-day demands that life presented as a matter of course.

Sam stopped the car and lit a cigarette. He gave all his attention to the feel of the cigarette between his fingers, watched the tip as he drew smoke into his lungs, knew the taste of tobacco on his tongue as he exhaled, and laughed out loud as he savoured total freedom from his earlier need to push the farmer and his horse and dray off the road so that he could get on.

For a couple of weeks he remembered to practise this simple exercise. He was happily impressed when, each and every time, this link to living in the present moment set him free of past and future angst. And it happened through making contact with any of the five senses, the simple act enriching his life by allowing him the power to get out from under all the stuff that clogged up the mind and any iota of creative thinking.

There on the beach he vowed to practise the exercise, using the senses to be free of the past and its aggravations. He would use it too, to avoid getting caught by the often nebulous fear and dread about something that might never happen.

Cold though he felt in his wet clothes, he was certainly refreshed from the skinny dip and began using the sand in his shoes as it rubbed against his feet to practise another moment in the present.

While he stayed with the exercise he felt free, released in the *now* from the shock, the pain and the resentment he had harboured toward the Republicans who had taken the life of Michael Collins.

He found he could smile, however wistfully, at the memory of his nerves jangling just a bit at seeing so many Crossley Tenders in the Four Courts area on the morning of The Rising – relief surfacing when he realised there was not a heavy commitment of soldiers on the streets. It seemed that British Intelligence had not prepared the army for what was to happen on Easter Monday 1916.

Walking the strand at Dunbla he found that his energy was slowly claiming its place in the ongoing story. He felt relief he had been rescued from the sea of inertia that had engulfed his dreams and his hopes for Ireland, and it was in this moment that he became certain that his life would never be the same again.

This was a strong feeling, though he could not have articulated how this change would happen. He simply felt sure and certain that his overall response to all that was going on around him was the catalyst that would point him in this new direction and give him the strength to do what he had to do.

Right away he felt an urge to go and write down the memories and the sequence of events – at least headlines and highlights of the years up to and since the Easter Rising. This appealed to him, to get some kind of journal going, memories, feelings, hindsight and whatever came to mind.

He would preface his journal of ideas with some lines about Collins – this eulogy and obituary, however unconventional, would be his letting go, emotionally, of his attachment to his dead hero. In this vein, Sam would write: *"The procession behind the coffin of Mick Collins was three miles long – he had his critics and made many enemies as he used violence to bring the Brits to the table, but surely this was evidence that he was loved and respected beyond believing. He was a man who never sought the public's favour, driven as he was by what he believed in, the right for Ireland to belong to the Irish. All that needed saying was articulated by the tears of Kevin O'Higgins, who on hearing of the killing in Cork wept openly, his idealistic heart shattered by the death of the young man on whom greatness had been thrust. God bless you, Mick."*

Picking up a stone and throwing it as far as he could across the ocean's surface, Sam let his mind go back to that Easter Monday morning when he had driven Collins up along Bachelor's Walk, the Liffey flowing by the passenger side of the motor car. This was just hours before Pádraig Pearse, Arthur Griffith, James Connolly and others prepared to launch an insurrection that would shake the British Empire for a long time to come.

Sam bent down to the shore and allowed a wave to wash over his hand. He allowed his memory to transport him back to the spot where he had jumped up onto the Liffey wall to dive into the river after a boy who had stolen his wallet back in 1902.

Twenty years later, he shook his head disbelievingly at the memory of tearing off his jacket and kicking off his only pair of good shoes as he prepared to go into the Liffey after the young fellow.

Those moments were etched onto his memory, uncounted seconds turning to minutes that altered the entire course of his existence – a couple of minutes in the river's fearsome embrace, three at the most from his lifetime, ensuring that his life was about to be turned on its head.

Now, just eight days after his wedding to Deirdre, he knew that the death of Michael Collins had ensured that Sam Sweet was facing another major change in his life.

A notion as to what that change might be had begun to arise, but not enough to say it aloud, articulate it even in his mind. He would let the hare sit, allow the thought to find its own small steps, certain of just one thing – he didn't want to talk about it, not even to Dee.

Deirdre commented on the elevation of Sam's spirits at breakfast the following morning. She had been late home from the Cork Street Clinic the night before. "You were dead to the world as I slipped into bed beside you. I cuddled into you and I was gone myself before I knew it."

As she had joined him at the table, he had risen with his arms outstretched and she had come into his embrace to contribute towards the kiss she needed more than anything else.

When she stepped back, breathless from the power of his great hugging way, she moved her head gently from side to side, as though wiping out the illusion that he had not been around the place for some time. Her smile grew as he shrugged and offered her his most disarming grin.

"I'm all right, Dee."

"Welcome back, dear heart. Sorely missed was my man." She kissed him again before they sat down to share their first meal in nine days, he looking across the table with such intensity it seemed as though he needed to burn her image indelibly onto his mind.

Touching his fingers on the table, she said: "Had there been no grief after what you two lads had achieved together, that would have made no sense at all."

Sam leaned forward to kiss her fingers, his eyes misting over as he looked up again. "Let's not forget that the work I did for Mick didn't happen without a fair bit of help from you." He grinned, sniffing back his emotions. "Especially on that afternoon in New Jersey – you probably don't remember." He was teasing her and she knew it and loved it. "When we had left Slim what-do-you-call-him?"

"I forgot his name about five minutes after you stopped the car," Dee said as memory transported her back there to that never-to-be-forgotten day in America. "You mean the man with the warehouse filled with weapons, guns stacked to the ceiling?"

"His name was Slim Levine," Sam smiled. "No more messing – that afternoon is branded on this old memory. Am I right in thinking it was you, dear wife, you, that asked me to stop the car?"

They began to laugh together and he reached for her hand.

"I pulled onto the grass verge of the open road," he said. "There was little or no traffic in the mid-afternoon.

New Jersey was so anonymous to our eyes it could have been anywhere in America."

"You turned to me," Dee said, her eyes shining, "and you said 'What're we going to do?' By way of an answer, I put my arms around you. My eyes were cloudy, clouding up with this heat inside me. I was beyond shameless." She lit her first cigarette of the day.

Sam declined, sipping his tea, wanting to stay wrapped up in the reverie that even after years never seemed tired or worn.

"I had a need, a desperate need to know you like I'd never known you." Dee shook her head in mock disbelief. "I was as free as the most promiscuous hussy."

They had spent hours in the sun of the afternoon on its way to evening. They made love again and again, Deirdre fascinated as she handled him, her eyes wide as her fingers induced tumescence, shaking her head once more in awe as he swelled yet again in the waning light.

"I love you, Dee," he said now.

"I know," she sighed and he could feel her joy. "And I love you."

"I feel as if I've been given new lungs, Dee, sort of released."

"I know."

"Something important has been added, some impediment has been shifted – I can breathe deeper than ever before."

When they finished breakfast, Sam rose and took Deirdre's hand. Without a word she allowed him to lead her up the stairs and into their bedroom. No word was said as they met each other in the sunlight that streamed through the open window.

Deirdre went to the Cork Street Clinic in the early afternoon – she would run the evening shift and stay that night with the children at the house on Merrion Square.

Sam ate dinner alone and later decided to walk down to May Murray's public house. The idea of drinking a pint or two of Brewer's Stout seemed like an agreeable idea.

There was a gentle twilight landing on the evening as Sam, to his surprise, came upon Séamus Byrne hobbling along ahead of him. "Should you be heading to May Murray's house, will you allow me to buy you a drink, Séamus? Goodness knows I owe you more than that." Sam shook the manservant's hand carefully, aware that the ageing Kerryman was plagued with rheumatism.

"Mister Sam, it'd be a pleasure to have a drink with you, God knows. I'm almighty glad to see you up and about and well as a mountain goat again. As you'd know, I was rent in the heart about Michael Collins."

Sam nodded his head and steered the chat away from the tragedy in Cork. He ordered a pint of Brewer's while Séamus settled for two drinks, a large whiskey which he would chase with a pint of his late master's brew.

Séamus talked about his life of semi-retirement – of how much he and Angela valued the chance to be caring for Kerry, the old woman of the roads. Sam felt warmed by the charity evident in everything Séamus said, but when the manservant drifted into pointing out some of the local farmers, Sam found that he had no interest. He knew none of the men drinking in the public house kitchen. Neither was there anything about them to suggest that they were prepared to be friendly – he had noticed since coming to Dunbla that the headland presented an essentially hostile environment to the newcomer.

He had spoken a few words of greeting to May Murray, a woman in her mid to late thirties. She was of a modest and agreeable way – his wish that her public house would continue to thrive, common courtesy. The kitchen-bar was crowded, May doing good business despite the turmoil of Civil War, a conflict sad enough and bad enough that it had turned brother against brother in the name of Ireland.

Some months later, Sam would reflect on the few hours he had spent in May Murray's place in the company of Séamus Byrne – images would stand up to be seen, moments to be remembered, so that he felt at times that his inner awareness was reminding him, yet again, that things are rarely as they seem to be.

At this time, Sam was completely unaware that May Murray had a plan to acquire a sizeable share in the division of the Brewer fortune. He could not have known that she believed she had the means to get her hands on a large part of this fortune including all the attendant properties at home and abroad.

4

August 1922

Pack Rowan was leaning against the wall one side of the open doorway when he saw the manservant from Dunbla House arrive in the company of a gent. He was sipping a pint of plain porter when the toff accompanying the Kerryman surprised the hell out of him by bidding him a good evening.

Sam had noticed the itinerant leaning against the wall of May's house as he followed Séamus in from the road. He was merely being civil as he bade the man a good evening, pleased to hear a civil response though he didn't catch the words.

Pack was so surprised by the greeting from the toff that he gulped his mouthful of porter, which delayed his response so that the words – "Good evenin' to yourself, good sir!" – followed Sam into the kitchen where May Murray was busily serving drink to some impatient customers.

Pack, who was currently doing casual work for May,

tended to linger by one of the open windows of the house – a public house since Seán Murray, deceased, father of May, had been granted a licence to sell alcoholic beverages from the kitchen of his granite-built home.

Seán, a sometime pugilist, had won the property by betting on himself in a bare-knuckle fight that eventually stopped after more than an hour, when his opponent could not rise from the dirt. Seán had moved into the house immediately and, through a solicitor with political connections, gained the drink licence for a tidy sum above the cost of the paper, allowing him to operate as a licensed publican. He had aged since the fight, never fully recovering from the beating he took from his opponent. Both men died within a year, with just weeks between their funerals.

Pack Rowan drank outside the house since tinkers, sometimes called knackers, were not allowed to drink inside with the farmers and others that were the backbone of May Murray's clientele. They were allowed inside the door to buy but had to imbibe off the premises.

Pack sneered at these bogmen, some of them only short of hay growing in their ears. 'If only yis knew, lads,' he let the inner chortle have a rip like a good fart, 'if only yis knew that Pack Rowan gets tucked up in the bed of the landlady! God, wouldn't that be 'Sally Come Home in The Dark'!'

May had been taken by Pack from the first moment she laid eyes on him. Being all too aware of the prejudice against tinkers that was stitched into the Irish mentality, she was very careful about keeping this part of her life private.

She had lived in England long enough to have shed some of the fear and the hatred of travelling people drummed into her by her father, but the old attitudes were solid as rock, and having no desire to change the world May's mind attended to her own business. She had her dream but it was not some kind of fairy tale – right now she was waiting to find out if Pack was the man to help her make the dream come true.

For months she had been waiting to find the right man to work as her partner. Within days of Pack's arrival at Dunbla, she had seriously begun to believe he was the very man for the job. Suddenly she was paying more attention to her appearance, intent on one thing – and one thing only – getting to know Pack Rowan. She had to find out if her intuition about him was correct since she needed a special sort of man to support her as she set about getting rich.

Meanwhile, she kept the house up to scratch – the goodwill and the building together would fetch a decent penny when the time came to sell it and get out of Ireland for good.

Pack had been polite from the start, putting his money on her kitchen table as he ordered his drink. She was taken by his lazy eyes, overt in their approval of what they saw as she served him his porter with a smile, and a hitch of her hips as she turned to serve somebody else.

May had responded to him warmly without even thinking about it – he was handsome in his rugged way.

But it was his aloofness that drew her like a magnet – she watched him and decided he was like somebody looking in, rather than being a part of what was going on around him. She saw that he was content in his own company, somebody who could keep his business to himself. Yet, he struck her as somebody with fire inside him, a passionate strain there to be kindled by the right woman.

Pack had treated her with the respect due to the 'woman of the house' – well aware that she regarded him with a knowing glint in her bold blue eyes. He observed how she watched his rough-hewn hands as they took the jug of porter from the table, wondering with a lazy smile how her customers would react if they noticed what had already begun to happen between the two of them.

When May offered him temporary work, he accepted with guarded enthusiasm. He would give good work for good pay, and he would expect to be well fed, he said without hesitation. When she began to talk about where he would sleep, he spoke up: "A straw bed in the hay barn, ma'am, that'll do me lovely, so it will."

Soon, Pack was labouring well for her on the forty acres she had inherited with the public house and, when she reviewed the work he had done, she had an even higher opinion of her softly spoken itinerant, and was more than ever convinced he was the one to be her partner in crime. She smiled to herself – it wasn't really a crime – it was more like an adventure with money at the end of it, provided they both played their cards right. You have to be bold if you want what I want, May reasoned, and she sensed in the big man of the roads the same kind of hunger that she had lived with for years. This was born out of the appetite you couldn't satiate with grub or booze.

May quickly realised she was paying him too much attention. From that moment on she would, every so often, actively withdraw her eyes as they followed his powerful stride through the open door – no sense in giving offence to her regulars to no purpose. Instead, picking up a couple of tankards from the long kitchen table serving as a bar, she'd saunter to the door like somebody checking the weather signs in the sky. Seeing what she was really looking for – her big, rough-and-ready tinker – she'd come back into the flagstoned kitchen and respond with a wave of her hand to the need of a man urging her to give him more drink.

Pack Rowan used his present name because it suited him for the time being. He was not a dyed-in-the-wool crook, in that he had no criminal record – but, on the West Wicklow border by County Kildare, several farmers thought badly of somebody called Billy Burden who had been paid for shearing and a rake of painting work that had not been completed though money had been paid in advance.

Pack had no formal education but felt smart enough in his own mind to think of names as just numbers made up out of letters. Only to 'the haves' did the name, 'the family name', mean a damn thing. He sneered at such rubbish – he had encountered men that would have died – the bloody fools – to protect a name given to them by God knows what kind of fool – the idea causing him to shake his head in bewilderment.

He felt the same way about this Civil War that was tearing the country apart. More fools shooting and killing each other because they had listened to some fool who had listened to some fool. Men dying for ideas that were not even their own. As usual, he kept his ideas to himself, so that even the regular drinkers allowed that he knew his place well enough not to earn himself a kicking from a crowd of honest men that knew how to deal with his kind.

Pack was aware that these small farmers, many of them getting their hands on land for the first time, were the issue of people that had been tenants for generations, while English owners were earning the title of 'absentee landlords'.

Many of these landlords sat in places like the House of Lords at Westminster, enjoying rents that had to be paid on time. If not, the tenant could find himself thrown onto the road, despite his plea for more time in which to make up the shortfall. Those who failed to pay joined the growing band of the dispossessed – 'the have nots' – adding their family to the line of travellers that had moved away because not to do so was to risk all kind of abuse, even death itself, at the hands of those who now slept well under what had recently been another man's thatch.

Pack was more than happy to be seen taking his tankard to sit outside on a bench, his mouth a grim line of satisfaction when he thought of how those drunkards inside would blanch if they knew what was going on at night between himself and Big May when they were joined at the hip.

When Pack was ordering a drink or paying over his money to May, he continued to make sure he did not have eye-to-eye contact with her. She liked to act dangerously at times – despite her cunning and her common sense it was like she wanted to wave their situation in the faces of the men she served and hated with the same degree of civility – but he knew that should the truth become public knowledge, it was he that would feel the lash, if only because she could claim he forced her into obscene behaviour and God alone knew what else.

At his behest, May reined in her need to flirt with danger though she did enjoy taking risks. He insisted she trim her way with him when others were there – she acquiesced by becoming more comely and personable, Pack admiring her ability to switch from one way to another without pausing for breath. He knew she was devious by nature, and he intended to discover just how bad she was prepared to be in the months ahead.

To May the legacy of the roadside house, and the drink licence to go with it, had been a blessing. It allowed her the financial freedom to return to Ireland as quickly as possible, where she could take all the time to hatch the plan that would make her rich for all her days.

She had felt no personal need to return to Ireland – it was in the interests of expediency that she came home. She had loved the gigantic experience that London had been to her, especially when compared to the bare-bones countryside around Dunbla.

Just days after May returned to the house her father

had willed to her, she took herself off in her pony and trap for a look at Dunbla House. Driving the pony into the vast estate, she smiled at the idea that part of this wealth already belonged to her.

Looking back on the first days of her returning, May had no doubt that the recently widowed Brewer woman would pay handsomely to keep hidden the happening that would destroy her life should it ever become public knowledge.

When the word blackmail had first come to May's mind she had demurred – it was more in the nature of a service that she was willing to render to the widow Brewer for a very large sum of money. And since the same woman had just married a rich Jew called Sweet – adding even more money to the heaps the Brewer family had always had – May failed to see any great difficulty in getting her share of what could truly be called enormous wealth.

As Pack Rowan leaned close by the open window of the hostelry the evening Sam Sweet greeted him, he sneered derisively at the idea that the likes of May Murray had the power to make him drink his paid-for porter by the roadside. Had his present situation not been as comfortable as it was – had the big woman not come cringing to his spot in the hayloft that night – he might even have set the barn on fire when he moved on.

He remembered how she had been before and after he had pounded on her bones, and he smiled in satisfaction at the thought that she was desperately in need of what he had to offer. Hence he had decided, as May plied him a gigantic breakfast after that first night together that he would journey no more for a little while. The cushy berth he managed to organise for himself in May's employ, and indeed, in her bed, suited him for the moment. He was more than content to indulge her lust while giving his own wanderlust a rest from the never-ending road.

The first time he laid eyes on her she had served him a drink in the early evening while the kitchen-pub was empty but for the pair of them. She was a fine woman, he allowed, an agreeable shape on her under a heart-shaped face and bold blue eyes. He knew in a heartbeat he would never trust her further than he could hurl a heifer – the eyes did their own dance, reminding him of the waywardness he carried within. He soon saw that she knew how to smile, and how to make the smile work for her around men, and when she gave a flick of her hips as she turned, like somebody unconscious of this, he knew that she knew, all too bloody well, exactly what she was doing. And that very first time he vowed to have her before he left the area, whether she wanted him to have her or not.

When she offered him work, Pack accepted – he was curious to get to know her enough to find out if he was right in his gut feeling that, public house owner or not, she was, in her heart, some kind of thief.

He worked hard for May for three or four days, ate a halfway decent supper each evening and drank the two pints of porter she allowed him as part of his board. When he wanted more he paid for it.

When she came to him in the hay barn acting like a woman scared out of her wits, he almost believed her.

She carried a lantern, affecting genuine fear, but he took it with a pinch of salt.

"I had a nightmare, Pack." She spoke in a manner that suggested she had known him a long time. "I woke up in a real dither and then I saw someone prowling around outside, and I got such a shock I had to come to you and ask you to have a look around out there, make sure there's nobody there with bad intentions on his mind."

Pack sat her down on a wooden box while he added more straw to his bed, creating a rolled-up rise of the stuff to act as a bolster. He took her by the upper arms without being too gentle with her and when she was lying there, the lantern hanging on a hook above their heads, he lay down beside her and said: "You just rest yourself there, alannah, and I'll make sure nobody's going to bother you."

She smiled up at him and he almost laughed out loud.

"Unless," he said in a deliberate way, "I end up bothering you myself."

May laughed in a manner that suggested he was incorrigible, and he patted her hand and let her see what was in his eyes. In moments her nerves settled down, and she lay there looking up at him like an innocent waiting for a lift.

Pack responded to the way her breathing caused her breasts to rise and fall, and decided why not? She was soft and round in the right places and he'd had enough drink to make him warm and willing to play her little game.

"I wouldn't do this for just anybody," he said, half joking but whole in earnest. "Only a lovely woman such as you could keep me from my sleep at this hour."

Her laugh in response to his suggestiveness was dry in her throat and he saw in her eyes how ripe she was for the plucking. Leaning over he kissed her on the mouth, May responding as though her life depended on it. Within minutes they were devouring each other, Pack kissing her with a ferocity that was the kind of beautiful abuse she needed.

He ripped her undergarment away and mounted her, she crying in pain and pleasure, gripping him in ways she had learned through a string of lovers during her time in London. At first he seemed remote, as though he was performing mechanically, looking in as he drove her to distraction. But gradually, as she took a bigger part in their togetherness, she became so totally open to him in every way that she could see, while they lay in the convalescence of each other's breathing, that she had made an impact on him, an impression that might well have sealed the as-yet unspoken plan as a partnership.

May was gone when he woke up in a wash of sunshine through the open top door of the barn. He gave her little thought – the job was solid for now – and went down to the water barrel behind the house.

Using a bucket, he doused his naked upper body. All too aware that she was there looking at him through the kitchen window, he stretched like a mountain cat, gasping loudly as the coldness of the water woke him up with a start, adding some stretches to his display, intending to increase the level of May's interest in him.

He saw her then moving about the kitchen as the smell of frying bacon came to him. Donning his only shirt, he went to go the woodshed to get logs for the kitchen. As he dumped the blocks down by the great open fireplace – big enough for men to sit in on little benches built into the chimney's side walls – he responded to her invitation to sit down and eat his breakfast.

As he began eating, he was more than surprised to see the result of the trouble she had taken with her appearance. Her hair had been washed and she wore carmine on her lips with a light dusting of face powder to lighten down the colour of her cheeks. He felt good that she might want to look her best sitting opposite him over the food – she was clearly taken with him. For his part, he was slow to admit, he wanted more of what had happened to them in the night before they fell asleep in each other's arms.

Remembering her power in their intimacy he felt himself harden under the table, slurping tea from the tin mug in his hand to shut out what he deemed to be the traps falling into place.

So, in his own quietly deliberate way, he asked her to tell him exactly what she wanted him to work on today – an effort to shrug off the sensation of his early morning sexual arousal. He focussed then on giving his attention back to serious eating, but as May went to get toasted bread from the fireplace, he found himself glancing about as he tried to decide where the hell she kept her money hidden.

Sitting opposite him at the kitchen table, May believed that her wait for the right man had come to an end. She could admit that his prowess in the lovemaking had something do with her desire to have him alongside her, but it was more than that. It was his way, his quiet, unfussy way of going about things – even in passion as he had been about to ravage her last night, with power enough to leave her craving more of the same.

She wondered was he some sort of criminal, had he a violent past? He was a bit of a mystery and free of any need to talk about himself – this appealed to her, especially in view of what she had in mind for them both. This thought stopped her speculation – noticing that she had already included him in the days and weeks and perhaps months that lay ahead, she realised she had decided without giving it any further thought that he was to be her partner in crime – not that it was a crime, not really. She was committed to him then – in her own fashion, of course.

Pack had never been an impatient man – the long years in prison, the slow ongoing search for the woman who had betrayed him and the mad dog that had murdered his mentor, The Vicar – nothing, not distance or time, got between him and his resolve that some day he would get even with the two people concerned.

For now, May was a cosy nook in which to live warm – he had to stay with her for a while, let her think she had a hook in him, that she would get to know him – whatever it took until he could manage to find out where she hid the money she made from the drink and the grub she served in the public house. When he knew that, he would take what was there and be on his way.

She had to be well heeled since she lived to make money – he had seen how she cherished the coins and the currency notes before she made them disappear into the box she used to hold her cash. As far as he could make out she never left the premises except to go out to the field behind the house to do her business morning and night.

Pack had been back to the headland of Dunbla for a month or more – a place he often thought of during the time in prison. It was not his home, this headland – the winding, twisting lanes and boreens of Ireland were that – he had never before lived under a thatch roof but beneath the roadside hedge and the trees of the woods, and under the odd bit of something pulled over you by the roadside to keep the rain from washing you away altogether.

Sipping his drink outside May's house, he felt the birds stop – he smiled – it was twilight turning to darkness, when the birds of a sudden quit moving and chattering – it was the same with the damned insects – one minute you could be eaten alive by midges, the next they were gone as though there was a pain-of-death curfew to be obeyed.

When Pack saw the woman bring the pony and trap to a stop outside the pub he wondered who she was. She was no spring chicken but she was a fine thing, the bounce in her step as she went inside was more than enough to get something stirring inside him – he liked the way this could happen around certain women. At the same time, he knew how lucky he was not to be locked up – that same urge had made him do things, take wild chances and some woman not willing to part the hairs had done so – because at those times he had to have his way.

He ran his tongue over his fleshy lips at the prospect of even seeing yer woman again for a minute. He heard her voice before he realised she was talking to somebody sitting right inside the window at his ear.

"Oh, come on now, Séamus, I've no time to reason with you nor have I the patience for it, and you've had a good drink and no harm done. So, up you get, and let me get you back to bed."

Pack realised she was the missus of the goat-faced Kerry man. Then he heard Séamus chuckle: "God love you, Angela of my heart's delight, you never lost it, and I thank the Man Above for you, and you still tryin' to get me into the bed."

There was a gentle thump and the woman said with a hint of irritation riding her words: "Séamus Byrne, you're going to vex me now in a minute. Get up again now on your feet and don't get my goat. I had to leave Kelly alone to come and get you home from here before you end up fallin' down in the road."

Her tone gathered the man's attention for he said with concern: "How is the old girl? Is she okay?"

"She's not the best tonight, so come on, and no more messin'."

"Just one for the road, alannah?"

Séamus Byrne had the sound of a fella three sheets to the wind, while Pack Rowan was taken by the excitement rising in his chest as the name Kelly landed on him.

He stood quietly in the semi-darkness under the three-quarter moon, watching the woman called Angela as she supported the Kerry Goat. He watched her heave him into the trap before she climbed up to turn the pony around and head back the way she had come.

Pack finished his drink and started to walk after the trap, staying on the grass verge as much as he could. He heard the woman urge the pony to "get a move on" heard the man start to sing drunkenly: "*I loved them all bar Maggie, 'cos she baked the currant cakes!*"

"You did in my eye!" Angela gave her derision enough force to float to Pack on the night air. "You weren't capable of loving any lassie, not till I plucked you from all the men available to me, took y'under my oxter and taught you the facts of life."

Angela's laugh on the tail of her banter was light and Séamus Byrne, who was now waxing mellow, acknowledged this with a syrupy charm that made her laugh even more.

"You did, alannah. You taught me everything I know including how to become a man in the art of 'how's yer father'!" His voice burst into a gurgle of wet laughter before a cough and a spit cleared his tubes so that he could speak again. "And I love you, Angela, till the next breath becomes the last. Oh, Glory Be! I have lived a life worth the trouble."

Walking fairly close behind the trap Pack could hear that Séamus was jarred enough to go to sleep any minute, heard the concern in Angela's voice as she encouraged him to stay awake till they got back to the house.

"I'm in no mood to be half carrying you in the door, Séamus. I've had a long day and I had to feed Kelly earlier – her hands are stiff with arthritis – and I pulled my back getting her into bed."

"Tell me something then, lass. Make me attend to you with something beautiful or juicy or bold and bawdy. It will be between you and me and the stars."

Séamus spoke as though reciting poetry and there was no doubting his feeling for the woman driving the trap.

Any hint of reservation that Angela had been carrying was diminished and dismissed by the words of the man she lived for. When she spoke there were tears on the cusp of her voice: "You kept me a woman by being a man at all times and I love you, Séamus. Me goin' on about Kelly, I'm concerned. I didn't want to leave her alone. She told me go on. She knew I had to come and find you, get you home where you belong."

A full-grown fox busily munching on the carcass of a hen turned to snarl as Pack Rowan sent her to death from a kick of his boot, the force of the blow lifting her off the ground. He pressed on without a blink, his own chest warm again at the mention of the name Kelly. He felt bile rise in his throat and he bent low to spit it from his mouth, taking no risk that the pair up ahead would know that he was following on behind the trap, his heart black as the night since it was scored by furrows filled with hatred for the woman who had betrayed him, a woman called Kelly.

The pony had responded to Angela's flick of the whip with a short trot – the animal preferred walking so that Pack caught them up again in no time. The lighted lamps on either side of the trap's breast provided enough light to get the couple home, in through the gates onto the Dunbla estate.

Pack stood for some seconds in awe since the moon had reappeared above the ocean and was lighting the land and the mansion – a magnificent edifice – that was now, according to May Murray, the home of the widow Deirdre Brewer and her new husband Sam Sweet.

When Angela stopped the pony near a cottage close to the great house with its Doric columns and the steps rising to the main door, Pack heard Séamus Byrne speak softly across the night. "Angela, love, you attend to Kelly. I'll look after the pony."

"Thanks, darlin'," Angela whispered with care, the soft air of the night carrying the sound to him so that he could hear it clear as a chapel bell.

He watched the ageing man totter some as he led the pony away towards the outline of barns and stables across the cobbled yard. Moving then on the balls of his feet, Pack Rowan silently reached the window of the cottage Angela had entered.

Angela and an old woman were speaking softly but Pack could tell from their shared demeanour that Kelly – for it was she all right – was assuring Angela that she was as well as could be expected.

The younger woman nodded her head in relief, her greying coppered hair visited by the odd blink of light from the oil lamps, as she began preparing a hot drink.

While the milk was warming, Angela brought Kelly some biscuits on a plate, Pack noting with resentment how comfortable was the home that his mother enjoyed, the home she had no doubt enjoyed during all the years he had been condemned to prison because she had betrayed him to the lawmen.

'You surrendered me to the po-liss, Kelly, a crime beyond anything a tinker could do to another, never mind their own flesh and blood. For a tinker to betray another to the police is the unforgivable sin. Because of your treachery, I promise you will pay for what you did on me.'

He wiped perspiration from his forehead with the sleeve of his coat, resisting the force of his need to burst into the room and kill the old bitch and the other pair too if necessary.

Simmering down he let go of a long breath: 'I've lived for a chance to pay you back, bitch! To find you and that cow was carrying my child, find you both and pay you what's owed to you. There's no rush now, no rush at all, now that I know where you are.'

Pack Rowan smiled grimly, fading into the night as the sound of Séamus Byrne's boots on the cobblestones from the stables warned him it was time to go, for the present.

5

September 1922

May Murray had never heard of the equinox – her schooling had been basic, the three R's ground into almost all the children, boys and girls attending the local school.

That was about as far as it went. Though, like the other children in the one-roomed school, May was also introduced to the Irish language – Gaelic. For one half-hour period a week, they shared a secret lesson – this had to be kept hidden since the first language of Ireland was English and the schoolhouse was owned by the Church of Ireland. This august body was a religious facility for the Ascendancy, known locally as West Brits.

Pack Rowan knew that the equinox was the time at which the sun crossed the equator. He knew that this happened twice a year, in the spring on the twentieth of March, in the autumn on the twenty-second or twenty-third of September – those being the points at which day and night are equal.

He had come by this information while reading a periodical during a house-breaking in Mayo some years before. The discovery took place while he was sitting on a toilet in the house he had just robbed, this being a pleasant experience when compared to squatting down behind another hedge in another field off another country lane in another county on another day, enduring an existence that caused him to wonder what was life about.

This philosophical thought didn't develop all that much but the anger that sprouted from its momentary appearance in his mind added fuel to his need to somehow improve his own way of living for the better.

Ever since The Vicar had taught him to read in Wormwood Scrubs, he had wanted a better deal for himself. Reading of the Russian revolution he had been amazed, his own new-found dreams and wishes being vindicated, that such a change could be made to happen. But then the vast hordes of deprived Russians had found leaders willing to die for their belief. The tinker in Ireland, even if he had family, was essentially a loner since he and his tribe were victims of the 'trust no man' school of thought. He determined though that whatever it took to make the right kind of changes in his life, he would match the demand. He would become one of those to whom he now had to touch his cap – he would set himself free of his present life – he would not be the tinker that slept under the hedge where every day was another challenge to beg, borrow or steal his supper.

On his last release from prison he had vowed

silently that he would achieve this goal or die. He was not afraid of death, or of any man that walked the earth. He had learned to read by dismissing his fear of failure – his guts and his determination to eschew the ignorance that had been his birthright seeing him through. Now he felt powerful in his mind, which, he reasoned, was where it really counted – he was free, and free of fear, he was a fighter who would fight to the death if necessary to reach the goal he had set for himself. Besides which, lad, he said to himself, there's two that you have to kill before you leave this earth – you don't do that, you'll twist and turn for eternity.

He had an incredibly reliable memory for facts, any and all kind of snippets of information, stuff he might have overheard, read in old newspapers – all of it seemed to hop into his mind and wait there till there was a need for it to appear.

He had been instantly intrigued by the facts about the equinox, his immediate response to what he read causing him to consider it as a very good time for things to happen for people – or for things to begin happening. As he viewed it, like, if those two opposites, night and day, light and dark, could be equal even for a minute, there might come a time when people like himself would be thought of as equal by all the good Christians all over Ireland.

Being a realist, Pack accepted the fact that the odd tinker doing a dirty deed – even he had to plead guilty on this score – had tarnished the good name of tinkers and knackers generally, but whatever the overall cause, he could put his hand on his heart and say he hadn't felt the benefit of a lot of Christianity in practice along the way his life had drawn him.

This experience, coupled with the opening of his mind under The Vicar's tutelage, gave birth to the notion that it was possible to get what you wanted if you went about it in the right way – and if you were prepared to do whatever was necessary, by which he meant, anything and everything to achieve your goal.

On a day in late September, Pack had driven May into the village to pick up the weekly food order she placed at Dwyer's grocery shop and to collect meat for a couple of days from O'Neill the butcher.

With the stuff bought and paid for, he placed the boxes May used to carry food onto the dogcart. As he packed the stuff carefully, a pony and trap drove past the cart. He gasped at the unexpected sight of the two women on board. The woman called Angela was driving while the old one with the white hair, his mother, wrapped up in a rug, looked to him like she wasn't long for this world.

For a moment he was disconcerted – if she was likely to die soon, it meant he needed a change of plan, like he couldn't wait too long to confront her. He had been enjoying the idea, the feeling of power to do with her whatever he wished – it felt so good at times he'd delayed taking her life.

He had been waiting for a sign – remembering the recent equinox. He had savoured its happening in his own private way, even spending some time each day waiting for something to happen. He knew not what he hoped for, but he couldn't resist a grim smile as he thought once again that if those opposites, night and day, light and dark, could be equal for as long as it took the sun to cross the equator, anything was possible, even for somebody like himself.

In that moment, May came striding out of the shop, her demeanour to all intents and purposes quiet and controlled, though he knew by the darting blue eyes she was all of a dither inside.

As he flicked the whip over the pony's tail and got the lazy nag moving, he asked her quietly: "You all right there, May?" He saw that her colour had heightened dramatically but, nonetheless, he kept his voice down. Nothing had changed in this respect – he was her employee and nothing more in the eyes of the locals. As yet there was no hint of scandal though there was talk going on all right: 'No, there's nothing going on with May and the Knacker. If he had his feet under the bed wouldn't he be drinking in the kitchen with the customers instead of sipping his pint outside?'

Up to now this was the total sum of local reasoning on the subject, aided to a great degree by the belief that no woman, but one of his own, would lie down with the likes of Pack Rowan.

"I'm all right, Pack." May sat straight, flushed up on the hump of some exciting thing that fuelled the powerful feeling that seemed to be spraying all over him.

Just the way she had hopped up onto the dogcart. Pack smiled when he considered that he had something to do with putting that spring into her arse.

"Get us back to the house like a good man," she said

softly, clutching yesterday's copy of the *Irish Independent* to her breast.

There was a chill in the wind that made him think again of Kelly and how brittle she had looked as she passed him by wrapped up against the cold – and he was bothered for a moment by a niggling need to dispatch her quickly when the time came.

He felt a certain resistance to the thought, having spent so many years promising himself that should he ever find her, he would make her suffer as he had done behind the prison walls.

While Pack took the food and the meat and some cleaning products into the house, May put on her apron and hurriedly began pouring drinks for the couple of farmers who had been outside waiting for her return.

From then until the early hours of the morning they were busy and Pack had no drink at all. He worked every bit as hard as May herself, turning the lamb cooking over the fire – slicing it up for men that would eat mutton on the hoof if necessary. He put in fresh barrels of stout, gathered the mugs and tankards to give them a wash in rain water before a shake to dry them and slap them down to be filled for another customer.

When they had the place to themselves, May poured stout for him and added a glass of whiskey for them both. As he went to drink she touched his mug with her own and, though he didn't understand what she meant, he responded before dropping the spirit down the hatch in his eagerness to enjoy the sensation it awakened.

Taking his stout he went outside and stood looking at the stars, listening to the night sounds of the countryside. He heard a fox bark nearby and then it was all quiet and he lowered the stout into himself wondering at the change that seemed to have come over May since she came out of the emporium with the newspaper pressed to her chest.

Not being a man who spent time wondering about such things, he flicked the end of his smoke onto the broken road, cratered in places after sunshine on top of fierce rain caused it to crack badly.

He went back inside and shut and bolted the front door. May was not in the kitchen so he walked through the house and headed for the barn.

As he crossed the yard, he heard her bedroom window being raised and when he glanced up she was leaning out, already in a nightdress and her hair loose about her shoulders.

"Will you come up a minute, Pack?" Her tone was free of the sound she made when others were present. She spoke as one person to another, no boss and worker, no suggestion the speaker was addressing a knacker. Without a word, Pack went back inside and up the wooden stairs to her bedroom.

May was smoking a cigarette as she stood by the small fireplace, bending then to throw another sod of peat on before she turned and pointed to the tray of drinks she had set up on the table under the second window backing onto the yard.

The room was soft to his eye, a woman's room, he acknowledged, with flowers from the bank outside the front door, cushions of different colours on the shabby couch and a couple on the big bed she slept in.

Pack took a glass of whiskey for himself and offered one to May. She nodded and accepted it with a gentle look in her eye, before she beckoned him to sit on the couch.

"There's something I want to talk to you about," she said, her voice turning all business on him. "It's an offer I want to make you." She looked at him with a directness that told him she was checking out his response to her initial overture.

He inclined his head slightly to suggest he was interested in listening to whatever she had to say.

"It's going to take some time to tell you the whole story but let me tell you this – if I'm right in what I believe, and I know that I am, there is a lot of money to be made, a whole lot of money. Will you settle for that for now and just allow me to tell you why I know this to be true?"

"Go ahead, May," Pack said without guile. "If there's a fella in the County Wicklow more interested in making money than me, I've not met him nor read about him in any paper or periodical."

He drank the rest of his whiskey, put the glass down and took a pull from his cigarette.

May sat down in a comfortable-looking chair to one side of the fire so that she was now looking at him from a slight angle. Her nightdress was a very pale blue affair with a white ribbon under the bosom part and though he was by now familiar with her breasts he liked the look of them very much as he sat there waiting to hear her story.

"When I left Dunbla, nine years ago now, I went

straight to London, got work at once cleaning for people. I got some good jobs and never was sacked from one because I never stole and the work was easy when you compared it to looking after my father and trying to keep him out of my bed nights. I never expected to come back to Ireland – and I knew I'd never lie down under the same roof as dirty Seán Murray again. May God forgive me for praying he'd burn in Hell's fire!"

She lit a cigarette and he poured himself a bit more of the whiskey.

"I made a halfway decent life, living in a room in Hammersmith, keeping myself to myself, until about a year and a half ago when I went cleaning for a woman calling herself Gloria Stein. A lovely-looking woman, reserved I suppose you'd call her, who said she had a son at boarding school. She was a professional singer doing concerts all over London and other cities in England. After a few months of me doing good work for her she asked me if I'd be interested in being what you might call her housekeeper. Times she might be away for a few days, then again at home for a week before the next concert. She said she liked me, was grateful to find somebody willing to work and that she would give me a decent home if I was interested.

"She didn't have to ask me twice, I can tell you. I had a lovely room in a very large flat in Chelsea, and when she wasn't off singing, she stayed home alone just like I did, and we never had need of a cross word between us in all the time I worked for her."

May smoked and exhaled before going on.

"One day I was cleaning out a wardrobe in her bedroom – spring-cleaning time as they call it there in London – and I took three boxes of books out so that I could scrub the wardrobe before putting them back in. They were dusty anyway, so I started in on them while the wardrobe dried. While I was lifting one of the boxes some of the books fell onto the floor and as I bent to pick them up I saw they were all the same – like, the same shape and colour and size.

"My curiosity got the better of me and I had a look to see what sort of books they were exactly. I didn't mean any harm, but when I opened the first one to hand, just opened it at random, lo and behold, what did I find myself reading but a page of handwriting with the words '*and may I never have to visit that house at Dunbla again*'."

May glanced at Pack who reacted slightly as he lit another cigarette without taking his eyes off her face. He was sitting upright, his body revealing his interest in the story she told, and she continued optimistically, feeling that she had been right about him being the man for the job.

"Over the next few weeks, I read all the books, journals they were, and I tell you, Pack, I cried bitter tears for that poor woman, tears that her story ripped out of my heart, with me wondering how she survived all that happened to her."

"Get to the reason she never wanted to go back to Dunbla House," Pack said quietly, seeing that May was close to tears in the memory of whatever she had read about this Gloria Stein, or whatever her name was.

"She got engaged to a man, Sam Sweet, the same man that's now married to the widow of Arthur Brewer. On that same night Arthur Brewer and Deirdre Doyle were celebrating their own engagement with a huge party at Dunbla House. Sam Sweet and Gloria were there but he had to leave early for a middle-of-the-night business meeting in Dublin. Gloria got a few jars into her – she was no kind of drinker – a Jewess with very strict personal rules about her behaviour. Add to that the fact that she hated Gentile men with a real passion."

"You got all this from her journals?" Pack was surprised by just how interested he was to hear where the story was leading.

"I did, and if you think this is good, you better hang onto your Derby, for it's only starting so it is."

May accepted the drink Pack brought to her, and she sipped the whiskey before carrying on with her story.

"That night, Gloria Stein – she was a virgin by the way, with no intention of ever giving any man his way with her until he had slipped a wedding band onto her finger – well, she got jarred and between the jigs and the reels she had a night of passion with Arthur Brewer who was so out of his mind from the wild drinking that, afterwards, he had no memory of her, who she was or what had happened between them. And I'm telling you they had some night of passion, believe me.

"At this time, Sam Sweet was Arthur Brewer's best friend, and the same Brewer in his right mind would never have stooped to seducing Sweet's woman. He was an absolute gent who'd never have dreamed of doing such a thing.

"Poor Gloria – my God – can you imagine, Pack? He'd been riding her like a stallion for hours, yet, as he left her, he was so out of his memory that he threw money on the bedside table, so far gone mentally that he thought she was a prostitute he was after being with."

Pack said nothing though he remembered some years back having such a feed of poteen that his mind and his memory had been wiped out for something like three days. He'd shrugged it off, putting it down to dangerous home-made hooch. At the same time, he wondered what the hell Brewer had been drinking to make him forget a night in bed with a lovely virgin.

May had a fresh cigarette going now and she went on with the story: "When she recovered from the shock she pulled herself together and she found Brewer on the veranda of the big house later that morning. He greeted Gloria as a gentleman would – he was charming and caring, apologising for being such a bad host, since he had no recollection of most of the evening. He was, he said, even now recovering from a memory loss the intensity of which had actually frightened him. She knew he was telling the truth, knew with every instinct at her disposal, that this gentle creature and her voracious lover of last night before were hardly one and the same person.

"Arthur blamed his memory lapse on a punch made by his great friend, a doctor, and said he should have known better than to touch the stuff again. He was courteous and caring, a gentleman as always, except for the time he spent being the sexual lunatic that ravaged a young woman, a woman he didn't know he was riding to death even as he was poking in and out of her. Gloria decided she had to marry Sam Sweet as quickly as possible."

"Because she could be pregnant," Pack said.

"Absolutely, she knew the wedding had to be as soon as she could get Sweet to arrange it. If she was pregnant by Brewer, she had to have Sweet believe it was his child and that she had conceived on their wedding night. Two weeks later they were married in the Registry Office in Petty France in London.

"When her daughter Sarah was born, Gloria got some bit of relief – thank God like, the baby didn't look anything like Arthur Brewer. Her son, Mendel, came a year later – looked like she did which was all right. But by now – now she knew she wouldn't have any more children – she was slowly losing her mind over that night in bed with Brewer.

"She felt desperate guilt for deceiving her husband who seems like a decent skin. Next thing you know, she gets this compulsion to shave her head, she straps down her bosoms, dresses all in black and she doesn't want her husband anywhere near her. She was like someone dead but still able to walk around and you can imagine what this did to her relations with her husband.

"Her mother-in-law lived with them and Gloria felt great love for the older woman – she had lost her own mother – the poor woman had miscarried and died after a kicking from her lover. All that kept poor Gloria from killing herself back then was her belief that her mother would never have wanted her to do such a thing."

Pack drank whiskey, saying carefully: "You sure you're not dressin' this up, makin' it worse than it was?"

"It's all there in her journals, Pack – all that had kept her going was the scribbling into her journals. She tore the heart out of me with her curses and her screams to God asking how he could do what he did to her mother – when they were on the way to Ireland, to keep a promise her mother made to her father who had been murdered in London while Gloria was in the womb. I tell you, Pack, that's a story to stop you dead, and I mean that. You'd need to sit with a stiff drink after reading it, believe you me."

"Did she keep the journals going up to the present time?"

"No. She stopped when Sarah was about eight years old."

Pack sat there biting his tongue to stop himself telling her to get on with the bloody story.

May smiled but turned her head away as she did so. Wouldn't do to let him see how pleased she was that he was so hooked on the story.

"Sarah Sweet was a bright girl, precocious, and got away with it because her father could see or hear no wrong in anything the child did. And Sarah had already said she wanted to marry Eddie Brewer, the firstborn child of Arthur Brewer and Deirdre.

"Edward, Eddie Brewer, was born ten months after Sarah. Even though they were just children, when

Sarah made this vow to marry Eddie, it sent a chill of fear through Gloria. She was hardly in her right mind like – if she'd been well she might have let it go, put it down to childer playing. But she actually began to worry that the young one and Eddie would end up as man and wife."

"I can see her head damaged after what she'd been through – she couldn't have been all right upstairs or she'd have given the young one a kick in d'arse, knowin' well the brats say more than their prayers."

As May watched him speak she was relieved that she had no motherly instincts. For all the good things she felt in him, she had no illusion that he would make any kind of halfway decent parent.

"She was half demented in a way," she said. "That's what I got from the journals, anyway. God love her, what she'd been through it was a wonder she wasn't in a locked ward. Even knowing that it would be ten years or more before a marriage between her Sarah and Eddie Brewer would be possible, she got so agitated that she was half-mad with the notion. This is her own statement in the journal about her state of mind."

"It's some story," Pack said. "But so far I'm not seeing where the money's coming from."

"I said before I started, I'd need you to be patient."

"All right," he conceded. "And what was it, to do with the *Independent*? You came back to the cart like you were very excited about something, with the paper pressed against you."

May smiled, delighted that he had noticed her excitement. "I was very thrilled, Pack, and I'm even more so now. I'm still asking you for patience. I've never said a word about any of this to a living soul and I'm only telling you because I think you're the man to help me turn what I know, and can prove, into the sort of money a person could retire on."

She paused and lit a cigarette, giving Pack time to comment or ask a question. When he just sat there sipping his drink she carried on.

"I want that money so that I'll never have to pour another drink, or serve another lamb dinner to the disgusting men that come into the kitchen below every day of the week."

Her demeanour had changed during this revelation and she drank whiskey again as Pack asked: "You say you have proof?"

She nodded emphatically: "Yes, I have. But don't pursue that for a moment. Let me drive the nail into the story and you'll see why I think it's worth a lot of money to the rich people who wouldn't want it known what happened all those years ago."

May was so convinced that she could turn this information into real money that Pack – who was more than interested in having a cut, if not all – remained quiet and smoked on a cigarette.

May finished her drink for the moment before she went on: "Finally, years later, when Gloria had simmered down a bit – she'd been like a fanatical Jewess for years – driving Sam half crazy with her need to be so much of a Jew that she was like a caricature."

"So what happened that stopped Gloria going totally mad?

"She found a new obsession – she fell in love." She held up her hand to stop his disbelief from becoming verbal. "Not with a man, nor a woman, nothing like that. No, she fell in love with an idea – the dream of a homeland for the Jews."

"You mean Palestine being the Promised Land?"

May was impressed but did her best to hide it. "You hit the nail on the head, Pack. Living in London now, doing concerts to make money to help the dream come true. That and her son, they are the only two things she ever talked about. Even the daughter, Sarah, she rarely got a mention when we'd be having a chat over a cuppa tea."

"You're right about needin' drink," Pack rose and poured whiskey for them both.

Taking the glass, May said: "Make yourself as comfortable as you can – the next bit of the story can't be rushed."

Pack sipped the whiskey and lit a cigarette. "You do tell it well. I'll give you that much."

May smiled, gratified that he liked her enough to be kind. Kindness and being gentle weren't that important to her in a man. Just as well, she had thought more than once since she became involved with Pack.

"Now we get to the part that everyone will want to keep in the dark. This is to do with the birth of the first child of Arthur Brewer and his wife, Deirdre, called Dee by all who knew her.

"Deirdre had gone walking alone – she'd been doing this compulsively throughout her pregnancy. The doctor that made the punch that caused all Gloria's problems – he was called Doctor Lote – he was the family physician, and he'd warned Dee not to leave the estate – she had plenty of land there if she had to walk – but on the fateful day we're concerned with, she not only left the estate, she ended up so lost she had no idea where she was, or how long she had been walking.

"Her baby was now threatening to come into the world – she was desperate enough to pray to God to help save her child. Now she was in deadly fear that the infant would die if it was born by the side of a country lane, and she not able to do anything for it.

"Moments later, an old woman of the roads – she told Deirdre to call her Kelly – there she was coming out of a field behind her camp by the ditch. She took this pregnant woman under the cover she had tied into the hedgerow, a kind of tent made out of tarpaulin or something, and in that tent Deirdre Brewer gave birth to her first child."

Pack rose and poured a whiskey. He drank it down and took another before he came back to his seat. May was curious about the effect this part of the story was having on him – he was not an emotional man – but he was more hot and bothered as he sat down again without saying a word.

"Deirdre lost consciousness, passed out, as her child came into the world. When she came around, Kelly was placing the child, a boy, at her breast.

"Dee promised the tinker woman she would make her life better from that day forward. Kelly asked her if she could include the name Edward or Eddie in those she would give her son. Said she'd lost a boy called

Eddie and that it was for his memory she was asking."

May was more than surprised when Pack rose and poured more whiskey without offering her a fresh drink. He lit another cigarette before he sat down again and she was of the impression that he was touched, moved in some way. He avoided her eyes and to her mind certainly looked like the story had reminded him of something that perhaps he had forgotten. She said nothing.

Rising, she poured whiskey for herself, sitting again without comment, anxious to keep him interested since she was now absolutely certain he was the man for the task that lay ahead.

"How did the woman Gloria Stein know all this? She wasn't there when it happened, if it happened, and how the hell do you know all this? She never told you, the likes of her don't be telling things to servants." Pack had spoken suddenly, as though he had no control over the words that ripped out of him, and he leaned forward as he spoke, his eyes glinting with curiosity.

May was pleased to see this – she had the hook into him anyway. "You'll get your answer now in a minute," she assured him. "I won't jump ahead to soothe your impatience. I have to tell the story in my own way."

"Get on with it so," Pack said. "That was a mistake earlier, me complimenting you on your ability as a storyteller."

May smiled and wanted to get up and kiss him but she knew this was not the time for stuff like that.

"Some time after the child being born by the side of the road, the Brewer woman moved Kelly into a cottage in the grounds of Dunbla House. It was then that Kelly told her what had really happened on the day she woke up to find her son Eddie at her breast. Not to put too fine a tooth on it, the boy, Eddie, wasn't the son of Deirdre Brewer. Her baby girl was stillborn, God love her."

"Where did the young fella come from?" Pack was on his feet for a moment or two before he sat down again, breathing down his nose.

"He was the son of a tinker girl that died the day before giving birth to him. She had been badly beaten by the child's father – that and a painful birth had been too much for her, only sixteen years old she was. Kelly was only after burying her in a shallow grave in the field behind the hedge when she saw Deirdre staggering along the road.

"She was praying, so she told Deirdre, asking God to help her find somebody to take care of the newborn boy. A minute later as she came out onto the lane, there was Deirdre Brewer about to drop her baby on the stones under her feet."

Pack stood up again and took more whiskey. She thought she heard him sniff, but dismissed the notion that he was weeping. He brought whiskey to her by the fire and somehow he seemed to be a little softer than she had ever seen him before.

He sipped his drink and without looking at her he said, as though he was covering up what he was feeling: "I'm still waiting to hear how Gloria Stein knew all this."

"You – I give up! Her husband, Sam Sweet, he told her."

"And how in hell's name did he know?"

"Deirdre Brewer told him. Sweet had known her since she was a little girl. They were friends from the start – only in later years did they realise they loved each other. He told Dee why Gloria was going out of her mind – the fear that Eddie and Sarah were blood relations.

"That was why Dee told him the truth about Eddie – so that he could put his wife's mind at rest. By all accounts that's the kind of decent woman she is – do anything to help anybody, especially her great friend. Sweet told Gloria the story – about the tinker boy given in place of Deirdre's stillborn girl. He only told her to maybe stop her driving herself into a lunatic asylum because she thought they were brother and sister."

May watched Pack as he lit another cigarette, his head shaking in total disbelief. "Sweet knew his missus opened her legs for Brewer and he didn't strangle the bitch to death?"

Pack's incredulity was a palpable thing, something May thought you could take a bite out of.

"That part doesn't concern our business, Pack, so unless you just shut up and let me get on with the telling, we'll be here all night." She sounded gruff but she was thinking he looked tired, like he'd suffered a blow that had knocked the wind out of him.

"This is where the newspaper comes in," May said with a hint of triumph in her voice.

Holding the paper by the light from the oil lamp she pointed at the headline over a short article set in a box on the lower left-hand side of the front page. Pack read for himself the words in bold lettering: **Trouble Brewing at Brewers**. He glanced at May, unable to hide his surprise, and she smiled gesturing to him to read on.

Pack read on: *"Rumours abound in the stock markets of the world but there appears to be some substance attached to the one emanating from the Brewers Brewery clan. This relates to a possible claim in which the Dowager Duchess of the Dynasty is to sue the estate, now a worldwide trader which was founded by the late Arthur Brewer on the banks of the river Liffey in Dublin but a stone's throw from the brewery of arch rival Guinness."* Pack looked up from the paper, his mind already rushing ahead in leaps and bounds.

May nodded, her eyes alive with possibilities. "I know in my bones that it isn't just a rumour, Pack. Everything is going our way. It's going to come to battle and we're going to be right in there to scoop the jackpot. Finding the journals was to me like getting my hands on the leprechaun's map to his pot of gold. It shone at me like my one chance to change my life, live the way I had dreamed of during the years of keeping house for others over in London."

6

September 1922

Scarcely a mile north of May Murray's Public House, Sam Sweet heard Dee's motor car pull up in the stable yard. He put his copy of the *Independent* into his desk drawer, no need for Dee to see this. As the article claimed, it was, after all, just a rumour.

Smiling now he dismissed the chagrin he'd been facing, warmed by his heartfelt response to his wife's return from the Cork Street Clinic.

Deirdre looked tired as she put her bag down on the kitchen table and when he embraced her she clung to him silently for several moments. He held her firmly but with a gentleness that meant so much to his wife – he said nothing, knowing that silence was what was needed until she was ready to tell him what was on her mind.

He heard a long sigh leave her and knew she was feeling better. He stood back and held her by her upper arms before he leaned forward and kissed her gently on the lips. He expected no less by way of return, but Dee surprised him by pressing her mouth onto his and putting her arms about him to hold him as tightly as she could. As he usually did when she kissed him in this manner, he responded with a rising passion that went on being a source of wonder to him.

Dee pushed him back then to stand gazing at him, her emerald eyes now releasing her tears.

"I am overjoyed, Sam – we're going to have a baby." She pressed her face into the sofa of his shoulder – his own tears came in the instant.

When they were able to move apart, both almost afraid that the dream might depart, they began to laugh together, he whirling her around the room in a dance of delight before he stopped suddenly: "Is it all right, to do this, dance?" He looked perturbed and she kissed his face.

"Oh yes, dear heart, it's perfectly all right." She leaned back, her hands on his shoulders and when he looked at her in a quizzical fashion she laughed and said: "I'm practising. Before too long this is where my head will be when you're holding me."

"You'll never be that big, Dee, will you?"

She pulled him close, chuckling into his shoulder: "I've no idea, nor do I care. I can put up with anything to have our child."

"What can I get you? You must be tired after the day at the Clinic."

"I'm fine, Sam. But I would like to soak in a warm bath."

He held her hand as he walked her upstairs and he ran her bath while she undressed in the bedroom.

The housekeeper, Madge Gallagher, had gone to bed – and the children were sleeping in town.

When Dee had been soaking for a few minutes, Sam appeared with a bottle of Veuve Cliquot. Perched on the side of the bath, he poured, touching his wife's glass with his own, a great grin spreading over his mouth. Dee sipped the champagne and looked at him, shaking her head slightly, acknowledging that the impossible had really happened.

Sam left the bathroom to go and fetch cigarettes from their bedroom along the landing. As he picked up the Gold Flake he was still swimming in the delight of the long-awaited news about the baby.

Back in the bathroom, he watched her as she lay back contentedly, smoking her cigarette. He loved the way she smoked – it was as though every single cigarette was a gift from the gods. Smiling broadly she suggested Sam slide into the bath. He needed no second bidding and moments later they lay facing each other, he using a cushion that had been waterproofed and made to fit around the taps behind his head.

"I almost fainted when Kathleen Lynn told me I was pregnant." Dee sighed, still tasting disbelief. "I thought I'd left it too long."

Sam felt some concern over the dark rims under her eyes: "You're thirty-six years old, Dee – surely you had time."

She shrugged her face: "Obviously I did, but, there was this nagging doubt – other times I thought I was trying too hard." She grinned and looked sheepish: "Not that I didn't enjoy all the hard work I put in." She laughed then: "If you'll pardon the pun."

"You know you've been doing too much, and I'm not referring to bed." He found himself grinning. "You're incorrigible – you know that, don't you?"

Deirdre pulled her bad little girl face and flicked some water at him. He was about to light cigarettes, managed to keep his hands out of the impromptu shower his wife had provided: "Seriously, Dee, you have been overdoing it. You will have to cut down now, without anybody, even your husband, having to remind you."

"I know, and I want to, Sam. The Clinic is a huge part of my life, but this baby, our first child, it means the whole world to me."

He poured more champagne: "I've decided to take things easier myself, Dee. To tell you the truth, I'm stepping back from The Cause and all that it implies."

Dee looked surprised. "Has something happened? Something special – something else that was awful – what – to bring you to this?" Dee reached and took the new cigarette he had lit for her.

"Perhaps it's to do with my age, I'm not sure." He exhaled and watched the smoke rise towards the ceiling. "I want to study, discover ideas that have been tickling my fancy for a while now."

"I think that's wonderful," Deirdre was clearly in favour. "You've worked hard all your life. Time for yourself now, why not? Have you anything particular in mind, as the basis of your studies?"

"As soon as I have a clear picture, you will be the first to know."

"Is it some kind of spiritual quest?"

"I can't articulate it just yet."

He rose and stepped out of the bath, then held up a towelling robe for Deirdre. She was delighted yet somewhat amused by the way he watched her every move as she rose from the water.

"You've started molly-coddling me already. Oh, I am going to enjoy being pregnant."

He offered her his arm and they moved on a wave of laughter toward the bedroom.

At breakfast next morning he made Dee promise she would take a week off from the Clinic. She agreed in order to keep him happy but in truth she needed to spend some time at Dunbla.

"I've scarcely talked to Kelly in a fortnight and I need to walk the land, spend time on the shore. Who knows? Do nothing for a complete morning!"

Sam hugged her close. "You know I would never tell you what to do. But this is a wise decision. Give yourself time to adjust to the baby – fewer hours spent at the Clinic would be the best way to work." He held her at arm's length. "Having said all that, I have to go to town, and I may stay at Leinster Road overnight." Sam still used his old house there on occasion.

"Is this to do with your decision to examine your life?" Deirdre touched his face. "I hope you will take time for yourself, Sam. Who knows, by working in a devious manner, I might manage to get you off for a holiday within the next couple of years."

"You might at that," he said, chuckling. "I have some changes to make and that could well be one of them." He laughed at Dee's expression of amazement.

"If you are serious, Sam Sweet, I will never say never again in my lifetime."

"You'll see, Missus Sweet, you'll see." He kissed her face. "John will drive me to Dublin – he'll stay up with me, come back sometime tomorrow I expect. I'll ring you on the telephone about supper time."

The meeting with Brendan O'Connor and Cormac Doyle took place in Sam's office at Portobello Harbour. Sam sent his secretary off for a long lunch hour, she having made sure that the three men would not be disturbed until their meeting was over.

Sam wasted no time in coming straight to the point. "I know that both of you have gone over." He had lit a cigarette before starting to speak and he was glad of it now as he drew smoke deeply into his lungs.

"The only reason you didn't hear it from us was because we were leaving you to grieve for Michael Collins." Brendan, the gifted speaker Sam had moulded into a first-class businessman, spoke on behalf of himself and Deirdre's brother.

"Just in case it slipped your notice, it was Dev's crowd that murdered Michael Collins." Sam held down his anger only because he remembered to rub his fingers on his trouser leg, the sense of touch helping him keep his mind in the present moment.

"That's not fair, Sam. He was killed in a gun battle," Cormac Doyle said. "I was there, Sam, right beside him when the ricochet killed him."

"If it was a ricochet," Sam said, suddenly feeling a little weary.

"As long as Collins lived we would have died for him," Cormac retorted angrily. "Without him we have to go with the others. Dev may have his faults, but he is the man now to lead this country forward. And what did you mean when you said, 'if it was a ricochet', Sam?

"Never mind that," Brendan said firmly: "Sam is not the only one wondering about that." Turning all his attention back to Sam, he asked: "What do you want of us, Sam? Where do we stand with you, as men like?"

"You don't stand with me any more." Sam felt a wave of sadness as he heard his own words, saw too the effect on both men but on Brendan O'Connor especially.

"What do you mean? What are you saying, Sam?"

"I left Deirdre in ignorance this morning. She's just learned we're going to have our baby. I couldn't tell her I knew this – I was afraid she might lose our child from the shock and the shame."

"Ah Sam, come on, what we did all along was for the country. This is the same – it's not for gain or fame. It's for Ireland, surely to God you know that."

Sam exhaled and pressed his cigarette butt into the ashtray before he said: "I've been reading some of Mick's letters – he saw much of this coming – he didn't say as much but I believe that when Dev backed off going to the Treaty Talks, Mick decided to risk his life by going instead." Sam waited a moment but neither of the young men spoke. "I always said that Dev knew Lloyd George would never surrender the thirty-two counties – ergo, he knew that whoever signed the Treaty accepting what the British were prepared to give, he knew that man would be the scapegoat – that he would surely be murdered – and clever Dev was not about to take on that role."

"Sam, this kind of talk serves no purpose. No matter how you look at it, either Dev or Collins had to go." There were tears in Brendan O'Connor's eyes as he continued: "I loved Mick Collins, love him now, but that won't bring him back. We have to keep on going."

Sam was smoking a fresh cigarette, exhaling to say: "I'll go to my grave believing Collins did the right thing. Total war unless he and the others accepted the offer that was on the table, that was a promise from Lloyd George – as it turned out, most Irish people wanted above all else an end to the conflict, a chance to get on with their lives, so Collins had done what most of the country wanted. But you're right about one thing, Brendan. This kind of talk serves no useful purpose. So bear with me, while I tell you what I want."

Sam sat down at his desk and glanced at the notes he had made.

"I am selling up – this business and all others in which I have any stake."

"Sam, for God's sake," Brendan's voice carried evidence of his desperation, while Cormac Doyle remained silent, almost as though he had no interest in what was going on.

"I will telephone Alex Gibbon and tell him to make an appointment with each of you. You will tell him what you expect – redundancy payout and the like and he will tell you what I propose. Joe is already setting up the process for the disposal of all my assets. You will be fairly dealt with, but as of today, there is no need for either of you to come into the office." Sam stood up and killed the cigarette butt. "I wish you both the very best."

"Is that it? After all we've been through together?" Brendan O'Connor looked devastated as he wiped away tears with the sleeve of his jacket.

"You'll be well rewarded for your input, Brendan. Have no fear of that."

"If you think that's what I was talking about, God, where have we come to?"

"We've come to the point where you have sided with the arch-enemy of the man murdered in Cork, the man we would have died for. Believe me when I tell you, after that, we have nothing more to say to each other. And that's my final word to you both."

Sam left the office and Brendan O'Connor sank onto a chair, his face drained of colour.

He glanced at Cormac Doyle who ground his cigarette under his heel as he said: "What did you expect? He's a Jewman."

"He was the finest man I ever knew, Cormac."

Cormac nodded his head, his expression derisive: "'Was' is the operative word." He moved to the door. "I'm going for a pint. You coming?"

7

London

October 1922

Some weeks later, at her London home on Eaton Square, Constance Brewer was attempting to control her temper as Sir Albert Whimby waffled on. Not that she disliked him but she hated with a passion the way barristers could rattle on. Even when they were contributing to regular conversation you would fancy they were being paid by the word.

Sir Albert promenaded on the Indian carpet as he did when playing with a jury's emotions in the courtroom: "The courts are simply backed up, old thing, more cases waiting to be heard than at any time in the last decade."

"Don't you old thing me, Albee! I'm certainly aged but I am not an old woman!"

Constance found herself cut off by a chopping movement from the ageing knight's arthritic hand while he chortled in silent derision, remembering that she was eighty if she was a day. "Desist, Connie, please, desist from looking like you are tut-tutting behind that mask of tolerance."

"I never tut-tut, Albee – how dare you suggest such a thing! And incidentally, you look somewhat ridiculous in those Cuban heels. I know they add to your height, but vanity –"

"Stop waffling, Connie. I wear them for my back. Good God, do you seriously think that a man of my age is bothered about looking two inches taller?"

"I know you better than you know yourself." She dismissed his effort to speak with a flick of her hand. "Now tell me how you are going to overcome the difficulty you seem to be having."

"I offer you the facts, forgive me should I not hide those and simply tell you what you want to hear."

Constance dropped her effort to continue politely, her irritation riding the waves of her discontent. "Albee, stop faffing – cut out the legal waffling, if you please. I have no interest in the details. Surely, a man of your power and prestige can get this matter into court without having to queue up for the privilege?"

"Constance, please, I have already explained to you, though once again it seems you have decided not to listen."

"I heard every damn word, Albee. I know that the defendant – your words not mine – that Deirdre Sweet's legal team have, through their expertise and cunning, ensured that this matter will not come before a judge until the New Year."

"Precisely, Connie, the old legal machine is grinding

to a halt and there's not a damn thing one can do about it."

"Talking to you is like talking to a deaf man, Albee. That's more than two months away, this is only mid-October, and I simply will not wait until the idiots clear out this backlog."

Constance stopped speaking as he raised his hand sharply in protest, his smile sliding away, his eyes like scapulars of boredom as he shook his head in mock defeat.

"If you insist on arguing with me when I tell you how things really are," he spoke as though he was hauling a loaded cart, "I'm going to ask you to seek the services of another lawyer."

Constance Brewer's rheumy eyes turned derisive, causing further fissures in her mask of paint and powder, her cosmetic effort never equal to the extensive wreckage caused by the lines of time, self-indulgence and the viciousness of her nature.

'What a pity,' thought Sir Albert, not for the first time in forty-odd years of friendship and social intercourse. 'Too many years, old girl, too much time spent in anger and resentfulness. Such a beautiful and magnificent woman – how I lusted after you!' This truth seemed impossible as he looked at her now, a caricature of the woman she had been. "I'm sorry, my dear – accept my practised endeavour or seek representation by another."

"Oh stop being so stuffy, Albee, stop being such a fusspot! Can't you bribe someone? Can't you, with all your power and influence, jump the queue?"

Constance set her jaw like a rock, knowing he would crumble as he usually did when she insisted on a certain course of action.

Knowing what she was doing, Sir Albert nodded his head in acquiescence, sighing wistfully as he made his way to the promise that she always needed to hear when she wanted something. "As usual I am as putty in your hands, Constance." He allowed her his *Giaconda* smile, knowing he would do nothing more. 'Let her believe what she needs to hear. I am sick to death of her.'

"Make sure you do, Albert," Constance warned him as though his life depended on it. "You stand to make a tidy packet of money from this case. And I know you need the money."

Sir Albert smiled: "Don't *we all*, old thing?"

He was being sarcastic but Constance missed the hint of derision since she was having a heart murmur at that moment. Taking a small bottle from the table by her hand, she held it under her nose and drew her breath in deeply.

In moments she seemed to have recovered for she said fiercely: "How dare you, Albee! My suing the jarvey's daughter and her Jew husband is not about money, it's about principle. Such people should never have been allowed into our way of life. And I am going to see they are booted back into the street and the gutters where they and their kind belong."

Sir Albert rose to take his leave. "When people say to me, Constance, 'It's not the money, it's the principle' – it's *always* the money." He took his hat and the cane he used to ease the pain from his arthritic hip. "And since I made some enquiries, I know that you are desperate for the money you may gain should we win the case. I know how you much you have left at the tables of the Carlton Club in the last several years."

He made a mock bow from the waist, a dart of pain in his kidney area reminding him that he was in his late seventies. "A woman of your age should have more sense." Seeing that she was mute with anger, he took his leave before she could launch an attack, reckoning that she was a decade older than he was, at least.

As soon as she was alone, Constance poured a stiff drink of cognac. She swallowed half of it in a gulp to help her dismiss the taste her barrister had left on her mouth. She hated him really, hated all barristers because she considered them charlatans who would never give you a straight answer, never commit really, and never quit putting their hand out to be paid, up front.

She was seething over the delay in her efforts to bring Arthur's widow to the law courts. Constance believed that her late son, Arthur, had been out of his mind when he married the daughter of a man born and reared in the top-floor flat of a tenement in The Liberties of Dublin city. To her mind, this area of Dublin was a notorious den of rebels and the kind of scum that inhabit any city. The thought that this seamstress, who had inveigled her way into Arthur's bed, was to live in the luxury of the Brewer wealth for the rest of her life brought a fist of discomfort to lodge in the old woman's stomach. She emptied the brandy balloon, vowing that it could not, it would not happen, not as long as she had a breath left to fight for the right to what belonged to her. Her son had been unfit to wed this wretched dressmaker and when he made his will he was further into delusion brought on by alcohol. Constance shook her head in bewilderment – how could her son have deserted his own people? How could he have betrayed all that the Ascendancy stood for? It was simply unthinkable.

Some time later, having told her butler, Johnstone, that she was retiring, Constance slowly made her way up the massive winding staircase to her bedroom.

Now and again her aching limbs reminded her that this nightly climb up the stairs of this huge house was beyond her, rather, but she dismissed yet again the nagging notion that she should sell it, move to a smaller abode.

Never! She was Constance Brewer, and this house was exactly the right size, with precisely the right address, for a person of her standing and she vowed she would die before people would know that she was as poor as a church mouse.

As she prepared for bed she was thankful that Thursday came around just once in the week. Her personal maid was off tonight and though she had left everything ready for Constance, the old lady found it no end of bother to get herself ready to settle down for the night.

8

October 1922

At the same hour on this Thursday night, May Murray was busily serving rough cuts of meat in thick beef gravy with potatoes she cooked in the ashes of the great fireplace in her public house kitchen.

She was tired, mentally fatigued from wondering, and worrying too, about how things were going with Pack over in London. In addition to her private concern that he might just have absconded with the money she had given him for his hotel and his other expenses, his absence soon had the locals making jokes, suggesting he had robbed May and departed in the dark "as tinkers do second nature".

The banter had ceased when she lied artlessly that Pack had gone to a funeral and was coming back to finish the work he had started on the back of the house.

Once or twice she almost let go of the calm she struggled to keep. She had been put to the pin of her collar not to throw her natural caution to the winds – a couple of her regulars had come very close to getting a face full of hot gravy as they belaboured the idea that anyone would be simple enough to trust a tinker.

As May prepared for bed, she was aware of how demanding it was – on your nerves and your feelings – all the thinking about how it would be if the old woman Brewer went for the proposition on offer.

Being a sensible woman, May had tried very hard to let the thoughts go away – between them nagging at her all day long, and herself wondering would Pack really come back, she was weary each night as she got into bed.

"But just imagine it," she murmured to herself in her bedroom mirror, "in no time at all, that rich old woman could hand over money enough to ensure that Pack and me would be free of financial considerations for the rest of our lives!"

She gulped at the boldness of her thinking but she laughed then at her reflection.

"What's the good in kidding yourself?" she said aloud. "You hope to God he's going to marry you!" May sipped her night-time whiskey: "And if he doesn't go for that, you could well end up living together like a married couple."

'We could move away,' she thought, brushing out her hair. 'Make a fresh start in England or America. No need for anybody to know that Pack was born by the roadside and that he spent most of his thirty-five years living at that same address.'

The weeks before he had sailed for England had been a trying enough time – so much to be done to get him organised and ready for what he had to do. 'We might have adopted a leisurely approach,' she admitted to herself now. But that wasn't the way of Pack Rowan. 'Once I'd given him proof of the story, convinced him it would stand up to any scrutiny, he couldn't wait to get to England and go looking for the oul'one with the power to make us rich.'

Although she was missing Pack's help around the place, May found herself thinking more about their nights together in her great bed. Shaking herself out of such reverie had become a necessity – she had found that her mouth went completely dry when she allowed her mind to linger on the power he had over her under the bed covers.

She forced herself to remember how they had shopped in Dublin for the right suit and shoes and shirts and all the rest of it. She smiled when she remembered just how well they had turned him out. Well, it had to be done properly – he had to look well off enough not to be thrown out as he attempted to get an audience with Constance Brewer.

May was all too aware of this as she paid for his suits and accoutrements in good heart. She believed utterly that her dream, backed up by their carefully worked plan could pay dividends in a very big way.

Pack had surprised her by his self-confidence about having to meet Constance Brewer.

"I have to be alone with her to tell her the story in my own way. That means I will be alone with her. Don't you sweat it, I'll handle my end of bargain and that's a tinker's promise to you, May."

He must have sensed a pinpoint of doubt – she certainly hoped he wasn't just blowing smoke like a lot of men did as if it was second nature, for he said deliberately: "May, look at me and hear me well. If the woman is alive, I will get to see her. I'm not saying I'll try to get to see her. I am telling you, as the man that shares your bed, I will see her."

May relaxed her face, wanting him confident that she believed him. She wanted to, but she could do no more than hope in her heart that he would deliver. Saying 'I'll just go ahead and do it' was one thing, but this rich old woman, living in luxury – she would have servants waiting on her hand and foot, day and night – so you couldn't just barge in there. Like, even if Pack showed up dressed as a gentleman, it wouldn't necessarily get him admitted to the house, even though he was, in May's eyes, very presentable and more than a fair bit handsome.

When they had committed to Pack making the trip to London, May had readily agreed to finance the operation. Her lover was willing to take the personal risks involved. Were things to go badly for him, the affair could turn out to be a criminal offence and he could face the possibility of going to prison. This caveat didn't deter him, not in the slightest. Again he seemed supremely confident that he would pull off whatever had to be done to take the situation to the next step.

May realised she needed to go as far as Dublin with him – and not just to help him in every way possible to fit the role of Constance Brewer's champion.

In truth she wanted to be with him, sleep with him,

feel him close and in and all about her on the nights he would be in the city. He was the most virile man she had ever slept with, and she didn't want him alone with her money in his pocket, and an empty bed in a hotel room waiting for whatever woman he talked into spending the night with him.

At the same time she had serious misgivings about closing her house for the few days she would be in Dublin, but she kept her thoughts clear by writing down the reasons she felt she had to accompany him.

She was going with him to give him what he needed every night as much as she did. She felt too that she had to be there – he would need her to dress him, give him the right kind of look. After all, he was going to be rubbing shoulders with people who didn't wear rubber boots and spit in public. In her own way she wanted to protect *them* by keeping him satisfied in the sexual department, and she wanted to protect *him* from things like having to choose a tie, which he would do anything to avoid.

And last of all, she wanted to protect her financial investment by booking his passage on the boat and by being there as he went on board, even giving him a wave as he was being transported down the Liffey to the open sea and England beyond.

Without saying a word to anybody, they left Dunbla of an early morning. As a gesture to Pack – she wanted to have his input to the idea of leaving the public house – May had expressed some concern about her customers: "Some of them rely on me now for the drink they need to get through the day."

Pack was hardly listening but he dismissed her concern without questioning whether it was genuine or not: "Just shut the house up and we go. They won't like it but you're the only open house for miles, so they'll be gasping in relief when you get back."

May later chuckled when she found his prophecy had been accurate – she had returned home and was scarcely in the door when she received her first customers, thirsty men grateful that she was back.

As she began serving drinks, May was more removed than ever from her life at that moment. This was not what she wanted – facing these people day in and day out for the rest of her life.

She thought of Dublin city which had impressed her – it was not on a par with London – but she was surprised by the number of people about the streets every time she went out, and the overall feeling that there was money could be made here.

For the first time she hadn't just been passing through the capital on her way to London – she was taken by what Dublin had to offer – great business opportunities, entertainment, the kind of privacy, even anonymity, you could never expect to have living in the countryside where all most people talked about was other people, and the weather.

She caught herself smiling the odd time as the day ran into evening – remembering little things and odd moments – like Pack's reaction when she told him to get the three-shilling haircut and shampoo in the high-class Gents' Tonsorial Parlour off Dublin's Grafton Street.

She would suddenly feel warm about him as she saw

herself scrubbing his back later with this thing called a loofah in the bath along the hall from their hotel room.

Her mind held the new smell from his body in the bed when they made love each night between white linen sheets, before she saw him off from the North Wall embarkation point.

Overall she felt happier than she had ever known herself to be. This confirmed in her mind that what was going on between herself and Pack was the right thing for her at this time in her life. Had it been unwise she would have been getting nudges from inside warning her to mind herself.

She had no misgivings either about her plan to get a lot of money from Constance Brewer. Standing back she couldn't see there was anything wrong about it – she wanted payment for information that anybody would be happy to have in their possession. Pure chance had put this valuable commodity in her path – she was just going with the natural flow of things in taking the next step.

Anyway, people who played hanky-panky with other people's husbands and wives, weren't they bound to get punished one way or the other?

The other thing was that Gloria need never know her journals had been replaced with books that looked exactly the same. Not that she'd notice – during the time May had been her housekeeper, the boss had never even glanced at the journals – they'd stayed buried under the other boxes in the wardrobe – she had found them by pure accident. When she said this to Pack he had called it a great stroke of luck.

They had eaten very well during their Dublin visit – May had cast aside her reservations about expensive places – caution to the wind, she said to herself – so that they ate a lunch at the Shelbourne hotel that cost three shillings and sixpence a head for the à la carte menu.

May felt such a thrill at being there that she asked Pack would he take drink with lunch.

"I won't, May," he said with such ease that she was instantly impressed. "No jar till I've had a chat with this Constance Brewer, just in case it might get in the way, mess things up."

The three days in the capital city had flown by as they went about the business in hand. They walked a lot – she saw many people cycling and Pack, who was devoid of interest in sightseeing, did his best not to get annoyed with May who *ooed* and *aaahed* at soldiers in uniform with rifles at the ready as they flew by on lorries that waited for nobody to get out of the way. May gaped at a handsome policeman who was directing traffic – horse-drawn carts and vans shared the streets with motor cars and the electric trams that floated by on tracks of steel, their power coming from overhead cables that stretched as far as her eye could see. She loved it all, liking Dublin more every minute she spent there.

"Stop pulling me back to look at things," Pack said gruffly after the third time. "I'm only interested in getting what we need to back up our story – then to get out of here and over to London and see if I can pull off the deal we want."

May ignored his gruffness, full of tenderness at how

kind he had been to her after their lovemaking in the night. He was a powerful man in every way but he had seemed to melt a bit, become gentler than she had known him to be so far, and for a fleeting moment she thought he might utter words of love to go with his uncharacteristically gentle way.

They took a cab from the small hotel in Rathmines to the Custom House, where they applied for a copy of a birth certificate – the all-important document that would supply the false information regarding the manner in which the eldest son of Arthur and Deirdre Brewer had come into the world.

They had an hour to wait before the Copy Clerk could provide the certificate. They used the time to check the details of Arthur Brewer's will at the office of Public Records, where a surprising number of people sought details of who had left what to whom.

They found a café where they ate deep-fried fish and chips and May smiled each time she took another look at the certificate secured from the office of Births, Marriages and Deaths. It was a simple document but worth so much money. Signed by an officer of the State over the given date and time of the birth of Edward Arthur Shane Brewer it would prove the false witnessing of those named as mother and father to the child. May pressed the paper to her bosom – every minute they were getting a step closer to making her dream come true.

When Constance had recovered from the task of getting

herself ready for bed on this Thursday night, she plumped her pillows before returning to the penny dreadful she had been reading. She sipped brandy as she picked up the racy story of a young woman ravished by a highwayman who convinces him that he must, having taken her, keep her for his woman.

Quite breathless at the prospect of what was to come as the handsome rapist inducted his mistress into the art of highway robbery, Constance heard no sound to alarm her. In fact, she only realised that a man had entered her bedroom when he coughed in a polite manner.

When she looked up she saw a tall, powerfully built individual of rugged good looks. He was quite well dressed and recently barbered and shaved, and she saw at once that he was displaying a revolver that was pointed casually in her direction.

Though she was into her ninth decade of existence, Constance could have counted on the fingers of one hand the times she had been rendered speechless. This was one such moment – she was so flabbergasted that she didn't notice the book slip from her fingers while she simply goggled at the intruder.

"You have nothing to fear from me, lady. That's a promise," Pack Rowan said quietly. "If you will hear me out, I give you my word you will quickly know that I am the bearer of good tidings."

"Who are you and what do you want here?" She had found her voice and was quite prepared to give this blackguard a piece of her mind.

Something about him – was it the fact that he had not threatened her? – was it the last words he had said:

"*I am the bearer of good tidings*"? – stopped her from yelling 'Help!'.

She could not have said in the moment – she remained silent now, taking him in, removing her reading glasses to see him the better as he stood ten feet away from her, the weapon hanging from his hand now down by his right leg.

"I come to you, lady, with important news, very good important news, in relation to your court case against Deirdre Sweet, formerly Deirdre Brewer." Pack spoke without inflection, his voice devoid of entreaty. "If you hear me out, I promise you, you won't regret it."

"Who are you? What do you know of this affair?" Constance took her time to study his demeanour and found him rock steady in what was a disarming barefaced way.

"If you'll allow me a few minutes to tell you the story, you will either be more welcoming or you will try to call the police. Should you be inviting me to sit down and carry on with the story, instead of yelling for help, I'll tell you my name and anything else you want to know about me."

Pack waited while she went on studying him, pleased to see that he had made her curious.

He was surprised by the energy in her voice. She looked like someone who had lived way beyond the three score and ten that the Bible allotted as a normal lifespan, but her voice didn't belong to an old woman.

"What have you to say to me then?" She lay back against her pillows, continuing to look at him, convinced that she was not in any danger.

Pack thought she looked like a lizard, her facial texture like diseased parchment, the wattle of skin under her chin repulsive to the eye. He lit a cigarette and took a good pull on it before he went on. "I'll begin by telling you that the eldest son of Deirdre Brewer is not the legal heir to her estate. And at this moment, it is her estate. It belongs to her because your son, Arthur, deceased, left all and every bit of his wealth to her to distribute as she saw fit, when Edward and Alfred come of age – Eddie and Alfie as they are called."

Pack paused, inhaled deeply, giving Constance time to digest the news he had given her, which, when you considered her position in this matter, could only be of the very best kind.

"I mention this," he continued in the same flat tone, "because I know you have been estranged from your late son's widow and unlikely to be party to this particular family secret."

Pack heard her intake of breath, smiled as she took her brandy glass from the bedside table and swallowed what was left of the spirit.

She looked at him now with serious interest, nodding her head as though life had become more agreeable of a sudden. Unconsciously, she spent a few moments licking her lips before she said: "As you knew I would be, I am interested in hearing the rest of what you came here to tell me." She held out the empty balloon. "But first, pour brandy, for both of us."

She never took her eyes from Pack as he obeyed her command, and when she told him to sit on the chaise lounge he did so with natural ease.

"Now tell me precisely what you mean when you say that Edward is not the legal heir to the estate. But first tell me your name." Constance sipped her cognac, and smoked deeply in anticipation, her jaded eyes never leaving his face.

"At the moment I'm called Pack Rowan," he said calmly. "Now, to answer your first question, the lad known as Edward Brewer is not the heir because . . ." He paused for effect and was not disappointed as she came forward off her pillows, her eyes squinting as though she was trying to burn holes in the space between them.

"Get on with it, man!" The old woman snorted derisively, unable to curtail her need. "Tell me how you can sit there and confidently inform me that Edward is not the legal heir of Arthur's widow?"

"Because he is not Deirdre's blood son, nor is he the blood son of the late Arthur Brewer."

Constance fell back on her pillows, taking some moments before she perked up on a serious drink of cognac. Enjoying the brandy as it threw fingers of warmth around in her chest she said firmly: "You have proof of this or you would not have come here, Pack Rowan."

"Yes, lady, you're right."

"You are willing to give me this information."

"Right again, lady. I have the proof that will win you your court case, all the proof you need, worth, as the man said, a considerable sum of money."

"Have no fear," Constance said glibly. "You will be well rewarded if what you say is true."

"I didn't come here to waste your time or my own,

m' lady," Pack said firmly. "I won't be getting any reward from you for the service I can provide. I will be getting a share, to be agreed, since you and me are going to have an arrangement, a business arrangement." He saw her stiffen at his high-handed tone but he continued relentlessly: "The labourer being worthy of his hire, ma'am, even more worthy when he comes bearing the gift of evidence that I have in hand, all that you need to win you your heart's desire."

Constance nodded her head in agreement, her eye jaundiced, her tone when she spoke suggesting that, despite her reservations, she felt respect for his directness. "All of that will be worked out to our mutual satisfaction. But tell me now, if you will, who is Eddie? Where did he come from if he is not the son of Arthur and his Papist widow?"

"He is the son of a tinker girl who died on his birth, fathered by the man you see before you here and now. Deirdre's child was stillborn." Pack lit a cigarette and leaned back on the drag to watch Constance Brewer perk up like a ravenous bird aware of the emerging worm.

"You have papers or something to prove this?" Constance could not listen to the voice inside telling her not to be too anxious since it drove the price up.

"I have papers and more, my lady. I know where the bodies are buried."

He let her soak that up for a few moments.

"I left the pregnant girl with my mother at the same spot where we rested for fifteen years at that time of year. The exact location is burned indelibly into my mind." He could see she was impressed and he smiled inside on the thought, 'Put that in your pipe and smoke it!'

Constance Brewer experienced a mild flutter of the heart. It was not strong enough to alarm her and she immediately drank the last of her cognac. She held her glass out to Pack Rowan then, waiting while he poured her another drink, her eyes never leaving his face. When he placed the balloon in her hand she smiled at him. "You must pour for yourself, Pack Rowan. We must toast our working arrangement."

When he came back to the bed they touched the delicate brandy balloons carefully, Constance saying in a formal tone: "To loyalty between partners and success to our endeavour!"

They drank the Bisquit Dubouche with great care and pleasure. In a moment, Pack, looked into the eyes of the old woman and said in a formal way: "I pledge my loyalty to you, my lady, and nothing will change that unless you do me wrong."

"That will not happen, Pack Rowan. I have the privilege of being a lady, born and bred. My word is my bond." Constance spoke with the haughtiness that had made her a laughing stock among her own class. This façade now masked her breathlessness, her heart again fluttering, her excitement pumping through her as she considered the fortune that was already on its way to her bank account.

"I accept your word, my lady, but since this is a matter of business, I'd be grateful to have your commitment on paper."

Constance raised her hand like a policeman and put down her brandy glass. Taking her handbag from the bedside table she immediately found her chequebook and pen, and with great care wrote in a slow deliberate manner a cheque which she handed to Pack Rowan.

"Does that satisfy you as a show of my faith in you as a man, and as my partner in this venture?" She already knew the answer to the question as she observed Pack checking that the sum of his advance really was One Thousand Pounds.

"Yes, my lady," he then said quietly, the respect in his voice somewhat overdone. "I am on your side and you will fare the better for having me with you, I promise you." He felt a sunburst of excitement as he thought of cashing the cheque – he felt so good he almost laughed out loud at the thought that his foresight and a fee of seventy-five pounds had ensured that the right identification papers to do so were in his pocket before he had stepped on the steam packet out of Dublin. On the other hand, he mused, he might keep the cheque and give it to May as a token of his honesty. That might be a better move. And, after all, there would be larger cheques to follow . . .

"I accept that," Constance said, pleased that he hadn't noticed she had dated the cheque three days hence. She had no choice since she had to deposit money before the cheque would be honoured. "You have my hand and my money, Pack Rowan, and though you are nobody's servant, you are bound to me by our pledge, sealed in the only meaningful way, with you pocketing my money. So, when will you return with the documentary proof I need to get on about my business?"

"I'll be back by the end of next week, ma'am," Pack said, the excitement still running through his veins like fresh blood.

"You will be returning to Dunbla at once?"

"Yes, ma'am, I came to London only to see your good self and talk with you as we have done."

"Very well, you must go now. I'm tired. But, Pack Rowan, as you have assured me you know where the bodies are buried, allow me to present you with a word of warning. I have thrown my lot in with you – let me down, or try in any way to cheat me out of that which I have paid a deposit on, and you will live to regret it. That's my solemn promise to you."

"I'm not educated, ma'am, but neither am I stupid. I bid you goodnight."

With those words Pack left the woman who had become a partner with May and himself – smiling as he descended the stairs silently to leave by the kitchen door forced earlier, without a soul knowing he had come to make a late-night call on the mistress of the house.

9

October 1922

At two o'clock on the day after his midnight meeting with Constance Brewer, Pack Rowan drank sweet tea and ate a bacon sandwich as he waited for Walter Guildford to leave his office and come to the tea stall for his lunch.

The day was like a harbinger for a severe winter with its biting cold rain showers and a rising wind that suggested to Pack Rowan it was a night for the high stool. He relished the thought – when his business with Guildford was over he would get a few hours' sleep before going out on the batter with some old pals that still lurked around Camden Town.

Within a minute he saw his old cell mate leave the run-down building by Fulham Broadway and cross the street to the tea stall.

As Guildford reached the horse-drawn tea wagon, he was salivating as the waft of frying bacon nudged his hunger.

Rowan knew that the dapper enquiry agent has seen him as he moved away from the serving hatch to make room for a team of workmen looking for grub. Moments later, as his eyes followed the hip movement of a pretty nursemaid pushing a pram, he was joined by his old cell mate.

"You look jolly well, old chap," Guildford spoke softly, his accent upper crust, but modestly so, the result of many hours copying the speech patterns of his commanding officer in the Coldstream Guards in the months before Guildford had been cashiered for cheque fraud.

Now in his early fifties, Guildford was a handsome man who tried and succeeded in looking nondescript. His suit of plain grey wool housed a slight frame of medium height, his curly-brimmed bowler his only nod in the direction of fashion.

"I'm good, Wally," Pack smiled knowingly, "and you're still out and about so you're doing all right for yourself."

Walter Guildford sipped his tea while he waited for his bacon sandwich. He was somewhat surprised by the quality of Rowan's attire – plain grey worsted suit, over a hard white collar with a narrow tie of dark red wool, his bowler held by his side.

Pack now lit a cigarette and moved his head to follow the progress of a handsome woman who was heading for the underground station.

"I see you are still interested in the ladies, Billy," said Guildford. "Or have you got a new name now?"

"Pack Rowan's the name, Wally, and I have some money for you in advance of more, if you get me the

information I need about somebody I've been looking
for this good while."

"If he's walking around he can be found. You know
my motto, Billy, sorry, eh Pack. How much did you
intend to give me, in advance?"

"Fifty quid. The job's worth one-fifty, depending on
how quickly you get the goods on yer man."

Guildford was pleasantly surprised. "Does your
man have a name?"

"Séamus O'Reilly," Pack said, wondering would the
penny drop. "He may even be using Jem Riley again.
With that lunatic, you never know."

Guildford looked pensive – Pack slipped the rolled-
up English fivers from his pocket and passed them
over.

"Séamus O'Reilly? Here! Wait a moment. Wasn't he
suspected of pushing The Vicar off the balcony that
time in the Scrubs?"

"He was, and he should have hung for it. And he
will, or worse, when I find him."

"You have no idea at all where he is?"

"Not a notion," Pack drank the last of his tea. "I'd
find him in a minute," he lied in an effort to keep the
cost down, "only I'm too busy to be runnin' around."

"So that aggravated burglary warrant's still hanging
over you?" his companion said with a knowing smile.

The look he received in response was enough to put
fear into the heart of any sensible man.

Guildford shrugged his shoulders, a suggestion that
he was merely making a joke. "So you think he killed
The Vicar?"

"I know he did, Wally. He hated Vic being a friend to me, resented him teaching me to read and write. And he hated me even more 'cos I stole his woman before I got nicked meself a few months after he did. He grassed me out that time, only I could never prove it." Pack sucked the last drag from his cigarette. "Anyway, I want to know where he is, and in a hurry. Like I said, I'll look after you."

"Give me another seventy-five now and I'll put one of my chaps to work on it right away. You'll have to make one further payment, of one hundred and twenty-five, when I deliver the goods to you." Guildford lit a cigarette. "How soon would you like a result?"

"I'll be out of England for a week or so," Pack said offhandedly. "I'm in importing and exporting, moving around a good bit. I'll telephone you when I arrive."

Pack took seventy-five pounds from the three hundred May had given him. As he handed it over he said: "Do well by me here, Wally, and you'll do better – above and beyond what we've agreed. I want Séamus O'Reilly or whatever he's calling himself. I know he killed The Vicar and he has to pay for that. Vic was the most decent skin I ever met and that half crazy bastard will pay the price for taking his life."

That same afternoon, at her flat on Cadogan Square, Gloria Stein was dismayed to discover that her journals had been removed from the wardrobe in her bedroom. This was bad enough – but there was also the puzzling aspect of a similar set of blank-paged books now lodging in her journal box. Was her memory failing her? Had she stored the used journals elsewhere? Or confused them perhaps with a set of spare blank journals?

No, she had no memory of ever possessing a spare set of such books. In fact, she remembered distinctly buying them one by one as the need arose.

She stood facing the mirror running the length of the wardrobe door, addressing herself, her head shaking in disbelief. "Who could have taken them? Who would have any reason to take them? And conceal the fact by leaving duplicates?"

Going into the kitchen she found Anna, her housekeeper, washing up after lunch. Gloria went to the Aga and poured herself a cup of tea from the ever-warm pot the Glasgow woman could not live without. Determined to remain calm, she squeezed a little lemon juice into the tea and sipped it for a few moments.

Then, as Anna wiped down the worktop by the sink, Gloria said: "Anna, I'd like to have a word with you about my journals."

When the middle-aged Scotswoman turned to face her she could tell right away that the housekeeper had no idea what she was talking about.

"I dinna know anything, Missus, about journals of any sort or description. What made you think that I would, if you don't mind me asking you, Missus?"

Gloria drank tea to cover her confusion. "I was wondering if perhaps you had moved them, put them somewhere else."

"Never saw them, Missus. Didna know they even existed. You dinna think that I –?"

Gloria raised her hand in a placatory gesture and the woman stopped talking. "I had no thought on the matter at all, Anna. Oh! Now I remember. I left them in a small trunk with some other things at a storage facility in town. Silly me! My memory is going to pot." Gloria blushed on the lie, scurrying to the bathroom to run cold water over her wrists to bring her temperature down.

As the water did its work she looked at herself in the mirror and said: "May – could May have taken them?"

Surely not! She had got on so well with her. The woman had been perfect for the job, ran the home with built-in ability and was always clean and personable and loyal to a fault. A woman in her mid-thirties, Gloria had always thought her a cut above many she had met while touring Ireland years before with Bill Boswell's Bohemian Band. She wondered how the Boswells were these days. They had not written for several weeks – she herself had been so busy touring the British Isles that she hadn't found the time to scribble even a few stay-in-touch lines.

'Shameful,' she said to herself in the mirror. 'Bill and Emily saved your life – they helped you come back to life when you lost Mama – you really must write to them tonight.' She confirmed this with a nod at her reflection. "But whatever has happened to my journals?" She asked the question out loud, not at all surprised that her mind provided no answer.

An hour later, having searched the flat thoroughly, Gloria knew without any doubt that the journals had been taken. She paused before allowing the thought to develop – appalled at the very idea: the journals had been stolen.

As she sank into her bath – she would nap for half an hour before preparing for tonight's concert at Wigmore Hall – she gathered herself together with a view to remembering when she had last seen the set of books containing the most personal and intimate details of her life.

To her chagrin she came to the conclusion that she had seen them about two years earlier just after she had taken May Murray on as her housekeeper. Not that she had mentioned the journals to the Irishwoman, but she herself had moved two boxes of books she could not bear to part with into the same wardrobe, placing them on top of the journals and thinking no more about it.

In a moment her world seemed to drop to the pit of her stomach, so that she found herself gasping for breath as she lay in the bathtub. My God!

"Those pages were written to take some of the burden from my heart. I never intended that another should read them. It's unthinkable!" She was so upset that she was speaking aloud in an effort to stay calm while she looked for an answer. "Why would anybody want the notes of a stranger who was, much of the time, on the brink of going insane?"

She made a conscious effort to release the tension that had built up – she had tonight's recital to think of. This didn't work for her. She knew in her heart that her journals had been stolen. And stolen by someone with the presence of mind to leave blank substitutes in their place. She lay back in the water and allowed the decision as to what she should do come to her in its own time.

"I have to talk to Sam about this. He will help me find out what the theft of my private journals means."

Driving to the Clinic on Cork Street, on her first day back after her enforced rest, Deirdre observed the newest evidence of the Civil War. In one ten-minute period she passed an orderly dressing wounded Free State soldiers – while both Free State and Republican men had stopped shooting to allow their wounded comrades to be taken away for medical attention – then, by the time she had driven to the next corner, she heard the rifles go back into action while she shook her head and asked herself had the country gone mad altogether.

Joan Ryan jumped up delighted from the desk and gave Deirdre a hug. Dee responded in kind, knowing what a strain her absence had placed on Joan's life day to day.

"You look so well, Dee!" Joan was surprised by how healthy she looked, doing nothing to hide the sound of relief in her voice. "You've been sadly missed, let me tell you." She put out her cigarette. "Sounds to me that the morning sickness could be over and done with."

"I'm keeping my fingers crossed." Dee found herself smiling grandly, simply because she was back at the facility she and Joan had managed to get off the ground. Just their first step, they believed, towards the day they would run a large hospital devoted to the health and care of mother and baby from conception, and for some years after birth.

Dee looked about the office which also served as a dispensary, and now and then as an emergency lying-in station, when the twelve regular beds were occupied.

"The first thing I suggest is that you take a few days off, starting tonight." Dee poured tea from the tin kettle sitting on the pot-bellied stove, smiling at the colour of it. "Lovely." She stirred in one spoon of sugar. "You could trot a mouse on that." She held the kettle up, offering to pour for Joan.

She shook her head: "It's a large brandy I need."

"And well earned is what I say. Teresa gave me a daily report while I was at home. Impressive is mild in the face of what you've been handling."

Joan's face slithered into an uneasy grin. "Did she tell you I punched Marie Carey's husband in the nose?"

"She mentioned it. Apparently you broke it." Dee was hiding her own amusement. "What did he do to earn a bloody nose?"

"It was in here. I was trying to find out how much he could afford towards Marie's keep. He was humming and hawing and I told him straight that we need all the help we can get. I made the mistake of getting too close to him. Next thing he grabs my breasts. 'Yiv a rare pair of dairies on you,' says he – jarred of course. I pushed him back – he started to unbutton himself. That was when I punched him." She sat down and shook her head. "I wasn't thinking, but I stepped on him, warned him if he gave any more trouble I'd bring the police into it – my jumper was covered in whatever goo he had on his hands."

"Poor Marie thinks he's God's gift." Dee sipped the tea.

"The real problem is so does he," Joan said, lighting a fresh cigarette. As she inhaled deeply Dee saw she needed to share whatever was causing her discomfort.

"Things are no better between yourself and John?"

Joan was breathing deeply to cut off the tears threatening to fall. "We want different things." She shook her head in a gesture of failure. "He is so hurt, poor John, such a decent skin. He's the innocent here." Joan shrugged and exhaled. "He insists that if I tell Simon it's over, he will never mention it again."

"He loves you. He wants to stay married to you."

"I feel such a rotten bitch when I see the pain in his eyes."

"Do you think you can let Simon go?"

Joan looked up at Deirdre as though wondering how she could even ask the question. Unable to come up with an answer, she drew deeply on the last part of the cigarette. "How did you stay out of trouble, you and Sam, for so long?"

Dee lit a cigarette before she spoke. "I loved Sam as a pal all my life – then as a lover – though even then we didn't make love for five or six years. I wouldn't risk breaking my marriage vows and he never made a move until I was ready." She took a long pull on her cigarette, savouring all the memories from that time. "I lost Arthur entirely when the drinking got completely out of hand. Then it just happened between Sam and me."

"You're the only one I talk to, Dee." Joan shook her head like someone trying to shed an unwanted idea. "The idea of having to give Simon up . . . I don't know if I could live, manage without him there."

Dee put down her teacup and came to where Joan sat on the chair. She drew her up and put her arms around her. In a moment Joan was clinging to her, her tears tumbling into the collar of Dee's work shirt and through to her skin. "I want you to get out of here this minute. Take the rest of the day, see Simon if you have to, but no more talk of what you just said. At the risk of sounding like a selfish bitch, I need you beside me right here."

Joan pulled her face back from Dee's shoulder to say with a very wet wry grin: "It was only the Clinic stopped me doing something really stupid in the last week or so."

Deirdre sat Joan down and came back with a face flannel. "Just sit still now and let Aunty Dee give you a wipe down."

"I made a mistake marrying John. He's the innocent one here, and I feel so guilty for the pain he's going through."

"Did you ever love him? Ever feel about him as you do about Simon?"

"He was just there, Dee, a good man, always attentive to me. And there was nobody else. So, when he asked me for the hundredth time to marry him I said yes. I didn't know then it was possible to feel what I feel for Simon." Joan stood up, sniffed back the threat of more tears. "I just don't know what I'm going to do."

"The one thing I do know," Dee rinsed the face flannel under the cold tap, "when you don't know what to do, do nothing. Make a cup of tea, take a bath, something, anything, but don't try to change things. Just leave them be for the minute."

"Now that I've got my self-pity in hand, can I ask you how Sam is? You said he was badly shook about Michael Collins getting shot."

"He's all right, more than all right, really. But will he ever really get over it, I wonder? He's getting out of business. Right now he's on his way to London to see his son, Mendel. Gloria has some problem she wants Sam to look into."

"You don't mind him going over to see his ex-wife . . . y'know?"

Joan was back to her old self and Dee smiled. "Gloria's only interested in earning money to help the Jews of the world get to their Promised Land. Sam and she get along well – it's a good thing, especially for the boy's sake."

"It's probably my own guilty conscience talking but I'd be worried about letting my husband go visit his first wife."

"She needs Sam's help. I don't know the details. But Sam will sort it out. To help Gloria and the boy, he'll go to the ends of the earth if he has to."

Joan shrugged: "You're a better woman than me, Dee. I'd be afraid, y'know?"

"There is no better woman than you," Dee said matter-of-factly. "Now go and get some air, and see if you can find a way not to want Simon so much."

With that she went into the ward, back on the job, back where she belonged.

Taking a cab from Claridges, Sam told the driver to go to Cadogan Square, not surprised that he felt no sentimental draw to the wonderful hotel where he and Gloria had spent their honeymoon night.

That was back at the end of July, fourteen years ago, after a quiet marriage at the Register's Office in Petty France, close by Buckingham Palace.

The wedding supper at the hotel had been something of a disaster because Sam had surprised his bride by having Arthur Brewer and Deirdre turn up that morning as witnesses.

Gifted actress though she was, Gloria had found it extremely difficult to hide her real feelings, going through the motions of a young bride somewhat overwhelmed by the day's events.

Sam, of course, had no idea at the time of what she was going through.

Neither did Arthur.

Some years later, while Sam and Gloria were trying to keep their marriage together, Sam had taken the liberty of reading his wife's journals – Gloria had given some of them to Esther, the mother-in-law she adored and cherished, to read, wanting her to know what she had come through in her young life. Esther had left one unattended and Sam had been hurting enough to take what he then considered to be a harmless peek. When he came to know what had happened to his wife, especially on the night of the summer solstice at Dunbla when Arthur and Dee celebrated their engagement, he was somewhat shattered, but not for long.

Yes, his self-esteem suffered, but on discovering the horrific life Gloria had endured at her mother's side, he was grateful he had stepped all over the rules of etiquette and common decency by dipping into Gloria's secret writings. Hiding the bruised state of his ego he had begun there and then to help his wife come to terms with some of the ghosts that were driving her to the brink of insanity.

When the taxi stopped on Cadogan Square, he paid off the driver and walked back to the corner. He bought a bunch of flowers from the street dealer who went on yelling about the charitable work she was doing by giving her wonderful roses away for next to nothing. Sam smiled, the moment evoking some of the memories of his own beginnings, buying and selling on the streets of the city where he had been born in what the Dubs called Little Jerusalem.

Gloria welcomed him to her grand flat in this exclusive enclave lying off Kings Road, Chelsea, and she thanked him for coming over from Dublin at such short notice.

Sam was comfortable in her company and found that he quite liked her now that she had quit being a zealot. He forgave himself the judgemental attitude but still tasted the dismay and the pain endured when at one stage during their marriage she had cut off her mane of wonderful blue-black hair. He had returned from work one day to find her hair gone, the bristles like a black skullcap that had been painted onto her head.

Gloria had also strapped down her magnificent breasts – forbidding him to touch them even when she granted him his conjugal rights, as she had come to think of lovemaking. Much as he admired her now, wished her well, he could not always shut out the bells tolling what had been the death knell of their marriage.

They didn't discuss the past any more, he restricting his curiosity about the future of his son – but just for the moment. His serious reservations about Mendel going to live in Palestine were on hold. He knew that should that ever look as if it was really going to happen, he would do what he had to do at that time.

Meanwhile, his daughter Sarah had become part of the Brewer household, the two boys Eddie and Alfie like her brothers, though the girl and Eddie continued to believe they would marry each other some day.

Mendel, allowed home from school for a week because of the outbreak of flu there, came to the table for his evening meal, as always polite but nonetheless distant from his father.

"Perhaps I could take you both to a play, or a musical if you'd like," Sam offered. "Do you like the theatre, Mendel?"

"I prefer a book worth reading, father. I enjoy my mother's concert performances – are you aware that her voice gets better year by year?"

Sam confessed he was not, saddened to find that his son continued to keep himself safely locked away from all, except, apparently, his mother.

Mendel had chosen to leave Ireland to be with Gloria as opposed to staying at home with his father and his sister. This had pained Sam at the time, and as he sat watching the boy – quite tall for a twelve-year-old – leave the table, he wondered whether his own growing lack of interest in Mendel had to do with the residual hurt from that first major rejection of him by his only son.

When they were alone Gloria quickly told him the story about the journals. Yes, she had searched the flat top to bottom, every nook and cranny.

Sam was not surprised by Gloria's conclusion that her former housekeeper had stolen the journals, since nobody else even knew that the books existed.

Sam was making notes when Gloria mentioned the woman's full name for the first time.

"May Murray?" His response was filled with surprise: "A woman of that name now runs a public house at her family home not a mile from our house at Dunbla."

Gloria looked at Sam, shock written all over her features. "Do you think she's the same woman?"

"She's a handsome woman, probably thirty-five or older, splendid bosoms, what the Irish call *a fine hoult* – as in the kind of woman men would like to have instant sexual relations with. She returned to Ireland on the death of her father who had secured a licence to sell alcoholic drink from his kitchen."

Gloria smiled despite her anxiety. "You have described May very well. It must be her."

"I'll verify it," said Sam.

Gloria shook her head in puzzlement. "But why would May or anyone take the journals? They contain the story of my personal life – I wrote in some detail while I was in danger of going out of my mind. I even wrote about the relief I knew when you rescued me by telling me that Eddie Brewer was not Arthur's son, that he had been born of a tinker girl the day before Deirdre had her stillborn girl by the roadside near Dunbla."

Sam waited, feeling no need to say that he had read the journals some years earlier.

"Why would May have taken the books, Sam? Have you any idea?"

Sam's mind was on the fact that in the very recent past his lawyer, Alex Gibbon, had heard through a legal pal, for a small consideration, that Constance Brewer was taking legal advice with a view to lodging a claim against the Brewer Estate for the return of her rightful portion of all and every share that the company owned throughout the world.

Shortly after this revelation there had been a mention of the story in the *Irish Independent*.

Sam saw no point in mentioning this to Gloria though he seriously considered the possibility of a connection between the act of larceny of the journals – convinced in his gut that May Murray was the thief – and the rumour, turned to fact, of a lawsuit.

"Why would May steal my personal memoirs?"

Even as Gloria repeated the question Sam could see realisation dawn on her – her mouth almost dropped open and it was a moment or two before she could speak. "Good God! The stuff in the journals could be used against Dee and Eddie and you and . . ."

"Yes. It could."

Pack Rowan returned to Dunbla as May was closing the house down for the night. He waited until she had doused the lights before he went around the back of the house and tapped on the kitchen window.

May was so overjoyed to see him she clung to him, her lips crushing on his mouth, her tears tumbling in the sheer joy of his presence. But when she took a breath her first words were: "Did you get a deal, Pack? Did you swing it?"

Pack nodded his head with a short laugh and she kissed him again, her tongue devilling in and out of his mouth, her body glued to him at his loins. He carried her up the stairs as if she was a doll and they fell onto the bed like a couple that would never be separated again. At some stage May cried out in relief and every so often her tears came like a deluge but no word passed between them and when Pack awoke in the morning there was May wrapped around him like a flag which, to his own surprise he didn't mind as much as he would have expected to.

May had no trouble about the fact that he had to return to England right away but she did suggest that he lie low for the few days before he left. "Best not to hand out any ammunition to the bad-mind brigade."

Not bothered one way or the other, Pack gave her the cheque from Constance Brewer: "I can give you my word there's a bigger one coming before long. I've signed it and she postdated it a bit, so just stick it in your bank. A bent pal of mine over in The Smoke says she's been selling off her jewels. There are paintings in that house of hers worth millions."

May didn't try to hide her elation: "It's going to happen so, Pack. It really is." Her eyes were wide in anticipation of all that was to come and she kissed him passionately, her feeling for him all the stronger now that he had brought home the bacon.

As he left Dunbla, Pack used the old bicycle he kept hidden in the woodshed. May hugged him close before she let him make a start: "You mind yourself for me, Pack."

Adjusting his shoulder bag, he nodded in the half-light from the open kitchen door. "I'm fairly handy at that," he said quietly. "Next time you see me, we'll be rich."

With that he was gone down the rough road with the relevant journals safely tucked away in his bag. May's heart was pounding in her chest with the excitement of it all.

'Imagine it,' she thought. 'I just went to the wardrobe to give the boxes of books a dusting-down during a spring-clean and now Pack and me, we're on the verge of serious riches.' She thought it was an amazing accident that had led her to this moment and all thanks to a few journals in which a heartbroken woman had recorded her thoughts and the overall pain of her life.

Who could have dreamed that so much could happen through a few journals?

Two days later, those same journals were the centre of attention in the drawing room at Constance Brewer's house on Eaton Square. At the moment, Pack Rowan waited as Constance Brewer and her barrister, Sir Albert Whimby, pored over a couple of the maroon-covered books.

Wanting to hurry them along, Pack said: "I left those books with you, my lady, to give you time to read them." He allowed his irritation to show: "My idea was that you would have read them before I came back here again today. This is wastin' my time."

"Stop being so damned uncivil, Pack Rowan! You have my money in your pocket!" Constance threw the words at him, her reaction to being chastised in her own home, but she almost bit her tongue trying to stop them.

"In the money, are we, old thing?" Sir Albert had a gleam in his eye as he savoured the prospect of a payment against her outstanding bill for services rendered.

"The journals have been read, Pack," she said in an effort to mollify him, at the same time ignoring the importuning of Albee Whimby who to her mind always had his hand out like a begging bowl. "I was pointing out some particulars in the penmanship that might well prove useful in court. So you hold a civil tongue in your head and show us the book that really matters."

"My point exactly, my lady." Pack was like a dog

with a bone. "This invaluable journal is only worth as much as it is because it can be connected to those two you hold between you, and the others that I have hidden in a safe place."

Constance released her resistance, her defiance wiped away by the rock-solid certainty in Pack's voice. He lit a cigarette and sat down close to them both. Before he could speak, Sir Albert held up his hand like a schoolboy seeking permission to go to the toilet.

"May I crave your indulgence, Mister Rowan," Sir Albert pleaded. "I have had a wretched day and I wonder if you would simply give me the gist of it, the salient point or points, which I can study from the actual pages in the next few days. If you wouldn't mind, sir, I'd be most grateful."

"As you wish," Pack Rowan rose and poured brandy for the three of them. As he sat down again he raised his glass: "Good health, my lady, Sir Albert!" He drank, revelling in the power he felt in the moment. 'For all the privilege,' he thought, 'for all you've enjoyed in your cushy lives, there you sit, waiting on the words of a wain born by a ditch, sitting there hanging onto every word of a tinker. Lovely.'

"Never mind the good health and jolly hockey-sticks, Pack Rowan. You have not delivered what you promised when you took my money." Constance leaned forward in her chair as she confronted him without fear or favour.

"Sit back and receive your entitlement, my lady, for within two minutes you will be hard put not to get up and dance a jig in delight." He held up his hand to forestall any further comment from her and ran his eyes over the pages again before he went on. "I have studied the journals, and I have put markers where you should read first. Here is the truth of Eddie Brewer's birth, known only to Deirdre Brewer, Sam Sweet and Gloria Sweet, since Arthur Brewer and his doctor are both dead." Pack cast a quick glance at the pair and found that they were in the palm of his hand.

"Deirdre Brewer had gone walking along the road from her home – this was against doctor's orders since her time was near. She was utterly lost when some hours later she felt her baby coming. She was desperate of a sudden and in terror that her baby could die if she did not get help in a hurry. She prayed out loud and moments later an old woman came out of a field some distance ahead, as Dee saw that there was a canvas awning fixed to the hedge. This woman – a tinker called Kelly by those that knew her – had just buried a dead tinker girl in the field. The girl died the day before giving birth to a boy child – Kelly took Dee in under the canvas out of the hot sun and when she comes back to consciousness, her baby boy is at her breast. What she does not know is that her own girl child had been stillborn, the old tinker woman substituting one for the other, having prayed herself all that morning for some way to keep the day-old boy alive. So each woman had been the answer to the prayers of the other."

Sir Albert cleared his throat and sat forward: "This story is documented there in that journal?"

"It is, Sir Albert, every word of it, and I promise you that whoever reads the story will be left in no doubt that it's the gospel truth coming to them off the pages."

"Of course the journals could have been written by anybody," Constance said, lighting a cigarette. "I am merely thinking of what the defence would say if the journals were the sum total of the proof we need to win the case."

"I've thought about all of that, my lady," Pack said, smiling conspiratorially. "Allow me to ask, what in your opinion, and yours, Sir Albert, is the one thing needed to nail the case down in our favour?"

"The old woman called Kelly," Constance said in the instant, while Sir Albert mumbled agreement.

"I've got her, my lady."

"You have this Kelly person?" Sir Albert was first off the mark this time.

"Indeed I do, Sir Albert, and what is more, she will testify on my lady's behalf."

"How can we be certain of that?"

"Oh, for heaven's sake, Albee, stop being such a fusspot! Pack Rowan has proved to be a man of his word and that's good enough for me. If you could get us into court with the same speed as Pack gets on with his business, I'd be a much happier lady."

"May I answer the question anyway, my lady?"

"Indeed you may, Pack Rowan. Indeed you may."

"I guarantee to deliver what I have promised, Sir Albert, because the old woman of the roads called Kelly is my mother. And she will do as I say, believe you me." Pack Rowan lit himself a cigarette and drew a deep satisfying smoke into his lungs. He sat back in his chair while Constance and the barrister absorbed this surprising twist and he savoured the thought that when this job paid off, he would then deal with Kelly, for betraying him to the law. After that he would go and visit Séamus O'Reilly who would die roaring for killing his friend and mentor, The Vicar, in Wormwood Scrubs.

10

October 1922

Constance Brewer was more than surprised when Albee Whimby suggested that he take her and Pack Rowan out to dinner. "A gesture of gratitude to Mister Rowan for providing such good evidence, Connie, don't you agree?"

They were alone in her study, Pack Rowan having left the room to – as he put it – "use the facilities", in the company of her butler.

Constance had taken the precaution of ringing for the little man to ensure that Pack Rowan was supervised at all times while in her home.

"Johnstone," Constance, at her most imperious, had said, "be a good fellow and show Mister Rowan to the nearest water closet."

When the two had left the study, Constance, waxing impatient, turned to her barrister. "Albee, kindly tell me in as few words as possible, what do you think of Mister Pack Rowan, overall?"

"He's a remarkable cad, I should say, a villain of real quality, somebody to have on the home team as opposed to the opposition."

"Do you think he can produce the old woman, our star witness, as he promised?"

"Why be so impatient, old thing? Despite your threats and incantations and the Lord knows what else, this case is not going before a judge until well into the New Year."

"I am not even going to grace that nonsense with a reply, Albee. You will come awake before long and perhaps be mentally alert enough to realise the kind of money we are considering here. When that moment happens you will talk to the appropriate bewigged buffoons and you will rearrange court dates." She raised her hand sharply: "Don't say it, Albee! I can see the negative smear in your eye. I'm giving you two weeks to find the right person to talk to – I'm serious, Albee, so despatch the smug sneer. If you do not measure up in that time, I will, on my honour, dismiss your firm and find someone who is in touch with how things are being done at this very moment, while you mutter it is impossible to fix anything. This country runs on and thrives on things being fixed every minute of the day. Now, what is this nonsense about taking Pack Rowan and me to dinner? What little scheme is this, pray tell?"

"There is nothing of the idler about the fellow. I am impressed by his industry in this matter – he has invested time and thought and cunning so he is a professional thief, a con artist rather than a robber *per se*. Chances are that he has a conviction or two. I thought I would give a pal, a Detective Chief Superintendent at Scotland Yard, a look at our friend while we were eating out. The more we know about the fellow, the easier it will be to dispose of him without too much fuss, when the time comes to share out the spoils."

Constance chortled for a few moments before she said: "You really are a dreadful wretch, Albee Whimby. And this 'old dodderer' performance you hide behind quite brilliant in the odd moment. You were always devious, yes. Your inherent knavery was always your most attractive quality."

Whimby seemed slightly surprised, sounding annoyed as he said: "You might have let me know. I wanted for years to have you in the feathers, but you never gave me an inkling you found me attractive."

"You see, you are a blasted fool as well. Good God, man, do you think I could ever have looked at you as a lover? I endured the marriage bed in order to solidify my place in the Brewer family. I hated all that rumpy-pumpy that Shane Brewer lived for. He was doing it with every servant that did not have a hump on her back. He brought prostitutes home and had mistresses all over every city we lived in. I let him carry on as long as he didn't seek my society in that respect. I only objected to him doing it with the servants, creating belowstairs gossip that had some of those kitchen cretins laughing at me behind my back. But my God, sex, never! And above all, Albee, much as I have enjoyed your friendship, never with a barrister!"

Whimby poured himself a brandy and drank it down. When he turned back to Constance he was himself again. "I have never been insulted with such style, old thing. Heavens, I thought, any moment now she will be accusing barristers of stealing a lady's briefs, if you'll pardon the pun."

"That's another thing," Constance assured him forcefully. "The awful jokes you make on a regular basis. It is not incumbent upon you to amuse people especially when you have no talent whatsoever in that area. Now, before our friend rejoins us, let me assure you he is going to be seeking more money from me. So listen to me, Albee, and please do hear what I am going to say. I am investing my jewels in this scheme. I am going to sell them because I will die before I will surrender what is rightfully mine to an illegitimate child, a tinker's illegitimate child, no less – while his foster mother, Deirdre Doyle as was – the daughter of a tramp from a slum who drove hackneys until he struck it rich – plays the Lady of the Manor. So, you go and find the right people to get us into court as quickly as possible. I will pay for that privilege and I will also pay you something on account, plus part of your fee for this case, in advance. If you fail me, I will not give you a penny, Albee."

Sir Albert Whimby nodded his head, poured himself another brandy and stood sipping it as Pack Rowan came back into the room.

Constance wasted no time. "So, Pack Rowan, what is the next step as you see it?"

"You and I need to talk, my lady." Somehow Pack gave the impression of bowing slightly from the waist when he gave Constance her title. "I have money to talk about, a sum of money that has to be talked about before we go much further with this scheme. I'm willing to tell you, ma'am, right now this minute, how much money I'm thinking about, to give you the chance of sendin' me packin' if you think I'm not worth what I want."

Pack looked at Constance Brewer all the way through his short speech, his demeanour one of calm and confidence, his tone reasonable, his manner as always in keeping with their relative positions in the social structure.

"Do you wish to tell me while Sir Albert is present, or shall I ask him to leave?" Constance knew which of the pair carried the power here and she had no problem that she might have hurt the feelings of one of the country's senior barristers.

"I'm quite prepared to pop along to my club, Constance," he said gallantly.

"There's no need for that, sir," Pack suggested respectfully, producing a slip of paper from a pocket in his waistcoat. He moved to Constance and held it out to her. She took it with a nod of her head and opened it. Pack was not surprised that she blanched a bit. Sir Albert, playing the gent, had turned his back and was passing the time by pouring himself another large brandy.

Constance put the paper by her side and gave her eyes to Pack Rowan.

"And this is merely a down payment, Pack Rowan. How much you are going to cost me overall is the question I find most intriguing."

"We'll have to let the hare sit on that one, my lady,

until we know just how many millions we are talking about all told. Does that seem fair to you?"

Constance nodded her head: "I will allow fair, Pack Rowan. Now, I have to make arrangements to have a certified cheque here in this house for your next visit. At which time you will receive what you ask for."

"That suits me perfectly, my lady. May I call you on the telephone in two days' time?"

An hour later, Pack Rowan was drinking a pint of Whitbread's ale while Walter Guildford sipped ten-year-old malt as though it was really too good to drink.

"We are working on it, Pack, and we will have a result in a week or so."

"If you're blowing hot air up my hole, Wally," he emptied the half-full glass, "you know what I can be like when I get messed about."

"I'm almost certain he has changed his name, so hold on, Pack!" Guildford raised his hand. "I have a lady friend who can get me info in minutes that would take a year if you go the legal route." He lit a cigarette, annoyed that he allowed his fear to show when he was in Rowan's company. But then he could never forget some of the fights he had seen during their prison time in the Scrubs, Pack being the one to walk away every time. "My guess is that Séamus got himself a fresh birth cert – that of a kid long dead."

"Any gobshite with a few quid in his hand can do that!" Pack was impatient but Guildford's look was that of a man holding a good hand, so he shut up.

"Do you remember the spoof I introduced into my phoney mind-reading act in the Scrubs?"

Pack nodded, unable to stop a sardonic grin appearing on his fleshy mouth. "You were so full of shit. 'Tell me your date of birth and I'll forecast your future.' Amazed me, but most cons went for it."

"Prison does funny things to people," Guildford chuckled. "I knew Séamus was forty-one, so when I went cruising the birth certificates of people already dead, I stuck to that age group here in London – you know Séamus wouldn't live anywhere else unless he had a powerful reason. Then there were the initials. Within three days my bird on the inside came to me with two possibles – checked out one, he died only last week – one of my ops is now checking out the other and my feeling is he could be our old friend, Séamus O'Reilly. So you be patient for another few days – I won't let you down."

Pack took a roll from his pocket, amused by the light switching on in Guildford's low-key eyes. "I have fifty here for you." Pack passed him ten fivers. "I want you to check out this lady here." He handed a slip of paper to Guildford: "She is a singer, a Jewess, and she works to earn money to support the New Jerusalem or whatever they call it. Find out all you can about her and be quick about it. There's a ton more if you do a good job."

"You don't need a partner?" Guildford offered, his eyes captured by the roll in Pack's hand.

"You got that one right, Wally." Pack grinned and threw a pound note on the table. "Have a drink or two on me. I've got things to do."

As he watched Pack leave the pub in St Martin's Lane, Wally's mind was busy behind the indolent eyes. He wanted some of what Pack was involved in – there had to be a way to get in. With that in mind, he scooped up the pound note and went out the door as fast as he could. Follow Pack, see where he was going.

He thought he saw Pack further up the street but before he could move off, a hand grabbed his shoulder and he was turned around to find Pack right in his face.

The big man didn't seem angry – in fact he chuckled at what he deemed to be the obviousness of most people. "You were about to sit on my tail, right, Wally?"

"Damn sure, I was, Pack. You're into something big and I would like to be in on it with you. If that's a crime – I plead guilty, Your Honour."

Pack let his shoulder go and nodded his head in understanding. "Following me won't do it for you. You do the job I paid you for, show me you still have it, and I'll find something worthwhile for you."

"That's good enough for me. I'll be in touch within a few days." Shrugging self-effacingly, he said with a rueful smile: "I should've known better than to try putting one over on you."

"Yes, you should," Pack assured him. "Now get going. You have work to do."

Two days later Pack Rowan arrived at the Eaton Square home of Constance Brewer and was shown into the study by Johnstone. As the little man closed the door behind him – the old woman waving to him from behind her desk – Pack once again had the feeling he knew the butler from somewhere on the wrong side of the tracks.

"Come over here and sit facing me where I can see you properly, Pack Rowan," Constance issued the order in a healthy stentorian voice that seemed remarkable in a woman of her age. "I have your money, a certified cheque in the sum of twenty thousand pounds." Constance paused with a shake of her head. "You are a remarkable man, Pack Rowan." When Pack remained silent, she continued: "Clearly you are not of the upper classes, hence it does not seem unreasonable to assume that you have never in your life owned twenty thousand pounds." She squinted at him, her feral eyes glinting admiringly. "Yet you sit there without any change in expression when I tell you that you are a rich man."

"It's agreeable, ma'am, a healthy down-payment against much more to come. I have had some money in my life – never felt any affection for it – I fought for it, fought with fist and boot for it, gambled to get more of it, and I agree it comes in very handy. It doesn't excite me though."

Constance placed an envelope on the desk and looked at Pack. "There is the certified cheque and now I would like you to give me the salient journal."

Surprised to see Pack shake his head, she took the envelope back into her hands and looked at him in puzzlement. "You don't expect me to give you twenty thousand pounds and allow you to walk out of here without giving me the journal?"

"From the moment I knew that you and I could do business, my lady, I have been faithfully copying the relevant pages of the journal."

Constance was more than surprised. "Are you being serious?"

"I was taught to read and write by a man who was a saint and a genius." He produced the book from the leather bag sitting on his lap. "See for yourself." He passed over the book and Constance was impressed by the penmanship. "Very well done, Pack Rowan, but you can't be asking me to take a copy of the journal while you leave here with my twenty thousand . . ."

"My lady," Pack said quietly, "why would I try to steal your twenty thousand? We have something worth millions, literally, the millions of the Brewer Empire. Do you think I would settle for so little?"

Constance pushed the envelope back across the table. "No, I do not." She looked at him now over her half spectacles: "You are some strain of villain, but I declare, you may be the first honest man I have ever known."

"My partner May, a strong woman but a worrier, my lady – I have to respect her wishes here. Otherwise I would give you all the books in a moment." He rose and closed his leather bag.

"She is a lucky woman to have a real man on her side." Constance was feeling tired and the words slipped away from her before she could stop them.

"Let me assure you, my lady, I am on your side now. If anybody should discommode you in any way, please let me know. Part of our arrangement is that you are now under my protection."

Constance smiled and raised a finger to delay his departure. He paused and she said: "How do you know I will not cheat you out of your share of all that money?"

Pack thought for several moments before he gave his answer: "In you I find a great hunger to go on living – taking on this court case, a massive undertaking, and you are like a hound straining against the leash." He smiled in a wistful way. "I know without thinking about it, that you wouldn't want to give that up."

"Give it up?" Constance said quizzically before her expression conveyed realisation: "You mean die?"

"Yes, my lady, that's it, exactly."

Pack left her with a smile and a wave of his hand and she sat there shaking her head, her mixed feelings giving her little in the way of comfort.

Sam wiped Deirdre's brow and refreshed the face flannel in the basin of warm water perched on the bedside table. She lay with her eyes closed, her breathing turning normal, her hand clutching tightly to his fingers. With the other hand he reached for a glass of water and brought it to her lips. She was well propped up with pillows and was able to sip the water.

"There you go, sweetheart," he said quietly. "That was a rough one."

"All the more so because I thought, only said it to Joan last week that the breakfast-time burps were over for this baby and me."

"Any point in my suggesting you stay where you

are?" Sam knew the answer in advance which Dee confirmed with a soft shake of her head.

"I'm grand, Sam, honestly. And today, well, Joan needs me. I'll stay in town overnight, if you don't mind."

"All I need to know is that you are looking after yourself and the baby."

"I am, love, I promise. And, if you fancied a whiff of the city, you could always come up later and we could have dinner at Merrion Square and you could comfort me with a Sam Sweet cuddle."

"That seems like a very good idea. But why is Joan likely to need you today, more than any other? Or am I stepping into strictly female territory here?"

"She was hoping to talk John into agreeing to some kind of separation, something civilised without all the grief they're going through as things stand."

"I'm not taking sides here but Joan might not find it so easy to be talking separation were their roles reversed. She is flying in love. Poor old John, his feet are like blocks of lead."

"She wants a separation agreement between them, Sam. The way things are in this country, she has no chance of a legal one. Even you – and you're the most broadminded man I know – there is criticism in your tone – you seem to be saying Joan is having sensation beyond the benefits of the marriage bed as though it's a crime. Their marriage never worked – it was over in no time. She has been very loyal when you consider that he wants a wife only as a housekeeper and a sometime companion."

"Being honest, I suppose I did mean something like that."

"Does that mean that if you were to go to bed with another woman, some woman you were very attracted to, it would be more exciting than what happens when we make love?"

"I'm afraid not, Dee."

"You're afraid not. What do you mean, you're afraid not?"

"Sorry if I'm a disappointment to you, love. It's just that, well, I'm a very boring old fart who actually meant every word he said when he married you."

Dee embraced him, chuckling emotionally as she tried to be offhand.

"There's no hope for us, wife. You know that, don't you?"

She nodded. "I'm afraid you're right."

Half an hour later, as she was about to be driven to Dublin, a local hackney sidecar came up the drive to halt facing the portico of the great house.

Dee saw Alex Gibbon jump down and ask the driver to wait. As he turned to her she gave him a wave and pointed him in the direction of Sam who stood on the steps. Having left her husband in fine humour she was too far away and too busily on the move to see the concern that registered on his face.

'What the hell brings Alex here at this hour of the day?' Sam wondered with serious misgivings.

In moments Alex Gibbon was marching up the steps to where Sam stood. "I'm in court in Bray later. So I'm hoping to kill two birds with one stone, if it's not an inconvenient time for you."

Shaking his hand, Sam was trying not to project

doom and gloom onto the morning. "Get rid of the hackney. I'll give you a cup of coffee and drive you to Bray. What about that?"

"Perfect."

Gibbon came back a minute later and they walked around the house and into the kitchen where a local woman was washing dishes.

"I was just about to have a nice cup of Bewley's," said Sam. Picking up the tray he added a cup for Gibbon, indicating that he should follow.

When they were seated in the drawing room, Sam handed Gibbon a cup of coffee and when they were smoking cigarettes he said with forced casualness, "Whatever has brought you here at this time of the day, it's got to be fairly serious."

"Yes, it is, Sam.""

"Tell me the story," Sam said, wondering what the hell was going on now.

Producing a folder from his briefcase, Gibbon put it in Sam's hand. "A lot of reading in there – I can crystallise if for you in about a minute."

"Has the dreaded Constance made her move?"

Gibbon shrugged philosophically. "Really, we've been expecting it ever since the rumour first surfaced in the newspapers."

Sam nodded, putting the folder to one side. "Tell me all."

"In a nutshell, Constance is suing Deirdre and Eddie for the return of every penny that is currently credited to the name Brewer, this to include all property, shares, investments, and all and anything else you can name.

All of it, so dear Constance claims, belongs to her by right. She is also claiming that Deirdre should be charged with perjury and misappropriation of Brewer funding and the devil knows what else. The main thrust of her argument is that Edward Arthur Shane Brewer – Eddie – is no such person by birth. That Eddie is not the heir, was not and is not the blood son of Arthur Brewer and Deirdre Sweet, formerly Brewer, née Doyle – that Eddie is, in fact, the son of a tinker man and a girl that died giving birth to him, a day before Deirdre Brewer's own girl was stillborn by the side of the road just a few miles from where we now sit."

Sam emptied his coffee cup. "Sounds very serious, Alex."

"I've talked to the leader of her legal team, one Sir Albert Whimby. He is adamant that she has a real case, that she can prove the allegation about Eddie's illegitimacy, and there are implications we need not go into right now that are far-reaching and likely to cause all kinds of commotion should they come to light."

"This man, Whimby. What do you know about him?"

"He's of the top drawer, well born, near royalty, all that – ruthless as a barrister, handles all kinds of bad people, and, it is rumoured, is not above playing very dirty tricks in order to win."

They fell silent for a moment or two, then Sam said: "I'm grateful you let Dee go on to town before revealing this. I'll spend the afternoon studying it and we'll have a meeting in town later this week. How is that for you?"

"Myself, everyone in the firm, we are at your disposal,

151

Sam – and I should warn you, our collective opinion is that there is a case to answer, a very serious case."

Sam rose. "Come on. I'll give you that lift to Bray."

Gibbon followed him out, very aware of the power in his client's stride and the new glint that had arisen in his coal-black eyes.

11

January 1923

Sam watched as Brendan O'Connor put his signature to the agreement terminating his connection with Sweet Construction. He watched him sign a second paper that ended his connection with any of the subsidiary companies that had grown from the original, the success of which had supported a range of innovative and successful companies for more than fifteen years. Sam sighed in regret – before their beginnings Brendan had given him the inside information that the Portobello Harbour site was going up for sale. Already involved in the revolutionary movement, Brendan was close to a fellow volunteer working for the Dublin Corporation. This man had given him the wink – Brendan passed the word to Sam who bought the land before anybody else got the opportunity.

Having proved how resourceful he could be, the young Dubliner – well rewarded financially for the tip off – asked Sam to give him a serious job. Within a few months of the deal being sealed, the value of the property had risen considerably – as a result the Portobello site had provided Sam with collateral against which he borrowed the funding to expand Sweet Construction. This had meant more staff and Brendan O'Connor was the first person to be offered a well-paid job with good prospects.

Now their journey together had come to an end but even as Cormac Doyle signed the paper and left the office without a word, Brendan tried again. He looked at Sam, his grief evident as the normally deep baritone voice revealed a husky soreness: "I'm making this last effort, Sam, a plea if you like." He raised his hand to forestall the interruption: "Sam, please, let me finish. This isn't easy. You and me, we risked our lives for each other. Cormac and me, we went over to Dev because he's the best that's out there after Michael Collins. With him we have some chance of pulling the dream together."

"The day someone murdered Mick Collins was the day our dream of a Republic of Ireland went into the ground too. You made your move. Neither of you thought fit to speak to me first."

"We couldn't talk to you about it when you were so shattered by Mick's death. I can see now we made a mistake there."

"What you did is your own business, Bren. It turns my stomach but you're entitled to do whatever you like. Before you go, I'll put the sale of Sweet Construction on hold for a few months. With your work record, you should be able to raise the money, or some of it – I'll help you if you'd want that, and I'd go guarantor for you as Arthur Brewer did for me a long time ago."

Brendan O'Connor stumbled from the office leaving Sam to wish that things were different. Another pointless wish, so many of them, bobbing about like flotsam and jetsam as the ongoing Civil War took its toll on the nation.

Who could have forecast that the conflict would reach the point where brother was killing brother? And there seemed to be no let-up as another act of wanton violence happened with every passing day – over six hundred Volunteers and Free Staters dead, more than two and a half thousand wounded.

The statistics weighed heavily on Sam's heart – men who had fought shoulder to shoulder against the British were shooting each other in the killing fields of the Irish Free State, where freedom was granted to a man only when a bullet or a bomb took him beyond the rules of the patriot game.

As the undertakers facilitated the needs of so many grief-stricken families, relatives and loved ones prayed only for peace. Ireland, having had no time to recover from the commercial devastation caused by the war with the British, was now brought to its knees in more ways than one by the Civil War.

In the seven years since the Easter Monday Uprising of 1916, thousands of acres of land had been out of cultivation. The population of the Free State was 2,750,000 of whom 130,000 were without work, while damage to property ran as high as 30 million pounds.

Sam shook his head as he left the office for his latest

meeting with the family solicitor, Alex Gibbon. He was learning to live with the numbing, shattering acceptance that the dream of an Irish Republic would never be anything more than a nebulous notion. 'So the things you did, Sam, the guns you bought that are now killing men on both sides – does it still seem all right that you did what you did? It was all for The Cause, sure, but that got lost somewhere, didn't it? A bit like you at times.'

He thought of the idealists, many of them men of lofty education and great spiritual beliefs who had gone to their graves, dying really, for an idea. Ideas were so plentiful, he thought as he hailed a closed hackney carriage.

He stopped for a moment before getting in, warmed by the memory of his first meeting with Victoria Brewer, she who gave him his first ride in a closed carriage driven that day by dear old Séamus.

Dear Vicky, friend and lover and mistress – his marriage to Gloria had not come between them – sweet and sour, lovely, wild and wayward – rest in peace, dear heart. He smiled, closing the carriage door behind himself. He had never hailed a cab of any description, never ridden in a hired conveyance before Vicky offered him that lift home to Rathmines.

He had been standing wearily, dripping wet by the Liffey after his abortive attempt to rescue the street-arab who robbed his wallet on that fateful day. His seemingly good deed had made such an impression on the beautiful Brewer heiress that she had tossed etiquette, and the rules of behaviour appropriate to a young lady of her standing, out of the carriage window.

As he sat back smoking, Sam thought now of Deirdre and how well she had been that morning. They had spent the night at the townhouse on Merrion Square – she had been free of morning sickness and they had breakfasted together. Later, as he watched her don her white coverall and fix the little round white hat she always wore at the Clinic, he savoured the thought of the little rebellion that his wife Dee and some other women had launched against poverty in Dublin. He wondered how many of the lamented idealists who had died for Ireland or were currently dying for Kathleen Ní Houlihan in the Civil War, had ever paid an actual visit to Poole Street, or any of its sister sewer-streets in the Dublin slums.

Poole Street was a foul, fever-drenched gut of stinking, falling-down tenements – such disgusting arteries were abundant all around the inner city. He would never have been there had it not been for Deirdre and her fellow volunteers – he went at times to protect the women who were giving their all to try and make a difference in a situation where the infant mortality rate would have shocked to their boots those who needed loftier causes to confront.

He wondered how it would be if an army of those same good and decent men, now dead, had taken up arms of soap and water, hauling not guns and boxes of ammunition, but blankets and bread and butter, while using both the fire in their bellies and their education to bring about legislation to drum out the slum landlords.

Hearing the criticism in his mind, he had to allow that he was like those men – too busy with loftier ideas, bigger dreams and higher mountains to climb. They talked of their willingness to die for nationhood, while young mothers and children were expiring daily in the face of indifference – the basic needs of the poor remaining way down on the list of priorities behind guns and ammunition and bombs. Places like Poole Street were the graveyards where people existed, hungry and broken and hopeless since they had been driven to expect nothing better.

Pack Rowan had slept late that same morning in 1923, May going quietly about her chores in an effort not to disturb him. Her energy was good this morning and she found she was looking forward to the day when, hopefully, alongside Pack she would go away from here, never to come back.

She had returned to Ireland only to gather herself together, and establish the business of the public house which she always intended to sell as a going concern when the time was right. She had needed too the time to consider how best to go after the dream that had presented itself to her when she had found Gloria Stein's journals in the wardrobe at the London flat.

She had never spoken about her idea, not to anybody. My God! In Ireland you'd want to keep your private business private – and, despite her claims that she was not committing a crime, she knew better than to take the risk of talking, the countryside being a hotbed of police informers and the like. It had all changed when she knew she had Pack – she smiled at how it had come about, now that they were actively making the dream come true.

Bringing logs in from the woodshed, glowing at the good fortune they'd enjoyed up to now, May tasted the agreeable thought that their success was like a golden promissory note for their future together.

This being so, she knew that their coming together – May smiled at the way those words had dropped onto her mind – happened at exactly the right time. To find Pack as he had come to the end of his tether in his given role of travelling man had been a great stroke of good fortune.

She was happy he wanted to change his life, she wanted him to put his gifts to work for them both, but she felt concern that he was acting in a superior manner. 'Hardly surprising,' she allowed, 'when you consider what he's achieved through his boldness with Constance Brewer. He said he'd get to see her and in no time at all he has her in the palm of his hand.'

But they had to go on being careful – that carry-on last night, him reacting against having to take his drink outside the house – "jumped-up shit-arses, all piss and rubber boots with their few acres" he called her regulars but only to her, thank God. "The state of them and their bloody caps hanging on the side of their heads like stinking ulcers!" She had not seen him so furious before.

She sighed, determined to make him see reason – she was not going to allow him to disrupt, even to throw away the chance to have a huge payoff by the end of the year – a God-sent passport to a whole new way of living.

He hated them, hated these men who actually stank like the cows and the pigs that they reared and butchered and, according to gossip, had sex with. But, when you considered what was involved here, he was going to have to put up with it for a little while longer.

She completely understood how he had felt – they hadn't managed to have a minute to greet each other when he returned from London. He was a tinker, and he worked for her when he was there – nobody would have so much as asked where he had been for the few days that he was actually in London. Nobody missed a knacker, a tinker – this section of the population being treated as though they were inferior beings in holy Catholic Ireland.

Of course, he had seethed.

'Wouldn't you know the bloody pub would be crowded on the night he came back with a pick-handle on him and my name on it,' May thought with a rueful smile.

Not that Pack Rowan had been celibate, oh no. He'd paid a visit to an old flame, Smarty, who lived and worked in Kilburn. Arriving unannounced he found some sailor rutting at her, his backside going like a fiddler's elbow.

Despite the attention she was receiving from the matelot, Smarty's boozy green eyes opened up like fresh oysters when she saw Pack standing there. She heaved the sailor off her voluptuous body and shoved him to the floor, her arms out to Pack.

"Billy Burden, you bastard! Where in God's name have you been layin' your pipe?"

"I've been abroad." He sipped at the whiskey bottle in his hand. "I never looked at another woman while we were parted."

Knowing each other as they did, this was a' very funny thing for Pack to say and they howled laughter together, like friends that were glad to see each other.

Meanwhile the seagoing man was climbing into his bell-bottoms. "I thought you was a square shooter," he said to Smarty, "or I never would have given you the time of day."

He sounded aggrieved and Pack didn't blame him. Deciding to let it play out, he drank more whiskey.

"Will you just sling yer hook and don't be keeping me from the on'y man I ever loved in my life. Go on with ye, I say!" Smarty looked ready to give her unhappy customer a fight he wouldn't forget.

Without a word the sailor produced a knife and held it like somebody that knew how to use it. "I'll cut that mattress off your head, you filthy whore! You have no honour – I paid you up front, so you give me back my dough, or somebody is going to be sorry!"

Smarty looked from the matelot to Pack.

Pack shrugged his shoulders. "He's right, Smarty. If he paid he's entitled to shoot his duff. So, I'll be off."

"Have you any money for me, Billy?" Smarty tried to look coy but the target eluded her.

"Did I ever come to you empty-handed?"

"Ah, don't get snotty, Billy! You're the only bloke I ever gave it to for free in me whole life. I only meant if you had something for me, give it to him and let him get the hell outa here. Just lookin' at you, I'm dampening to the ankles."

Pack took a pound note from his pocket. "Will this do you, pal?"

The sailor whipped the pound note with a grin and an expression of genuine appreciation. "Fair play, mate, that'll fill the bill nicely."

"Ah Jesus, he on'y gave me seven and six! Here you, maggot-mickey, give me the change!" Smarty threw him big eyes and a sexy smile – as though this was going to make any difference.

Pack wondered how somebody living her kind of life could be so short of cop-on.

"God bless you, mate!" The sailor gave Pack a salute and was going down the tenement stairs even as Smarty came up off the bed with mayhem in her eyes.

"Save your energy, Smarty," Pack said quietly. "And no shouting or I'll be forced to give you a slap or two."

She slithered close to him and placed his left hand on her right breast, which, despite her way of life, was like that of a young woman in full bloom. With the other she was touching the lapel of his jacket. "I never noticed it before, Billy, but when you're dolled up you could pass for a gent so you could."

Pack gave her a five-pound note and told her to clean herself up while he undressed and had a couple of drinks. She went to a corner of the room and he heard water splashing before she opened the window and threw the contents of the basin down into the street. She was giving her hair a vigorous brushing as he stood naked with the whiskey bottle to his lips. He held it out to her and she drank deeply and belched like a sophisticated Bedouin. Without even blinking she put the bottle on the table and fell to her knees before him.

He heard her sigh as she fondled him and then she said with a hint of inebriated reverence in her voice: "I swear to God, Billy Burden, yer such a man as could turn a Christian girl into a cannibal!"

"A penny for your thoughts, Pack." May's voice was soft and wanting as she came to him outside the pub, after the last customer had gone staggering along the broken roadway.

The scent of her perfume, thrown on in the first moment after she closed the pub door, overcame his reverie and suddenly he was aware of her nearness, the mound of her breast against his shirt, the melting animal presence of her wiping everything but his wanting from his mind. His body went its own way and she was there, ravenous as he was, her anger and her hunger matching him at every turn, causing him, even as they pulled at each other's clothing, to see how very alike they were in so many ways.

Pack's fleshy lips were like a magnet to her need. She put her arms around his neck and they were wildly passionate, like people trying to devour each other. He pulled her forcefully up into his arms to stalk across the narrow strip of road and to the field opposite the house. He fell to his knees, dropping her down on the wet grass of the night, and without foreplay of any kind began ploughing roughly, his hunger for her making no room for consideration which, there and then, suited May down to the ground.

He moved fast and with a fury she had never known in any man before and she could not believe how he brought her so close to orgasm in so short a time. But, make her come he did, while he let go of a cry that had been a long time buried deep, the ripped sound of a man-bird that had flown to some place it had never been before.

Afterwards, they washed each other's backs with hot water, taking turns in the tin bath she housed on the back wall of the kitchen. They sipped beer, May so overjoyed from the moment he handed her the certified cheque for ten thousand pounds that she was like somebody who had lost her mind and discovered happiness.

"Deposit that in Dublin in your own name. Be all over the countryside if you bank it locally."

"Don't worry. I have a cousin in Dublin who'll take me to her bank." She fought not to show him the adoration she was feeling, in case her crushing need for him might frighten him away. That he would bring a cheque for so much money back to her, surely it was a sign that they had some chance of a future together? Her mind was dancing little polkas of delight but her down-to-earth, pragmatic self had to ask him the question that wouldn't quit. "Were you worried carrying all that money around, Pack? Was that why you bought the certified cheque?"

"In the Scrubs I devoured the library for eight and a

half years, came across an American writer, a sort of spiritual psychologist I supposed you'd call him – name of Emerson, a genius of a man – he claims that the mind asking the question already knows the answer." Pack gave her a smile that was colder than she, in her euphoria, realised. "You just proved the great man right."

"You learned an awful lot from reading books, didn't you?" May's response to this was like a double-edged sword – she loved how he talked at times but she'd have settled happily for a straight answer.

"How you use what you learn in books, that's what matters." Pack kissed her breasts, his lips and his teeth at her nipples, a vein in his neck throbbing so that she wondered was he under a strain he didn't want to talk about.

She found him insatiable on that first night home, and she was more than happy to have him take her again and again. In between they drank beer, she wondering did the money do it? Was it getting the money and it only a down payment? Did that do it? Was it that that could make him hard again in a few minutes even after the second time?

She had loved what happened between them from the very first time he took her in the hayloft, but now, tonight, he was like a heavenly demon capable of pumping himself into her until there was nothing left lying there but his skeleton.

She chuckled at her fancy, knowing she was fairly jarred. She knew too that her desire for him, always active, was even stronger and more energetic that usual, and she accepted that in her own case it was the money that gave her senses a hoosh, sent her up there to greet his every movement, no matter what new heights he scaled.

Into the night, they were pleasuring each other, every so often, one or the other bursting into a bout of wild laughter as they took another glance at the certified cheque for ten thousand pounds.

Pack had allowed May to believe this was the total down payment against the future earnings, saying nothing about the rest of the money deposited in his new London bank account. The name on the account matched that on his new passport – bought from a dealer he had served time with – his mind already set on the plan to disappear entirely when he had millions in his own name.

He did this without a thought entering the process. It was his way – fix your own corner first and always, see what happened after that.

The following morning at breakfast, May said: "Pack, soon as we get our share of the big money, I'm selling up here, going away from Ireland for ever."

He looked at her over the tin mug he liked to drink his tea from. He nodded his head gently and she saw what she deemed to be an interested look in his dark eyes. Drinking coffee today to celebrate their good fortune so far, she said: "We make a very lucky team, wouldn't you say?"

"Have to hand it to you – you're a hell of a damn woman." He smiled, the compliment offered in a very casual way, as though saying 'so far so good' but nothing more.

"Did you think me stone mad when I started to tell you the story about the journals?" May sipped from her coffee cup, her eyes suddenly flinty since she sensed something she could not identify but which made her uneasy. Not getting an answer she said: "Tell me, what's on your mind?"

Pack killed his cigarette and said quietly: "I have to deal with Kelly. She has to pay for what she did to me."

This bothered May and she was unable to just let it go. "For the sake of the money we're going to make, would it not be worth while to just let her alone, Pack? Sure, she's a harmless oul'one! What do you need to do with somebody like that?"

"You've no idea what it was like being in prison year after year. To add to my torment – I'm a human being and the thought of my kid, where it was – God, I didn't even know if it was a boy or a girl child! But, apart from the great wrong she did to me, Kelly is witness to where the girl is buried – and where Deirdre Brewer's child is buried. And there could be money in that knowledge, too."

"How do mean, more money?" May's concern was shelved for the immediate moment.

"Whatever happens between Constance Brewer and the estate – even if she gets all she wants – and we get our share – when it's all over and done with – do you think Sam Sweet and his missus are going to want the world and his wife to know they buried babies they never even legally registered or baptised or anything?"

May regarded Pack in awe, shaking her head as though unable to believe anybody could be gifted to such a degree. He smiled, bathing in the warmth of her response to his idea.

He rose from the table, stretched his arms wide, making sure she had no trouble seeing that he was aroused. Catching her glance at his loins he said: "All this talk about money makes me horny."

May stood up and nodded: "There's a pair of us in it."

With a sweep of his hand he cleared the table, cups and mugs and all the breakfast stuff flying in all directions. He grabbed her and threw her onto her back, pulling her legs up over his shoulders. May shuddered as he peeled away her underwear and she just let him take her with him wherever he wanted to go.

12

February 1923

Kitty Daly untied the stretched canvases from the butcher's basket of her bicycle. She placed them in the narrow hallway of her house in Waterloo Mews and came back out onto the cobbled lane to take in the bike. She was about to shut the door when a man came hurtling in off the street, kicking it closed behind him even as he fell onto the bare boards.

"Please!" he said – the word a plea for her help even as he passed out.

Kitty stood looking down at him but only for moments – his badly beaten face turning her into an immediate ally, regardless of what he had been involved in.

Pushing open the door of her junk room, she put the bicycle inside and, insightfully, decided to do the same thing with her visitor. She hauled him into the box room and in a minute had him hidden by several of her unsold paintings. As she came out into the hall she was startled by a banging on her front door.

Removing her rain jacket, she threw it into the boxroom, leaving the door open. She ripped off her woollen jumper and held it up against her chest and neck. Giving her tousled auburn hair a good rake with her fingernails, she opened the street door just a little. "Who's there? And what do you want?" She played it 'curiosity mingled with vague annoyance', ladling her natural Galway accent on a bit since most men seemed to like it when she talked that way. Even though she was nervous as she let the door open a bit more, she smiled inside as she thought of the money her snooty mother, Pauline, had paid out to all comers in an effort to make her daughter sound posh.

"Would you kindly open the door a little more, please, ma'am?" came a breathless voice. "I'm a police officer."

Kitty pulled the door open. She hid her gasp of surprise when she saw the fine thing standing there in front of her, all hot and agitated, and all the more attractive for the revolver hanging from his right hand.

She acted as though she was carefully covering her bosoms, while she allowed the copper enough to gather his attention. Glad as she was to have a shape that made men drool, she thought it amusing how most of them were martyrs to the breasts. Times it didn't seem to matter what was in back of them in terms of good looks or a nice way about you – big tits turned most men into some kind of jelly.

His reaction was exactly as she had expected it would be – he registered surprise that turned into lusty appreciation while he went on trying to keep his mind on the job. Just like every other man she had come across in her life.

"We are in pursuit of a fugitive, eh, Miss. We have to check the houses here to see if he gained access."

"Ah, Jesus Christ. I didn't get to sleep till five this morning! You woke me up – banging on the door there. Have you got identification on you?"

Looking somewhat embarrassed in front of the uniformed man standing by, he produced a warrant card bearing a good likeness of him alongside the name Patrick Doyle with the rank of Detective Sergeant in the Covert Branch of the Dublin Metropolitan Police Force.

"Thank you, Detective Sergeant Doyle. Sorry I can't help you. Is this man dangerous?"

"He was part of an IRA unit that was robbing a bank in Donnybrook. Yes, you could say he's dangerous." He put his warrant card away and conceded regret for having disturbed her. "I'll be in this area for some time – I'll let you know if we find our man."

"If you have an office, Sergeant, I could ring you on the telephone – that's if I see your man whoever he is." She made no bones about being interested in him as a man.

He was flattered and scribbled his details down on a page torn from his notebook. "My office number – I don't have an instrument at home."

He smiled self-consciously and her heart melted as she bit off a bawdy rejoinder to his apology.

"Not on a sergeant's pay," he said: "That's Dublin Castle," he added before asking, "May I have your name?"

Kitty was enjoying herself – she could see he was

hoping it was Miss as opposed to Missus. "I'm Kitty Daly."

"Thank you for your time, Miss Daly. As you no doubt know we have a very uncivil war going on between the Treaty side and the out-and-out Republicans. Both sides are robbing banks to pay their way – it's up to the DMP to stop them causing havoc in the lives of ordinary decent people. This means we sometimes have to disturb people who have every reason to be fed up with it all." He gave a shrug of his fine shoulders – registering his helplessness in the matter. "Good day to you." As he said the words he seemed to bite down on his tongue, while she smiled, pleased that he was already thinking of seeing her again, however it was to come about.

With those words he left and she went upstairs to her living area which also served as a studio. Slipping on her jumper, she risked peeking out of the window overlooking the lane. She saw no sign of the good-looking copper and went down the stairs to open the boxroom door. Pulling back the paintings, she found that her visitor was conscious and clearly in some pain. She moved his jacket aside and saw some blood. Opening his shirt she found an open flesh wound about three inches long, a crust of blood beginning to form about it.

"Whoever you are, and whatever you've been up to, you need to go to a hospital."

He shook his dark head adamantly, his blue eyes pain-marred, his chin set against this idea.

"Well, you can't stay here. My life is complicated

enough without having some bank robber come to stay. Anyway, I don't think that policeman believed a word I said."

She watched him force his body into a position where he could see his wound.

"It's only a flesh wound," he said, the effort to speak showing her just how much pain he was in.

"The bullet tore the surface flesh as it went by. Could you find me some kind of bandage, a piece of cloth, anything I can use to bind it till I get to somebody who'll fix it up for me?"

"Let me help you up from there." She didn't wait for his approval and he allowed her to haul him to his feet. Sweat was dripping from his forehead but he made no sound. "Do you think you can get up the stairs?" He nodded and she said: "I can give you a hand."

They got to the living area without having to stop, Kitty knowing it was quite an ordeal for him. As they moved towards her bed in the corner he seemed to stumble. She grabbed him as he did the same thing to her so that they found themselves swaying in an embrace that caused some bother to them both.

After what seemed ages Kitty managed to say: "Take your time. Lean on me while we get you to the bed." He nodded and she knew that the accidental meeting of so many body parts had had the same disturbing effect on him.

"If I can just sit on the bed and you could bind up the wound, I'll make my way. I don't want to be the cause of any trouble for you."

She sat him down and he gasped audibly in relief.

Pouring a glass from a half-empty bottle of cheap wine, she came back and watched as he drank it down the hatch.

"Sorry, I've no hard stuff. Have to watch myself around it."

She found an old linen sheet which she had already torn up as a surface for a painting. That was recently, on another day of being flat broke, and so fed up about it she was practically willing to sell herself to some rich old guy just so she would have money for canvases and paint and some personal stuff like silk underwear. As she usually did when she thought about the lack of money in her life, she prayed, jokingly, to a God she didn't believe in. 'Oh God, just send me a sugar daddy, a nice cuddly man in need of a bit of comfort once or twice a week! I'll be a whore for the painting, and sleep well for being supported without having to be married – to have to belong to somebody who thinks he owns you because you were daft enough to let him slip a little band of gold onto the third finger of your left hand.'

Kitty tied the makeshift bandage and stood back to admire the result of her efforts. She was at once very impressed by the patient's body which bore two scars that had cost him more than the present hit. He was naturally muscular, his body's definition like a work of art, his face brooding under a wild thatch of shining black hair. The impact he made on her created a rush of urgency to get him down on canvas.

She gave him the last of the wine and he drank it down. He found cigarettes crushed in their package in his jacket pocket and she straightened them out for him.

She helped him sit at the table and she put an ashtray between them.

"I want to paint you," she said right away. "My name is Kitty Daly but don't tell me yours. It's a superstition of mine, in your case particularly, you being a bank robber." She lit a cigarette, excited by her belief that he was the perfect lost soul at this moment, like somebody with a strong crucifixion quality about him, something so strange, so powerful, that she had to leave him intact with his anonymity, if the work was to be worth a damn. "Will you let me try getting you on canvas?" she asked with a modesty that was all an act.

"If I said yes, would it mean I could stay here for a few days – till I can move about without looking like I'm in agony?" He looked at her, a demonic glint in his pupils, and she felt the need to paint him become even more demanding.

She nodded her head, drew on the cigarette and went on looking at him. "Yes, you can stay here, strictly business, you modelling for me, me providing you with shelter. I'll give you Board but there won't be any Bed."

"Bed and sex would be the last things on my mind right now. Where would I sleep?"

"I have sleeping bags and spare blankets. We'll make you as comfortable as we can. And by the way, it had nothing to do with you as a man that I said no bed. I can't be objective enough to be involved in the painting in the right way if I'm having an affair with my model – nothing personal."

"I have money to buy drink and cigarettes," he said, trying to keep his eyes off the shape of her now that she had got his mind thinking in that way. He felt a pang of guilt and he hated himself for it.

Bloody women! Grainne was the same – take something and twist and turn it till you ended up saying sorry for something you didn't do. Like she had made it sound like the kid would be the answer to their unspoken prayers. He fumed. Shite! I never prayed for any kid.

He'd been putting off telling her he didn't want the child. He could go out and shoot the enemy, take his life in his hands, get shot at left right and centre, but he was afraid of what Grainne might do when he told her it was no go. He believed now she had tricked him, telling him it was safe when it wasn't. He had always been careful in that department. Well, if she had tricked him, if she was in the family way, it was her own funeral.

Some days later, Cormac Doyle missed a family funeral because he was lying low still in Kitty Daly's mews house off Waterloo Road. He was the only one of the Doyle family not present when Molly Harney was laid to rest shortly after her eighty-fifth birthday in Mount Jerome cemetery at Harold's Cross.

Just a week earlier, Deirdre and her mother Elizabeth had driven down to Cullen Lower – Molly having agreed to let them take her back to Dublin to celebrate her birthday.

Arriving at the cabin where Elizabeth – Lizzie – had been reared, they found Molly ill and in no fit state to be moved.

"She's not long for this world," Elizabeth said softly to Pat on the telephone from the hotel in Wicklow town. "If you want to see her again, you'd want to hurry down. Get word to the boys and be sure to tell Mary." She hated being forceful but in recent times her husband's memory was about as reliable as the weather.

Molly found enough strength to tell her niece: "I'm ready to go, Lizzie, been waitin' a long time." She passed over with a tiny smile on her deserted mouth, as though she had caught a glimpse of the God she believed in with every breath. She died in this belief, as she had prayed, believing in His guidance on that morning back in 1885.

That was the morning when she believed that God showed her that she had to get Lizzie away from Wicklow and up to Dublin City where all would be well.

"God works in strange and mysterious ways," Elizabeth sighed by the deathbed, her rosary beads between her fingers. "She sent me off blind to Dublin, her faith in God our only hope. Imagine her having the faith to send me for a job that didn't exist. Your father a total stranger meeting me at the railway station, working his sidecar as usual, and the pair of us never separated again from that minute on."

"She was an easy woman to love, Mammy, the kindest of the kind." Dee was moved deeply but holding onto her tears for the most part, wanting to be there as a support to her mother, not as any kind of burden.

Elizabeth's eyes let go their tears and she said: "Thank God we got her to Arklow that time. You remember, when you got us all down there to hear Gloria Rose singing." Moved by the memory, she smiled tearfully: "Do you remember how she was over the moon? Such a simple thing, meant the world to Aunt Molly, God be good to her."

Deirdre remembered well that night in Arklow. She sat with her fiancé, Arthur, Sam beside her with Vicky in tow, while Gloria, the woman who would be Sam's first wife, kept the audience spellbound with her magnificent singing, and her heart-wrenching performance as Lady Isabelle in the melodrama *East Lynn* by Mrs. Henry Wood.

At Mount Jerome, as the funeral party moved away from the open grave, Sam walked between Elizabeth and her husband, Pat Doyle, who was now his father-in-law. He provided them both with the security of his strong hands as they traversed the wet and slippery ground between the gravestones. He was also keeping an eye on Deirdre who, though showing her pregnancy, was in fine fettle alongside Sarah, and her own sons, Eddie and Alfie.

Sarah caught his eye and they shared a gentle smile, she burrowing a bit more into Dee as though telling Sam yet again how much she loved her stepmother. He noticed that Sarah's free hand was held by Eddie, while Alfie walked like a boy needing to run and yell and break something. Sam smiled – no doubt about it – wouldn't take a mindreader to work out that the two boys had not been sired by the same father.

At that very moment he caught sight of a couple who had been on the fringe of the family, surprised as he recognised May Murray in company with her hired man, Pack Rowan.

What on earth were they doing at the funeral of a woman they didn't know? Surely they would hardly have known who she was – so what the hell were they doing by being present at the graveside?

Seeing him glance their way, May repeated her complaint about running the risk of attending the funeral of a woman they had never met.

"I don't care," Pack whispered the same answer she had received earlier. "I came to take a look at my son." His eyes were on Eddie Brewer even as he spoke. "And I don't care what they know, that's *if* they know about me and you and what we're up to – before long they're the ones'll be scared of us. Now stop annoying me, May!" His son was tall, carried himself well and had a beautiful lassie held by the hand – like father like son he thought, dismissing a dart of anger. 'He doesn't even know I exist. He will someday – even if they pay us off to keep it all quiet. Someday I'm going to tell that lad he's mine."

Sam glanced again at Rowan and May Murray even as he helped Pat Doyle – an old man now with very little to say for himself – and Elizabeth, still full of life, into the Rolls. At the same time he found himself remembering Gloria's face in that moment at her London flat when she came to believe that the housekeeper named May Murray was the only person who could have stolen the journals.

As he got behind the wheel of the Rolls he knew for a certainty that the woman across the graveyard with Rowan was the very same person who had robbed his ex-wife of her precious, dangerous journals.

He made a mental note to talk to Alex Gibbon tomorrow about this very interesting development. He wondered was Rowan simply a lover of the woman or had she roped him in to help her deal with the tricky business of turning her thieving of the journals into a money-spinner?

He waved at Paddy Doyle – recently promoted to the Covert Squad as a Sergeant of Detectives.

Paddy had earlier admitted to Sam and Deirdre that he had no idea where his brother Cormac was at the present time. "Neither did I expect to see him here, Dee. He's on the run which means he's lying low."

"How recently have you seen him?" Deirdre leaned on Sam and he put his arm about her waist.

"Without knowing it, I was chasing him for a while the other day. I thought he'd been shot – he was on the bank raid in Donnybrook – but I suppose not, since he managed to outrun the lot of us."

"Come on, Paddy," Deirdre had said testily. "If you didn't actually see it was Cormac –"

Paddy had cut her off. "The copper with me saw his face before he gave us the slip."

"Are we going back to Casimer Road, Dee?" Sam asked now, half-hoping Dee would say no, the appearance of May Murray and her handyman at the funeral making large demands on his thinking.

"We have to go." Dee pressed his hand. "We won't

stay long."

"It's fine, love," he said quietly. "I just want to see you sitting down in the warm."

Over lunch the following day, Sam told Alex Gibbon about seeing May Murray and Pack Rowan together at the cemetery.

Alex wrote down Rowan's name. "I'll check it out and see if he has a record." He put down his fountain pen. "You're convinced this is the same woman that Gloria employed? The woman who, most likely, took the journals from Gloria's flat."

"It's just a feeling, Alex, but I know it. In my water I can feel it. She is the one. Just as I believe that this Rowan man is her lover. Something about the way they were at the funeral. They were a couple, if you understand me."

"Didn't you say earlier he was a tinker?"

"Yes. Nonetheless, Alex, I'd bet money he's her man. A woman who could recognise the chance to get her hands on a fortune, who then finds backing in the shape of Constance Brewer no less, such a lady is not going to bow to convention when she wants a taste of forbidden fruit."

The main course arrived, beef on the bone for Alex, a Dover sole with boiled potatoes and garden peas for Sam – and both men tucked in heartily.

Later, Alex Gibbon informed Sam: "The court case is due to open on the eighteenth of April, unless some kind of settlement is reached before then."

"Deirdre told me last night she will have nothing to do with a battle over money or property or anything else."

On the previous evening Sam had tried to talk to Dee about the overall situation, since he had to meet Alex and decide on a plan of action.

Deirdre had stopped him before he got very far. "You and the children," she patted her tummy, "and the Clinic, Sam – family and my work, those are the things that matter to me. You can involve yourself in this court business if you want to – you might actually enjoy it – I don't care about the money, I have enough of my own – I don't care about the brewery or anything else, except that Arthur wanted his children to have what he deemed to be their right."

Facing Alex Gibbon across the lunch table, Sam shrugged: "Dee meant what she said."

"What about you, Sam? How do you feel?"

"Ask me again when we've concluded the arrangements with Brendan O'Connor and Cormac Doyle."

"Since your stepchildren are involved you may well find yourself embroiled whether you want to be or not. As your lawyer it's up to me to point this out to you."

"Let's take it a step at a time, Alex. I will do what I have to do." He finished his coffee. "One thing I am sure of: there's never a dull moment."

"There's another thing. The letter and package that Victoria left for you – as per her instructions, they were not to be opened until the twenty-seventh of February, nineteen twenty-three."

"That's next week," Sam said more in surprise than anything else. "My goodness, how swift the moments turning to hours become years."

A shaft of sadness rent his heart as he remembered Victoria, the first great love of his life. His melancholy mood came with the memory of Vicky's last hours. How he had raced to the nursing home in Bray, knowing that she was unlikely to live through another night . . .

He had been met at the front door by the nervous nurse he had talked with the day before. "Thank God you got here for her, Mister Sweet. She hasn't got long."

A nursing sister was wiping Vicky's brow as he entered the sick room. Seeing him, the middle-aged woman nodded her head in commiseration, slipping silently from the room.

Sam moved to the bed, touched Vicky's hand. In a heartbeat, her eyelids fluttered, he saw a glint of the bright blue eyes – first seen by the Liffey – before mucus drowned them again and she was once more the broken woman breaking his heart to see her like this.

"I knew you'd come, dear Sam." She fought, getting the words out with difficulty. "I was just waiting for you."

He felt the skeletal fingers as Vicky tried to grip his hand. "I'm all right, Sam. Don't be too sad. I'm fine, honest."

"I know you are, darling." His eyes spilled tears without restraint. He held her hand, heard as she sighed quietly, this gentle ululation the last sound she was to make.

He saw the light go out of the wasted eyes, her fingers fell from his hand and he knew she had passed over. For a moment he felt that a wedge of ice had been driven into his heart and he bent and kissed her wasted fingers. He saw a picture of her smiling in the bed after a glorious night together, the shaft of pain left him, and he knew Vicky was relieving him of anything but warm memories of their time together. "You'll always have a resting place in my heart, Vicky."

They had become instant kindred spirits – her wayward way – like Sam's – born ahead of its time. Honest enough to be selfish at times, she opened the door to a future he could not have dreamed of – so many wonderful memories of her wild and irrepressible spirit that he would harvest down what years he had left to mourn her, even happily, now that she was at peace.

He had wept copiously as he drove away from Bray, crying out a wish, a prayer filled with pain: "Mind her!" to whatever power might hear the words. "She was a god's gift to this world."

13

February 1923

Mendel Sweet wanted to go back to school by himself but since his mother was not going to see him again for several weeks, she insisted on travelling down to Ramsgate with him.

"I thought you would enjoy my company." She hid the wicked smile that adorned her mouth as she set about teasing him. "But I suppose most boys want to cut the apron strings when they're twelve years old."

"It's not that, Mama, and you know it. And you might remember that in four months' time I will be thirteen."

Gloria turned her face to him and he grimaced as he realised she had caught him with her teasing. "I won't be seeing you till well into March, darling – besides, each time I visit you at Townley Castle, I like it the more, and that allows me freedom from the nagging concerns mothers are heir to. Would you deny me that sliver of comfort in my old age?"

He came to her and she hugged him from within her

being, knowing that the grace to feel was a double-edged sword. In this respect, nature had been especially generous to her – she flew on his nearness, usually bereft then for several days as she parted from her son until the next time. Time did nothing to dilute the sense of loss –and to Gloria, the price seemed more than high. Mendel charmed her by being free of the need to indulge in guile – he was an open book to her – his eyes had not yet lost their inherent innocence.

Like shiny brown buttons they lit up inside each time they landed on her own as she came to visit or when he arrived on her doorstep for a weekend break. Those weekend visits were happy times for mother and son – they crammed in plays and musical shows – Mendel enjoyed both when they were well done, despite his rejection of his father's offer to take him to the theatre – they shared the books they were reading, and, of course, played chess. Mendel won all the time with such ease that her heart sang for the brilliance that ensured her very next defeat.

She had no difficulty in accepting that her world revolved around her son and her dream of a Homeland for all Jews. Her singing had become a major part of her active living – since she and Sam had separated and divorced, she used her talent willingly to earn money which she donated to the cause – in truth, singing for its own sake paled beside her feelings for her son and her dreams of their future together in the Promised Land.

Sometimes she had to remind herself that she had a daughter, Sarah, who would be fourteen on her next birthday – the girl had chosen to live with her father in

Ireland – and had openly declared in her own precocious fashion that she did not want to live in Palestine, nor live with her mother who was obsessed by that idea.

Gloria believed that it had worked out for the best – with her busy schedule of concerts and the travelling that touring involved, she failed to see Mendel as often as she wished – had Sarah been at some other school in England, the pressure of making time to visit her would have been that much greater, and she couldn't have faced that. She found it equally hard that Sarah had made it all too clear that she wanted to stay with her father, that she wanted to live at home in Ireland for the rest of her life.

Gloria's thoughts moved onto the back burner as the driver of her hired motor car drove into the grounds of Townley Castle School. She was once again caught up in the feeling of helplessness, within minutes of letting go of her son she would once again have to accept there was not a thing she could do about it.

To her surprise, the car pulled to the side of the cobbled driveway, and she saw the driver try to tap on the glass screen that separated them before he slumped over onto the front seat. The car stopped and in a moment she and Mendel had jumped out.

Mendel opened the driver's door.

The man lay lifeless, his eyes wide open, his face a startled question mark. Gloria knew he was dead as she stepped back to gather herself through a deep breathing exercise her instructor had taught her.

Mendel stood looking at the corpse until Gloria took his arm firmly.

"Darling, do you think you could run and ask matron to telephone for an ambulance, a doctor, something. Perhaps they could send the nurse down here. This poor man has passed away."

Even as the boy nodded, a man riding a bicycle stopped before them. "May I be of some help, madam?"

Gloria found herself looking at a man over medium height, a fine figure of a man, his stature enhanced by a full beard that spread onto the lapels of his tweed jacket worn over corduroys, the ends of which were held tight above his ankles by metal clips.

"Yes, please, Mister Jameson."

The man raised a hand in friendly greeting. "Good day, young Mendel – excuse me, madam – you have a problem here, I take it."

Within half an hour, due entirely to the caring energy and willingness of the man Jameson, the corpse of the deceased driver had been taken along to the school infirmary, while Gloria dictated the details of the event to a uniformed policeman who had arrived on his bicycle and taken charge.

As Gloria waited for a taxi to take her to Ramsgate station – she had missed the train she had intended to catch – Jameson came to her in the headmaster's study. He had brought a tray of tea and watercress sandwiches and a small selection of delicious-looking pastries that she had no intention of ignoring.

"Are you certain I am not discommoding the headmaster, Mister Jameson?"

"You have my word, madam. He it is who gives the main lecture on Thursday afternoon." He paused while he poured tea for her. "French or science this afternoon, I can't remember which, when, in my view, the lads would benefit no end from a good talk about English grammar. Your son, ma'am, is the only boy in his form who knows what a split infinitive is."

Gloria sipped tea: "I want to thank you, Mister Jameson. My son tells me you are a good friend to many of the boys – it seems to me he values his talks with you more than any of the teaching staff."

"He's a very special lad, ma'am, gifted and gentle – during some of his breaks he will come and find me in the garden – it's been said of me that I have green fingers – he likes to talk of books and writers and theatre – he is capable of topping any class on any subject to which he gives his time and attention. In his case, should he do the regular studying, punch in the hours, as someone said, his success is simply inevitable – a case of 'how big will it be?' as opposed to 'will it happen?'." He broke off as though embarrassed by his own effusiveness. "Forgive my familiarity, ma'am, but Mendel, your son, we have become friends, and I am here only to serve in any way I can."

Gloria woke up on the train, surprised that she had drifted into a nap. She found herself smiling a little as she remembered Mendel's embrace and his promise to write every other day – he asked her if she had liked Mister Jameson and he was very pleased as she responded without criticism of the man with the green fingers.

Jameson had taken the time to show her the castle and its environs and she enjoyed the Scottish burr on the hem of his speech. "This was a genuine castle, ma'am. The crenellations and those grey battlemented towers, they are the real thing. It is claimed," his voice dropped, his tone carrying a fair deal of doubt, "that Queen Victoria once lived here as a girl."

As the man went on describing in general terms the sterling qualities of the school, Gloria noticed that he ignored any mention of the fact that it was a Jewish school, though he did emphasise the fact that it was designed on the lines of Eton and Harrow. He talked with respect of the headmaster, avoiding mention of the fact that he was a Jew. She reasoned that he was doing this because he assumed she knew all about it, since her son was a student there. But something told her this was not the case. Within a few minutes she realised that his observations, apparently natural, had the ring of words practised to eschew any acknowledgment that the school was in fact a Jewish school. This struck Gloria as anti-Semitic and she found herself wondering about what else he might be hiding. The huge beard and the mane of hair suddenly seemed to her as a mask until she allowed that she was being fanciful, adding a hint of drama. 'Just like an actress,' she chortled inside, before letting the conjecture go. But before she drifted off the sleep again, she made a mental note to keep Mister Jameson to the forefront in her letters to Mendel – no harm done in responding to an instinctive caveat, be it fanciful or not.

Even as sleep claimed her she was smiling at herself, a hint of derision in her humour – 'You have been like some neurotic old woman since you found out your journals were stolen.' Her inner voice countered: 'Sam didn't think you the least bit daft, and whatever else he is, Sam Sweet is nobody's fool.'

"To hell with Sam Sweet!" Pack Rowan informed the nightscape of Ireland's capital city.

He flicked the butt of his cigarette into the Liffey estuary as the ferry to Liverpool began the overnight to 'Little Dublin'. The nickname had nothing to do with the size of the thriving west of England seaport – it related to the number of Irish people, a great many of them Dubliners domiciled there from the turn of the century and before.

Rowan was glad of the cold February night. The bite in the wind helped grant him real privacy as he stood by the rail on the passenger deck, his fellow travellers preferring the snugness of the smoke-filled saloon bar.

He had warmed himself with whiskey from the half bottle in his pocket, fed up with himself since he had not managed to cast off his concern about Sam Sweet. At another place in another time he would have got rid of the bloody man, but he didn't think it was smart for the man to have a fatal accident, not right now.

This restriction troubled him – mates in Dublin had painted a very clear picture of the successful Jew so that Pack knew he was not somebody you should mess with.

Rowan had been impressed, he grudgingly admitted, by the casual manner of Sweet's surveillance of May and himself when they had gone to the Doyle family funeral. He knew they should have left the funeral alone – against his better judgement he had allowed sentiment to cloud his thinking. Yet a lingering fancy to see his son had camped on the edge of his mind. Aggressively he dismissed it with a derisive spit into the sea before it gained a foothold that might cause him to do something else as stupid as going to the cemetery at Mount Jerome.

He felt a dart of aggravation as he watched the port being swallowed up by the distance, this arising as he remembered May wanting to shut up shop again and make the trip to England with him. He felt like giving her a slap for being so stupid but when she said, "I miss you bad when you're gone, Pack," he chomped down on his temper and played the game. Bloody women! They had a way of worming themselves into your shagging veins if you didn't watch out.

"Don't you think I have feelings?" he responded instead. "Oh, I'm just a bloody tinker so how could I have?"

He had intended to sound hurt and it worked because she threw her arms around him, cuddling him rather than lying in passionately. "I don't know how I manage to stop throwing the drink in their faces when I hear some of the things they say about tinkers, and me having to be civil as I serve the stinking bastards!"

Her tears were warm on his neck which annoyed him, but because he had no patience with this kind of chatter, he picked her up and carried her upstairs.

"That's one sure way to shut May up for a while," he

said to the night, smiling as he threw the empty bottle at the invisible ocean.

The whiskey sat well on his taste buds and he licked his lips. Might as well get inside, nice and snug in there, a night for the high stool really. Who knows – a fella might just come across some poor woman in need of a bitta comfort. He chuckled as he made his way across the deck – wouldn't be the first time he provided balm to a female heart sore and lonely to be leaving the homeland.

Gloria Stein put the receipts for the concert money into a desk drawer and locked it. Since the discovery that her journals had been stolen, she had become very security-conscious. This had led her to use her profile in the concert world to apply for a permit to own a handgun. This had been granted and she was in the process of finding somebody to teach her how to use the weapon. She had felt so violated by the loss of her journals that she was intent on ensuring that she would be a victim no more.

Checking the morning post she found a letter from Sam, who, good to his word, had been checking up on May Murray. "For the life of me, I can't remember whether or not I asked you if you had a snap, a picture of the woman when she worked for you."

Gloria permitted herself a smile, not unhappy to discover that Sam had his memory lapses too. Her manager, Ruth Davis, had suggested just today that her memory might be in need of a little romance to give it a jolt. Ruth had been introducing Gloria to one man after another on a fairly regular basis – she being of an earthy spleen and convinced that all females needed what she called 'a rub of the brush' every so often.

Gloria quite enjoyed the company of some of the men Ruth found for her, but she had not been in the slightest bit interested in forming a relationship with any of them. There were nights – when she had taken a glass or two of wine before going to sleep – she had lain in a state of reverie, wondering about this and that, and what if this had happened in a different way. The total sum of her dozing reflections was summed up by an overall feeling of immense gratitude to Sam for his caring and his understanding in their debacle of a marriage.

He had been a very special man, and had she not allowed herself to be taken by Arthur Brewer on that long ago night of the summer solstice at Dunbla House, they might well have had a marriage made in heaven.

She was relieved that at last she could view her seduction – ravaging more like – by Arthur from such a distance that it no longer made any claim on her sense of wellbeing. Thanks to Sam she had paid her dues for that folly.

All in all, she felt very fortunate to have the life she now lived, and she didn't even have to think that it was due to her relationship with Mendel. That was a given now – he was all and everything, the air that she breathed first thing, her last sigh at night, her every reason to live a good life and to keep working for the cause of Jews worldwide. The energy that it took to fuel her considerable work schedule came to her through her feeling for this boy who returned her fervour with his golden loyalty. When this mixed bag of feelings and responses had worked their way free of her mind, she dropped Sam a note saying sorry, no picture of May Murray.

Not that, so his note had claimed, he needed one. He knew she was the journal thief who had opened up all their lives to the most serious threat they were ever likely to have to face.

Sam read Gloria's letter – she had no photo of May Murray – and wondered if Mendel might have one. Sam had sent him a camera for his tenth birthday, the boy had been taking pictures ever since. He had been fond of May – there was a good chance he would have a picture of her.

Sam sent a note off to his son at his school in Ramsgate, just before he went into his meeting with Alex Gibbon at the lawyer's office on Kildare Street to discuss the contents of Victoria's will.

"Before we get into any discussion, Sam, I should tell you that I know the contents, since I drew up the papers for Victoria."

Sam nodded his head, his mood sombre.

Alex went on: "I've left you a letter opener – I have set aside this conference room for the next hour. When you are ready to talk, or have need of anything meantime, just give the bell a tinkle. Do you need anything else from me before I leave you in peace?"

Again Sam shook his head, his heart swelling as Alex left the room. In a moment he was blinded by tears and his breathing convulsed once or twice as he tried using the opening of the package to distract him from the emotional turmoil that had invaded his morning.

Spreading the documents out on the vast polished oak table, he soon found what he was looking for, a letter in Vicky's own hand. He pressed the notepaper to his lips and wiped his eyes, leaving his hankie on the desktop, not at all sure he wouldn't need it again.

As he began to read, it was as though he was listening to a gramophone recording of Victoria's voice, and indeed, he had to put the letter down for some moments.

Sitting upright he drew long deep breaths in through his nose in an effort to quell the threat of another fall of tears hovering, as though waiting to drench his resolve to be calm and dry-eyed.

Finally, a cigarette between his fingers, he was able to commence reading her letter to him.

'My dearest Sam – My friend and lover, mentor, tutor, guide and giver of all things good, I have passed on, or you would not be reading this.

'I have spent some time thinking about how I would feel if our situation was reversed – I know that I should be sad beyond words – knowing how close we were, and having tasted a different kind of nearness in our later years, I should be missing you terribly even after all the time since my demise.

'So, let your sadness do its dance, allow your tears their waltz as the seasons of my destiny have arranged that I pass *over before you, for which I am truly grateful. Sad I am to be leaving you but sadder still were I the one left behind. Myself and dear, dear Arthur, we usually meant well but, dear heart, we tended to gloss over things that needed attention, dismiss others when we might have been more caring, and to generally behave irresponsibly, though of course Arthur had genius thrust upon him when it came to the brewery and his other business pies, but I'm afraid we need you there, left behind, to sort out the cracks and stuff we left behind.*

'Therefore, thank God you are now reading this which is my legal document to you along with the others that Alex Gibbon deemed necessary to enable you to carry out the task – I trust it will not appear daunting to you – truly not for the sake of money or property but as a matter of principle.

'Arthur felt all of this when he finally realised that he was going to die young, that his profligacy would demand redemption long before his span of three score and ten came into view. Which is why he asked of me – should he go first – that I take on the role I am now passing on to you. It has to come to you, Sam, since you know it all – you have lived in the shadow of the damage that Constance Brewer inflicted upon her twin children through her total indifference to the wishes and even needs that are a given in the life of every child. Our mother was not a fit person to bear that title – she never once set foot in a nursery – she refused to breastfeed us because it would damage her figure, which, paradoxically, she never used for anything that would have required her to be wrinkle-free (forgive me, Sam, for being so wicked) – but I once heard Lisa O'Brien (Arthur's heart-mother, God bless her) say, not knowing that I was within earshot – that "Missus bloody Brewer got a body made for mortal sin and

all she did was shut up shop once she had the two children to cement her position where the money was concerned".

'Poor Father who came quickly to hatred for Constance, excluded her from parental duties when she later tried to control us – more from fear of our import in the family situation, than from any shred of motherly love. Arthur and I, or course, played on father's guilt – he gave us a free hand, he even agreed that we could be tutored at home – he never forgave himself for being such a disaster as a father – and truly, after a time, all that existed between Constance and her twins was hatred.

'She was, of course, a very stupid woman, and when she threw Lisa out of the house because she and my father were lovers, she threw away whatever chance Arthur had of being a normal boy. I was born tougher than he, and in truth, he and Lisa were closer than any mother and son I have known in my lifetime with the exception of yourself and Esther. You two had a wonderful mother-son relationship which I envied at times, and I have to say her generosity to Gloria from the beginning of your marriage was something channelled directly to her from some heaven somewhere.

'However long-winded this is, I am not going to apologise, for this is truly my final goodbye to you. So bear with me, dear heart.

'Arthur felt that at some stage Constance would come back into the Brewer orbit – she has a most unforgiving nature and she swore more than once that she would make us pay for eschewing her. As I've already said, our dear Arthur feared that he would go first and he felt that her attack on the status quo might come into play at this point. This was the reason he appointed me as Chief Executor of his estate – Alex

Gibbon has tied up all the loose ends, and things are knotted tightly in an effort to ensure that whenever and however the attack comes from Constance, it will be to no avail.

'Arthur agreed with me – my own health was on the wane at the time of my appointment as guardian of the Brewer fortune – that if I felt it necessary – if my health deteriorated in a serious way – I should appoint you to take my place. He did not suggest that I ask you, he took it as a given that you would step into the breach, since you were, and have been for so long our dear and trusted loved one.'

At this point, Sam had to take a break in order to simply indulge his need to weep, to allow what felt like a waiting deluge to power its course out of the body and heart and the mind, and he sat there for several minutes like somebody whose heart had been shrapnel-rent by this explosion of grief.

When the tears ceased he blew his nose, had a long drink of water, smoking a cigarette through, before going back to Vicky's letter.

As he picked up the pages his only wish was that he could have communicated somehow to the twins that he was honoured beyond imagining to have been chosen for the role he now accepted so willingly.

As though reading his mind, Victoria continued, her once steady penmanship a tad shaky:

'Knowing you as I do, I expect you are feeling honoured by the responsibility both Arthur and I place on you in this moment. Please feel the degree to which the feeling is reciprocated, dear man. You have allowed us feel blessed by the closeness we have enjoyed down some decades. The honour has always been ours and we have loved you as we

have from the earliest times of our laying eyes on each other.

'When you face Constance you will be meeting someone who considers only one point of view – her own. She is a consummate actress when she wants something badly enough and she is ruthless to the point of being capable of almost any criminal act. If this sounds hyperbolic, step back from it. Don't take it on board, Sam, but remember I said it, and that I would not offer anything here that was not for your benefit.

'At the risk of sounding like Constance, I tell you she was jumped up, pumped up in a way to appear good enough for her role as wife to someone such as Arthur Shane Brewer. Having taken the part as it were, she played it to the hilt – Lisa summed it up one day when she said: "Put a beggar on horseback and they'll ride to Kingdom Come." That was Constance Brewer and I can assure you that she was incensed to the point of insanity that Arthur chose to wed Deirdre. She was also obdurate in her Jew-hating. She was born with this character defect, Sam – surely it can never be a personal thing – and she never forgave Arthur for having you as the best friend of his life.

'Before I stop, I charge you with taking on my role here – all you will have to do is sign some papers and be ready to fight the court case of your life.'

Sam had to stop reading again and he lit a badly needed cigarette. He was almost stunned by Victoria's prescience. As he sat reading her words, the situation she described was into production. He was shaking his head in disbelief as he went back to reading.

'I am also asking you to set up the sale of the twelve paintings I have left behind. They may well be the work of my

life – whatever money they earn is to go to Dee – she is to have a free hand to spend it in any way she sees fit, and you and I both know where it will go. She is a heroine of my life and I thank you again since you brought her to us when she was the emerging young designer who offered the bower of her decency to those of us in need of such an arbour.

'Alex has assured me that all is in order. I pass it all on to you, Sam – may you feel as you read the last lines I will ever write, the love that I feel for you, a love so powerful, so universal really, as to be beyond the personal. To me you have been the channel through which all the power of the Universe came into our lives.

'My last words are: "Sam, God broke the mould when he made you." To which, knowing you, I expect you to rejoin: "No, Vicky, he broke the mould and then he made me anyway."

'I am smiling now as I think of you. Is there no end to you, Sam Sweet?'

Vicky

Sam sat and made no attempt to move. There was no point. There were tears that would not be denied and he resisted the pointless attempt to suppress them. As they flowed he could feel the heat of them on his skin and he welcomed them, in the knowledge that had he not felt such an extreme sense of loss that Vicky had passed over, the whole of his life would have been a complete farce

14

March 1923

A couple of days after St Patrick's Day, Mendel Sweet's reply to his father's request for a photograph of May Murray arrived on Sam's desk. A wry smile distorted his mouth as he cut the envelope – his son's penmanship got ten out of ten but the pace at which he posted his mail needed some attention. He sniffed at his own impatience – what's the hurry, Sam? This case is going to be on your plate for some time.

In truth he was grateful that Mendel had replied at all – any breaking of the ice coming from that direction was more than welcome. The snapshot fell from between a single folded page of a school jotter, Sam not needing a second glance to confirm that May Murray in the snapshot was the landlady of the public house at Dunbla.

He sipped his morning coffee and smoked a cigarette – he had smelled this from the first time he heard her name from Gloria's lips in London. In that moment he had questioned the speed of his conclusion – but then, it had landed on him – there had been no working it out like some kind of permutation – his dart of insight, prescience, foreknowledge, call it what you will, he mused, had been God-sent, suggesting to him that he was meant to be involved in the intrigue that Constance Brewer had set up in order to steal the Brewer fortune from its rightful heirs.

There and then he knew that he would not – whatever the cost to him personally – back off the emotional commitment he had already made in his step-children's interest.

He got up from the desk, having decided a walk would do him good, help him to get the mind awake and working constructively.

It was a cold morning but he was feeling warm with satisfaction as he slipped the snapshot into his pocket.

Moments later he answered the telephone to a call from Alex Gibbon. His lawyer was feeling good to impart the news that his closest old school chum, James Gatling, would be acting as Second Chair to Sir Albert Whimby when they got to court.

According to Alex, this was very good news since his friend, a compulsive card player, always in need of money, was happy to pass over valuable inside information at a reasonable price. "We already owe James a few quid, Sam. He confirms your suspicion that the bold Pack Rowan is a major player on old Constance Brewer's team."

Sam smiled grimly at the news, expecting no less. He had felt the chemistry between Rowan and May

Murray, would have sworn the pair were lovers, tight as ticks, the tinker the muscle and the driving power behind the publican's lust for riches, however they were to be gathered.

Alex said he had heard from this source how Rowan had cemented Sir Albert's belief in the near certainty of success against the Brewer estate.

This had come about as Rowan, pushed by Constance Brewer to really prove his worth, had said without equivocation: "The lad called Eddie Brewer is the son of myself and a tinker girl that died giving birth to him."

When Constance Brewer had pushed, yet again, for proof of a more tangible nature than Rowan's word, he had replied with an offhand sense of conviction: "No problem, my lady, I know where the bodies are buried."

"But what does that mean, Alex?" Sam asked. "I mean, we all know that, metaphorically speaking, 'where the bodies are buried' is a smart way of covering a multitude without anything actually being given away."

"True," Alex agreed. "And of course it cut no ice with the dreaded Constance. Gatling says she demanded to know exactly what Rowan meant."

"Did he reveal anything more?"

Alex had been somewhat amused by what came next: "He assured them that at their next meeting he would reveal all. When the old dame pushed him still further, he assured her that he was more than willing to reveal everything, but, he would like to talk it over with his partner, not wanting to offend the lady in question."

"What did Whimby and old Constance think of that?"

"Whimby didn't bother with it. He is impressed with Rowan's solidity in their discussions. Gatling himself is more than surprised. He tells me that the tinker talks like he is the boss, that he runs the show."

"He sleeps with May Murray, I'm sure of it. My source tells me that May tries not to moon over Rowan when they are working the pub together. Séamus Byrne, who is rarely mistaken in matters relating to fornication and sexual behaviour generally, tells me that May fails more often than not. Sorry for going on, Alex – do make your point."

"Sir Albert, who is a lot sharper and craftier than he pretends to be, believes utterly that Rowan was not speaking metaphorically when he said he knew where the bodies are buried."

On hearing this, Sam experienced extreme disquiet and agreed to meet Alex the next day. He was bothered to such a degree that he went to the sideboard and poured himself a brandy. Drinking it down, he quietly used his sense of taste to bring him into the present moment.

Breathing more easily, he went back to the desk and lit another cigarette before he considered the consequences that could arise for him and Dee and the others, should Pack Rowan have been speaking literally.

My God, he mumbled, smoking heavily now, if Rowan was speaking literally, it had to mean that he knows of the secrets contained in the Pets' Cemetery.

Sam recovered his calm by the time he slipped on

his Wellingtons, but his street-self could feel it in his water that Rowan knew more than he himself could have imagined.

He knew via Gibbon's lawyer friend with the gambling addiction that Rowan could read and write – Sam thought that praiseworthy in a deprived person and tinkers certainly came into that category – and that he was also somebody who could articulate an argument in a clear and forthright manner. "Sure of himself about everything he says," Alex had related.

Sam had lost his enthusiasm for the morning walk – he fretted since there was no denying that this particular tinker and his partner May Murray could create havoc if they ever took the information from the stolen journals into the public domain.

Rowan could read and write and argue his case. But, before the tinker had ever learned the alphabet or put pen to paper, he had been part of a people who spoke and argued and bought and sold and sang and recited a language that was steeped in poetic doggerel and simile and metaphor, with exaggeration and hyperbole and imagination laid on with a trowel, loquacious as even the most uneducated among the Irish seemed to inherently be.

But did that necessarily mean that Rowan was speaking wildly or metaphorically when he said he knew where the bodies were buried?

No. The kind of ability that Rowan was demonstrating in his dealings with a titled barrister and a dowager like Constance Brewer led Sam to believe Rowan was being literal when he had said that he knew where the dead mother of his own child, and Dee's stillborn baby girl, had been laid to rest.

The very idea that this could be true sent an aggressive chill along Sam's spine.

As he donned his raincoat, Sam's calm had turned cold – this was what happened when he was faced with daunting odds – and he was able to say to himself without fear or anger or any concern for his own future: 'It can't, it just can't be allowed to happen – there has to be a way out of this mess, and I have to find it, stop this runaway train before it destroys the lives of those I love and care for.'

This produced a busy butterfly of panic which he quelled immediately by standing still and pressing his feet against the inside soles of his rubber boots.

He also rubbed thumbs and forefingers together, asking himself: 'To whom does this fear arise?' Hearing the answer 'Me', he asked: 'Who am I?' staying with this question until his breathing had turned normal again.

Calm enough now, he felt so very grateful to be aware that the sense of touch could bring instant stillness to the busiest mind – smiling as he remembered the day when he had grabbed the steering wheel of the car as a reflex action to discover, by accident, that his mind had gone still, the resentment he felt to the driver ahead of him eschewed without his making any conscious decision to this effect. Staying now with that same sense of touch, he stepped out into the chill of the March morning.

He now set about considering just some of the

damage that could soon be assaulting all their lives were the truth to come out. First of all, he allowed that as a general principle he tried to live hand in hand with the truth, though he could admit that more than once he had indulged in what he called concealment of material fact, this euphemism used when he was keeping somebody in the dark.

Sam jammed his favourite corduroy hat down on his head as he walked across the stable yard towards the cottage Séamus shared with Angela. He was allowing himself another glance at the line of accusations they would face if the bodies in the Pets' Cemetery were exhumed, and he was stunned by the pictures showing up in the space behind his eyes.

He and Deirdre, Séamus, Angela, Kelly, not forgetting Cormac Doyle, would be liable to be accused of all kinds of things including murder, quite literally. He stopped and held onto the gate of the cottage, practising deep breathing as the subsidiary charges roll-called themselves out in the echo chamber of his mind.

'And let's not forget a trivial thing like fraud on a grand scale, Sam. After all, it is a fact that the boy named Edward Brewer is not the son of his mother and his deceased father. And by the way, those who will be accused alongside Deirdre Sweet knew this for a fact, and . . .'

Sam pressed his feet against the inner soles of his boots and savoured the relief he felt as the hint of panic returning disappeared into thin air. He lit a cigarette and tasted tobacco on his tongue. But the force of his earlier reaction to the possible charges he and Dee and the others could be facing exploded all over his sense of wellbeing and, for a moment, he imagined himself reading in the *Irish Times* of someone accused of such a list of criminal activity. How would he, as a reader of the newspaper, see it? Surely he would ask himself: 'How can the accused be anything but guilty? With so many accusations made against them, surely they have to be guilty of something and possibly guilty of everything on the list?'

And yet, by the cottage gate, knowing all that had taken place, Sam could say for certain that no crime had been carried out by the accused, Deirdre Sweet, beyond falsification of a birth and a burial certificate.

He would argue to any jury anywhere that two of the three people shot dead in the Washington hotel in 1920 had been killed by accident – Cormac Doyle, in the name of the republican cause had made a mistake – the third, a British officer, had been shot dead by Sam himself in order to save his own life. His part in the killing had to be a case of self-defence, and Cormac, as a Volunteer in the IRA, should be treated as a revolutionary and not as a common murderer.

Even as he rationalised the overall picture, Sam could practically hear a jury start to chuckle, the muted laughter becoming something else as the collective amusement of the twelve exploded all over the courtroom. And what bothered the hell out of him was that Sam knew if he was one of those jurors he would be among the first to laugh.

He shook his head and blew through the circle of his

lips, seeing the air vaporise instantly, knowing that should the truth come out, it was naïve and at least fanciful to think that any of the accused were just going to walk away with a slap on the wrist.

When it came to light that the bodies of Arthur Brewer and Lisa O'Brien had been removed from the dead British officer's hotel room, that they had been buried under cover of darkness on the Dunbla estate, this would hang their chances of being found innocent of anything, never mind everything.

The thought of being hanged turned his blood to ice but there was no denying that such an outcome would be very likely indeed. The fact that Cormac, as an IRA Volunteer, had gone to the rundown hotel to kill a British Army officer, had in his panic shot Arthur Brewer and Lisa O'Brien, and that he Sam had been forced to shoot the Englishman to save his own life – none of this would stop his death by hanging. And worse, Dee had to be implicated in some charge relating to 'after the fact' which could mean she would be treated as if she had pulled the trigger that killed all three people.

He quelled the flowing thoughts and permutations, thanks to the taste of tobacco on his tongue, knowing he would not allow it to happen. He would not allow this to happen because he could not, and he could not since it was insane that Dee be punished for saving the life of the boy motherless and bound to die had chance not sent her to keep him alive with the milk her stillborn girl had no need of.

This permutation ensured that Kelly would end up before the courts, the old woman being guilty of collusion with Deirdre in the falsification of the registration of Eddie's birth. She was also involved in helping Dee bury her stillborn daughter without the girl's birth or death being recorded as required by law. And in back of all the unbelievable carnage that would ensue so far, there was yet the question of the charges that Séamus Byrne and his partner, Angela, would face when all 'ifs and buts' were ironed out and laid before a judge and jury.

Sam's mind reeled under the development of the hell-sent images that were flying off the conveyor belt of truth that, in prime working order, merely presented the facts without prejudice, and without falsification of any kind. Sam stood still, accepting the fact that no amount of courtroom skill on the part of barristers could present a case for the defence that was anything more than a token effort.

So whatever was needed to prevent a gigantic miscarriage of justice he would have to introduce into the situation. Implicit in this acceptance was the unspoken thought 'by fair means or foul', since, strictly speaking, the application of the letter of the law here would ensure that everybody charged would pay the severest penalty that the law allowed at this time. Which was tantamount to saying that his beloved wife and the others that had by-passed the law in the name of justice – and this included himself – would die swinging on the end of a rope. This, he vowed with all his might, could not be allowed to happen. And it would not happen, not as long as he had a breath left in his body and the finances to buy whatever it took to see that just once, the law would not prevent justice being served.

With this torrent of conflict under some kind of control Sam pressed on to the door of the cottage where Séamus was living out his last years with his woman, Angela.

Opening the door to Sam's knock the Kerryman failed to hide his surprise. Sam himself was taken aback that an impromptu visit should have given Séamus such a shock – it was only when he caught a glimpse of his face in the mirror over the mantle that he saw he was sweating on what Séamus had deemed to be "the coldest one of the winter yet, Mister Sam".

When they were sitting either side of the fire sipping from mugs of strong tea, Sam munched on one of Angela's home-made biscuits, pleased to find the cottage as comfortable as any man could wish for.

Because it was impossible to keep in-house situations from the staff, Sam spoke as though Séamus knew why he had dropped in to see him.

"We have a serious problem, Séamus, and I am going to need all the help you can give me."

"I knew she'd come back to haunt us some day," Séamus nodded his head, his face in a cloud of anger and resentment. "I met some quare people in my time, Mister Sam, but Constance Brewer takes the biscuit so she does. You tell me how I can help in any way to stop the bitch robbing Arthur Brewer's fortune from his children and his widow." He gently bowed his head at Sam. "We can't let her get away with that. The boss'd be spinning in his grave so he would."

"It's about all of that I will need to talk to you. I have some notes to make, so that when I come to you to talk, I'll know exactly what I need from you, if you can help me."

"Have no fear on that score, Mister Sam. I'd give what life's blood is left to me to put a stop to the gallop of Lady Muck."

"I wanted to be sure before I came trundling in here asking questions. This is your home and I came only because I feel we have had a rapport for a good many years."

As he was about to leave, Sam said: "You know that fellow, Rowan – he works with May Murray at the tavern?"

"I know who you mean, Mister Sam."

Sam saw that Séamus had gone tight in the lips and that his chin had hardened and that his hands had turned to fists on his lap.

"Would you know if he has made any kind of contact with Kelly recently?"

Séamus was simply stunned. "How in God's name did you know?"

Sam nodded his head in satisfaction. "I thought so, Séamus." He came back to the fireside and put his hand on the old Kerryman's shoulder. "Do you trust me, Séamus?"

"With my life – Angela's too, Mister Sam."

"We are going to have to use all the guile we can find to handle what is going on. I'm not yet sure how we are to go about all that has to be done, but I will come back to you when I've worked things out."

He left the cottage and walked up the hill, glad of the rubber boots as the long wet grass washed them clean of what mud had been there when he left the house.

He stood on the headland, where for many a morning hour last autumn he had sat viewing the shoreline curve at Killiney, the beach then, from his bird's eye view, like worn tweed, as though only the energy of the tide could wake it from its early morning torpor.

He loved this place and he realised as he looked down the slope of the land behind him to the Pets' Cemetery, that there was not much he would not do to hold onto the life he had come to know.

He thought of Arthur, the gentlest man that ever drew breath – in sobriety – torn from all this by the excess of violence that had spilled all over him to take his life.

Arthur was buried down there, Lisa O'Brien too, and the tinker girl taken in childbirth. Lying with the young tinker was the tiny bundle of Deirdre's first child. Eddie Brewer had been given to Dee by the tinker woman Kelly, the motherless lad replacing the stillborn at the breast of the woman who was now Sam's wife.

"Whatever it takes, we have to hold on to our secrets. We have to, and we will." Sam words were taken by the biting bluster of the March morning as he staggered for a moment, moved on steadily then, glancing now and then to the sea below to his left.

It now looked so different from the autumn colours he had loved to see as early as possible after first light.

How muted and different it looked in the grip of a vicious March day, as though reminding him that change was inevitable.

He felt anger as he vented his thoughts onto the morning air: "If Constance wins this court case our way of life as we know it will be over. The terrible beauty of Yeats will apply very much to all of us and I could get the rope or a life sentence, worse than death." He almost staggered as the truth of their situation hit him like another killing blow. "I won't let that happen. Do you hear me, Arthur? I won't let Constance do this to us and to all that you stood for!"

He fumbled for a cigarette and drew smoke that made him cough, so that it was almost a minute before he was back in full control of his breathing.

The pictures in his head, the implications that fell all over his wellbeing, took him to a point in his resolve where he knew that he would die before he would let such a thing happen. No crime had been committed – even Cormac's intention to kill the officer in that hotel room was in the name of the war with the Brits, but who was going to believe it? When the pictures of what had happened were presented in the eloquent prose of a grand master of procedure such as Sir Albert Whimby, there could only be one outcome.

Sam killed his cigarette and turned back to go down the hill passing the Pets' Cemetery on the way to the house. His anger had strengthened his will not to be drowned by a chain of events that had landed on his life the day Arthur and Lisa had been shot. He was now more grateful than ever that he had survived many a daunting situation. He had mettle when it came to standing at the coalface – now he needed to sit and work out a strategy that would keep the dogs of law from tearing his life to pieces, in full view of the world and his wife.

Kitty Daly opened the door of her mews on Waterloo Lane and gushed with pleasure as Paddy Doyle said: "Do I look like a happy fella?"

She laughed and kissed his nose. "You sure do, Detective Sergeant! Give me some of those."

He allowed her take the two bottles of wine and the fruit basket and chucked his head to indicate she should get on up the stairs. He kicked the street door shut as he moved to follow her, and he made no bones about enjoying the pendulum nod inside her ankle-length skirt.

They abandoned the wine and the other stuff on the huge table and fell into each other's arms, their mouths locked.

When she pulled her head back to take a good look at him, she said breathlessly: "Nobody French-kisses like you do."

He laughed and pulled her closer. "I thought I was the only fella in Ireland actually doing it."

"And you a copper!" Kitty laughed and went about opening a bottle of wine.

Paddy took off his suit jacket and hung it on the wall-rack. "So who have you been kissing, behind my back?"

He said it half-joking, but she knew from the set of his back that he was wholly in earnest.

"If I had been kissing anybody, it would still be none of your business, Paddy Doyle. Now, are you going to be a pain in the arse, or are you going to stay happy?"

He accepted the glass of Beaujolais and touched it to hers. "It's a treat to see you and I'm keen to feel happy – not something comes naturally to the Doyle men."

She drank and watched him over the rim of her glass, his attention on the bouquet of the wine, and she felt good to be looking at him. His looks were regular, his eyes hazel under strong blue-black eyebrows, his hair the same colour falling to one side off a forehead large enough to suggest a big brain. She hardly knew him, but she believed she had known him in back of present time – felt he had been a lover of hers in another life. She had never said this to him – he didn't like the way she talked – a bit fast and loose he had said one night when they were both drunk. She took no time in telling him to go to hell and get out. He had returned a week later to apologise and ask her if she would let him take her out to dinner. He had a modest way about him that endeared him to her. Of course he was the exact opposite to herself, but then she was used to being a beauty and a target for almost every man she came across, and she made no bones about being happy to be good-looking with a shapely body and good health and talent, and a willingness to go with life as far as it wanted to take her. She knew about herself that despite any feeling she might ever have for any man, her wants and desires were as nothing compared to her commitment to her freedom.

They had already dallied with how she was, and how he was, and she hoped they could enjoy each other as two free people before he started to make demands that she be his girlfriend, his woman, or whatever way he was likely to put it. She would be nobody's anything, though he interested her very much, she wondering how much of this was due to the fact that he had not yet tried to get her to go to bed with him.

Times she wondered if he had ever been to bed with a woman – he would not be the first she had come across, rather to her surprise, in the city.

When she had arrived in Dublin two years earlier she had expected that every fella would have long since stopped being a prick virgin, the reality being nothing of the kind. 'Never underestimate the power of oppression,' she had reminded herself more than once since then.

She left him drinking and stepped into the tiny bathroom to wash paint off her hands and freshen her face.

He smoked a cigarette and had another glass of wine. He was fascinated by her and he could admit this to himself. He was not easily impressed but it was easy to be enamoured of her – she was so lovely to look at and to be with, and he felt a desire for her that was strong enough to make him want to make her his own.

He backed off the idea since she had made it clear she was not in the market for a husband, and though it didn't suit the shape of his future plans, which indeed included her, he respected her for her forthright way, wanting all the more to have her for his wife, because of it.

His eye fell on the canvas under the sheet on the easel near the window. Without a thought he rose from the aged chaise-longue and put down his wineglass. In a moment he was drawing the cover off the painting and a moment later he stood there in a state of shock as he looked at the demonic good looks of his brother, Cormac.

Paddy was so taken by the painting, so stunned, that he didn't hear Kitty come back into the studio.

"I don't like people looking at my work until I invite them." He started to apologise but she cut him short. "I didn't warn you off looking if I wasn't here, so it's not your fault. If you weren't curious you wouldn't be a flat-foot, and in the Covert Squad at that."

Paddy was lighting a cigarette and she watched him draw smoke deeply into his lungs.

"What is it, Paddy? What's the matter?"

"Your friend, who is he?"

"Even if I knew I wouldn't tell you."

"What do you mean? I only asked his name."

"I never get the name of somebody I want to paint, not until the work is done."

"You could be a lover with someone without knowing their name?"

She chuckled. "Another rule of mine, I never get involved with a client or a model, not while I'm trying to put them down on the canvas. I have had sex with somebody without knowing his name. It was a wild thing to do, during my experimental period. As a rule though, I like to know them first."

"Like to know who you're waking up with, right?"

219

He was trying to be funny but missed, and knowing this she let it go without retort.

Truthfully she said: "I never let them spend the night. I don't like people here in the morning. It's something to do with the nuns, Catholic shame, guilt, you know." She emptied her wineglass. "So, are you cooking or am I?"

He laughed. "Me cook? Sure I can't boil an egg."

"Another one," she chuckled. "Another mother's boy sent out into the world looking for his mammy with sex." She kissed him and he hugged her tight.

"I want to keep you tucked away all for me," he said awkwardly: "I know you don't want it but right now I can't help it, Kitty. I'm in a state about you."

Pulling away from him she took a cigarette and got it lit before she said quietly: "I like you a lot. I know you're good and that matters to me. But, you'd better get to the point where my way is allowed into the picture. Otherwise, and I'd be sorry if it happens, you and I will not be seeing each other, whether it be as friends or lovers." He started to say something but she cut him short. "I'm twenty-nine years old. I am free, white and over twenty-one. My feeling this minute is one of sadness, knowing you'll never be able to deal with my past, even though it's none of your business."

He nodded his head and killed the cigarette butt with unnecessary force. "I hear you, Kitty, and again, I'm sorry. I've never said this to a woman before but I feel such love for you, I want to own you."

"That's what I mean, Paddy. We are dead as dodos. Nobody's going to own Kitty Daly, so have a glass of wine and go and don't come back."

"No, I don't want that. I want you to be patient with me, give me time, help me with all your caring, and I know you care for me. Put up with me till some of your knowledge, your worldliness if you like, rubs off on me. Some day, surely, you will want to marry, settle down?"

"No, I won't," Kitty flared at him, "and I don't want you to ever tell me that or anything else that I am likely to feel in my life. You talk of love. My God, Paddy, you don't know what you're talking about. *'Love is not love that alters when it alteration finds, nor bends with the remover to remove'* – sorry," she smiled apologetically, "that's –"

He surprised her with: *"Oh no, it is an ever constant mark that looks on tempests and is never shaken."*

She smiled at him, and he could tell she was delighted with him and he pulled her close and she kissed him with more abandon than before. Her hands were on his lower back pulling him to her with all her strength and she was in no doubt as to his need for her.

As she pulled her mouth away to gasp for more air, he moved from her and she was put out. "What? What is it?"

"Your model, Kitty, do you really not know who he is?"

"I told you." She went no further, very put out since her own need to make love was every bit as strong as that she had felt in him.

"That's my brother, Cormac," he said. "You had him here hiding that first day when I came to the door, didn't you?"

Kitty's shock was evident. She lit a cigarette and

took a long drag. "Are you going to arrest me for harbouring a patriot?"

"Don't be daft!" He lit a cigarette for himself, his eyes flaring with anger. "He may have started out with idealistic intentions. He is now a criminal who hides behind the Republican movement to make what he does seem respectable."

Kitty was shocked to silence.

He went on: "In my heart, I knew that first day that you had let him in." Paddy was speaking like somebody who could not believe this. "I knew, in my bloody bones, I knew. I felt it. And I colluded with you because you were so beautiful. I just let it go, wanting only to know you." He was stunned, literally.

She said: "You knew you were chasing your own brother?" She was pouring drink, trying to still the shake in her hand.

"The policeman with me saw his face before he gave us the slip. But I would have known it anyway – because nobody else could ever outrun me like Cormac did."

"Which he did carrying a flesh wound from a bullet," She handed him a drink as though he was a customer and she the barmaid.

"I didn't shoot him, thank God." He put the glass down and covered the picture. "He was always mad for the United Ireland idea. More to best the father than from any idealistic motive, at that time, like. Later he meant it, believed in it, told me he would die for it. I thought he was mad."

"You're so different. What does he think of you being a flat-foot?" She had calmed down, let go of her anger.

"He is no fan of the police. I wanted to be in the force since I was twelve years old. I never said. The father had an idea of me running a shop, learning how to be in the retail trade. Nothing wrong with that as a way of living, but I wanted to help society in some way, not going around fighting for a united country, but day to day, and I knew I'd be a good copper, which I am, except when I let my desire for a beautiful woman cloud my judgement and make me a fool that can think of little else."

"You might feel different if we go to bed and see how we work out sexually." She opened her eyes to him, giving herself to him there and then.

He looked at her with pleasure, surprised, she thought, and somehow different.

"You are a remarkable bloody woman." He was grinning in a shy way. "I suppose this is the part where a sophisticated young flat-foot would take his clothes off?"

"I'd say it is." Kitty killed the cigarette without taking her eyes from his face. Then she began to remove her clothes and Paddy found himself doing the same blindly since he was hypnotised by the boldness of her.

They fell onto the bed and she accommodated him quickly. He gasped out loud as she took his erection into herself and she let him lie still for a few moments before she did more than breathe. She had been right, he was a virgin, or close and she didn't want him embarrassed by a premature orgasm.

Pulling her mouth free of his lips she held his face, their mouths just inches apart. "I like you more than

I've ever liked any man, and I think you a fine fella. And I want you, have for weeks now. Take your time with me now. There's no need to rush. We can do this for the next week if you have the time and the energy. I'm a bit in love with you, too. So come on now. Let's see how we get on with these two fine bodies!"

15

December 1923

Sam Sweet was having a tough time as he walked the carpet outside the bedroom door where Deirdre was about to produce the first child of their union. All his good intentions to stay in the present moment had gone right out the window – what if this and what if that – and would the baby be all right? His head thumped and he knew he couldn't stand this for very much longer.

The date was the twenty-first of December and his watch-hands pointed at twenty-eight minutes past seven. It was morning and Sam wanted to be in there with Dee, comforting her in some way. But, like many a man before him, he had deferred to the wishes of Dr Kathleen Lynn, who at that moment was urging Dee to push and push again.

Sam thought about going downstairs to have a cigarette but he was afraid that the child would arrive while he wasn't there. His anguish was short-lived since the first cry of the newborn reached him through the closed door. Quite shocked, he sat on a chair to one side of the door and felt tears on his face. Wiping his eyes, he then blew his nose, vowing that he would be a better father this time around.

At that moment, Kathleen Lynn, the heroine of Dee's life, opened the door as Sam stood up wanting to run inside. She bowed her head slightly to look at him over her spectacles, her presence inducing in him a sense of awe, she being something of a saint in his eyes, too.

"Your lady wife has given birth to a lovely, healthy baby, Mister Sweet, and you are welcome to come in. Forgive my stance re your presence at the birth. I need to give all my attention to mother and baby without concern that the father might drop down in a faint." She stood aside as Sam, nodding his head in gratitude, tears of joy resisting his need to suppress them, passed on in.

Dee, pale and somewhat worn, welcomed him with a brave smile and a gentle embrace, her own tears touching his skin as she kissed his mouth.

"Never have I felt such love for you," he said in a whisper. "And you are all right?"

"I'm all right, Sam. It was no cup of tea but I am, yes, I'm good and I'll be better after I've had a rest."

Kathleen Lynn came to the bed bearing the newborn child and Sam stood to hold his baby daughter for the first time. Her face was beetroot red and scrunched up like a walnut under a cap of blue-black hair.

"You're quite comfortable, Deirdre?"

"I am, Kathleen, thank you. I want to call her after you if you wouldn't have any objection."

"Why, my dear, I'd be honoured. You have talked

this over with your husband?" The legendary doctor seemed a shade uneasy.

"Oh yes, Sam and I agreed on it last night."

"Deep thanks to you, Doctor," Sam said, giving the baby to Dee. "We are honoured to have you in our home. Now, I must go and tell Sarah and the boys."

When he got downstairs, Sam smiled at the sight of the huge Christmas tree that spread itself across half of the great hallway. He passed on into the kitchen and poured himself a cup of tea, taking a long drag on a Gold Flake. Exhaling, he vowed with real vehemence that nobody was going to kill off the life of his family. Nobody was going to turn his newborn baby into an orphan whose parents had died on the end of the hangman's rope.

At the same time, about a mile from the great house where Dee suckled her daughter, May Murray was adding a small drop of brandy to her cup of tea in the kitchen of her house, now called The Dunbla Tavern.

May felt she needed a little help to deal with the fact that Pack Rowan had taken the first steps to leaving her. She drank slowly, savouring the taste of the mixture. He'd wait of course until they got their full share of the money when Constance Brewer took that fortune from the Brewer estate. Oh yes. He was not going to go anywhere until their share of all that Brewer money was safely lodged in some bank or other in the name of Roger Gregory.

In truth, she felt dumbfounded – the shock of finding the passport, brand new, in the name of Roger Gregory in Pack's shoulder bag, had deprived her of the power to stop her dream crumbling about her ankles.

In a careless moment she had upended his black leather shoulder bag and found herself holding the brand new United Kingdom passport.

Moments before as she got out of the bed her sails had been billowing beautifully in the fresh wind of last night's sensational love making. He had set upon her with all this sexual magic upon his return from London, and now to have all that joy and bliss shattered by the evidence of his disloyalty to their agreement and their love was like a kick from a mule.

There was also a lodgement slip from the Westminster Bank, Hammersmith, in Pack's new name which simply solidified the unwanted truth that she held there in her hand. She was heartsore as she put everything back as it had been before she knocked the bag over and she went downstairs to try and gather herself together, find some way to bring him back to his senses.

It was the more hurtful since they had made love all night which was as powerfully, joyfully demanding as it ever had been with them: "To keep you going till I get back," he had chaffed, since he was returning to London immediately with the last of the journals for Constance Brewer.

She accepted that he was withdrawn, secretive by nature, and that he might be keeping the news of his latest identity quiet until he felt the time was right to tell her. She dismissed the notion that he might have just forgotten since he would have been tired after the boat journey – regardless of what was going on he had a memory like blotting-paper.

She poured another brandy into the tea and took a good drink of it. Alongside the deep personal hurt she was enduring, she felt badly let down. On top of this, above and beyond those two personal wounds, she was, as his business partner and the creator of the opportunity that was actually paying off before it got properly started, angry beyond words – angry enough to commit murder. She was stunned by the revelation, conscious of the change in her way of thinking since this could never have crossed her mind just a few months before.

Hearing him call her name she went to the foot of the stairs. "Are you wanting a mug of tea?" she called, in what she hoped was an offhand way. No matter what he might have been up to, she didn't want to get on his wrong side – in a fight with Pack there could only be one winner.

"A mugga chah, yes, and bread, May."

When she took his ham sandwich and tea up on a tin tray, he was down on the floor, coming up and going back down again, even as she came into the bedroom loft.

He quit the push-ups when she put the tray on the locker his side of the bed. On his feet he stood before her naked, the magnificence of him turning her mouth dry in an instant. Trying to remain calm, she went to her dressing-table and foostered with her toiletries, simply because she didn't know what else to do.

As he slurped the tea and bit into the bread she glanced in the mirror, surprised to see that he was rampant again. His expression was benign as the hot drink and the sandwich did their job and May put some lipstick on with serious attention, in an effort to keep her eyes off his erection.

"I've something to tell you, now I've demolished that sandwich." He sounded happy in himself and had another swig of the tea. She turned around to face him, simply unable to stop her eyes from going to his loins. He was grinning, sweat all over him from the exercise. He put his hand under his hardness, as though he was weighing it. He was grinning now like a man free of worldly cares. "This fella," he said, glancing down, "the minute I do a few push-ups he comes up like Tower Bridge. He must think I'm at it with some invisible lady, would you say?" He was amused by himself and she found herself taken along. It was not often he made a joke and she felt close to him again for a moment, though she remained a prisoner of the violent anger he had engendered in her with his double-dealing.

"I've a new name I'll be using in England, May. Got word from my pal, Guildford – there's a warrant out still for Pack Rowan – a burglary that went bad when the householder came at me with a hatchet – I didn't kill him but he got hurt bad enough.. So over there, I got a passport and bank account and all. So from now on, while I'm in the UK I'll be known as Roger Gregory."

May felt so relieved she burst out laughing. He grinned at her, bouncing his erection on his open hand, a blatant invitation to sex that May would not have turned down had her life depended on it.

"I'm delighted to meet you, Roger," she said cheekily, "and what do you call your friend there?" She nodded at his handful.

"You may refer to himself as John Thomas," he said, moving closer to pull her to him. "Now, after you bringing me grub, wouldn't I be an ill-mannered brat if I didn't show a bitta gratitude?"

Gently, he pushed her back onto the bed and as he pulled her underwear away he was like somebody obsessed by one thing and one thing only. In the moment, May was breathing like someone in fright but feeling so lucky because she had never felt so wanted in her whole life.

"I'll give you 'Sally Come Home in the Dark', May." His uneven breathing matched hers, while he somehow found the wit to ask: "Would you go for that, May?

"I would," she said breathlessly, "in a big way. And thanks for telling me, about the new name."

He looked at her as though he didn't know what she was talking about, his breathing distorted now as he began to move in and out gently, taking his weight on his magnificent arms.

She felt him pulling her along with him but she couldn't take part as she wanted to until she had his assurance. "You won't dump me when we get the money, will you, Pack?"

Looking annoyed, he stopped moving and she half expected a slap for interfering with his pleasure. "We're partners, so we are. Nobody dumps their partner because they made money. Anyway, even if we were broke, what you give me in the bed would keep me chained to you till I forget how to do it. Now shut your gob and get your share of the ride."

Shutting out all her doubts and fears, and the anger

that had earlier consumed her, she wrapped herself around him, taking the bittersweet bliss that he could bring her to in a minute. With her eyes closed tightly she held onto him, her heart wrapped up in all the love he was giving her.

For his part, even as he ploughed her furrow, he felt good he'd sorted out what could have been a real problem. Had he not come awake in time to see her put the passport back in his bag, things could have been very awkward. He smiled down on her, delighted to be where he was in the minute, and began to alter his move, slow, slow, quick, quick, quick, seeing the power he had over her as she embraced the seasons of his rhythm.

May was drowning in bliss as he changed the pace of his thrusting, altering his force so that he touched her like a feather that became a battering ram in a second, before going gentle again to make a slow withdrawal almost all the way before he sank once more into her body and her mind.

May was outside and above everything but the sensation he sent shooting through her, while she unwittingly showed him that he had all power over her, including that of life and death.

The brewery at Kilmainham had spread to such a degree that Sam felt he was seeing the latest malt house for the first time. This wasn't so – he had been there for its opening with Arthur, one of the last jobs they had designed together. He had been so busy since that time he had forgotten what a magnificent building Brendan

O'Connor and his crew had built. The red-bricked, oblong giant was a monument to industrial development, the first of its kind to accommodate rail cars as they fetched and carried all that was needed to manufacture the stout that rivalled Guinness almost bottle to bottle, pint to pint, both in Ireland and England and much of the continent of Europe.

Most of the Brewer senior staff members knew the story of Sam Sweet and Arthur Brewer – how they had formed an unlikely team some twenty years earlier, the Dublin-born Jew and the leading figure of the Ascendancy. The two men had altered the face of the old brewery with their innovative style and Sam's inherent gift of marrying the practical with designs that were also aesthetically pleasing.

Meanwhile, Arthur had pressed on with his dream that each and every brewery employee would, after seven years of service, gain possession of shares in the company. At the time this had caused a major rift between Arthur and his mother, Constance Brewer, the consequence of which was about to unleash itself upon the company in what could be a disastrous blow to both the present and the future of the brewery Arthur had created in his own idealistic fashion.

Now the new Chairman and Managing Director was about to take over the running of the company at a crucial time in its history. Even as he entered his office for the first time, the newspapers were running the story of how Constance Brewer, mother of the late Arthur Brewer, was taking the company to court to sue it and its officers for the return of all things named

Brewer which she deemed to be her legal entitlement.

The emergence of the story, though admittedly muted at this time, indicated to Sam that Constance had organised some kind of public relations firm to bring her stance to the notice of the general public. This, of course, added pressure to her claims for justice, since psychologically people would feel that she had to have a good case – nobody in their right mind would risk the enormous expense of mounting a court case unless they were certain they were going to win.

Nuala Parsons greeted him as he entered the office block.

"Good day to you, Mister Sweet. I am Nuala Parsons, your private secretary. It's my pleasure to meet you."

Sam shook her hand, noting the firm grip of the handsome lady before him, a picture of elegance and class in her tailored suit over a white ruffle-fronted blouse.

"If you'll follow me, sir, I'll show you to your office." They walked through a small forest of desks and he noted that all eyes were on their work, sure and certain proof that the silence was some kind of buzz because the new boss was actually on the job.

Sam smiled to himself. If only they knew. He was thinking of his business training – pushing his own little handcart around the Dublin streets, until he was doing well enough to buy a pony to take his place between the shafts – buying and selling bric-à-brac, books, furniture in need of repair – anything that he could sell on for a profit. His education had been derived from the books – he reckoned he had read over three hundred books during those early years before he sold them on at some kind of small profit. His mother too had read the same stories so that they had a wealthy meadow of things to talk about, which made up for the fact that his father had never had a word to throw to a dog.

Esther it was who had read Shakespeare and helped him when he studied the parts he found obscure – she it was who cooked his dinners every day and who he was able to keep with him and his first wife, Gloria, until she passed away.

Within thirty minutes of his arrival he was chairing an extraordinary board meeting – half an hour later he was totally in control of Brewer's Brewery and all its subsidiaries, with the goodwill of his board who knew that it would take a united effort to thwart the ambition of Constance Brewer to usurp the position of each and every one of them.

Sam had put it very plainly: "Gentlemen, we are being challenged by a lady who is no lady, a woman who had already employed the most devious means of bringing this company, and all who sail in her, to its knees." He apologised for the mixed metaphor just to show them that he knew something about the language and he drew a smile or two in doing so, which told him he was going the right way about things. "Constance is prepared to use material that was stolen from the home of my ex-wife by a man with a criminal record – my enquiry agents have produced to me a record of her bank statements for the past five years and I can assure you that the lady is living on her wits, and more recently her jewellery. Due to an addiction to roulette, Constance Brewer is a pauper living in a house worth a king's ransom. She recently sold precious jewels to pay the couple who are in back of the robbery and to finance the acquisition of further information that, were it made public, would do this company no good at all."

Sam paused for a cigarette and found that most of the men present were happy to light up.

In a minute he continued: "Gentlemen, I am a product of the Dublin streets, blessed to have had a mother who helped me educate myself and from whom I learned the black and white meaning of right and wrong. I now have to admit that sometimes there are shades of grey in relation to what's right and what's wrong, and it is only fair to warn you that I would never employ Marquis of Queensbury rules in a fight in an alleyway against an opponent that never heard of them."

Flicking ash from his cigarette he went on: "We are in a fight with someone who will not play by any rules other than those she creates, in the interest of expediency. This lady and those who are representing her have no scruples – principles are for fools and integrity is a word that hands your chance of victory to your opponent. The only aim of these people is to win, to win at all costs, and, gentlemen, unless we do the same thing, we will lose this upcoming court case."

He paused to let those words sink in and he waited a full minute before continuing: "I propose to fight like an alley cat – and in order that you gentlemen are not to be burdened with details you do not need to know, I take it upon myself to carry the burden of whatever is required to bring us through this fight in one piece. I do this for all of us but mostly because it was Arthur's wish that this be so – his executor and my dear friend, Victoria Brewer, told Arthur that she would pass the role on to me in the event her health failed. Arthur agreed. So on behalf of two of the finest people I have ever known, and on behalf of my stepchildren, Edward and Alfred Brewer, and the widow of Arthur, Deirdre Sweet, to whom I have the honour of being married – for all of them, and for all of that which meant so much to my departed and much-loved friends, I take on the mantle of defender of the family Brewer against the onslaught of a mad old woman with a heart filled with hatred who never forgave Arthur because he eschewed her. I am going to do what has to be done. I will do it anyway, but I will do it the better if you will trust me by giving me your agreement, indeed your blessing, as I go into the fray. Incidentally, the fees related to the position of Chairman and Managing Director – those monies will go to the Lying-In Hospital on Cork Street run by my wife Deirdre and other gentlewomen who help those women less fortunate that themselves. I now ask you to raise your hands first for Nay and then for Aye."

Sam was immediately astounded to find that not one hand was raised against his proposal. He was quietly moved and bowed his head before he said: "Gentlemen, I am honoured by your faith in me, and I promise you, I will fight to my dying breath if necessary to see that justice here will be done, regardless of what the law proposes. I thank you one and all."

The following evening, Sam and lawyer Alex Gibbon were shown into the drawing room of Constance Brewer at her house on London's Eaton Square. Initially, the meeting was to take place at the offices of Sir Albert Whimby, but James Gatling had telephoned and rearranged things to accommodate the old woman who was recovering from a bout of influenza.

The two men were silent as they waited for the others to arrive, both looking about with appreciation of the quality of the room's paintings and objects d'art. The lamps had been lit, adding shadows to the wall hangings that were placed between pictures by Matisse, Monet, Manet – Sam thought he saw a Rembrandt on the far side of the large room, as Alex Gibbon turned to him saying quietly: "She may be cash poor but we are sitting in the midst of a huge fortune here."

"The poor old dear couldn't live without her art." Sam's tone was laden with sarcasm and as Alex smiled in response Sam said: "My agents assure me that anything of value was bought for its resale worth. Constance is, apparently, a paid-up member of the Philistines' Club. She has only been given such leeway at her banks because of the wealth we see around us."

The door opened and both men remained quiet as James Gatling pushed Constance Brewer's wheelchair into the room.

Sam was vaguely amused to note that her claw-like fingers were wrapped around a brandy balloon, a chortle riding on his mind as he thought: 'Well done, you old bitch. Rehearsing for the court room, are we?' – not amused at what this picture of the frail old lady could have on a judge from her own class who might well be nearly as old as she was.

Alex introduced Sam and James Gatling. The middle-aged old Etonian was a man who would sell his soul for the right sum, but he produced a handshake that had been rehearsed for years to establish its owner as a gentleman of integrity and character.

Constance inclined her head as Sam bowed slightly, while she looked at him as though he had recently come from under a stone in her back garden.

Alex Gibbon got down to cases immediately, he and Sam having agreed to keep it brief and depart as soon as possible. Neither had much hope that things would go their way but knew there was only one way to find out.

"You are dealing, madam, with Mister Samuel Sweet," Gibbon began in a formal way.

"I know who he is," Constance spoke as though she had a rancid taste in her mouth. "Feel free to be less formal, Mister Gibson."

Alex glanced at Sam who flicked his eyebrows. By mispronouncing his name she believed she had relegated him to the stature of the Jew who sat beside him, or so Sam thought.

"Mister Sweet has taken over total control of all Brewer holdings worldwide," Alex said, expecting a rejoinder from the old woman.

"But not for long, Mister Gibson." Constance smiled and Sam thought she looked like an ailing frog.

Alex decided it was time to step on the old bitch. "Mister Brewer and I have come here in good faith, madam, as professional gentlemen bearing an offer that would seem to deserve the bounty of a respectful hearing."

"Oh, get on with it, man. What offer? What are we talking about here?"

"To spare your good self and the entire Brewer legal team boundless time, effort and expense, on behalf of Brewer's Worldwide, I am to offer you a very serious amount of money as a yearly pension for as long as you live."

Constance looked enraged, then somehow gathered herself together sufficiently to yell at her lawyer Gatling: "After you have shown me out of this room, would you be so good as to show these men to the front door?"

Before Gatling could move, Sam stood up and said: "We have a second offer, madam – a lump sum buy-out for the estimated cost of all lawyers, court's time, every penny that this case will cost either Brewer's Worldwide, or your good self. We are in possession of a rough estimate which at this time is being refined. I promise you this is a considerable amount of money."

Constance sat back and looked at Sam. "So the greasy Jew comes to beg. The man whose wife whored for my sick son Arthur, whose daughter Sarah may well be a Brewer, while Edward Brewer, first son of Deirdre who was Arthur's wife at that time, is very definitely not a Brewer – I imagine you would add your own personal fortune to that of Brewer's Worldwide in order to keep such a scandal from the public domain." She stopped and took a sip of brandy from the balloon resting in her hands. "So tell me, my Jewish adversary, do you seriously think that for the cost of this event – it surely is an event, such a court case is a cause célèbre, yes? – I am to forget the indignity imposed on me by my insane son? When I win this case, and attain my rightful position as sole owner of Brewer's, with myself alone deciding what will go to the grandchildren when my time comes, I will be chuckling yet, all the way to my coffin I should imagine, at your naiveté. Now I ask that you leave my house and prepare well for the fight to come. I have nothing more to say to you, except, 'I will see you in court'."

"When this is all over," Sam said quietly, "you will not be able to say we didn't make you a fair offer to step away. I accept your stance. And now I warn you that, as you have dealt with the devil to arrive at a position you deem to be unbeatable, I swear to you on the life of your son, Arthur, a great man and a wonderful gentleman, I swear to you, I will be there to see you brought to your knees. You are an evil old woman and should it become necessary to squash you like the bug you are, I will have no hesitation in taking that honour upon myself. And just for openers, Connie, I bring greetings from an old admirer of yours, Sir Ralph Dorning." Sam paused to allow the other men time to see Constance turn pale under her broken make-up. She tried to remain calm but her initial reaction was so strong that there was no way she could hide her fury and the terror that had shattered her equilibrium.

"I bid you good afternoon, ma'am. Let's go, Alex."

Sam hurried from the room knowing he and the defence team would have a real fight on their hands.

As their taxi took them away from Eaton Square he came into the present moment by rubbing his thumbs and forefingers together. Quietly then he decided he had wasted enough time on emotion. This case would be won on evidence and that alone. Tears and breast-beating might very well earn some Brownie points with a judge, but in the heel of the hunt it would be the evidence, or the lack of it, that would decide the winner.

Evidence or the lack of it – he let the sentence roll around on his tongue and decided to keep this mantra before his eyes from now on. He made a mental note to devote some time each morning to further reading of the *Upanishads*, his ongoing need for some kind of spiritual back-up raising its head the more so since the meeting with the dreaded Constance Brewer. He repeated the words again in his mind – evidence or the lack of it – just six words that had touched some small spark inside him. He didn't know quite what it meant, he didn't need to, since experience had shown him that if he left it alone while he simply kept it under observation, its meaning would be delivered in the moment he was meant to receive it.

He turned to Alex. "What we have to do now is devise a plan, a plan that will be an ongoing series of very good reasons why this case must be kept out of court for as long as possible."

Alex smiled brightly. "I was thinking the same thing, old man. I expect you have some ideas as to how we are going to achieve such an impasse?"

"Yes, I do," Sam said evenly. "Constance is up for an alley fight – well, believe me, old dear, you are going to get one! Now, let's get along to Simpson's for one of your stodgy public school lunches."

Part Two

16

May 1924

Deirdre Sweet was making a pot of tea in the private kitchen of the Lying-In Clinic in Cork Street when Joan Ryan staggered in the back door, anxious to put down the two-gallon can of milk.

"We didn't need that much," Dee smiled and put the lid on the china teapot given her by her mentor, Kathleen Lynn, on the day the Women's Clinic opened for the first time.

"This will be one of the most important items in the Clinic," Kathleen Lynn had said as she hugged Dee and wished well to her great venture.

"It's an adventure, really, Kathleen," Dee had said somewhat in awe, knowing that she had been heading towards this moment for a long time.

She gave Joan a hand now to lift the two-gallon can onto the worktop alongside the deep sink.

"You didn't carry this from Jimmy Halpin's?"

"Jimmy left it at the end of the lane." Joan pulled a rueful face. "I won't do it again, Dee."

"I'll talk to Jimmy. He delivers it in here to this kitchen or we get our milk from someone else."

"But he's the only farm that's this close to us," Joan said.

"Sit down, you!" Dee pointed at a chair. "Sit down and drink your tea." Her smile was large and she sipped from the china cup, a present from Sam.

The two women seemed to let go the same sigh in the same moment, the sound enough to send them both into a rapture of laughter that was laden with relief.

Through most of the night they had attended the difficult – at times, seemingly impossible – birth of a boy born an hour before. He would be called Jason, so his mother said, a twelve-pound-ten-ounce bundle that had dangerously refused to budge – his mother seriously in danger of losing her life. She had been in labour for twelve hours, was utterly exhausted and didn't seem to have a push left in her, when Dee nudged Joan Ryan and whispered: "I'll be back in a minute."

Dee had gone out of the back door. Dawn was showing its face to the city, but between the Clinic and Smith's public house on the other corner, the narrow lane was hidden by the twin storeys on both sides and quite dark yet.

Moving a little way from the light thrown by the gas lamps in the kitchen, Dee leaned back against the wall. She clasped her hands together and she began to weep silently. A few moments later she found enough voice to ask for help. "Dear God, if you are there, please hear my plea! It is arrogant of me to attempt to make a bargain with you, but I must for the life of this young mother – she has two children that need her – she lost her husband in the Civil War – she will surely die if we cannot help her deliver her baby as soon as possible, like now.

"Dear God, I have ignored you. I have lived as an agnostic, as though you did not exist, but if you will grant me this wish – help us to save this life – I offer you my heart and soul, all of which are yours anyway, to do with what you will.

"Lord, we have to succeed here. We have to make this Clinic work – not for gain or profit or recognition, but that we might encourage others to do the same thing in another place. This city is awash with the need for more humane compassion for the suffering women who want no more than to bear and rear children despite severe lack in their lives.

"I have to go back. I have to be there for Mary Kearney, twenty-three years old, widowed and as of now, of no fixed abode. Thy will be done, O Lord. I pray that you will hear my prayer, and promise you I will give what is left of my life in devotion to you and to this work which is in its own infancy."

Dee pulled herself away from the wall, felt her sweat run down her body and took several deep breaths before she hurried back inside.

Remembering the moments in the lane on that night, Dee sipped her tea, smoking a cigarette. She nodded her head in agreement when Joan Ryan said: "Poor Mary, so exhausted and you gone out for a minute. And next thing, nearly frightening the life out of me, her eyes open and she lets out a yell and started to push, and you were there beside me, and I thought the veins in Mary's forehead would explode and then the yell increased and she heaved like I've never seen a woman heave, and the next thing there he was, that lazy lump that wouldn't move for love nor money!" Joan emptied her teacup. "Somebody was praying for us."

Dee smiled and wiped away her tears, silently chiding the God she had hidden from up to that time in the laneway, smiling wistfully as she whispered to her Maker: 'But then I was taught that you gave a person whatever time was needed to come to the knowledge of you.'

"You should go home, Dee," Joan's voice put an end to that great moment, the memory of the split second in which she stepped in out of the cold. "I can manage until Sheila Fitz and Connie get here. You're all in and you have been here since noon yesterday."

"I'm too tired to argue."

"I'll telephone for John O'Toole to drive you home."

Joan left the room and Deirdre got down on her knees. And she heard her own voice for the first time in too many years saying: "*Hail Mary, full of grace, the Lord is with thee. Blessed art thou amongst women and blessed is the fruit of thy womb, Jesus. Holy Mary, Mother of God, pray for us sinners now and at the hour of our death. Amen.*"

Dee was still praying when Joan came back to the kitchen. She stopped just outside the door and was instantly in tears as she saw her friend and her mentor and the woman she admired most on earth, finally let go of her resistance to God. Joan made the Sign of the

Cross on herself and went back in for another look at Mary Kearney and her fatherless lump of a son.

John O'Toole, driver to both Sam and Deirdre, lived with his wife Lucy in the mews flat at Merrion Square. Warm-hearted Lucy served as cook-housekeeper while the children attended school in Dublin, providing Eddie and Alfie and Sarah with all they needed during the week. John returned to Merrion Square each night regardless of what time he finished driving his employers home. His presence provided the security deemed necessary since the house was a treasure chest of valuables and works of art, including a library that could boast some of the early works of Oscar Wilde, who had been a neighbour, signed by the great man himself.

This was behind the townhouse which Arthur had wrested from his mother's grasp by giving her the mini-mansion on Eaton Square in London. It was this act above all else that had been the final nail in the coffin of their non-existent relationship – the day she was driven away from that house was when her consuming hatred for all things to do with Arthur had claimed its place for all time. Sam Sweet could not have known it but it was the expulsion of Constance from this most prestigious address that had spawned the dilemma he now faced as the old woman put all her energy into finally reaping her revenge on her late son.

John O'Toole woke instantly as the extension telephone from the main house rang by his ear and thirty minutes later Dee was being driven out of the city. Since there was little or no traffic the car ride was smooth as silk and Dee didn't even notice how quickly she drifted into a light sleep that ended only when John stopped the car outside the kitchen door at Dunbla.

She found Sam in the kitchen drinking coffee and smoking a cigarette as he scribbled busily, pen to paper.

His embrace was like a balm, and she kissed him soundly on the lips before he sat her down to a cup of tea he readily prepared within minutes.

"You look all in." He seemed to stand some way behind his words. 'I'm totally on your side, Dee, but could it be possible, just possible, you are doing too much?"

"We are doing so very little, Sam, but I take the point. You're right. I should not have been there when Mary Kearney went into labour. I should have been at home here with you since I'd been there all day. It just happened. Sometimes things get away from you and then . . ." She stopped, pulling a face, and held up her hands in surrender. "Sorry, dear heart."

Sam poured the tea, took toast from the hot plate of the Aga, buttering it and pushing the plate to rest by her hand.

"I'm being bloody selfish, of course," he said. "I want so see more of you. But, more than that, I don't want you to have a breakdown, ruin your health, and the women you are helping wouldn't want that either."

"I'm sorry." She sipped the tea. "I will try to be more balanced – the Clinic shouldn't interfere with our life. The two – family and work, they have to complement one another."

Sam chewed a piece of toast and Dee, sensing he was reminding her to eat something, did the same. He pushed a dish of Angela's home-made plum jam forward and she smiled as she smeared it onto the toasted bread.

"Besides," she said, chewing, "you have this whole court case in your lap because your wife has dumped it there." She reached for his hand: "Have I been a dreadful bitch of a person over it?"

The warmth of his heart seemed to reach her through his fingers and she was close to tears as he stood up and came to her and lifted her face so that he could kiss her lips lovingly. She put a hand to his face and gave him her mouth. Much of her tension had left her by the time he pulled his head back: "A kiss with plumby crumbs is not to be sneezed at."

She stood up and embraced him fiercely as though for a moment she thought she had lost him.

He held her close but drew his head back and gave her a knowing look. "I was under the impression you were close to exhaustion."

"I was. I was flat as a pancake when I came though that door." She held him still, her eyes with that glint he had come to know so well.

"Things have changed, I see." He made no effort to still the familiar gleam she loved to find in his eyes.

"I feel I could say the same thing about you, Sam Sweet." She put her hands on his lower back and pressed him closer. "Oh yes," she said with a knowing smile distorting her mouth. "You've changed in a big way since you pulled me to you."

Sam looked astounded and made the most of it: "I pulled you to me?" They laughed together and he took her hand. "Should I live through this madly exciting time, Dee, I need to talk to you for about an hour, before you head off back to Cork Street. Is that all right?"

She nodded her head and allowed him lead her from the kitchen. As they went upstairs, they met Madge Gallagher, the housekeeper, coming down. She had worked for Sam since Gloria had left – she was smiling gently now.

"Does the heart good to see you so happy," she said.

Quickly they were together in the bed, Dee crying out softly: "Just make love to me, Sam, no performance, just, oh God, shut up, Dee. I love you, Sam. I love you, love you, love you . . ."

Later, he sat on a bathroom chair as she lay up to her ears in the hot water. "I can handle the time when you're away, Dee. That being said, I don't want to miss a moment when it's possible for us to be together."

She reached for his hand. "I can remember as if it was yesterday when you came to our cottage in Long Lane to put in a window for Mammy. You were about sixteen and I was four or five and I thought you were a hero or a god or one of those people in the stories Mammy read, like Fionn or Cuchullain. Have I ever told you that before?" Laughing he leaned over and kissed her breast while she answered her own question: "Only about a hundred times, Dee!"

She howled with glee and then, from the sheer devilment of being alive and happy, pulled him into the bath on top of her.

Deirdre slept till just after two in the afternoon and arrived downstairs just as Sam, back from his walk, was taking off his rubber boots in the pantry.

"I thought I heard a lorry," she said, a quizzical tone to her voice.

"I'm sorry, love. Didn't want to wake you."

"It's all right. I had enough sleep. What was it?"

"We're going to have a couple of tennis courts," he said affably, following her into the kitchen where she stood with her back to the Aga.

"For the children really," he said, "but no reason why you and I can't knock a ball or two about. What do you think?"

"That's a lovely idea. You are a dark horse."

"Are you going back to the Clinic today?"

"No. I need a few days off. It's not a sprint we're involved in at Cork Street, it's a long distance run, and you are right, I have to pace myself or I could end up being sick in some way. I've prayed on it, and I seem to have heard an answer."

Sam looked at her as though he had misheard her words.

She smiled ruefully and took his outstretched hands in her own: "I made my peace with God last night."

His face lit up and he squeezed her fingers in a gentle way: "If you're happy about that, so am I."

"Look," she said with enthusiasm: "Why not slip back into your boots? We can walk the land, go down to the beach, you can show me where the tennis courts will be, and I can hear what you have to say to me about the court case. How does that sound?"

"That's the best idea I've heard yet today."

* * *

Sam Sweet's Journal –
May 1924

'This in an attempt to record all that happens, in relation to the claims of Constance Brewer. An effort to get things written down in sequence, so that I won't have to repeat it verbally, over and over, as Dee and I make every effort to get our story straight and keep it that way. Besides this practical reason, I'm thinking that in years to come the children will want to know about certain things – this court case will surely be high on the list of their inquisitiveness – this makes the exercise even more valuable. And it's a protection job as well, against having to rely on memory which has its off days.

Speaking of the children who are fast becoming young adults, I have to record that Kathleen – who is now five months old and beautifully formed – is a blessing in our lives, a young lady who is already springing the odd surprise. She certainly surprised me as I changed her napkin yesterday – for the last time, let me add – Nanny standing by in case I made some dangerous mistake such as dropping my daughter on her head.

Nanny's watching brief was rewarded, if not in any way she might have expected, but much to her amusement, when Kathleen delivered into my hand a package, an experience I have no wish to repeat, much as I love her, while giving thanks to the gods that her bodily functions are in good working order. Enough said on the subject.

Needless to say, my position as Chairman and Managing Director of Brewer's Worldwide, and my role as Keeper of My

Wife's fortune – Dee's estate – are keeping me busy and beyond.

Dee insisted I take on Power of Attorney relating to her interests – she is just too busy with her Lying-in Clinic and just doesn't have the energy to become involved in the battle with Constance.

Just weeks into the fray, I am already enmeshed in what might well be called skulduggery – not that I have broken any laws, yet. But, through those well-known ploys in which law people indulge with impunity, I have already ensured that the case was put back twice, this adding a tad more muscle to the weight Constance is already bearing – not that there is enough pressure in the universe to force her to quit now that the bit is between her dentures.

I felt good about forcing each postponement. We had loud and vociferous ranting by the opposition, the disdain of the judge who, by all appearances, seems to be sitting on a case of piles, which on reflection is probably the perfect punishment for anybody who would take on such a job. I'm being flippant. A lot of good men do that kind of work in the interests of society, making less money than they did while barristering or whatever they call it.

I began with the most obvious ploy of them all: ill health. Ill health, complete with verification by a notable medical personage (for a significant fee) is, as far as I can make out, the first excuse used, worldwide, to cause delay. And since every legal eagle has used it at one time or another, it does not come up against too much resistance. Some drum-beating, of course, but a token really. An example of live and let live, I suppose.

The second delay was granted since I agreed with Alex Gibbon that a recent accident resulting in the essential *witness being confined to quarters for the immediate moment was the way in which we should continue.*

This claim gathered respectability due to Professor Whatsit who takes the word of the person seeking it, Alex Gibbon. This is par for the course, Alex engaging somebody of his own kidney, his own class. These chaps indulge in what is practically schoolboy ritual: "We are all gentlemen, gentlemen, are we not?" and some more of this old-school-tie waffle that passes for meaningful input.

Here is just another example of Alex Gibbon's value on your team – Eton and Cambridge. The Oxbridge connection, comes in very handy when you need a solid, well reared, wonderfully educated man to come on board. Someone such as Alex is an absolute godsend – who better to find all his old school chums, he knowing all of their character defects, since he lived with them while they were being taught to be the most excellently corrupt people of power that the country has yet been blessed with.

The cardinal rule appears to begin with 'never say anything you don't have to say' followed by a sleight of tongue that is a language all to itself. Alex told me as little as possible of what wasn't said between himself and the medical professor. It's strictly on a need-to-know basis – even the fee, cash for convenience, please, no receipts, keeps it all neat and tidy.

I have so much going through my mind at this time I can't always remember it in sequence. But it does come back and then I write it down, if only to give the children a good laugh someday.

At the moment, I am holding in abeyance that delicious old chestnut 'A Change of Counsel'. This will arise, when I really need another postponement. It will come about due to a serious – fictional – disagreement as to how the defence should be so very precisely handled. This is an expensive move to arrange – there is much to be earned by a legal team from a case designed to run for weeks at the law courts in The Strand.

Not that we in Ireland hadn't got courts capable of handling Brewer v Brewer Worldwide but since the Civil War ended and this case has been on the books since last year, it was arranged then, and not unreasonably so, that it might be safer all around to have the case set down in London.

May 26, 1924

It's quite late but there is no sleep on me so I thought I'd scribble a few lines. After a late dinner with Deirdre, we spent an hour with little Kathleen. Dee likes to bathe her and talk with her and share some of Nanny's evening duties. "It's important that she knows I'm here each evening. She sees you during the day and you are very good with her, Sam." Dee smiles, shaking her head a little. "I don't know why I felt surprised when I saw how eager you were to have an input. That's just you, isn't it?"

We are happy despite the Sword of Damocles hanging over our heads. Dee and I have made a pact – I will not discuss anything with her about the case unless it is absolutely essential. I'm glad of this because it's going to get nasty, and since there is little she can do until I need her to corroborate my story and that of Séamus and Angela and indeed, Kelly, why bother her with the day-to-day stuff?

I am writing a separate paper for Dee – this will include

our story in relation to all the things we are likely to be charged with, when we really get down to the brass tacks of the accusations by Constance and her team of experts.

When I say our story, I mean just that. As I write it, I give Dee the pages which she studies on the way to and from the clinic, provided she doesn't fall asleep on the way home. Doing it this way will give us the time needed to digest the nooks and crannies of our very worthwhile story. I suggested this way, a gentle ongoing familiarity with the events rather than an intense learning process at the last minute before going into court. When you think of the kind of pressure lawyers can inflict on people sitting nervously in the glare of the spotlight any courtroom is to the uninitiated, one would be very wise to be well prepared.

Of course, one might well ask the question: 'Why do you need a story? Can you not just go in and tell the whole thing as it happened?'

The answer to that one comes up a resounding 'No!'. The story as it actually happened cannot be used in our favour. On the contrary, it could hang the lot of us.

'But you know, Sam, you know that no serious law was broken – that justice would best be served by throwing out the claim of Constance Brewer and her cohorts.'

'Well, of course, I know that, but when it comes to the law, we learn that things have to happen in a certain way or you lose. I mean, why else did all those Eton and Oxbridge graduates spend years learning how to bend the rules due to a legal loophole that ordinary everyday people know nothing about? They endured all that bunkum to win, to win and consequently earn heaps of money and become lords and things, while poor Joseph Soap returns from the courtroom feeling that a soft *pillow placed in the gas stove could well be the best place to lay his head in the immediate moment.'*

Clearly, the case is taking up great heaps of my thought processes and were it not for my Senses Exercise, which I use a great deal, I should have no peace at all. I speak of this because as I came into the study just now I was thinking about the end of the Civil War, and indeed, about the cost of it, and the further cost not yet worked out.

It started because I dropped a book in the hall. As I picked it up, I disturbed my marker which was a letter from Michael Collins. I'd been keeping this near me – I kept returning to it to get another taste of my late, lamented mentor, who though gone is far from forgotten.

This is just one of the letters he wrote me while he was in London for those months during which the Treaty came into being.

How would he have received the news that the Civil War has ended? I know he would have cheered and applauded – in my view he carried a weighty heart from the moment it was launched in October 1922. That was when the arch-enemy of the Treaty, Dev, was elected President by the Anti-Treaty faction that are to be the army of the new Irish Free State.

The Civil War was the inevitable outcome of an order from Liam Lynch (a very brave man) who was military leader of the Anti-Treaty crowd. His order was that any Dáil deputy who had voted for the Treaty was to be shot. The same thing applied to every soldier of the Free State army above the rank of lieutenant. When Deputy Seán Hales was shot dead and Padraic O'Maille, Deputy President, was wounded, a reprisal on that same night was the execution of four leading Anti-Treaty members. These ruthless acts by people for whom I *bought arms in Germany and the United States of America, did bring the initial terror to a halt – you still had members of the Provisional Government sleeping in government buildings, their hands close by their revolvers. It was a terrible time, enough to turn the stomach and the heart and make you wish you were somewhere else rather than in Ireland.*

When Liam Mellowes was shot dead it tore the heart out of the Republican movement and those opposing the Treaty stopped fighting on May 24, 1923.

The end of the Civil War – the official end, that is – is being regarded generally as a blessing and who in his right mind would not endorse this response?

But, even as I write, I am reading of killings on both sides of the Peace and it remains to be seen whether the secret conflict – the war between one-time comrades who chose opposite sides and who have not forgiven those with political views different to their own – will spill back into the public domain.

The Civil War was regarded by ordinary people as a public outrage while the combatants created statistics fit to horrify anybody keeping up with the day-to-day toll on men, women and children.

And this time, the British are not to blame, well, not for the day-to-day revenge killings that litter the pages of the newspapers. On the Treaty side there are men who did not accept the findings of their own authority, soldiers that were satisfied that Michael Collins was indeed shot, accidentally, by a bullet at Béal na Bláth in County Cork on August 22nd. 1922. Those disbelieving men were loath to let go – this not being their only grievance. Their opposites among the opposition were of the same mind, hence the ongoing killings.

Just two days ago, I attended the funeral of a good man shot to death, two minutes after we had shaken hands as he was going to Mass, a man who risked his life daily that peace might be achieved without another shot being fired, without one more death happening in the name of the Irish Free State.

He was not a friend of mine – we were on opposites sides until I resigned when my mentor Michael Collins was killed on the day that my wife Deirdre and I were finally granted the right to marry by the Roman Catholic Church.

I shudder to think how long it will be before the country recovers from the Civil War. The loss of life – over 650 killed, more than 3,000 wounded. These are cursory estimates – the figures relating to the cost economically will not be worked out for some years but the total waste is likely to be horrific.

I had to make these notes today. It feels like a minor exorcism and I intend that this will be the last of my notes on the Troubles and the Civil War and my minor involvement in it. Whether I shall manage to keep my word remains to be seen, but that is my intention. The heart remains bruised but it will recover and, meanwhile, I have to get on with finding the wit and the will to take on a ruthless opponent who will stop at nothing to get what she wants.

The question in my mind right this minute is: how far am I prepared to go to ensure that Constance in her anger does not win?

Since fighting to win will surely involve me in some skulduggery – I know this because I know Constance will stop at nothing – actions I will have to take that would be deemed wrong, as in unlawful, in order to overcome the law which in this case will almost certainly allow a thieving old woman to steal, legally, all that belongs to others. If I work by *the letter of the law, our side stands no chance of winning. This victory for Constance Brewer would be a travesty of justice. In order to get justice for the wish of Arthur and Victoria, and to see justice done to Arthur's children and his widow, I have to circumvent the law. I have no problem with the concept – that of doing something that is regarded as unlawful – in order to prevent the instruments of law being used for a foul low-down purpose. Even though one may not be able to prove that Constance and her crew are willing to tread all over what is right by basing their case on stolen journals provided by people of criminal intent, one of whom claims to be the blood father of Eddie Brewer whose real mother died through being brutally beaten by the same man, I have to say my blood boils at the thought of this deadly assault on the lives of so many decent people – but I can't lose sight of the fact that they have a case. But what I will remind myself of each and every day until this business is over and done with is this: they have a case and I have to ensure that it becomes a case they will not win.*

I'll leave this for now. I have some notes to make for Dee – I will begin coaching Séamus and Angela and Kelly in the very near future. Meanwhile, I must talk privately with Kelly – have her tell me what her son Pack Rowan had to say when he dropped in to see her."

17

June 1924

"To keep it as simple as I can, Kelly, we – that is Deirdre, Séamus, Angela, and you and I – we are all going to be taken to court by Constance Brewer. Her intention is to overturn Arthur Brewer's wishes and should she succeed, this will deprive Edward and Alfie and Dee of whatever Arthur left them."

Sam paused to give her time to understand exactly what he was saying. She was an old woman now and the washed blue eyes had lost some of the sparkle but there was nothing to suggest that her mind was on the wane.

"That wouldn't be right, sir," she said with a quiet firmness that brooked no argument.

He smiled, charmed by her vitality – she had recovered from her hip injury which laid her low for some weeks, Sam thinking that another woman of her age might well have gone under. So perhaps the hard life on the roads had given her a toughness not found in most people who slept every night under a solid roof.

"Unfortunately, Kelly, the question of right or wrong will not enter the mind of Constance Brewer. She has been given an opportunity – by your son, now called Pack Rowan, and May Murray whose house is now known as Dunbla Tavern – a chance to steal from her son's widow and his children, what is their God-given right."

"But how can she, sir? Doesn't the law protect what Mister Brewer wrote legally?" She had moved in her chair as though irritated by what she had heard.

"It's too complicated to explain, Kelly, but it happens that justice is often the loser in a contest with law. What I want to do, if you will bear with me –"

Kelly raised a hand to stop Sam. "I will do anything, sir, anything you require me to do to see that Deirdre and the children get what they're entitled to. You have no need explainin' a word to me, sir. Just tell me what you want."

Sam inclined his head in gratitude and the old woman sat back, not a shred of doubt touching her.

"The day Deirdre found you – the day you found each other, Kelly, you were about to pack up and move on, am I right?"

He paused as her eyes registered his words, the nod of her white-capped head accepting them before she said quietly: "You do have it, sir, and you have it right."

"Seeing that Dee was about to give birth, you took her into your shelter and helped her through a very difficult time, forcing her to keep her eyes on you even when she was on the brink of lapsing into unconsciousness. Have I got that right, Kelly?"

Again the old woman nodded her head, her white fringe moving on her forehead. "You have, sir. I kept her talkin' and grippin' the hem of the cut-off sack I wore as a sort of a waistcoat. Afraid, sir, so I was. If she closed her eyes on me I might never have seen them again. She could've died on me, sir."

Sam nodded, trying to ensure that his appreciation of her worldliness didn't get in the way of the job in hand.

"And you delivered the boy, Edward, right there by the side of the road?"

"I surely did, sir. I'd swear on a stacka bibles."

"You were alone with your belongings by the roadside a mile and a half or so from Dunbla House, am I right?"

"It'd be a terrible walk for a woman about to give birth, sir, but I couldn't say exactly now what the distance'd be."

"That's perfect, Kelly. You'll be a great asset to the cause." He smiled encouragingly seeing by the raise of her chin that she was pleased. "It will be suggested by the legal team working for Constance Brewer that you substituted the boy called Edward Brewer for the stillborn baby girl of Deirdre Brewer. They will claim that you had buried the young mother of the boy who had died in giving birth to him. They will say that you left her in a shallow grave some time before Deirdre landed on you by the roadside."

He paused to check her response to this. There was none and he pressed on.

"If this were true, Kelly, and it was accepted by the court – you and all of us who helped in such an extraordinary situation, would face some very serious charges. On top of this, I could face other charges that could well include murder, concealment of bodies after they had died, and the devil knows what else. Dee would be implicated in this also since it might be suggested that I brought Arthur's body and that of Lisa O'Brien back to Dunbla for burial in the Pets' Cemetery there."

Kelly sat through his short monologue without any sliver of reaction that Sam could see.

"There would be other charges too, Kelly, but suffice it to say that certainly Dee and myself would be in grave danger of going before a criminal court facing a charge of murder and as accessaries after the fact of murder, and God knows what else."

"We can't let that happen, sir. Leaving yourself out of it, Deirdre is a saint and we must do all we can to protect her from the madness of that woman."

Sam nodded and prepared his next words, only to be interrupted by the old woman who asked: "How is it, sir, that them legal men that work for Constance Brewer got hold of a story we know to be nonsense?"

Sam admired her steel, her lack of anything in the nature of tension or strain as she took all he had said in her stride.

"My responsibility overall, but brought to light by the fact of May Murray stealing a set of journals kept by my ex-wife Gloria at her flat in London."

Kelly was appalled. "A girl from here did the likes of that? Merciful hour!"

"Indeed," Sam agreed, opening his cigarette case.

The old woman's interest was palpable, and when

he held it out to her she took a cigarette with a smile of appreciation.

"We'll have a smoke and I'll tell you how that wild story of Gloria's ended up in the journals stolen from her by May Murray."

Kelly exhaled smoke and tapped the ash into the palm of her hand. "I remember her da, a hard, mean man, won that house in a fist fight – him and the other man died within a twelve-month. The same man was a womaniser that'd steal the eye outa yer head and come back for the eyelashes." She drew on the cigarette again and moments later she said: "No lie to say the apple doesn't fall far from the tree, sir."

"You're very good, Kelly, to give me your time and the support we're going to need to keep the dreaded Constance in her place."

"No need to thank me, sir. Sure, Deirdre, may God bless her all her days, didn't she take me off the roads to give me a home for all me days." When she smoked again and exhaled, she looked at Sam with a steady eye. "Whatever you have to do, sir, do it. It can't be wrong if it keeps Constance Brewer from creating hell in the life of our own Deirdre, who is God's gift to this earth, so she is. I'll give you my support, sir, all the way. I'd give my life for that lassie, God bless the day I met her."

Pack Rowan walked into the working men's café by Fulham Broadway to join Walter Guildford at a table for two. He indicated same again to the girl behind the counter and sat down.

"This better be good, Walter."

"I think it is, and sorry to hear you're being held up by the opposition."

"That's for your ears only. I wouldn't have told you, only I was three sheets to the wind when you got me on the telephone. So, what's the story?"

"Jem Riley changed his name to Séamus O'Reilly. He did time in that name too, in Durham. While he was there he wangled a job in the market garden – a cushy berth – and my mate that celled with him said he turned out to be a natural at growing the veggies. When he got out he had a decent reference saying he was a fine market gardener and could be trusted to deliver a good day's work for a good day's pay."

"You better not be about to tell me that this is it, that it's all you've got." Pack stubbed out his cigarette as the waitress arrived with his fry-up and a mug of tea.

"It looked dodgy for a week or two." Walter blew a smoke ring. "Then I got an idea, rang this agency that finds employment for ex-cons."

Pack was eating ravenously, his eyes on Guildford who had to turn his head from the sight of so much food disappearing into Pack's mouth at the same time.

"For a day or two I ran into a dead end. Then I had a little brainwave. Riley had such a liking for changing his name that I wondered if he'd gone and done it again. Checked it out and lo and behold, the old leopard hadn't changed a spot. I'd guess he organised that by Deed Poll, then gave someone a few quid to type up his references in the same name. You know how slow people are to check up if they need you in a hurry. Jem got lucky." Guildford had a smile on his careful mouth as he said: "He is in charge of the market garden at this poncy school for Yid kids in Ramsgate."

Sam Sweet and Kelly were smoking another cigarette and he was pouring tea he had just made for them both. He sat down and made sure all was just as she liked it before he said: "Now that you know the whole story, Kelly, are you still in for the journey, whatever it takes?"

"I am, sir, have no fear of that. And don't doubt I'll keep my end up when we go into the court."

"I'm hoping against hope that we can avoid that, Kelly. It would be best all around." Putting down his cup he drew on his cigarette and continued: "Have you the energy to tell me what transpired when your son, Pack Rowan, came to see you?"

"I'm not surprised you know about that, sir. I told Séamus knowing he'd pass it on. It wasn't for me I did that. I knew he'd be up to no good, sir, and him knowin' I was here, livin' with rich folk, that'd set somethin' off in his mad brain, some way to get his hands on money, usin' me and anyone else he could lay hands on to help him rob all he could."

"Did he give you any idea of how he came to know you were living here? Did he see you with Dee or what?" Kelly rarely set foot outside the gate of Dunbla House but Dee took her out in the trap once in a while, a trip to Killiney village or on to Bray of a fine day.

"He was always listening to other people while they'd be chatting, sir. Never knew what you might hear, he'd say – loose lips can give you information you can use – you can barter it for something you want to know or you can get a few quid from somebody who needs what you know." She put down her cup. "He heard Séamus and Angela in that May Murray's place – Angela had driven down in the trap to bring Séamus home – he was half jarred and he was delayin' her, it was me and the hurt to me hip she was worryin' about – Edward, you call him Pack, he remembered every word and had a dirty eye on Angela – he is a bad man around women. He followed the trap home and when he looked through that window he saw Angela lookin' after me, God bless her. He knew from then where I was – knew he could get me any time he wanted." She said this with a hint of sadness coating her voice.

"Are you afraid of him" Sam said quietly.

"I got a shock when I saw him, sir. I gave him to the po-liss, y'see. After he beat up the girl carrying his child, sir, he ran off, leaving her to die in my arms and her baby left without a mother to feed and mind him." Kelly looked at him. "I can't mind her name at this moment, sir, but it'll come back."

Sam allowed her see he was delighted with her – they both knew that the girl had died, that she had indeed been buried in the field behind her shelter. Kelly moved on from there without any prompting from him.

"He swore he'd take my life for giving him to the po-liss, sir. Tinkers can hate one another, sir, but the idea of snouting to a po-lissman about one of yer own – they don't go in for that no matter what, sir."

"I understand, Kelly."

"So I got a shock when he walked in here and I was ready to meet my Maker that night, sir."

Sam poured more tea and said nothing until she had taken a drink.

"Did he hurt you that night, Kelly?"

"No, sir, though I thought I was in for it. He had a wild temper when he lost it, sir. Tinkers breed a lot of tough men and he was harder than most."

"Did he threaten you?"

"Right away he told me he could kill me in a breath. Said I deserved to die for giving him to the po-liss. I told him: "Get on with it then and shut up the oul' gab. I'd sooner go than try to live with knowin' you was there waitin' for a chance to take my life without gettin' in trouble over it.""

"You're a very brave woman," Sam said, making no effort to hide his admiration. "What on earth did he say to that?"

"Plenty of time, that's what he said, sir. Plenty of time to give me time to think about it. He was always full of cruelty, sir, even as a wee lad he'd hurt an animal deliberately, never a listen when I'd tell him stop it and leave the poor thing alone."

"I'm going to arrange some protection for you, Kelly."

She seemed about to argue with that but Sam once again gave her a gentle halt signal with his hand. "We are going to have security people anyway, Kelly. The new tennis courts are going to be built, and we are building some new homes, cottages and small houses. We will have valuable equipment all over the place for some little time. And since you are of more value than all of that, I will make sure that Pack Rowan does not bother you again."

Kelly accepted this without demur, saying, "I hope we'll talk some more about the story I will tell, sir. I do have it, but a bitta practice wouldn't go to waste'd be my opinion."

"A woman after my own heart," Sam rose and shook her hand gently. "I'm going to fight for all of us, Kelly, and I'm very happy to have you on my side."

Kelly smiled and he was moved to kiss her cheek before he took his leave.

Pack Rowan and Walter Guildford were drinking in a pub called The Rum Pot on Old King's Road. It was just after six in the evening and the place was fairly crowded, a mix of working men on the way home and a smattering of artistic types, some of them actually wearing smocks with paint stains, and an ageing prostitute that Pack had used in the past.

They had been drinking quietly for a couple of hours, Pack in a good humour at the news about Jem Riley – the thought of getting closer to him to pay him back for The Vicar's death warmed him up – and he was more than ready to buy drinks for the enquiry agent who, as Pack said of him "could drink the knobs off a coffin".

Earlier, Guildford had reminded Pack that he had talked of bringing him into his deal.

"I know what I said, Walter. But that's on hold, thanks to another delay in getting into court." Seeing the other man's face drop, Pack actually took the trouble to reassure him. "Meanwhile, I'm offering you something else, a nice little scam that I think of as a sprint." He ordered the same again and said to Walter. "I am going to supply the readies to get the thing going and I want you to be the man to front it. I'll give you wages up front and I'll give you a third of whatever gelt we come out with. Interested?"

"Once there are *readies* up front, I am always in, you know that about me. What are we talking about here?" Guildford had leaned forward, taking small draws on his cigarette as though his pulse had just quickened.

"I never met anybody like you when the few pounds are mentioned," Pack Rowan chuckled harshly. "Tell you there's money in it and you palpitate, so you do."

"Comes from being broke too often," Guildford made no apology: "Too many times coming out of nick with not a bob. So tell us, what is this scam?"

"You find premises, cheap and cheerful. We pay three months' rent. We get a bank account, cheque books, all of that by sticking say a thousand quid into the bank. Then you go out and find them that want to buy stuff at the right price. When you know what people are looking for, you buy that and you sell it to them for cash, below the regular price."

Guildford started to smile in appreciation. "We pay for the first couple of lots and we lose a bit on the resell. We put the money in the bank and then we go for a big one. An order you will have pre-sold for say ten, twelve thousand. This time we have cleaned out the bank account, and we just disappear into thin air with ten or twelve grand for a few weeks' part-time graft. What do you think?"

"I think I like it very much," Guildford said in a moment. "Right up my street, you could say."

"It's only to keep you sweet. You have more ability that this little scam takes. But I have to be patient with the court case – that end of it is out of my hands. But we're going to win that when we get it to court and I am going to be holding a very serious amount of money. Then I go legitimate, and I will have you as my number two on real readies and me on your side. What could be better than that, Walter? Go on, tell me."

Walter opened out his hands in total surrender and his grin grew some as Pack slid a hundred pounds across the table.

"I presume you want something done about Jem Riley?"

"Let me think about that. Tomorrow we'll head for Ramsgate and take a gander at the toe-rag."

"I know you're too smart to get into trouble for what you're going to do to him, Pack." He sounded troubled and Pack was not the least surprised when Guildford went on: "I'm right about that, right?"

"When I think of that toe-rag my blood goes on the boil. I want to grab him and eat his heart out. And here I am sitting here and ordering another drink. And do you know why, me oul' flower? Because I am going to be very rich and nothing or nobody is going to stop that happening. Not even me by going off half-cocked because I'd like to. Like has nothing to do with it. From here on in, I weigh up everything. Riley will get it, make no mistake. After what he did to The Vicar in the Scrubs, I couldn't live with myself if I didn't see that he died hurtin' real bad. So don't fret yourself, you won't get in trouble because I won't be copping any aggro from the law. There's too much at stake to do anything stupid. Much as I hate Riley, I don't hate him enough to throw away my chance to be money rich for the rest of my life."

The drinks arrived and Pack told the waitress to give one to the lady with the feather in her hat.

A few minutes later the lady herself came to the table. "I thought it was you, eh –"

"Tony," said Pack.

She sat down and Pack made no bones about ogling her breasts which would have been difficult to ignore. "Tony," she said in her own demure way, "how nice of you to remember me. Good health." She raised her glass and Pack looked at Walter. "So, Tom," he said quietly, "call me at the hotel by ten in the morning. Tell me where to meet you for our little trip. I'm looking forward to it."

Walter finished his drink and stood up. "Good evening." He made a little bow from the waist to the woman with the feather in her hat, glanced at Pack Rowan and said: "Till the morning then."

When he left Pack turned to her and said: "I'm in need of my quiet hotel room and your company – I thought that on the way we would pick up a bottle or two and see how things unfold. What would you think about that?"

"It seems like a jolly good idea, Tony," she said, smiling grandly since she had just remembered what a massive lover he had been the last time they had taken each other over the jumps. She put a hand on his thigh, feeling better about the evening. She had no memory for names but she tended to remember men who were very active in the feathers. And this Tony had been a divine monster.

Brendan O'Connor was deeply moved as he and Sam hugged each other, both of them silent – holding back tears in this special moment of reconciliation.

They lit cigarettes and walked around the paved garden path circling the house at Dunbla. The silence between them was essential so they took their time, allowing what was to come to do so in its moment.

"Before anything else, Sam, thanks for helping me get Sweet Construction going. I know I wrote you a letter, but what you did – to go guarantor for my bank loan – nobody could have expected that kind of generosity, especially as you were so disappointed in me."

As always, Brendan had spoken straight from the shoulder.

"Those days are behind us. I felt what I felt and I went with it. You did the same. All I want now is for the secret war, the shootings, to stop on both sides. Enough people have died – the price of this Free State is already becoming far too high." Sam sniffed, and smoked desperately.

Brendan waited and they walked. When he thought

the moment right he said, "In your telephone call you just said 'I need you, Brendan' – so here I am. Those words meant more than you know. So, tell me, Sam, how do you need me? What can I do to help you?" He punched Sam's arm: "Just for a change like."

Sam tucked his hand under Brendan's left arm and they went on walking. He gave Brendan an edited version of his situation – the looming court case and the ruthlessness of Constance Brewer. He told him about Pack Rowan – the complications that now surrounded the birth of Eddie Brewer – the deadly ramifications of the deaths of Arthur and Lisa O'Brien – and his plans to remedy that problem.

Neither of them needed reminding that both Brendan and Cormac Doyle had helped him with the burial of Arthur and Lisa on the Dunbla estate. They had been involved too in the fake funeral of Arthur in Deans Grange cemetery, the coffin containing eleven stone of rocks and sand in place of Arthur's corpse, "It sounds tricky enough, Sam, but so far I don't hear anything we can't manage." Brendan stopped and they both lit fresh cigarettes. "But you're dead right where this thing could go to – like, we could be up for murdering Arthur and Lisa. If we weren't somehow involved in it, why would we have buried them here?"

They walked on and Sam told him how his private enquiry agent had discovered that Constance Brewer had already paid over twenty thousand pounds to Pack Rowan, the son of Kelly, the old woman who had rescued Deirdre the day she gave birth by the roadside.

"This Pack Rowan is a smart customer, very hard, I

would say, and capable of anything. He intends to kill old Kelly for giving him away to the police. According to his mother his real name is Eddie Kelly – but my latest news from London is that he has a bank account in Hammersmith, passport too, in the name of Roger Gregory." Sam explained further that Rowan's mistress was May Murray. "She runs the local public house – she recently deposited a certified cheque in a Dublin bank for ten thousand pounds."

"So Rowan, he gave his mot half of what he got from oul' Brewer. That's a fortune and they're looking at the kind of money they'll have if they can overturn Arthur's will." Sam nodded and Brendan went on: "These are ruthless people, Sam – there's nothing they wouldn't do for the kind of money that's involved here."

"Deirdre will play no part in this, though she may have to go before a court at some stage. It just depends on how far they can go with the thing. But, you can see why I've decided there is not a lot I won't do to win this case."

"You have to think like that, Sam. If you didn't, you might as well throw your hat at it. This thing won't be won wearing boxing gloves. This is an alley fight with boots and chains and no rules except 'do what you must do to win'."

"So you'll come on board?"

"I've already done that." Brendan blew his nose to relieve his emotional response to Sam's need for his help. "Nobody is going to destroy you while I'm alive and kicking. And I'm not forgetting I could be in there with you, on maybe a murder charge, with accessory after the fact thrown in as well."

"How much time have you got today?" Sam asked.

"All day and whatever else you need. I have two good right hands working the shop while I'm here. I gave them your telephone number in case they need me."

"It's just that this is so complicated – we'll start talking again after dinner, see how we go from there. Is that all right with you?"

"I'm looking forward to seeing Deirdre again." He was a shade anxious. "Does she know I'm going to be here?"

"I told Dee I needed you – she was relieved I'd left the past where it belongs. She was championing you back when I used to give you a tanner for bringing me a cup of tea at the workshop in Mountjoy Square."

Brendan was smiling in memory. "Great days even if the rasher had to grease the pan sometimes. God, I remember Victoria Brewer coming in and that gown that Dee designed for her. The way Victoria's breasts flowed above the material." He chuckled at the memory. "I wasn't right for a week after. And Arthur, such a nice man, one look at Dee and I could tell he was in love with her." He looked anxious until he realised that Sam had no problem with the fact that Deirdre had loved Arthur back then. "I hear good things of the Cork Street Clinic," he went on. "She's not having any problems in the slums these days?"

"Not at the moment," Sam exhaled smoke. "You were there when she had troubles at the start, but we sent out a message – a few blackguards that thought they were tough. They were hurt enough to get some sense. The only trouble Dee has now is from the Catholic Church."

"The Church doesn't do anything like enough to help the poor. Even so, they don't want anybody else doing it either. It's a joke that they could be giving Deirdre grief."

"Right now she is about to start turning my old house on Leinster Road into a sort of halfway place for mothers of no fixed abode. She has a twenty-three-year-old widow – a Civil War widow – with three children, and she has put her up at the Brewer house in Merrion Square while Leinster Road is being organised. There are so many people in this country living in subhuman conditions – you'd wonder how all these priests and bishops – how they can eat so well that they shine with health and the benefits of the best food and drink in the land and people starving under their noses. How do they sleep at night knowing people are dying of dirt and disease and even malnutrition, while they preach to them God will provide, instead of finding them somewhere to live where they can wash their children and God alone knows what else?" Sam took a deep breath: "I'm sorry to go on like that but at times, my God, the situation seems so hopeless. And yet, we can't throw in the towel. We have to keep on trying to help those that can't help themselves at this particular time."

"Are the 'white-collar workers' ever going to wise up to the notion that a bit of help is worth forty-five sermons?" Brendan spat a bad taste out.

"God alone knows," Sam said. "Here, what's the word on Cormac Doyle? Is he on your team?"

Brendan was sceptical, as though he wondered if

Sam was pulling his leg. "He's out there – been in the Civil War a hundred per cent. The word is he won't quit anything – robbing banks interests him more than working for a living. They say he's like a driven man – even them he soldiered with are staying clear of him." The Dubliner then said quietly, "He told me how you got the British officer in the Washington Hotel – that it was him shot Arthur and Lisa O'Brien."

"Less said soonest mended." Sam was trying to shake off the memory of the night Michael Collins and his guerrillas wiped out the cream of British Intelligence. "If those two deaths come to light – anybody looking at those bodies – a blind man would see they were gunned to death."

"We should've stuck to the original idea. Lose them both in one of the construction sites."

"I couldn't do it to Dee. She wanted so badly to have Arthur close by. He was her husband and she loved him like a good wife should. She felt too that since Lisa had been more mother to him than ever Constance was – that girl kept him from cracking up – she should be buried with him. I couldn't argue and I didn't want to. I loved Arthur like the closest brother a man could have – he put me on the road to all I am today – I'd have given my own life for him in a split second – but now, now we have to deal with the mistake we made in bringing him here."

"Absolutely," Brendan said evenly. "Sentiment comes off the stove – the bodies of Arthur and Lisa have to go – so that there'll be no chance of anyone ever finding them again."

Sam nodded his head in agreement. "I want you to

know how much it means, you and I working side by side again." Sam released a heavy breath as though he realised for the first time just how much weight he had been carrying all by himself.

"What Arthur did for you, you did for me. If I'm honest, I'd have done the same for you." Brendan stopped and smiled wryly. "The tennis court idea is a good one, a great start to getting working men in and around the place before the shit starts flying in this direction."

Sam smiled. "We need the courts anyway. The children ride and swim and whatever, but a game of tennis is a bit special."

Before dinner Sam poured whiskey for Brendan, a glass of white wine for himself.

"Are you saying the idea of the tennis courts arrived in all innocence like?" Brendan asked then. "That it had nothing to do with finding a way to hide what has to happen to tidy up the Pets' Cemetery?" He was grinning disbelievingly and Sam started to smile himself.

"I thought it was straight, but, who knows? When you open the lid on the devious part of your mind, who can say what might slip out while you're wondering what to use in a given situation." Sam turned serious and said: "Dee has gone back to her religion after all her years as a Free Thinker. If that's what she wants, I'm happy for her. But it couldn't have come at a worse time."

"How do you mean that?"

"It means I have to keep secrets from Dee. She can never know that there isn't anything I won't do to put Constance Brewer down."

Brendan felt Sam's unease at the impact of his own

words, his voice so calm and detached that it was all the more sinister.

"My God," Sam whispered, "it's even bothering me, so what would it do to Dee to know that I'm thinking like this?'

Deirdre had been about to enter the room and could not help hearing what Sam was saying. She stood frozen to the polished floor of the hallway for a moment before she turned and went quickly back upstairs.

18

June 1924

Before going back down to join the men for dinner, Deirdre spent time in the nursery with Kathleen. She was calm, giving to her daughter all of her attention, except for the thought of what she had heard Sam saying earlier as she had been about to enter the study.

She cherished the times she could spend with her baby daughter, all the more so since she was sometimes gone overnight at the Clinic – enjoyed so much taking Kathleen for her bath before sending her off to sleep on a lullaby sung to her as a small child by her own mother, Elizabeth.

Sam's words seemed to have burned themselves indelibly onto her mind: "It means I have to keep secrets from Dee. She can never know that there isn't anything I won't do to put Constance Brewer down."

She had been stuck to the floor outside the open

study door, simply unable to tear herself away in time to miss the sound of his voice, so calm and detached that it made him sound sinister.

"My God," Sam had whispered, "it's even bothering me, so what would it do to Dee to know that I'm thinking like this."

Now as she left Kathleen to go and freshen up before joining Sam and Brendan O'Connor, Dee knew that Sam meant well. This was something you could take for granted where he was concerned – it was just the way he took life on. This meant that to think and talk as she had heard him do was a painful thing for him to deal with day in day out, and God alone knew how long the whole affair would linger before it was resolved one way or the other.

When she had finished her toilette she knelt by the bed and prayed, asking God for guidance. "Help me help the most wonderful man I have ever known. Let me guide him, support him in every way – help me release my judgmental attitude and just leave it all to him, since he always means good. I am in your hands, Father – show me the way."

During dinner she wondered what Elizabeth would do or say in her situation. Her mother had been a rock in relation to her father's business dreams, she the guiding hand that moved Pat Doyle in the right direction without the big man ever being aware of it.

Putting down her wineglass, she said in an offhand way: "This thing with Constance, Sam, I was thinking, and I'd be interested to hear what Brendan might have to say, as well as you . . ." She found she was nervous and took another sip of wine before continuing: "Because our main concern is the possible effect of all this on Eddie and indeed, Alfie – obviously, Brendan, if the truth ever comes out it could have a devastating effect on Eddie in particular." She stopped, somewhat puzzled as Sam held up his hands to stop her: "What is it, love?"

"If the *story*, Dee – 'if the *story* ever comes out' – this is how we are going to turn this whole thing around. You and I, we concocted a *story* to relieve Gloria, who was in danger of losing her mind. Keep trying to think of it like that, please, darling."

Dee felt irritated but she pressed on: "All right, let me just say this straight out. What if we – that is you, Sam – what if we made Constance an offer that might appeal to even her rather voracious appetite?"

Brendan was clearly open to hearing what Dee had in mind. She wasn't so sure about Sam, but then she knew he had been burned by the manner of Constance Brewer's rejection of his previous offer.

"What are you thinking of?" Sam asked.

"Suppose we said that we are privately willing to arrange that she will end up with a fifty per cent share of Brewer's and all that means."

"An awful lot of lolly," Brendan sighed. "She could very possibly go for that."

Sam looked from Brendan to Dee and slowly he began to smile. "That just might do it, Dee. It just might work the miracle." He turned to Brendan: "She never lost it."

"Don't be talking!" Brendan was amused, and Dee thought she detected a shade of relief in his Dublin accent.

286

"If she takes it, can we make it happen?"

"Anything is possible, Dee. It could cost you a pretty penny."

She cut him off. "You know I don't care about that. Let the accountants do their worst. If it would stop Eddie and Alfie hearing –" she stopped with a wisp of a smile, inclining her head towards Sam, "if it would stop Eddie and Alfie *hearing the story we concocted*, and it would get you out from under the weight of all this, I'd surrender every penny in the morning. Be sure about that, Sam." She looked directly into his eyes. "I'm not happy that you have to be so involved in something like this. You've worked all your life. You're entitled to your retirement, time to get on with your studies and stay alive for me and the children for another forty years or so."

As she finished speaking all three of them were wrapped up in the gentle hush of their collective emotional response to what had been said.

"You're one lucky bastard!" Brendan turned to Dee quickly: "Sorry, Dee – the language."

She waved away his apology.

"It's hard not to envy this guy at times," he said.

"So will you give it a try, Sam? Use all that charm God gave you, and have another crack at the dreaded Constance?" Dee was smiling, full of hope that the offer might just make the nightmare go away. "I don't want you having a heart attack on me. And, at the risk of sounding original, we all know money isn't everything."

Sam remained moved by Dee's offering. "I'll go to London this week and beard the old lioness in her den.

Leave her a dossier showing her the extent of the company's holdings. That might well shorten her cough. It would be the best thing all around if she went for it."

They left the matter rest there, Dee feeling the better for her suggestion. Sipping wine and hoping for some good news of Cormac, she pressed her old friend, Brendan for news of her young brother. When she saw the glance exchanged with Sam she knew that the news was not going to be good.

"Dee, you mean the earth to me. You were the best friend possible in the time I worked for you."

She stopped him by leaning over to touch his hand. Seeing tears in his eyes she said: "There's no need to worry. Whatever you can tell me, I only want the truth."

"Very few know this. Cormac is out there. He's robbing banks and he's shooting at the coppers trying to arrest him."

Dee thought of Paddy, shuddering at the thought that one could end up killing the other.

"You knew Gráinne, did you, Dee?"

Dee shook her head and reached for a cigarette. Sam held a light for her and then lit his own.

Brendan clearly felt more than awkward. "She and Cormac were sort of steady – at least he led me to think they were. She was like him, intense as he is, y'know? Anyway, he got her into the family way and he threw the head badly when she told him. He cared about her, Dee – inside, he's a very decent fella."

"It's all right, Brendan. You can tell me."

"She was shattered when he told her he'd never bring a child into this world. He was off his head – he

288

left her without a kind word. I only know this because he came in my window recently for a bed – told me the next morning when I gave him a lift into town. Dee, Gráinne took her own life. She went into Tara Street baths and slit her wrists in the hot water." Brendan sniffed while Dee wiped her tears away.

Sam went to stand by Dee, his hands on both her shoulders, his love for her a palpable thing, his heart a wound he carried for her, his eyes going up to the ceiling, his expression an indictment of the notion that a loving God could allow such a thing to happen.

Cormac Doyle took the drink from Kitty and sat down wearily on the chaise longue in the studio.

She sipped her wine, looking at him guardedly, trying to hide the fact that she thought of him as a special somebody. "That's a terrible thing to happen to you." Her breasts swelled with compassion for him. "It's not your fault. You couldn't have known she'd do that to herself."

"I wish I was dead." He emptied the glass and looking up at her said: "I can't believe the power of Catholicism. I mean, Christ, I know better, and I can't get out of this, get away from all the pain I create, I can't do that because I am some kind of fucked-up Catholic."

She put down her glass and came to kneel by him where he sat. She put her arms around him in a friendly way and he began to weep. She found that her own tears needed release and she held him tightly, kissing his head and neck, trying to bring him some moment of comfort, amazed in the moment by the strength of her desire to make love to him.

He turned to look at her and she thought him the most beautiful man she had ever seen. The moment stamped its claim on both of them and a second later they were like two people trying to eat pieces of each other.

Through the night and into the next day he came into her in the bed, a man driven by his inner demon, plundering her much of the time in his need to pass away from the effort he was dumping on his heart and his mind. For Kitty, the sensation of this new experience seemed to be turning her into the kind of wanton she had read about, but couldn't believe in.

When she finally washed herself down in the following afternoon, she gasped when she looked into the mirror over the sink. Her lips were so swollen she looked like she had been severely beaten while her neck and shoulders carried love bites and bruises that would take weeks to heal. Examining her breasts she found her nipples bruised and discoloured and tender under the face flannel. It was the same down below. She would feel sore for some days, at least. Looking back into the mirror she saw her face burst into smile, her wounds lit by the glow of how good she felt in the moment. She got dressed carefully and went down the stairs and out the door, off to buy food and drink and cigarettes for the man she felt some kind of breathtaking love for.

An hour after his arrival in London, Sam Sweet was waiting for his agent, Prod McLoughlin, to join him at the Ritz Hotel. As he arrived, Prod, as usual, made Sam think of a big jockey. His slight frame looked as tough as teak, Sam reckoning he would be a handful in any kind of fight. He was a neat man, carefully checking out the occupants of the tea lounge before settling in.

"I've got Rowan's hotel nailed down for you, Mister Sweet," he said after they had greeted each other. "I can give you the names of the women he hires night after night – and I can reveal that at this moment he is visiting Constance Brewer at her home in Eaton Square."

Sam gave him a grin and patted his shoulder. "I always believe in picking the best, Prod."

The fact that Pack Rowan was with Constance Brewer at this time gave Sam an idea. Standing up, he cancelled the order for afternoon tea. "We'll talk as you walk me over to Eaton Square," he told McLoughlin. "I hadn't planned this, but I want to meet Pack Rowan in Constance's company. Now is my chance. Can you meet me back here at five?"

When Johnstone the butler saw Sam Sweet standing on the doorstep his expression remained calm, the man in charge. "Ah, Mister Sweet, I realise you have a meeting arranged, but you are three quarters of an hour early. Madam will not be at home until the appointed time."

Sam put fifty pounds in the butler's hand. "You can say I barged in on you." As he spoke, Sam did just that, pushing past the little man who hurriedly pocketed the notes before closing the door.

A moment later he was confronting Constance and Pack Rowan.

"All right, go away." Constance dismissed the butler and looked down her nose at Sam. To his eye, she looked like she had been exhumed and warmed up for a little while in some kind of oven. But there was nothing fragile about her response to his rudeness, nor the weight of her voice: "I was correct in expecting no better from you. I do expect an explanation for such a lack of courtesy."

Sam briefly studied Pack Rowan, who could have passed for a successful executive, his charcoal grey suit, white shirt and plain red tie, shoes shining like black mirrors, a testament to industry and general good taste. "Good afternoon, Mister Rowan. We have not been introduced but we would have seen each other at the Dunbla Tavern the odd time." Sam drew near to Rowan even as he spoke, and found him impressive indeed.

"Glad to meet you, sir," Pack said as though he meant it, shaking the outstretched hand firmly without any need to present more than a reasonable grip.

"I do apologise, truly sorry to interrupt your meeting." He turned to Constance. "I ask your pardon, madam, not my normal form to barge in but I am desperate for time – an enquiry agent to meet – a certain bank manager to see – I pray that you hear me out."

Sam paused, noting the instant interest in Rowan's eyes though he saw no such change in Constance. "May I carry on?"

"No, you may not, Mister Sweet. You dare force your way into my private study with your Jewish business tactics – how dare you!"

Sam had expected no less, but his armour was

blistered by the vehemence in the old woman. "But, madam, I swear I had no intention of giving offence," Sam tried, knowing in his heart he was on a loser here.

Constance turned to Rowan, her tone now conciliatory. "Mister Rowan, would you be kind enough to step outside while I deal with this uncalled-for situation." She rang a bell, remaining silent until Johnstone appeared clouded in just the right degree of sheepishness, Sam thought.

"Johnstone, please take Mister Rowan to the drawing room and serve him some refreshment."

Sam could see that the very last thing Pack Rowan wanted was to be excluded from whatever was going to be said here. But, he had the grace and the *savoir faire* to withdraw without demur. For his part, Sam was most impressed. Considering Rowan's background, Sam gave him ten out of ten for good behaviour – the well-dressed man of the roads had certainly made use of his time in prison for self-betterment..

When the door closed, Constance gave Sam her attention.

He averted his eyes as much as possible. Her skin and an odour he found very unpleasant made him think of a lizard.

She now regarded him with a jaundiced eye before ordering him in a vehement tone, "Get on with it, man!"

Sam took a moment, wondering if he should make any further attempt at an apology. He decided against it since the old woman's opinion of him mattered not at all. "I am empowered to make this offer – lawyers and accountants have given me the necessary documentation – for your consideration. So without further ado here it is: Deirdre Brewer, in whose affairs I have Power of Attorney, wants you to know that, in the interest of all concerned, but most particularly her children, Edward and Alfred, she is prepared to offer you a half share in Brewer's Brewery Worldwide, including all associate companies, investments and the like. In short, madam, half of all that is Brewer's – with the exception of the legacy to the two boys from their father, this more for reasons of sentiment than finance."

He saw the interest the offer evoked in the bloodshot windows to the mind of Constance Brewer, but she quickly pulled the curtains, determined to give nothing away.

Sam opened his briefcase and removed a folder. "All the facts and figures relating to the value of all that is Brewer's are here, madam. I'll leave this with you and await your reply to the offer."

Constance was ignoring Sam's conciliatory tone but he felt her mind was racing as she worked out roughly just how much money was involved here. Sam was picturing how Pack Rowan would have been reacting to such an offer – he could practically hear Rowan telling Constance silently with every pore in his body to say yes and stop being such a damned old fool.

"You'll hear from me when I'm good and ready," she said finally. "There is principle involved here that cannot be bought with all the money in the Bank of England. Now leave me. I have matters that need my attention."

Sam inclined his head and was about to leave but, he found he could not, not without sending one more salvo across her rusting bows. "Madam, you may think what you will of me, but hear this: you would be insane to turn down this offer – I believe we can beat you in court, but I give you my word, this gesture comes from Deirdre who, like it or not, was your son's lawfully wedded wife, and is the mother of his two sons, Eddie and Alfie. She makes the offer with a view to keeping private matters in the family – is particularly keen to protect her sons from the very likely scandal this case will most certainly generate in the gutter press on a daily basis.

"And finally, madam, the stuff of possible scandal is not confined to Deirdre's position. You yourself may want to consider the possible fall-out if Sir Ralph Dorning – who has not a penny to his name – were to give his story about how Ellen, his beautiful young sister, took her own life. He tells me she was so utterly devastated – abandoned by the woman she married in an alternative wedding ceremony at Dorning Hall, on a Midsummer's Day, all those years ago. You and I, madam, we both know why Ellen Dorning committed suicide." Sam deliberately hit the last two words, finding some satisfaction as the picture he had painted seemed to land blow by blow on the wretched brow of Constance Brewer.

The old woman rallied well, once more regarding Sam will ill-concealed hatred. "You are a foul creature, sir. The man now sitting in my drawing room, someone that spent his life sleeping by the roadside, he is a gentleman to his fingertips compared to you. You epitomise all that is wicked and evil in the Jew. Now leave me. We shall not meet again until you face my lawyers in a court of law."

Sam felt nothing and almost smiled as her eyes opened in surprise that he was not already on his way out of the study.

"Leave me, I said!" Constance was suddenly fuming.

Sam felt her anger was pumping up out of the fear that his scarcely veiled threat had uncovered. "Your opinion of me is of no consequence, madam – this is a matter of business. I advise you to take the offer. Should you decide not to do so, what you have experienced here today is a shadow of the pain that will come to you. You will not live to destroy Deirdre and Arthur's two boys. Believe me, when your lesbian wife took her own life, she left letters, and I have seen them in the hands of Sir Ralph Dorning."

Constance could hardly find her voice in the well of anger that sent her body quivering. "Get out. Get out, you fiend! I shall have the law on you!"

"Sir Ralph did not approach you with an offer to sell the letters – he felt it would be pointless since you have no money. My agents have statements from your bank to prove this. You have gambled every penny of the money that your late husband, Arthur Shane Brewer, left to you, and it is your desperation to feed your gambling addiction that has turned your well-known intelligence into a mush of madness that will take your life before you ever see a penny of Arthur's legacy to Dee and his children."

Sam stood for a few moments as Constance gave all of her attention to finding the next breath.

"And now, madam, I bid you good afternoon." As he reached the door he turned back and said casually: "A copy of the offer has been delivered to the office of your legal team. At this time, I felt no need to alert them to the possible inclusion of the tragic story of how your beloved Ellen ended her own life." He gave her a smile. "There's plenty of time for that later."

He found Johnstone standing in the hall and the little man let him out of the house without a word being said.

It was a dull London day, the sun losing out to a cloudbank coming from the direction of Victoria, but to Sam it seemed like the best of weather. It was not cold and he felt sure he would get back to the hotel without rain pouring down on him.

There was a spring in his step as he headed for Hyde Park Corner and the short walk down Piccadilly to the Ritz. But, he was also being troubled by a niggling doubt as to how he had behaved back there with Constance Brewer.

'She has to go for it, surely,' he thought. 'Even if she wanted to be evil and cruel, surely Pack Rowan has enough influence over her to make her see what a wonderful offer she has been given. Unless,' he pondered, 'she is serious about the principle part. She couldn't be, not with many millions on offer. She couldn't be that insane, could she?'

At Hyde Park corner Sam his eye was captured by a small Indian man in purple and pink silks over white shoes. The slender colourful creature seemed to be dithering, unable to decide whether he should risk life and limb to cross the dangerous corner. In the instant, Sam knew a sense of danger and he moved towards the little man. The Indian was so intent on looking one way he lost sight of a bus that was tearing towards his position.

Hurling himself forward, Sam did not yell out in case the cry sent the man under the wheels of the omnibus. He managed to grab him even as he stepped off the footpath, hauling him to safety while the tips of his white shoes literally scraped lightly against the side of the speeding monster..

Sam put the little man down on the footpath and to his surprise heard him chuckling in delight.

Seeing that the face of his rescuer was a study in perplexity the Indian bowed, his hands joined before his face. Then he smiled again, addressing Sam in a delightful sing-song voice. "I am alive, good sir, all thanks to you. I am alive and deliriously happy that this is so."

"May I be of any further assistance to you, sir?" Sam wasn't certain the little man had the right to be so happy after a brush with death. The little man's glee was so evident however, that it simply brushed this caveat from Sam's mind.

"Which direction do you walk in, sir?"

"I'm going along to the Ritz Hotel," Sam said.

"Oh yes, I know the Ritz. I stayed there many times in another life." He bowed slightly. "May I impose on your company until you reach the hotel?"

"You may indeed, sir." Sam felt the fellow was more normal now, no longer as manic as moments earlier when he was positively bursting with ecstasy.

As they walked, his companion was reaching into his shoulder bag. Having found what he was looking for he stopped walking and offered Sam a small book. "It is but small offering of gratitude, dear sir. You kept me from death at the corner and I am most happy to make your acquaintance."

"I am Sam Sweet, sir," said Sam, offering his hand.

The Indian's grip was firm though the dark hand was not large. Sam looked into the oil-burned eyes of his companion and for a moment, incredibly, everything seemed to stand still. It was as though a sense of oneness, some spiritual connection had wrapped around them, something he had never experienced before.

The Indian smiled and nodded his head. "You are open, Sam Sweet. Today you are ready to walk the road of few travellers and I am delighted to be present as this good fortune lands upon you." He put his hand out again and Sam found he was shaking it in quiet joy as his companion said: "I am Asham Zadapeer Gopal. My small book is the key to living. My name and address are printed there should you ever wish to get in touch with me about your future life."

This was said in such a matter-of-fact way that it attracted Sam's attention instantly. "My future life, sir – in what way do you mean?"

"Have I made a mistake, Sam Sweet? I felt that you had already started on a journey in search of yourself." Asham Zadapeer Gopal seemed to be genuinely surprised. "You have become aware in recent times that this life is not what you thought it was. Is that not correct?"

"Well, yes." Sam looked into his eyes. "I am starting a study – for some time I've needed to know more about truth – the truth about myself. Much of the time I feel isolated, no longer connected with people and things I once thought the bedrock of my existence." Sam was more than surprised to be confessing such to a total stranger.

Reading his mind, Gopal said: "I am not a stranger, Sam Sweet. I Am That – That Which Is, same as you are." He took Sam's hand and shook it. "I must leave you now. I know you will contact me when you have read my book."

Speechless, Sam watched him hurry away with a short-stepped shuffle that was taking him along towards Piccadilly Circus. He shook his head, a lack of understanding perched on his shoulder, the small book clasped in his hand as he went into the Ritz.

He found Prod McLoughlin waiting for him in the tea lounge and, having ordered refreshments for them both, began telling the enquiry agent what had happened at Eaton Square.

"She did well to get Rowan out of the room," Prod said. "Had he heard what you had to say, he would almost certainly have twisted her arm, even while you were there."

"Exactly my thinking on the matter, Prod." Sam poured tea for them both and bit into a watercress sandwich.

"I know she went up in the air on you," Prod said, "but surely, surely when she has had a drop of brandy she'll see reason, take the money and hobble off to the Carlton Club to lose some of it." McLoughlin sounded so matter of fact. "All we have to do is be patient. She has to come around, unless . . ."

"Unless she's gone insane altogether," Sam said, while the enquiry agent nodded in agreement. Sam considered this, sipping tea as he weighed it all up. "At first when she started on about it being a matter of principle, I dismissed it as the waffle I thought it was. My guess is she is not long for this world – no denying she wants money because she has to gamble. The hatred towards Deirdre and the utter lack of motherly feelings for Arthur's wishes, that's what makes me wonder just how far she will go before she throws in the towel here."

"Her eruption when you spoke of her 'marriage' to Ellen Dorning – I would have thought that might do it."

Sam agreed. "I thought so too. Now I'm not so sure. It's, well, I can't be sure – it's like she's blotted it out, like she's found a place in her mind where it never happened."

McLoughlin drank tea and said: "Your lawyers, they'll be working with her team to sort it out. You can bet all the legals will want to settle. They get paid right away without having to do the work."

Sam agreed. "So for the next God knows how long, we're in a waiting place."

"Indeed, but there's something else you should hear about. The court case aside, I need to talk to you about something else." He seemed hesitant and used the ritual of lighting a cigarette to buy time.

Sam said: "Tell me, Prod. What's going on?"

Exhaling smoke, Prod said: "I need a few minutes to give you the details."

"Go ahead," Sam said, wondering what this was about.

"It involves your ex-wife, Gloria," Prod said.

"Something to do with this Palestine business she had got herself into?"

Prod shook his head: "Nothing like that."

Before he could press on, a page-boy came to the door of the tea lounge announcing: "Telephone call for Mister Sweet, telephone call for Mister Sweet!"

Sam was already rising as he said: "Is Gloria all right, Prod?"

McLoughlin nodded. "Yes, it can wait."

Sam said, "Are you free for dinner?" Prod nodded his head. "How about you join me here for dinner? Seven okay?"

"Fine," McLaughlin walked into the foyer behind Sam who was already heading for the telephone.

Brendan O'Connor's voice came down the line with a guarded greeting. He was still active in the IRA and like his compatriots never trusted that 'the Branch' weren't listening in. "Just to say that the clean-up has started, and to ask when you're due back in the Emerald Gem?" Brendan kept his tone conversational and Sam went the same route.

"Expected to leave here in the morning, but I may be delayed for a day or two. If you need me to be there, I will go ahead and get out tomorrow."

"No, you attend to your business. All is well here. The team of lads are all dedicated workers."

This meant that Brendan had gathered a team of IRA Volunteers around him to begin removing the evidence from the Pets' Cemetery. Sam thought of this event as a sacrilege but it had to be done – he simply couldn't take the risk that the evidence would be found by people working for Constance Brewer. Were that to happen it would solidify her case to such a degree that he and those he loved would be major players in a tragedy.

Sam pulled his mind away from the gruesome possibilities lying there and gave his thinking over to the work already under way at Dunbla. The 'dedicated workers', as Brendan had called the IRA Volunteers, would be paid for their labour – if they wished they could donate their earnings to the ongoing Cause, but they were free to keep the money.

In a sense, Brendan and Sam had agreed that up to a point they had to dupe the Volunteers. Of course this was to be done without malice, the need to get the evidence out of sight for all time forcing them to reveal only that part of the story that made it incumbent on the IRA men to get involved. This meant that Brendan – a high-ranking officer in the Dublin Brigade of the IRA – could tell them, without prejudice, that Sam Sweet had been the extra man on the night that the assassination squad of Michael Collins had wiped out the cream of the British Secret Service back in 1920.

Sam agreed that Brendan was free to tell the men how he had to take out the officer to save his own life –

this necessity the result of Cormac Doyle shooting Arthur and Lisa O'Brien by mistake.

As he ran a bath in the hotel room Sam felt relief that Brendan had got things under way back home. Then, as he was about to get into the hot water he remembered the little Indian man and the small book he had given him as they walked along Piccadilly.

He poured a drink from the half bottle of Courvoisier he'd bought coming over on the ferry from Dublin's North Wall. Catching his reflection he smirked wryly at the mirror: "I know. I'm getting far too fond of the old cognac."

Glass and ashtray perched on the flat rim of the hotel bath, he slipped into the water and sighed in release. Luckily, he left the book on the bathroom stool – it might have been destroyed otherwise, for within a matter of seconds, he was having a snooze without noticing, while the water not only filled the bath but overflowed.

Fortunately, he woke up before any serious damage was done, his gratitude for the little book's safety so palpable that he knew he must read it right away. Smiling he wondered if Asham Gopal hadn't caused him to drift off in the bath, in order to help him to begin reading the book. "Nonsense!" was the next word that came to mind and he left the matter there.

19

September 27, 1923

Sam sipped a glass of Brewer's stout in the saloon bar of the ferry-boat. He had just spent an eventful few days in England and he was now jotting down guidelines for writing up the trip in his journal.

His dinner with Prod McLoughlin had been more than rewarding. As always the food at the Ritz was excellent, he and his companion sharing a Château Briande and a couple of bottles of Côte de Beaune that left both men replete, though they did enjoy a couple of Rainbow cocktails, courtesy of the management, something new in Sam's experience, and enjoyable.

Prod McLoughlin ate his food with such gusto that Sam found himself munching away at the same pace. He was anxious to hear what Prod had to say and had no objection to getting dinner out of the way first.

When they were settled in the lounge Prod began his story. "It may take a few minutes. My sister, Rose, a decent woman, widowed, very bright, has a great job in the Public Records Office. She's been having an on-off affair with a Walter Guildford. He calls her and they sleep together. When he doesn't call she goes out, picks up a man in a pub. She finds it almost unbearable to sleep alone. I fear that some night – the wrong man, y'know – she may never wake up again. Rose tells me she doesn't care. Living the best way she can, 'If I'm to die for it, better than taking my own life.' What can you say, Sam?"

Sam found himself impressed by the acceptance in his companion. How large the smaller man seemed of a sudden – free of claiming any of the limelight for himself – a caring friend rather than a heartbroken brother devastated by his sister's manner of living.

"When Guildford is doing well, he is good to Rose, and she is not above enjoying the material benefits that come via his generosity from time to time. Recently he's more affluent than usual – when he's had drink he boasts to her, brags about the kind of people he knows, works with. Most are criminals, certainly night people living in the shadows, to his liking. Rose claims he has an inherent hatred of the settled, middle-class way of life, thrives on being accepted as a minor villain. Uses his licence as an enquiry agent, as a means of gaining information – sells it to criminals who will earn from it.

"He told Rose the other night he and a man called Pack Rowan were well into something that could earn all kinds of money. When she aired her doubt he asserted, vehemently, that he would benefit from the millions Rowan was going to earn shortly. Meanwhile, Guildford is the front for a scam Rowan dreamed up – they were already making their first monies from this. Rowan has changed his name to Roger Gregory – Guildford made his own enquiries with some help from Rose – she has contacts in banks and all kinds of institutions and these people work very much on a quid pro quo basis – Gregory has ten thousand pounds in his bank account, has a new passport in the new name. Originally he deposited a certified cheque for twenty thousand – the money came from Constance Brewer by the way – and then bought a certified cheque for ten thousand made out to a lady, May Murray. Am I going too quickly for you, Sam?"

Sam shook his head and sipped his cognac. "Go on, Prod, you're grand. I'm right there with you."

"At Walter Guildford's request Rose turned up a man called Séamus O'Reilly. She says that Rowan has been looking for this man for years. Now it turns out that this O'Reilly has got himself a new name as well. He is now Joseph Jameson. The word from May is that Pack Rowan was delighted when Walter told him he knew where this Jameson was holed up. It seems O'Reilly alias Jameson was in Wormwood Scrubs with Rowan, who wants very badly to kill him stone dead."

"Was Rose able to find out why, Prod?"

"An inmate, The Vicar, was Rowan's mentor in the Scrubs. Apparently, The Vicar taught him to read, write, coached him in etiquette and cleanliness, all that. He was queer, The Vicar, and Rowan may have looked after him in that area to pay for his education. Rowan swears he knows that O'Reilly threw The Vicar off a gantry in the Scrubs, killing him – he has vowed to kill the man called O'Reilly now Jameson if it's the last thing he does."

"The way you say, 'the man called O'Reilly' – what is that about, Prod?"

"O'Reilly was an alias – Rowan knows the first name, the name behind that first alias, and I have Rose now turning things upside down to find it so I can tell you."

"D'you think Rose will be successful?"

"She's a bit abnormal, Sam, but when it comes to the work she's so committed it'd scare you."

"Why did you think it so urgent for me to hear all of this, Prod? There's something else, isn't there?"

The enquiry agent nodded his head and looked up at Sam. "This O'Reilly now called Jameson – he has become friendly with your son."

"How can that possibly be?" Sam was so shocked that he almost rose from his chair.

"He's the Head Gardener at a Jewish school in Ramsgate, and according to Rose, he and the boy became friends in the past year. And, from what I hear, he has met your ex-wife, Gloria. I thought you should know."

Sam was smoking nervously, sensing the Pack Rowan involvement. Rowan and May Murray were popping up all over the place. Perhaps May had talked Rowan into kidnapping Mendel. Perhaps they thought it could be a lever to force Sam as chief executor of Brewer's Worldwide, to be certain Constance got the exact deal she wanted, or Sam would not see his son again.

Sam had no idea where Jameson, or whatever his name was, fitted into the picture. But sitting there with McLoughlin as this latest strand unravelled, he knew that he had to talk to Rowan, he had to get to him and let him know just how much money was ready and waiting to be picked up once the old woman signed her name on the dotted line. The sudden sense of urgency present in the thought arose because he intuitively felt, and believed, that as yet Constance was keeping the tinker in the dark.

Sitting in the gently swaying saloon bar of the ferry to Dublin, Sam allowed his mind to return to the train journey he and Prod McLoughlin had taken to the town of Ramsgate in Kent.

Arriving at his son's school by taxi, Sam left Prod in the car while he found the House Matron. Clare Morton bade Sam sit down in her office, offered him refreshment which he declined, and produced a short note which she held between her fingers. "Madame Stern took Mendel with her on her latest concert tour. He'd had flu and we agreed that a holiday would be good for him. A couple of days ago we received this letter from her. She has been laid low in Turkey with some virus. She says that Mendel is in perfect health and 'having the time of his life' and that she will have him back here shortly. He will have private tuition during part of the hols to catch up."

Matron Morton made no effort to show Sam the letter, nor would he have expected her to do so. His ex was entitled to demand that she and she alone should be privy to anything other than general information about her son's welfare. For a moment Sam tasted resentment but he knew it was just an old habit and not worth the houseroom.

Returning to London with Prod McLoughlin, he was content enough that his son and Gloria had come to no harm. He would talk to her when she got home, find out what, if any, was the connection between Mendel and the gardener called Joseph Jameson.

In his London hotel room, Pack Rowan was lying back smoking a cigarette in the dark. A flash of intermittent light altered the shapes of the room as a neon sign advertised Bovril from across the street.

Beside him in the bed was someone called Lily, who was sleeping after some very physical sex. Her gentle snore suited Pack Rowan down to the ground because he needed to be quiet, to be left alone with his thoughts.

For some time since Lily had left his arms, he had been trying to connect Joseph Jameson aka Séamus O'Reilly to a toe-rag he had first known in Wormwood Scrubs as Jem Riley.

Jem Riley, the half-mad bastard Riley who had been so jealous of himself and The Vicar – Riley who never forgave the defrocked Church of England man for spurning his sexual advances in the Scrubs. 'Bastard – he hated me getting an education, envied me having

310

someone to get tucked up with at night. Hatred and envy, what else can you say about Riley, a dirty stinking low-life who'd give criminals a bad name.' Pack exhaled smoke. 'Where the hell did Riley get Joseph Jameson from? From a birth certificate in the name of a man or a child that had died, where else? But what was the thinking behind it?' Then it struck him. Riley liked to brag about being a legendary drinker, a poet and all kinds of other things. And he'd been doing a ten-stretch for a grievous-bodily-harm job he did on a punter he was robbing – the face had fought back and Riley had to kill him to get him to quit fighting. The word landed: Jameson. Jameson Ten. Riley and his love for Jameson Ten, the best whiskey ever to grace the inside of a bottle! All the time it was bloody Jameson, Jameson, Jameson!

Pack gave a whoop of delight as the answer landed on his consciousness. He stubbed out the cigarette, excited enough to be violent, his energy now burning in his loins even as Lily woke up with a start.

"What? What's the matter, Tony?" She put her hand out as she sat up in the bed and she laughed as her fingers landed on his erection. "Mmm," she said with real appreciation. "I can see why you're so delighted."

"You're the most exciting woman I've been with in years," he said with such sincerity that she was overcome with desire for him. "Now let's get this into you before it takes me for a walk or somethin'."

She laughed hoarsely as she felt him press in and Pack began going through the motions, only short of grinding his teeth. Lily could feel the drive and the energy that to her mind made him some sort of legendary lover. But then she could not have known that his excitement overall was the result of the pictures his mind was throwing up, pictures of how he intended to make Jem Riley suffer before he finally put out his lights.

Sam Sweet was not surprised when Alex Gibbon said on the telephone that as yet there was no response to the offer made to Constance Brewer. "It wouldn't be in her nature to make things easy for us, Alex."

When Deirdre got home from the Clinic she was very distressed and he, almost afraid to ask, poured her a brandy and made her sit down across the fire from him. "You look worn out, my darling. Would you like to take dinner in bed?"

Dee shook her head, and he realised that she was quietly shedding tears. He got up and went to her side, wiping them away with his handkerchief, pressing this into her hand before backing off and allowing her be with her grief.

After a while she said: "We lost a girl of eighteen years old today. A sweet beautiful creature beaten by a man, beaten so badly that her son was stillborn. We did everything we could: we fought for her life, I prayed, I promised God anything he wanted from me." She blew her nose. "Nothing, nothing worked. We lost her."

Sam said carefully, "I think you need a break from the Clinic, Dee. I –"

"Oh for God's sake!" Her anger was palpable, good manners and her ability to reason that he would always mean well, deserting her. "Can't I speak of what I am feeling without you turning it into a lecture about my health, the risks I am taking working with women who may be bringing God knows what into the Clinic?"

Sam held his temper, this kind of retort not entirely unexpected. Deirdre did need a break from the Clinic was how he saw it. She needed this, not only for health reasons, but so that she could let go long enough not to be, well, he stopped trying to compromise, so that she would not be bloody well addicted to the place and what went on there.

He rose to throw some turf on the fire and he turned to Dee. "Forgive me, Dee, I meant well. And I do understand how you feel." As the words left his lips he felt guilty for the lie. He did not understand, but, feeling it was what she needed to hear, he was servicing the moment.

Deirdre looked up at him, sniffing back any further tears, her eyes flinty now, though she did not sound angry when she said: "I don't think you do, Sam. I'm not blaming you for that." She shook away something she decided not to express. "I'll take a bath – you have your dinner. I'm not sure I'll want to eat."

He was about to reason with her, but she stood up at that moment, touching his arm briefly with her hand, as though she was trying to rebuild the bridge between them.

Sam ate a good dinner and was ready to go to work when Brendan O'Connor arrived after his own working day in the city. The Dub had eaten before driving to Dunbla, so Sam put on his rubber boots and waterproof coat and they left the house.

Walking up the hill towards the Pets' Cemetery, they passed a huge space already flattened at the base of the incline. This would accommodate the two tennis courts. Three men were working here under lights needed as the evening settled down for the night.

Climbing up the land they reached the Pets' Cemetery. The team organised by Brendan were well into the work. There were six of them digging in the area Sam had earlier marked off on a plan of the graveyard – at the rate they were working he expected them to find what was there before long. He turned to Brendan: "As soon as they strike oil, give me a shout. I'm just going up the hill for a minute."

As he climbed towards the early moon he had mixed feelings about the next hour or so. His mood was uneasy as it always was when he felt resentful towards Dee. Here he was up to his neck in the middle of a seriously criminal offence – on the bottom line it was grave-robbing – with a more demanding task ahead of him this night – the next few hours enough to age a man – and she comes home in a mood. He stopped the thought right there, ashamed to even think about Dee in such a tone. He became calm by standing still, all of his fingers touching as he joined his hands like someone praying. He was moved to tears. 'Whatever happened to *in sickness and in health* and all that, Sam?'

He stepped on the admonition by rubbing his thumbs and forefingers together. His mind was still, his peace helped by his sense of sight as he stood on the rim of the land with the sea below like dark ice highlighted by a highway of cream light provided by the moon.

Some minutes passed without a circling thought finding landing space on his mind. He came then to the notion, not for the first time, that mind was just a collection of thoughts, that in effect mind was not something like the brain which you could see and touch, it only existed when thoughts came together. This gave him pause – it was such a wild sort of thing to think. But it felt right and he had the idea that he was verging on something important. He stopped the flow as he heard Brendan O'Connor give him a call from below.

Coming down the hill he was anxious but relieved to find that Brendan had given his Volunteers a break. They could be seen further down the land where they were now eating the sandwiches and drinking teas and beers that Séamus and Angela had provided.

Brendan stood by the gate of the little cemetery, stepping aside as Sam came through. At a dimly lit area at the far end, Sam stopped and looked into the pit three feet deep that O'Connor's volunteers had dug out. He saw the canvas sheaths in which Arthur and Lisa O'Brien had been buried. Alongside this was a tarpaulin wrap-around in which the tinker girl and Dee's stillborn girl had been laid to rest.

Sam's throat constricted and he had to light a cigarette. He needed the activity to occupy his mind for a second or two, and then the cigarette to smoke in the hope of finding relief from the grief and the guilt and the fear that had invaded him when he thought of what had to happen next.

Without a word, Brendan found the drums of petrol

the Volunteers had brought to the site. Sam cut into the canvas cover holding Arthur and Lisa while Brendan did the same with the second parcel. Now both men began pouring petrol over their responsibility, Sam stepping back with tears coursing down his face.

For moments he felt he was drowning in the sense of his own loss – Arthur, the best and most noble friend and dear old pal, Lisa – Arthur's early saviour.

Both men now added twisted newspapers and kindling wood, lots of it, all over the open graves. Brendan was lighting tapers made of newspaper, passing them to Sam.

In a matter of minutes the fuel was creating a blaze and both men were throwing turf and several shovelfuls of coal onto the flames. They stood smoking as they watched the fire in the pit, but after fifteen minutes there was no hint, no sign, nor any smell to suggest that the heat was enough to do the job.

"Oh God, this is disastrous," Sam said wearily, his eyes stinging painfully.

"Looks like Plan B so," Brendan said, while Sam envied him his objectivity.

"We'll have to use the steamroller," Sam said, anxious to get things dealt with tonight.

"She's ready and waiting," Brendan said affably. He indicated the corner nearest the pit where a small steamroller rested in the shadows. "Let me get Jimmy up here. He's kept her warm, so it shouldn't be long before she'll do what has to be done." Brendan touched Sam's arm. "Have I ever failed you when you needed something doing?"

With tears in his aching eyes Sam said no and shook his head.

"Well, I'm not going to start tonight. So, take it easy. We are going to get this job done tonight." He called down the hill for Jimmy to join them.

Sam could only shake his head in admiration – what a bloody man! To have considered the situation in such a complete way, a way that Sam hadn't even thought of until circumstances left him no choice.

He was not looking forward to what had to be done, but this job had to be despatched with all the haste possible. As he heard Brendan giving instructions to the Volunteer called Jimmy, Sam walked back up the hill knowing Brendan would call him when things were ready.

On the rim of the land, he sat down feeling very weary. It was now ten o'clock and he expected that he had an all-night vigil ahead of him. Watching his cigarette smoke swirl around for a moment or two before it faded, he realised there wasn't a breath of wind and he felt grateful for the calm. To be so close to Arthur and yet so far – he wept in the knowledge that all the blotting out of the pain that his friend's tragic death forced on him, didn't solve anything. The pain didn't go away just because you buried it. It just stayed low until something brought your guard down and you hadn't the energy to keep it in the darkness where all your demons lay.

He saw himself, yet again on that awful night in 1920. Hurrying into the Washington Palace hotel as Cormac Doyle came out like a man who hardly knew where he was going.

He had called Cormac by name and when Dee's brother turned, he hit him hard enough to drop him to the ground, leaving him there against the buttress of the hotel railings. Filled with dread, he stepped into the lobby of the run-down hotel.

The first thing he saw was the open door of Room 13 at the top of the stairs, and he knew as he bounded up and into the bedroom what he was going to find. He vomited as he saw Arthur and Lisa shot to death on the bed. His legs gave way for a moment and he involuntarily slumped to the floor, his hand knocking one of the brass knobs off the cast-iron bed frame. He threw a mumbled prayer to a god unknown – "May they rest in peace!" before he tried to get up. He was pushing his hands against the floor, but he couldn't make it. His hand touched something hard and cold and as he looked to see what it was, the door of the bathroom opened and a man came out fast, moving to a chair near the window. Sam saw that he was reaching for a gun sitting there in a holster. In that moment he found he was holding a revolver, and instinctively raised it as the officer started to spin around, arm outstretched.

His shot took the man in the forehead, sending blood and tissue splattering all over the window and the faded wallpaper, the body going backwards to hit the wall.

His adrenalin was now pumping so hard that he was on his feet before he knew it. He stuffed the revolver into his pocket, and moved to the bed. Poor Lisa, she had been shot in the face, unrecognisable was the only word for it. He gave one of her hands a pat.

"God love you," he said, as he heaved Arthur's body up off the bed and tossed it over his shoulder.

He could hear some movement up on the next floor as he came out onto the landing. "Stay in your rooms!" he yelled up the stairs. "This is the police. There's been a shooting!"

Coming out onto the street, he kicked Cormac to bring him around. Dee's brother shook himself and sat up and Sam yelled: "Cormac, bring the woman off the bed!" Cormac paused, puzzled, and Sam said with feeling. "You shot her, you stupid bastard! Now go and bring her down here, or I'll shoot you!"

He placed Arthur on the back seat of his car, covered him with a tartan rug, and closed the door. As he opened the boot of the car, Cormac arrived with Lisa, wrapped in a sheet. He helped him shove the body in and slammed the boot shut.

A few moments later, they drove away from the hotel. He was keen to get out of the city as quickly as possible, but he drove steadily to avoid attracting attention.

When they reached Blackrock, he had things worked out enough that he was able to tell Cormac what they had to do.

"The way it happened, nobody needs to know about that," he said, nudging him with his elbow. "Do you hear me, Cormac? Nobody needs to know what happened."

"I shot Arthur."

"Arthur was in the wrong place at the wrong time, and Lisa. We have the bodies, so nobody need ever know what happened. Now stop looking like you want to kill yourself, and tell me you're with me on this. Tell me you can understand what I'm saying to you."

"I failed in my mission. I didn't get the officer."

"He's very dead, so you got him, right? Only you and I know how it happened. The other thirteen of these very special English spies are gone for their tea, along with your man. Mission completed." He got a cigarette going, took a deep drag from it and passed it to Cormac. "Jesus knows the extent of the retribution it's going to bring down on our heads." He lit one for himself. "You shot him, Cormac. Tell me, say it." He inhaled deeply as he waited for confirmation from Dee's brother.

Cormac nodded but he needed more.

"Let me hear you say it. You have to say it, believe it, come to feel it, whatever it takes. We have to get our story straight and stick to it."

The young man exhaled a wall of smoke and then he said quietly, "I shot him."

Sam glanced sideways, saw him begin to relax, shrug off his melancholia, but not yet free of concern.

"Arthur was Dee's husband," said the boy. "What are we going to tell her?"

"Arthur got hit in a shooting on the street," Sam said firmly. "We only found him because we were looking for him all night. The pair of us spent hours looking for him. Have you got that?"

Cormac looked at him, no longer shaking in terror. "You're a cool customer."

"We found him on Sackville Street. That's close enough to Monto for Dee to buy it. Oh shit! I forgot about Faires, his driver. Where the hell was he?"

"He's one of us, Sam. He had a mission just like me. Knew Arthur wouldn't need him all night. He'll be over at Lisa's house now, looking for him."

"We tell Dee we found Arthur on Sackville Street, between Nelson's Pillar and the bridge on the east side. You OK with that?"

"Yeh." Cormac was subdued but he was back in control. "What about the body in the boot?"

"It's something I won't be showing around. We'll have to dump my old friend into some wet concrete. You and Brendan, get something fixed for tonight. I'll drive by when it's dark, and we'll give Lisa a midnight burial. The job the bullet did on her – she wouldn't want anybody to see her. And she knows I'm doing the best I can in the circumstances. She was a good girl, and I always loved her like a real pal should."

As they turned into the drive of Dunbla House, Cormac said, "You're probably right about reprisals. Lloyd George's piles could explode when he hears about this operation."

Despite all that had happened, Sam chuckled and punched Cormac in the arm. "You hold onto the sense of humour."

Cormac gave him a nod behind a look that told him the lad would be all right now.

"You're right there, about the Welsh Wizard's piles," Sam said. "But no matter how heavily they come down on us, the world is watching, and this will bring the Brits to the table. They'll sit down with Dev and Collins after this." He turned to look as he heard Dee come out of the house. "But do you know what, Cormac? I don't honestly know if we'll ever really be a republic, like we dream about when we're in our cups."

He took Dee in his arms as she turned from the sight of Arthur's body on the back seat of the car.

"We brought him home, Dee. We might be grateful he never knew what hit him."

She was weeping but she knew he was right. "God love him," she said, her tears touching Sam's neck.

"Paddy Lote will sign the death certificate and we can bury him here at Dunbla," Sam said quietly as he took her towards the house. "He's home for good, Dee."

"He loved the Pets' Cemetery," she said weeping. "We'll lay him to rest there, it's so peaceful and still. Can we do that, Sam?"

"We can do anything you want, Dee. You're the boss around here now."

Later on, as Sam and Cormac were about to take the body of Lisa O'Brien away to dump it into a bed of concrete on one of Sam's building sites, Dee had said no. "Lisa was the heroine of Arthur's heart – she mothered him when he was bereft – let her be with him in death. We'll bury them both here together."

Lost in the memory of that time Sam had no idea how long he sat on the rim of the land, his feet pointing at Killiney beach and the somnolent sea under the moon, wondering why the well-meant deed had turned so sour. Some rules of law were broken, yes, but nothing to deserve a yoke of such magnitude as a guilty-of-murder verdict would guarantee. He sighed, ditching his natural reserve to do anything wrong, vowing silently that no matter what it was going to take, he was going to do with all his might. This farce which could destroy all and everything that mattered to so many people, it had to be stopped.

Brendan's hand touching his shoulder and the quietly spoken words: "That part is done, Sam," drew a sigh of relief from him as he climbed to his feet with a helping hand from his protégé. As he welcomed the strength of the younger man he was wondering if this was what old age was like, a foreign land where every limb could ache at the same time.

"I'm sorry, Bren. I was back there somewhere."

Brendan squeezed his arm, the gesture assuring him all was well. "I was trying to cover whatever we might come up against. There's a trawler out of Wicklow that's skippered by a pal of ours, one of our own. He's sitting offshore now waiting for me to give him a light. When that happens we can haul the, eh, material down to the beach. He'll send in a couple of boats – just you and me row out there. When we go on board we go out a good few miles and drop the bits and pieces down deep. And they are all bits and pieces Sam, there's no way to dress that up. We do it this way, it'll mean the problem's been cleared up and you can rest easier. Does that sound okay to you?"

Sam nodded his head and embraced the man he had known from a youth. In the moment he knew that a threshold, some kind of Rubicon had been crossed. He had always avoided thoughts of the time when you, as a man, accepted that you were no longer *the man*. There, up on the rim of Dunbla, he not only accepted the inevitable, he found that he welcomed it, and he felt closer to Brendan than he had ever been to his blood son.

20

Summer 1924

Within a matter of days, the Pets' Cemetery at Dunbla had been returned to its original state, now giving a resting place to just the remains of dogs and cats that had died or been killed on the land. Of the bodies that had been removed there was no trace and when Brendan O'Connor and his team had added ready-made mature flowers and bushes to the grave area, the little burial place looked like what it had become: a private, quiet haven for the family pets.

The bodies of Arthur, Lisa, the young tinker girl and Dee's stillborn baby had been taken out to sea as Brendan had suggested. Much of the flesh was contained in netting so that fish could get at it – some parts had to be weighted with rocks before being dropped overboard into water more than a mile deep. Even as day came burgeoning before a splendid sun the skipper of the trawler spent some hours circling, taking time to be certain that nothing of the night's work could be seen.

It was as a result of that night's work that Sam invited his protégé to come down to Dunbla and spend a couple of days with him. Now that the first major step had been taken to neutralise Constance Brewer's assault, Sam wanted to sound out his thinking on other steps that might yet have to be taken.

When Brendan had freshened up and hung up his clothes, he and Sam took their first walk of the weekend.

Dee had been the first to welcome Brendan – they had made their peace and there was no need to speak again of the fact that he had gone over to the Anti-Treaty side in the Civil War.

"I hope it will be a nice break for you, Brendan," Sam told him the moment they were alone together. "A few days in the country while the good weather lasts. But, I have my own reasons for asking you down at this particular time."

Brendan looked quite the country gent in twill trousers under a Norfolk jacket and a soft check tweed hat.

"If the worst comes to the worst," he said by way of response, "we could kill Constance Brewer."

Sam looked at him askance. This really did hit him for six and he held his hands out in front of him in a defensive posture. "My God, don't even think such things!"

Brendan was imperturbable. "Are you saying you haven't given it a thought? Then what did you mean when you said there wasn't anything you wouldn't do to put Constance Brewer down?"

Sam was silent and lit a cigarette.

Brendan smiled. "Of course that's what you meant! After what we came through, the Uprising, The Tans, wiping out of the Spy Brits, the Civil War? And you, the risks you took in and out of the country buying arms – how could you not have looked at every possible way you might make this diabolical intrusion go away?"

"I have to go on believing that Constance is stalling out of pure badness. She hasn't a penny to her name – surely she has to take the offer when you consider the money involved."

"Right now you are in the clear about Arthur's death. You didn't shoot him, Cormac did. He told me that himself. But you covered it up, the same thing with Lisa, to save Deirdre as much pain as you could. Jesus, Sam, you could swing as accessary after the fact. And you know what, while you were buying arms, risking your life, doing all you did for Mick Collins, Constance Brewer was eating caviar. Some people might well think she deserves shooting, including me."

They walked on, Sam stunned that Brendan's committed involvement in the IRA had brutalised the Dubliner to such a degree that he could talk calmly about the violence he would so willingly inflict upon the dowager of Eaton Square.

Revulsion arose in his throat then, his shock having turned to horror as his power to rationalise deserted him. "For God's sake, Brendan, bitch though she is, Constance is an old woman."

He found it difficult to speak further and Brendan said, "So what can I do then? I know you don't care about the money, Deirdre or you. I know Dee would die before she'd risk Eddie being exposed to the scandal. And I'm sorry to sound so diabolical. Just tell me what you need. I'll do anything it takes, Sam, to make sure Constance backs off."

Sam held a match to Brendan's cigarette, clamping down on his need to express vehement objection to the horror picture the Dubliner had presented to him just minutes before. But he decided to let it pass. Brendan might acquiesce, accept that such thinking was way out of bounds, but it would just be behaviour. He was as he was, had had to be so when sending others out to kill and be killed. Like it or not, the dogs of war remained bedded down in the minds of men long after they had hung up their weapons and put their uniforms aside for all time.

"Don't think I don't appreciate what you're saying, Bren," he said, 'but right now we have to wait, give Constance the time to rub our noses in it, hoping she will, before too long, revert to type, take the money and run."

Cormac Doyle was completely at a loss, his face quivering, tears sitting on his eyelids, his breathing a laborious thing. "You said you loved me."

Kitty stood, her feet wide apart, anger adding dark pinpricks to her amber eyes. "Shut up the poor mouth for Jesus' sake! I meant what I said, but that doesn't mean I'm going to take off from here, my own place, my studio where I do the work that's more important to me than any man could ever be."

"I have to get out. That's my only hope. If you meant what you said you'd be right behind me on this." Cormac was upset so badly that he couldn't hear the fear riding high on his voice.

Kitty sat down to discover she was out of cigarettes. She took a deep breath, willing herself to hold her temper, and then she said quietly: "You yell at me once more and you can take off out of here right now and don't ever bother coming back." She didn't even glance at him as she spoke.

He fell to his knees, almost sobbing. "I'm sorry, sorry we're having this row. I can't think straight." He rose quickly as though forced by some inner urgency. "I can't stay here and I can't go without you. You've given me back the life pumped out of me when Gráinne topped herself."

Kitty said quietly: "It always comes back to *you*, doesn't it? Jesus, you're such a child." She stood up impatiently. "I'm going for a walk. I need to be free of all this emotional shit."

"Oh God! I can't even take a walk with you since they saw me in Baggot Street last week!"

Kitty was slipping on an old light raincoat that hardly complemented her bohemian skirt, olive green blouse, her bangles and her earrings. She didn't notice or if she did, she didn't care. "I meant what I said about loving you. That doesn't mean I couldn't get by if you left me. I don't want to own you any more than I will be owned. I feel intensely about you even when I don't like you, like this minute." Then she was gone down the stairs, the front door banging behind her as she took off.

He sat there helplessly, his guts scrunched up in the fear that he had driven her away from him. He drew his knees to his chest and rocked forward and back holding down the cries torturing him. With a sob he looked up and said savagely: "It's you, isn't it? You're paying me back. Gráinne took her own life 'cos I wouldn't marry her, and you're blaming me, punishing me for that!" His shoulders slumped and he fell sideways on the chaise longue, his knees coming up into the foetal position.

Sam and Brendan O'Connor walked down to the Dunbla Tavern on the Saturday evening of the Dub's few days in the countryside. In the afternoon, they had gone up to the Pets' Cemetery to check out how the mature plants and young trees were working into the soil. The place was alive with colour, the edges masked by the hardy privets Arthur had planted when he first bought the house.

Going down the hill to the pub, Sam felt easy enough to cast a nod of gratitude to a god unknown. He was delighted that Brendan was by his side – the help he'd been given to hurdle the first major fence in the convoluted dilemma that remained staring him in the face, he would never forget. The regular workmen – part of Brendan's own commercial mobile building unit – had returned and were working on the tennis courts. The Volunteers had left on the night, as unnoticed as when they had arrived. Sam had insisted that money change hands, knowing that no amount could pay for the removal of the weighted rusting glove that had been wrapped around his heart, choking off so much of the energy he needed as the skirmishes with Constance pointed inevitably to a battle royal.

Brendan took the money on behalf of the others, and no more was said about it. Now in the autumn-like evening, he was more than ready for a few pints of Brewer's, while Sam – though concerned that Dee was again going to be at the Clinic all night – felt that two or three cognacs would do him no harm at all.

"Tell me that again," the Dubliner said as they strode from the house along the broken road toward the tavern.

"I believe I'll go to India," Sam said, wondering if he really would take off for a while when the threat of Constance was no longer on his plate.

"And this is because you read a little book by some Indian you met in London? Have I got that right?"

"You certainly have," Sam said, pleased he wasn't boring Brendan to the point where he'd gone deaf. "I read his book and it showed me that so many things that have arisen in me, in the past few years, are but the tip of the iceberg when it comes to the truth."

"How do you mean 'the truth', Sam?" Brendan didn't wait for an answer: "Like if you say trees have leaves, that's the truth, isn't it? Do you mean that kind of thing?"

"That trees have leaves is true, Bren, but it's not the truth."

"Y'see, that's exactly the kind of double talk that pisses me off about these religions and philosophies and whatever they're called. They have an answer for everything. Like if it's good, God made it happen, but when you get floods or famine, that's not God's fault, that's nature throwing the head!"

In May Murray's public house, Sam noticed the small changes that went along with the new name. The Dunbla Tavern boasted a short bar counter complete with foot-rail. This was set between the fireplace and the front window to one side of the door – shelving had been added to a backing panel fixed to the wall, bottles sat on the shelves, leaving enough room left for May to work the bar without having to step outside.

As he paid for their drinks, Sam saw Pack Rowan come in from the back of the house with an armful of large logs – evenly cut he noticed – to place them down at the hearth before throwing several into the healthy flames.

Rowan was wearing dungarees, his shirtsleeves rolled up to reveal arms that looked as strong as steel hawsers. He returned several times with more firewood before he accepted the pint May put up for him and made his way through the front door to have his drink in the only place allowed to him – outside.

After they had renewed their drinks, Sam asked Brendan to join him outside, the bar-kitchen being full enough and noisy enough to make anything like normal conversation difficult.

The evening was retreating before the onset of darkness but Sam had no trouble seeing Rowan who stood alone off to one side from the front door. "Give me a minute, Bren," he said quietly: "I need to test the water."

Pack Rowan affected surprise as Sam arrived with a cheery: "Good evening to you, Mister Rowan. I was wondering if I might exchange a few words with you."

Rowan responded affably: "Of a certain, Mister Sweet. What can I do for you?"

"I was wondering if you have had any indication from Constance Brewer as to whether she intends to accept the generous offer I made to her on the day I met you at her home on Eaton Square?"

Sam had decided to come straight out with it, ask for what he wanted, instead of playing games. He felt certain that Pack Rowan's eyes narrowed some but the diminishing evening light might have been playing tricks on him.

Rowan sipped his pint, his eyes sliding onto Sam's face. "I've heard nothing up to the moment. Not that there's any reason the old woman should be telling me anything. I've nothing to do with your goings-on – that's between herself and the Brewer estate, Mister Sweet."

Sam remained true to his original approach: "I have a deal of respect for you, Mister Rowan – like myself, you're a man's pulled himself up from the lower end of things – no silver spoon for you, and let me say that at this moment I carry no ill intent in my enquiry."

Opening his cigarette case he held it out and Pack Rowan helped himself. "I'll be very direct. I know the part you and May Murray have played and are playing in this little drama. I know that May stole journals belonging to my ex-wife and that the pair of you colluded with Constance Brewer in the kind of blackmail it's hard to nail down."

"Now hold on, sir," Rowan protested quietly.

Sam cut him off: "Please, hear me out. At this time I'm unconcerned about the possible rights and wrongs here. Truly, I don't give a damn about any of that. I'm only interested in having the very generous offer I made accepted so that we can get this whole mess cleared up." He allowed a moment or two for this to land. "I mean it. The money involved is considerable, some people would say huge. The offer has been on the table for a month." He smoked and exhaled: "Unless Constance Brewer is so eaten up with hatred that she is willing to risk all – she has to be of diminished responsibility to you, as her partner in this affair, should she decline the offer. I'm speaking to you now, man to man. You do understand I am not interested in bringing any of this to the attention of the police. I simply want a boy called Eddie Brewer to get on with growing up without his world being torn apart by the stigma of the word 'bastard'."

Sam spoke in a very deliberate fashion about the son Rowan had sired with the tinker girl that had died in the arms of his mother, and he saw him blink a couple of times to cover the reaction in his eyes

The tinker smoked and exhaled, before slowly turning his eyes back to Sam: "Not that I admit to being involved, Mister Sweet, but what sort of money are we talking about? The offer like?"

"At a very conservative estimate, Mister Rowan, we are talking about twenty-five to thirty million sterling." Sam let the figures roll off his tongue as though they were heaven-sent. "That sum would grow over the years, the offer being that Constance and her partners would own fifty per cent of all things Brewer from the moment the contract has been signed, sealed and delivered."

Sam had meant it earlier when he had openly admired the travelling man's development in a society that didn't care that much about people who slept by ditches, many living and dying without ever knowing a fixed abode of any kind. Now he saw the immense quality of Rowan's steely nature.

To mention such an enormous sum of money at a time when a first-class blacksmith might earn a pound or slightly more in a good week – Sam was trying to think as Rowan might well have been doing in that moment – had to be akin to the man who had known no miracles in his life hearing of the opening of the Red Sea and taking it literally. Very simply, it had to evoke an experience that might well interfere with the shape of his mind.

Rowan didn't even blink, used a moment or two to grind the cigarette butt under his boot, and said in his usual steady baritone: "Anybody turning down such an offer would have to be tuppence short of a shillin', Mister Sweet."

"Being blunt, I felt you hadn't been advised of the offer. Since you and May Murray instigated the situation, it seemed to me that you should have been the first to hear what was on the table from the old woman of Eaton Square."

"I wondered why she asked me to leave that day." He shook his head. "I didn't hear there'd been an offer.

334

like. I can't even imagine as I stand here before you how anybody could do anything but jump at the money you just mentioned to me."

"All right," Sam said conspiratorially. "It's none of my business how much of that sum would come your way, but you are entitled to know what's there. Now, do you think you can light some little fire under Constance? She hates me, my wife, all things Brewer. That doesn't entitle her to cheat you and your partner out of your share of a considerable fortune."

"I say fair play to you for telling me, Mister Sweet."

"In truth, I have no feeling about it one way or the other. I simply regarded it as mutually good for both of us. I just want the damn business over and done with. All I want is to protect the children from possible exposure to this kind of scandal." He stopped before he continued: "An innocent young man's life – the life of *your son* if you are telling the truth – could be ruined and for what? So, Mister Rowan, man to man, will you shake my hand on an agreement to go and talk some common sense into Constance Brewer?"

Pack Rowan extended his hand and Sam shook it. "You can leave the witch to me, Mister Sweet."

Sam nodded his head and then he said in a quiet voice: "One thing having nothing to do with the other – I know who you are – I know your mother and I wouldn't want anything to happen to her."

"Why would anything happen to her, Mister Sweet?" He now displayed a mask that allowed the world see his cunning nature, without giving it enough to accuse him of the same.

Sam smiled. "You're a gifted man. I hope you get your share of the money. That being said, you could throw it all away should you keep your word to kill Kelly because she informed on you to the police a long time ago."

Pack Rowan smiled as though he didn't quite understand. "This is all blather, Mister Sweet. I'd never touch a hair on the old woman's head. You have my word on that."

"I hope so, Pack, because should you commit that dreadful sin, I promise you – and like you, I have been to many hard places in this life – I give you my word that you won't walk away from it scot-free."

"Mister Sweet, you've just given me the best reason I ever had in this life to stay out of bother. Surely you don't imagine for a minute I'm going to jeopardise getting my hands on my share of a fortune? If I harboured any anger to the mother, the thoughts of the life I can have with all that money has cut it out of my memory, and that's my promise to you."

"I'm very glad to hear it, for truly I wish you well. So, I take it you'll be paying a visit to the old woman of Eaton Square?"

"You can bet good money on it, Mister Sweet. I'll be ringing her doorbell hours after I get off the ferry. And I'll make it my business to let you know how I get on."

He offered his hand in an agreeable manner and Sam shook it. Bidding the big tinker man a good night then, he returned to Brendan at the bar.

"Went okay?"

"Yes," Sam said. "He's a remarkable fellow for a

tinker. And I really believe he is the key to this deal being completed in the very near future."

"Fair enough," Brendan pressed a glass of cognac into Sam's hand. "I hope it keeps fine for you. But listen Sam, he's a tinker, a knacker, and to him you're like a Boer to a black South African, and don't you forget it."

Sam sipped brandy, refusing to allow Brendan's prejudice to interfere with his hopeful mood.

True to the promise made to Sam Sweet two nights previously at the Dunbla Tavern, Pack Rowan was standing at the front door of the Eaton Square house when the butler, Johnstone, opened it.

"Good afternoon, sir. I'm not at all sure that madam is at home." He spoke with more than a hint of courteous regard, having no desire to annoy any man that towered over him.

Pack Rowan smiled and stepped forward with serious intent. Johnstone, who had learned the art of survival during several incarcerations at the expense of the government, moved adroitly aside, while Pack closed the hall door.

"You go and fix me a drink of strong tea like a good man. I'll slip you a fiver on the way out. And have no fear of the oul' one. I'll tell her you tried to stop me."

Without taking his eyes off Rowan, the slender man in his black frock coat moved away and Pack went to the drawing-room door, turned the handle and walked in as though he owned the place.

Constance, drinking from a balloon of cognac, felt

startled for a moment, but recovered in an instant before bringing the glass away from her face.

"I've not been exposed to such bad manners before from you, Pack Rowan. What the hell do you think you are doing?" She waxed like somebody that was furious, but her ardour waned when she saw that he had no time for polite behaviour or the lack of it.

"You've been a very bold woman, Constance."

"Constance? Constance?" she stuttered, hardly able to believe her ears. "How dare you, Pack Rowan! Have you lost your reason?"

He came to within three feet of where she sat and he stood there like someone restraining a very violent urge. Constance Brewer knew enough about survival to be terrified and she did not have to wait long to know why the big man was so furious.

"You have been sitting on an offer from the Brewer estate, an offer worth anything between twenty-five and thirty million, and you could not be bothered to tell me about this."

She could see that he was dangerously angry and as his breathing became more audible, she looked at him with all the guile she could muster. "Come now, Pack. I thought we had agreed that I would handle that end of things." She attempted to smile but found her lips uncooperative due to the fear that had almost frozen her face.

"You are either so vicious that you cannot get off your own hook, or you are insane. The offer is beyond worthwhile, beyond dreams. It is wonderful, and I tell you now that you are going to accept it, and you are going to pay me my fifty per cent, or I swear to you, old woman, you will die a very slow and painful death, and that is my promise to you. Do you understand what I'm telling you?"

Constance felt frozen all over. She tried to reach for her brandy on the table near her hand but her movement was so limited in the moment that she gave up. Rowan put a cigarette between his lips and began to slowly draw smoke into his lungs. He pulled up a chair and sat down, averting his eyes from Constance to allow them to wander over the drawing room and its contents.

His only previous encounters with rooms such as this drawing room in Eaton Square, London, had been in several great country houses in the Irish countryside, palaces owned by men that lived in London and elsewhere. He had sat on Chippendale chairs more than once, not knowing what they were called until later when he found pictures in books that reminded him of this or that burglary. He had lounged before a marble fire surround before, the fire lit by himself in the dark of night and the place empty but for him. And he had seen all the paintings an eye could wish to see with frames he had broken up for firewood. He had burned paintings too, his way to relieve the anger he felt at being forced to live a million miles away from such luxury.

He had ached for a taste of this, this being the norm to the people living in such magnificent homes, that is, when they weren't living in one of the other lovely houses they had dotted around the globe.

"I was not hiding news of the offer from you," Constance said firmly. She was finally capable of reaching for her brandy glass and she was now working on him, knowing she had better convince him of her loyalty to their partnership or she might not live to gain the victory she wanted more than anything ever before in her long life.

"You knew about it four weeks ago and you have been sitting on it ever since. We are partners and if you forget that again, your life will come to an end." Simmering with barely controlled rage, he said with an intensity that terrified her: "Hear me well, Constance. I have killed men over trivial things that seemed important in the heat of drunken argument. I will not hesitate to snap your neck if you deny me my share of a fortune by being a damn fool."

"I can't see that a few weeks should make any difference," she lied. "The offer is still there – it has not run away."

"Enough of this," He yelled so wildly that some of his spit landed on the old woman's face. He stood up from his chair and made it his business to tower over her, to kill any resistance she might yet be harbouring. "You hate with such power that you couldn't accept the offer. You no longer have the privilege of refusal at your disposal."

"I resent you talking to me as though we are equals." This retort was not quite how she would have chosen to admonish him for daring to talk to her in such a way, but she was so terrified that she hardly knew what she was saying.

"Don't bother with your high horse for me, ma'am. You were bloody glad to have me as your equal partner when I brought you the chance to get your hands on wealth you never tasted before. Not even you. Well off as you were, I know for a fact that your husband never gave you any real money." Seeing how she was looking at him askance, he chuckled. "Are you really surprised that I know all about you, Constance Brewer? I used part of the twenty thousand you gave me against my fifty per cent of whatever money came out of this golden opportunity that I brought into this room. I laid out money to find out all about you. I even know you were an alternative young thing before you left Ellen Dorning to marry the Brewer money."

She didn't say anything, and he stood closer still as he said quietly: "I am right, am I not? You gave me twenty thousand against fifty per cent?"

Constance nodded her head though it killed her to do so. But she went through with this farce, knowing that she would die before this reprobate would get his hands on fifty per cent of anything.

"Not good enough, old woman. Let me hear you say it." He stood, his foot starting to tap gently on the Persian rug under his boot.

"I gave you twenty thousand pounds against fifty per cent of whatever money comes out of the court case."

"You need to correct that, Constance Brewer. Just leave out the bit about the court case – there isn't going to be any court case."

"But –"

"Stop there." His huge hand was by her face, his index finger like a weapon close to her skin. "What is it you English say? 'But me no buts and uncle me no uncle'? Have I got that right, Constance Brewer?"

She could almost taste him he was so close and she used her smelling salts to stop herself from passing out. The heat coming from his body, the way his strength seemed to permeate the air about her, all of it made her feel that she was going to throw up unless he moved away.

Sensing her obvious discomfort, smiling at the power he had used to induce it, Pack Rowan stepped back and away from her and stood with his back to the fire. He held her gaze which she could not, not for the life of her, break off.

"As I have said, I know all about you, Constance Brewer – I know about your lesbian marriage – how you abandoned your lover, your wife, because you were chosen by Arthur Shane Brewer to be the mother of his children. I know that your partner took her own life because you deserted her."

There was a knock on the door and Constance managed to find enough voice to say "Enter!".

Johnstone had arranged a tray set for two. He placed this on an occasional table some way from the fire. Pack smiled warmly as the little man left as silently as he had arrived. Rowan loved the way he could get what he wanted simply by telling people what to do – no need for them to say a word, but simply do what they were told, and all would be well.

He noticed that the little butler had ignored the eyes of his mistress and hurriedly left the drawing room, stepping all over the servant ritual by going out of the room without waiting to be dismissed by madam.

Pack Rowan poured tea for two and brought a cup to Constance – one spoon of brown sugar and a slice of lemon – fixing his own with three sugars and a dollop of milk. As he stood sipping the tea, his eyes remained fixed on her.

"Just in case you have any doubt about accepting the offer, let me tell you what will happen to you. I will take you up to your bedroom, and I will rip every stitch from your body, and I will pound your bones until your heart explodes. If you linger beyond what time I can afford, I will take these two," he held up the thumb and forefinger of his right hand, "and I will slowly squeeze the life out of you. Do you understand how important it is to me that you sign the agreement immediately, Constance?"

Fighting for breath, her veins crawling with disgust, and simply unable to stand it any longer, Constance said: "Yes, yes, all right, all right, I will call Sir Albert Whimby and tell him to accept the bloody offer! Now, I hope you are satisfied." She was shaking so much that some of the tea spilled onto her silk dress, burning her leg and causing her to cry out in fury as she hurled the cup and saucer away from her.

"You hope I am satisfied." Pack Rowan shook his head. "I won't be satisfied until I know the ink has dried on the deal and you show me the figures on your bank statement just before you hand me a certified cheque for half of the total amount."

She sat still and he went and poured her another cup of tea. When he brought it to her she took it with a gentle "Thank you".

He said: "Just let me hear you repeat that part, about the cheque to me for half of the total amount."

This time she wanted to throw the hot tea in his face but instead she looked up at Pack Rowan with a smile. The smile was enough to turn his stomach but he held her mucus-lined eyes. "I will give you a certified cheque for half of the total amount received from the Brewer estate. Does that satisfy you?"

Pack nodded and smiled: "It'll do for now. But again, when I have the cheque, the certified cheque, then and only then, will I be satisfied."

She saw how pleased he was with himself and it put her mind on edge. She sipped the tea in case he saw in her face evidence of her decision to see him dead at her feet before she gave him another penny.

"Now," he said as though he owned her, "call Johnstone in and tell him which room he's to make ready."

Constance brought her head up so quickly that she hurt her neck. "What? Make ready for what?"

"Stop playing the fool! You're going to annoy me again? Not a good idea. Tell Johnstone to show me to my room."

"But that's preposterous. You can't stay here. I'm not having . . ." Her voice trailed off as she saw him pick up a Ming vase she had been planning to sell to finance her desperate need to play roulette.

Before she could even cry out in despair, Pack Rowan let the vase slip from his hand. The small cry Constance made was muted by her realisation of the power he had over her, even as he bent quickly at the knees and caught the vase in his other hand. Smiling at her, he placed it back where it belonged and said agreeably, "Now be a good woman and tell the butler to show me to my room."

"How long do you intend to stay?" Constance wanted to bite her tongue. Tacit in the question was her admission of his power over her.

"Till we get the deal done, Constance, then I'll be gone with the wind and you won't ever see me again."

Johnstone accepted the instructions from madam without the blink of an eye or the slightest change in expression. As he left the room, Pack lit a cigarette and when he offered one to Constance, to his surprise she accepted. He poured a cognac for each of them and though her mouth was a pencil line under her nose, she nodded her head and downed her drink, clearly for medicinal purposes.

"You have experience of such matters as this one." Pack was sitting comfortably, like a man just beginning to taste the wonderful result of his labour. "So how long would you say before we are splitting a very large cheque?"

"It will take ten days at least for all the paper work – when the principals have signed, another week – so two to three weeks in all."

Pack smiled and sipped his cognac: "That'll suit me just grand, so it will. Gives me time to clear up a number of outstanding things. Then it's the high life for me till the day the heels go first."

21

October 1923

Sam Sweet tried hard to curb his exasperation as Deirdre, turning away in tearful despair, said: "I'm only saddened that you felt you had to talk to that man. My God, he's a monster – he and that woman running the pub – they were willing to have Eddie destroyed."

Sam, tempted to go and comfort her, knew this wasn't the time. Quietly he said, "The law – the legal profession – to its core operates on making deals, Dee. Civil Court is always the last straw. I thought this was the best way to bring this outrageous criminal imposition to a conclusion."

Dee turned back, wiping her nose: "I know you meant well, and I hope that what you went through will not have been wasted."

"All Rowan is interested in is sterling. Unlike Constance who is so hate-filled she would jeopardise her chance of getting the money for the pleasure of bringing you and your family into disrepute."

"It's you I'm worried about, Sam."

Sam wasn't listening. He continued talking, still having difficulty in not allowing his temper to get the better of him. "So hate-filled that she feels nothing but contempt for all of us, even Eddie, a wonderful boy anybody would be proud to call son. But Dee, if that were to happen, if she got her day in court, that would merely be the beginning of a whole new nightmare. I'm sure you remember this, but so that you understand why you sometimes have to lie down with dogs, I urge you listen to me. You and I, and others even more innocent than we are – all could be before the Criminal Courts on such charges that would make our blood turn to ice in our veins. Dee, I have done the best I could in this matter. I admit to being caught by the power of that old woman's will to destroy – my God, someone actually offered to take her life to stop her, and I can only say thank God I was capable of turning them down. Up to that moment, it seems to me now, I felt there was so much for this family to lose that I believed deep down that Constance should die, that she should be killed."

Deirdre stood looking at him, her face masked in disbelief.

He, in an effort to placate the horror that possessed her in that moment, said: "I have been under great pressure, Dee, and feel I will be until I hear that the deal is a done deal."

"It's not fair of me to judge you, Sam, I'm sorry for the fact that I have been doing that. After all, who was it said to you 'Deal with it for both of us, for all of us'? I walked away and left you to deal with that she-devil."

Deirdre walked over to the drinks table and poured brandy for Sam.

He accepted it, waiting while she attended to her own drink, expecting that she would raise it, that they would share an unspoken toast, but Dee simply sipped the brandy and lit a cigarette. Sam felt a dart of pain go through him – that they were so far apart shocked him, one of their more meaningful private rituals being that they would always be totally open and honest with each other. This was now apparently forgotten as she shut him out of this ordinary small moment that in fact loomed suddenly like a huge block between them.

Dee was silent because she was simply stuck for words. Her mind felt bruised, but not only by Sam's admission of collusion with Rowan who was a criminal. Her concern had more to do with her inability to realise that his involvement in the revolutionary movement had brutalised him to the degree that he could harbour for even a second the idea of somehow causing the death of Constance, though she herself now faced the memory of having vowed to her morning mirror: "I could willingly kill that bloody woman!" Of course she had not meant it in the literal sense but had to admit that she had been forced outside the borders of what she deemed to be normal behaviour by her need to protect her family and the people whose lives might be torn asunder should Arthur's mother get her day in court.

She heard Sam say, his voice sounding like that of someone talking to himself as though he was getting his thinking in order, "I chose to see Pack Rowan as an ally

– he has been poor all his life – yes, he is a criminal and I held out the money like a carrot, knowing that he had real power where Constance is concerned. Truly, good or bad, he is a powerful man. I got him on our side – he will bring Constance to heel – we will be able to put all this behind us and get on with our lives the same as before."

Deirdre was shaking her head and Sam went to her and tried to put his arms about her to comfort them both. She held his arms apart, resisting his embrace and he felt shocked. "You're wrong, Sam. It will never be the same as before. That's what frightens me so much."

"Dee, that's not fair," Sam's protest was cut short, Dee stopping him by holding her hands palms up towards him. "I'm not blaming you, Sam. My God, I have to accept responsibility for my own behaviour. It was I that left it all to you because I had my life pictured as I wanted it to be – you, the family, the Clinic, all neatly lined up in order – I'm sorry for being so precious, so thoughtless. I felt horror, nothing less, when you spoke of wanting Constance dead. My God, I yelled something similar to myself in the mirror one morning!" Dee stopped and downed her brandy. "I've been thinking of how your work with Michael Collins – the work we did together as we bought arms – I thought of how that must have brutalised you for you to be able to even think like that."

As Dee paused to light another cigarette, Sam had a memory flash of himself shooting the British officer in the Washington Hotel, something he had done without a thought, and he felt silent inside as Dee went on speaking.

"I left you at the very coalface of this dreadful situation while I could yell the same thought to myself in the bathroom mirror." Tears slipped from her eyes but she sniffed and continued speaking, "I am so sorry, Sam, horrified that you arrived at such a pass and equally appalled that the same thing happened to me only in a more *respectable* way. You see what I mean? I got caught by the awfulness of our predicament just as you did, only I blotted it out by obsessing on the Clinic, leaving you in the firing line but expecting you to behave like the nice man that you are even when others were making up new, dastardly rules as they went along."

She turned away, sobbing once more. About to touch her shoulders, Sam pulled back and left the room.

Going into his study, he went to his desk and sat down. Ignoring the fact that his breathing was a bit distorted still, he found he had let go of the antipathy he felt towards the wife he loved so much. Lighting a cigarette he found the little book that Gopal had put into his hand on Piccadilly. His mind was racing. He had tried to excuse the words "I believed deep down that Constance should die, that she should be killed" which had shocked Dee to the core.

Sitting at the desk, drawing smoke in as deeply as he could, he knew he had meant every word. He had distanced himself from the words for Dee's sake, and wanted to mean the denial, but he didn't. He did accept there was no going back to the other side of the night he shot the British Secret Agent with Cormac Doyle's IRA issue revolver.

He poured a brandy, drank it down, accepting that much as he would wish it, he was not the same man who had run up the stairs in that awful flophouse intent only on bringing Arthur home safe and sound.

Fingering Gopal's book, using the sense of touch to come into the present moment, he poured another brandy. But he had to go back to that room in his mind. He had to see if there was any way for Sam Sweet, builder and entrepreneur, to turn back his inner clock. Was it even remotely possible that he might emerge without feeling so tarnished by that night's happening? Could he feel clean again and not be shattered as he was by Dee's horror that he could go and lie down with a dog like Pack Rowan? These thoughts now invaded his mind so that even though he tried the sense of touch defence against them, he failed. His defence that he wanted nothing for himself, that he put aside his overall worth as a human being, in order to beat Constance Brewer, turned rancid in his mouth.

He didn't even dislike the bloody woman. All he sought was the most expedient route to force her to let go of her madness. All he wanted was that she accepted the deal so that they could all go home. In this way he tried to fight the feeling that he was invaded by the fleas that live hidden behind the everyday coat of all animals, including man.

When Sam left Dunbla for London he did so with a heavy heart. This was the first time he and Deirdre had parted with even a hint of distance lying between them.

His sadness, he accepted, was due in part to his sentimental nature, but he knew there was more to it than that. On the ferryboat from Dublin's North Wall, he settled down in a corner of the lounge and began catching up on his journal. The bar would not open for another half hour or so – he opened the book and unscrewed his fountain pen, settling for a cigarette until he could have a brandy or two.

Under the dateline, *October 7th 1923*, he began to write.

'I've not stopped trying to make allowances for Dee coming home from her Clinic days in ragged order, more often than not. Her vocation – indeed her devotion – is without doubt a demanding one – but she is a steadfast woman, the finest I have known. If anything, she has become even more of a firebrand than she was that day in Poole Street at the beginning of her journey through Dublin's slums.

'That day I could have killed a man – God, I'd forgotten how tumultuous my heart was as I faced this huge lout in that stinking tenement room. As I write these words I am stunned that I could have forgotten those moments with my heart shuddering under a fierce desire to take his life. This was the same feeling I knew when I talked about the idea of stopping Constance Brewer no matter what the cost. I was not thinking of actually killing the sad old woman but I have to admit that the same demanding passion, providing the familiar taste of bitter almonds to my tongue came with its shame riding on its coat tails.

'I had to be very hard on that young man who had exposed himself to Deirdre who was there in that stinking tenement room to take his woman – to the Brewer family home in

Merrion Square, as it turned out – that she might deliver her child, due at any time, in a clean and warm situation where the infant was less likely to contact any one of a number of diseases. This lout not only refused to let his young woman leave the hovel they shared, he exposed his penis to Dee who had to run from the room for fear of being raped even as I came up the stairs to check that she was safe .

'He was a big man but I hurt him badly. I'm ashamed to say I had a need that he fight back, that he give me further excuse to beat him to a pulp. Right now I am hot, beginning to sweat as I swallow the bile that came with the package. It never occurred to me that he needed help as much as his young woman – he was lost as I vented my spleen and wished him to give me good cause to inflict more injury upon him.

'Deirdre was proud of me back then – her father had been quite a hard man – earning his early living as a jarvey he had to deal with all kinds of customers, and he did so in the currency of the streets as I had done often enough as I fought to hold onto my hard-earned pennies. So she was no stranger to the notion of violence, but, God, how stupid can a man be? To have mentioned the wish that Constance be dead! I had overstepped the bounds of what was allowable in her mind – had trodden all over her idea of reasonable behaviour in hobnailed boots.

'In this moment it seems, if not childish, certainly immature, to be so concerned about the division between Dee and me. She is working too hard – her youngest brother is wanted by the police – her mother is slowly dying – and we have this diabolical intrusion into our lives by an old woman so full of hatred that she is a health risk to those that have to stand near her. For myself, I am admittedly impatient to have the matter over and done with. In my heart I believe I did the right thing in talking with Rowan – it's easier to deal with someone wanting money than with one wanting to wreak havoc in the name of revenge. But just because one feels that one did the right thing – talking to Rowan man to man – one has no right to expect universal acceptance of that stance. I now accept this and allow Dee her position without any further wish to make a song and a dance of it.

'Ah, I see the bar is opening. Time for a cognac or two to help me prepare for my trip to Ramsgate. I hope the return of my son and his mother after their sojourn in Turkey will work out as expected.

'Meanwhile I must live with how I am, for the present at any rate. The more I read and reread the little book that Gopal gave me, the more I realise that I am standing still and not necessarily in the light. I want more – even the desire 'I want more' is part of the dream I deem to be real. For now I must press on with all the skill I have developed as a fully involved player in this game of life. I have to deal with things that demand action and perhaps ruthless action – what we had to do when we took the bodies from the Pets' Cemetery – my God, it doesn't bear thinking about. So, please God, let this next few weeks be the foray to the final furlong of this race to keep the lid on things best buried for all time.

Pack Rowan was chuckling to himself as he sat on the train taking him to Ramsgate. By his side, Walter Guildford gave him a curious glance which the tinker noticed. Since he was practically tingling with elation – this elevated state had been dancing through his veins from the moment he knew that the settlement with the

Brewer lot was imminent – he felt he had to let
Guildford in on the source of his amusement.

"I keep remembering Constance Brewer's face when
I told her I was going out of town for a couple of days.
She looked like her piles and all her other ailments'd
gone flyin' out the winda."

Walter smoked his cigarette without comment. He
wasn't happy about making the journey, not at all
comfortable with involvement in anything that was
likely to turn violent. Pack had assured him this was
just a fun run – an exercise to give their quarry an
unhappy time before Pack returned to pay him back for
the death of The Vicar.

"All very well – *just an exercise*," Walter knew he
was moaning but he didn't care. "So why have we got
a couple of Soho's most notorious leg-breakers sitting a
couple of seats back up the carriage?"

"You'll see when we get there. Now shut yer cakehole,
quit moanin' or I'll throw you out the winda." Rowan
affected his half-joking, whole-in-earnest demeanour
which, from experience Walter Guildford knew could
turn all too real in the blink of an eye.

He took Rowan's advice and closed his eyes. The last
thing he wanted to do was annoy the Irishman. Pack was
so close to the big money you could taste the sensation
coming off him, and since Walter also knew that Pack
gave you what he promised you, he was looking forward
to a serious windfall in the very near future.

Constance Brewer allowed Johnstone to feel the full

force of her impatience as he faced her in her bedroom at noon on the same day. "What do you mean? They haven't been back to you? You said you knew the right people for this particular commission."

"As per your request, madam, I went and talked to some acquaintances from my previous life. They put me in touch with a certain individual. I made him a proposal. He was interested but said that he would want two thousand for the job."

He was perspiring and trying hard not to look at his employer. The old woman had woken up just a quarter of an hour earlier – minus even the slightest toilette, she looked like a ragged old canvas painting of a very bitter matriarch who hated all that she could see. The telephone rang and she waited while he lifted the instrument.

"Brewer residence. Yes. Oh! Oh yes, hello, this is Mister Johnstone. Yes, ehm, I see. All right. Yes. Please, please hold on a moment." Looking somewhat relieved, the butler placed his hand over the instrument before turning back to face Constance.

"Madam, this is the party I was talking about. He finds he can take the job on – he wants me to go to him this afternoon with the agreed fee, two thousand pounds, after which he will carry out the job within two to three days."

Constance gave Johnstone an old-fashioned look. "He expects the full fee up front? Does he take me for a moron?"

The butler demurred: "Madam, trust me, you are not in a position to bargain. This man is a law unto himself – he is willing to take this on because of my connections – to be blunt, he is not stuck for work." He spoke again quickly into the phone: "Do bear with me a further moment, sir – I am having some trouble connecting with the other party. Thank you for your courtesy."

Constance snorted derisively while Johnstone stood like a statue, his hand covering the mouthpiece of the telephone. "This would be the best connection I could ever have made for you in this area, madam," he said, his rising colour confirming the extent of his embarrassment.

"Oh very well," Constance snorted in disgust: "Say yes, you'll take the money to him."

"Are you absolutely certain this is what you wish me to do, madam?" Johnstone could not hide his doubts now that the irrevocable step was about to be taken.

"Just get on with it." She shook her head, mumbling, "If I pay him the full fee, how can I be sure he will deliver?"

The butler was appalled: "Madam, this man has a business, a reputation. If he was not a man of his word, he would be unemployed within a week. He guarantees satisfaction."

Constance threw her hands up in annoyance and he spoke into the telephone to make arrangements for the delivery of the fee. She simmered over the outrageous cost but she trusted her butler's hearty recommendation. Putting the cost aside, she had a better taste in her mouth as she savoured the belief that Pack Rowan, the thorn in her side, would be removed for all time, come the weekend. Imagine the brute threatening her with death by sex – what a monster! Well, he would pay for daring to terrify her.

Johnstone the butler left the study and went upstairs to his room. He was sweating and needed to take a bath, hoping this would help him get rid of the anger that was eating him up.

When the old woman had first broached the idea of having some professional person – as she put it – remove the obstacle that Rowan represented to her peace of mind – she admitted to him that the Irish tinker was quite capable of killing her without a blink of the eye. Johnstone, who had never been any kind of saint, was appalled.

"There's no need to be coy with me," Constance had warned him: "I know all about your prison record. Don't you think I checked you out before I employed you?"

"Perhaps so, madam, but that was a previous life as far as I am concerned. I have not associated with any kind of villain for almost ten years."

As he ran a bath he felt like strangling the old bitch. He had tried to divert her insistence that she needed his help – keep her from going down the road of no return – she had chosen to ignore how he felt about the matter. 'But if the thing turns turtle and she finds herself in trouble, who'll be the first one she names to the law? Me, Muggins, that's who.' He felt sick in his stomach as he confided his concern to his reflection in the bathroom mirror.

He was so bothered by this unwanted situation he

had to sit on the bath and try smoking a cigarette to calm his nerves, give him time to think before he went about obeying her order. His acceptance of the fact that, once you went down that road, there was no way to turn back had paralysed his will to go on.

At four o'clock that afternoon Sam left Sotheby's having made the final arrangements for the auction of Victoria's last work, a twelve-painting sale which had already caused a stir in the art world.

The dealer at the art auction house had just told Sam confidentially that they expected several of the paintings to break records. Sam felt good that Victoria was going to achieve the fame her work deserved, though sadly she was no longer around to enjoy it. She would have been the first to admit it was her own fault that this situation existed. "I was too busy seeking sensation, Sam – that was me, and so what? Had I never painted any of my pictures, in time somebody else would have done so."

The money earned by the art work, as per Vicky's will, was to go to Deirdre's Clinic and Sam hoped that the windfall would enable Dee to employ more skilled help – they needed to revert to some kind of normal home life before the drift towards separation became a real threat.

Heading for the Ritz he was thinking about Gopal. As he turned from Bond Street onto Piccadilly, he found to his astonishment that the little man was coming towards him on the footpath, arms wide, a great beaming smile lighting up his face, his laugh such a gleeful thing that Sam greeted him with a hug, something he hadn't even thought about before it happened.

"My friend, Samuel Sweet, I knew you would find me today! I am so happy to see you!" Gopal pulled back. "It is good you can give and receive a hug. People that are too embarrassed to share a hug, they need help to get in touch with their feelings."

"I'm glad to see you, Asham," Sam said with feeling, "but I wasn't aware that I was looking for you."

"I know that, dear boy, but you found me all the same which is just as wonderful. Have you time to visit with me – we could share tea at the Ritz?"

Sam looked at his wristwatch. "I have half an hour before my next meeting – tea seems like a very good idea."

"Some day, Samuel, you will dispense with the timepiece on your arm. I feel very strongly that this is the road you need to travel." He linked Sam's arm and together they crossed Piccadilly and entered the hotel.

Constance Brewer was annoyed as she moved awkwardly to answer the telephone – what in heaven's name had happened to Johnstone?

"Hello."

"Let me speak to Johnstone."

"Who are you, and how dare you talk to me like that in my own home?"

An audible sigh suggested that her caller was asking some reliable deity to grant him patience. "Are you the woman he works for?"

"Yes, I am. And who are you, may I ask?"

"He was to come see me, free o'clock at the latest, dahn the East End."

"Well, he left here in plenty of time."

"In case you 'aven't noticed, lydee, it's nah four, so at the very least e's an houa layte. Supproisin' since he'd be aware Oi don't loike to be kept 'angin' arand."

Constance was silent simply because she didn't know quite what to say.

The awful Cockney accent came back on the line: "Oi fink your man Johnstone 'as gone and done a runna." With that the caller slammed the telephone into its cradle, Constance reacting to the vicious sound of the impact.

"Done a runner?" Her face dropped and she screamed to the empty room: "Isn't there anybody left in this world that one can trust?"

At five o'clock, Pack Rowan told Guildford to pull up short of the property Joseph Jameson had driven into. They could see him get out of the van, watched him walk back down to the gates which he closed shut, using a lock and chain to secure them. He then turned back and walked up along the side of the weather-beaten Georgian house before he disappeared into what was probably the kitchen.

"He's in for the night," Guildford said with the practised ease of a man that had experienced many a stakeout.

"You're dead right," Pack agreed. "So, let's get a move on till we see somewhere to buy grub."

He glanced at the leg-breakers in the rear-view mirror. He knew them by reputation to be very good bad eggs. "When Walter and me go for our grub, I'll give you the readies to get fed and find a B&B for the night. Let's say we meet back here for ten o'clock, give Jem time to settle down with a jar and the telly."

There was no response from either of the two men, not that Pack expected any. As they approached a well-established hotel on what seemed to be the main street, Pack told Walter to pull over. Pulling out a wad of money he passed fifty pounds back to the heavy known as Sniff Colgan. "Have a meal, a few jars. Nothing heavy later. I just want to put a real scare into yer man."

When he and Walter had checked into the hotel they went in to the dining room. Sitting down, Pack said affably: "Have whatever you like, Walter. They're practically counting my money at the Bank of England." He laughed and ordered pints of bitter for both of them: "We'll leave the shorts till later."

At the Ritz Hotel in London, Sam was writing down details of his address and home telephone number for Gopal. "When you say you will come and visit, I'm sure you mean it."

"When I say I will come, I will come." Gopal's singsong Indian accent caused the stir of a head or two in the august lounge of London's finest. "I am hardly going to lie. How can I offer to be your guru, your spiritual guide, and lie to you about a visit?"

"Indeed," Sam said. "Asham, I have been thinking

of taking a walking trip in India, perhaps a trek through the Himalayas, see if I might get in touch with some kind of spiritual experience. Does that seem like a worthwhile idea to you?"

"A walk in the mountains is always a good idea, but to go there looking for some kind of spiritual awakening or whatever, is the height of nonsense."

Sam's surprise registered so strongly that Gopal burst out laughing. "Oh Sam Sweet, you are a dear man! I am saying no need to go for that purpose. God, the Absolute, Brahman, whatever name you apply to the Supreme, it does not reside in the Himalayas – the Power is everywhere, dear friend, even here in this stuffy English hotel with all the snoots that peer down their noses at my funny accent."

"You make it sound so easy," Sam said, wishing he could have kept the note of complaint from his tone.

"Simple, my dear man, simple, which is not to be confused with *easy*. And yes, the truth is simple. Which you will come to understand before long once, the fervour I sense in you will ensure it." Asham Sadapeer Gopal beamed a smile of love and caring and patted Sam's hand as though he were a seven-year-old boy. "You are already a good student and, since I see myself as a wonderful teacher, you will soon stop labouring under the misapprehension that *this* is all there is." He opened his arms and moved his head to indicate their surroundings. "What we think of as It, The Real Life, it is but a drama for the enjoyment of the Absolute. Now Samuel, what was the significant phrase in the sentence which began with my praising you as a student?"

Sam gave it a moment's thought. "You said: 'I see myself as a wonderful teacher' – am I right?"

Gopal clapped his hands in delight. "You are two hundred per cent right, Samuel Sweet." He was simply delighted and incapable of being polite and low key, as the tone of the room seemed to demand.

Sam, relieved to have understood something, said: "I'm glad."

"But what did I mean by that, Samuel? What did I mean when I said: 'I see myself as a wonderful teacher'?"

"You were not being egotistical. You meant that because you have come to your natural state of total Awareness, that you simply witness Gopal in his role as a wonderful teacher."

"Bravo, bravo!" The little Indian was more elated than ever. "You have studied my book – you have a feel for what it contains. You are open to change and I feel so good I could dance on the table." He smiled wickedly and said: "It's perfectly all right, Samuel. I am only playing with you. I never dance on tables, not any more."

Sam looked at him for some moments. "I am in pain in relation to my marriage, and I have had fears about where I have allowed myself to be led, blaming circumstances rather than taking responsibility. I want to change all that."

"We all thought we were alive until the pain of existence forced us to look for the truth. Educated, indoctrinated, call it what you will, we came to believe that education, success, wealth, fame, were the ingredients for a happy life – we were to *look out there* and go after what we wanted. Samuel, it is time to begin looking within – there you will find your truth." He rose abruptly and said "Now I must dash, it is half past six, yes?"

Sam looked at his watch: "That's remarkable – how on earth did you know to the second?"

With a deadpan expression, Gopal said: "I simply looked at the clock on the wall over the door behind your head." He now began to laugh again and this time every head in the lounge turned to look at him, most faces showing annoyance and resentment. Gopal leaned down and whispered: "Look at the moneyed and the successful and the famous all around us, Samuel. And be warned. I will see you in Ireland within two weeks."

With that he whisked out of the tea lounge and was gone while Sam sat back and lit a cigarette. He exhaled and blew the smoke-ring away and took another drag. He was very thoughtful now, gently but suddenly aware that at the ripe old age of fifty-four he was going to have to turn everything he had ever learned on its head.

He sat back and considered the prospect that his thinking would have to endure the shock of a one-hundred-and-eighty-degree shift. He took a long drag on the cigarette, asking could his life, his lifestyle, cope with such a profound change. In the moment he remembered that it was Ralph Waldo Emerson that had said: *"The mind that asks the question, knows the answer"*.

22

October 1923

At ten o'clock that same night, the man Pack Rowan knew to be Jem Riley suffered a rude awakening, since his great mattress of a beard had caught fire. He was stunned for a moment but the lethargy induced by too much alcohol fled as he started to beat at the flaming hair with both his hands. Hearing laughter, he thought he was having a nightmare. Moments later, he came to his senses and realised that what was happening was all too real.

Two faces – East Enders, he thought – were there in front of him, one of them throwing water from a bucket into his face with enough force to knock him back into his armchair as the flames died in his beard. Peering up at them Riley did not see either of their mouths move.

But a voice that belonged to someone who was having a jolly time said: "Mister Riley, I presume."

Startled though he was to hear his real name reach him in this way, he gave nothing away as he said: "I'm not called Riley, boss. The name is Jameson. I swear to that on my old mother's grave." He didn't have to fake the Scottish accent, having used it so long that it was second nature.

He looked at his wrists as they were yanked together by one of the Cockneys. One to one he would have given even this hardchaw a fight for it, but he knew enough to know when you couldn't win.

"We all like the accent, Jem, we really do. But save yer breath 'cos I know who you are. Start using the scissors and the razor, lads."

Riley's heart skipped a beat as he felt his ankles being bound and, though he felt it pointless to say anything, he had to give it a shot. "There's some mistake here. I'm nobody. I work as a market gardener."

"At Townley Castle School, Jem, we know that. We know all about you. Get on with the cutting."

Bracing himself to experience all kinds of agony, Riley suddenly realised through half closed eyes that one of the faces was cutting away his facial hair. "What?" he protested in despair. "What're you doing?"

"We're takin' away that privet hedge you've been hiding behind. We want the world to see you for what you really are."

"It's all a mistake," Jem pleaded. "You're mixin' me up with somebody else." The scissors moved around to the other side of his face but he didn't dare move – so far he felt halfway lucky they hadn't cut his throat.

"We're tidying you up, Jem. Because we're goin' to come back, maybe daytime, maybe night-time, it all depends on how busy we are. And you were such a sight we wonder how the boss at the school could let you go about like that."

Riley said nothing, listening as best he could while he was being assaulted in this way, for some hint in the voice of the lone speaker. His effort was interrupted by a rough and heavy hand slapping soap all over his face. Then a huge hand was rubbing the soap in as though he was trying to alter the pattern of the nose and facial bones. It was all he could do to stop from crying out – he hurt like hell but his pride wouldn't let them see that, not for now, anyway.

"All right," the Voice said quietly. "You are about to be shaved so keep your head still. You get cut, it'll be your own fault."

He froze as the razor slid down one side of his face, holding his breath as it stopped before coming back up to go on down the other side. He shut his eyes in case it was a wind-up – get him to think he's not in real trouble, but cut his bleedin' throat when you get there.

He was suddenly dazed by his predicament and had to hold on tight not to shake himself up enough to plead for a release from whatever was going on. He knew better. These were not kids that were now cutting his hair off, the shaving over it seemed. He bit down on his need to do anything – whatever was going on, he had the feeling that he'd be lucky to survive it

Finally, when he was beginning to believe he was close to the end of his tether, they quit, untying the binds at his wrists and ankles. He was shoved back roughly into the chair as though he was being reminded his ordeal had not yet come to an end.

The dim light in the kitchen allowed him see the two faces that had worked on him, but he got no glimpse of the speaker.

"Shut your eyes," a face smelling of whiskey said harshly into his ear. "Open them afore I tell you, I'll slit your gullet."

Jem shut his eyes. There was silence. How long he remained like that he couldn't have said but finally, after he had called out a few times, he knew he was alone in the old house.

He opened his eyes and waited. There was no reaction and he stood up, his knees hurting him, and staggered to the deep kitchen sink and threw water from the tap onto his face and head, lowering his head then so that the water ran over the back of his neck which, at times, had been so tense during the abuse that he thought it would crack.

Now he looked in the old mirror over the sink and he saw they had left him clean-shaven, his head close-cropped as ever it had been during his various stays in prison. He stood there for a minute, appalled by the power they had enjoyed over him, frightened when he thought that they could come back any time. What was it about? What was going on? Who could want to put the frighteners on him? What had he ever done except survive?

He looked into the eyes of his reflection and then like a flash he came up with a name that made him shudder. 'The crossborn bastard of a tinker, Kelly. He swore to get me over The Vicar. Swore if it was the last thing he ever did, he'd pay me back for wasting that mincing old queen with his poncy accent and him teaching that stinking knacker the King's English, if you don't mind. That's who it is, Kelly. Probably got a new handle by now.'

Turning from the mirror he lit a cigarette, took a drink of Jameson and said aloud: "It's him all right, sure as crab apples give you the trots." Energised by the impact his belief powered through him, he took another drink and vowed, "Let the bastard come. Let him come back like he promised. Next time he won't find Jem Riley like a sitting duck!" He swung back to the mirror and yelled at his image: "*Come on, Tinker Kelly!* Come and face me and let's see if you can back up your big talkin' promise! And may the Lord Jesus help you! It'll be more than your hair I'll be cuttin' off the day we meet again!" Riley grabbed the bottle of Jameson Ten and he put it to his head, drinking the last inches of spirit before he gave a frightening yell and hurled the bottle into the fire.

Going into the parlour, he lifted the worn carpet and used his knife to prise up a cut of the floorboard underneath. He came up with a shotgun which had been hidden there for quite a while, took it into the kitchen and went to work preparing it for action. From this minute on he would be armed, carrying the gun for his own self-protection. Next time Tinker Kelly and his leg-breakers tried to shit on him like they'd done tonight, he would blow their fucking heads off. And laugh afterwards, the bastards!

Elizabeth Doyle had been suffering with angina for

some years, more years than anybody could say – but she didn't acknowledge she was ill until she had what appeared to be a heart attack. In fact, it turned out to be an attack on the heart, in that it was about clogged arteries rather than the heart itself being a sick pump.

Mary Doyle had been her mother's nurse night and day for several months, coming home from the convent where she had been working towards becoming a nun. Mary herself was certain she had a vocation – the holy women that mattered didn't see things the same way, so that it was only a matter of time before Mary returned to civilian life. The need for a full-time nurse to her mother provided the perfect opportunity and the gentle young woman, the youngest of the Doyle quartet, soon found that she was happier looking after Mammy than she had been during her time at the novitiate. It was through this experience that she decided to give the nursing a go sometime in the future.

Deirdre found some time each working day in the city to go and be with her mother and Mary. She and Elizabeth had always been close but though she felt great love for Mary, she had found it difficult to establish any kind of sisterly relationship with her. When Mary had said goodbye to the veil, Dee hoped it might open things up between them.

Elizabeth was not confined to bed but said often, "I'm getting to be an old woman now," and Dee wondered if she needed to spend quite so much time between the sheets. "I lived the first twenty-eight years of my life without sheet or pillowcase, so I'm making up for all I missed," she would say in good spirit.

Her mother's cheerful acceptance that, apart from some light relief, the medical profession could do little to cure her condition, often brought Dee to tears, and several times on her arrival from the Clinic, she found Mary in the kitchen weeping in her quiet way because "Mammy just said she'd be glad to meet up with Aunt Molly again – that she might even get to see her own mother and father for the first time in heaven," or some similar sentiment.

Elizabeth had never been less than devoted to the God her Aunt Molly had introduced into her life when she took the tiny baby girl into her hovel of a home on the death of her parents.

No matter how many times Dee heard the stories of Molly's fight for survival at Cullen Lower in County Wicklow, she never tired of them, and though she had never been close to her father, she had given him great credit for his decency towards the saviour of his wife.

"Wasn't she great altogether, Mammy? And so brave the way she sent you off to Dublin that time?" Dee sat by the bed holding her mother's hand, prompting her really.

"She was great right enough, Dee, and mad as a March hare. Mind you, I was insane myself that morning. Eamon Coyle had tried again to have his way with me, swore he would sooner or later. I was ready to swing for the same Eamon Coyle and Aunt Molly could see it and hear it when I told her that if he came near me again I'd geld him or kill him stone dead. God love her, praying for guidance on her knees with this fella trying to rape me every time he found me out in the field gathering wood or carrying a bucket of water from the well. She told God about writing off to a house in Dublin – the parish priest gave me a good reference – people looking for a domestic servant – the letter gone six months since and not even a reply – and then I come in the door like a lunatic and tell her about the murder in my heart for Eamon Coyle.

"Remember now, Aunt Molly was waiting for a sign, expecting God to show her something to help keep me from killing a fella with rape on his mind. Feeling guided by the Almighty, Molly tells me I'll be working in Dublin by the weekend.

"The heart is a wonder, Dee, when it can come through the days that followed Molly's lie and my belief that there was a job waiting for me in a fine house in Ballsbridge. We hardly knew what to say to each other – like, well, it was like our hearts could only cast the odd glance at each other – it was like we daren't talk about the parting of the ways that was there ahead of us in a matter of days. Words – we nearly left them alone entirely – the feelings in the air in that shell of a cottage, they sat there between us like warnings of the pain to come if we accepted the possibility that what hours were left to us might well be the last we'd spend together.

"Molly drove us into Wicklow town on this old flat two-wheeled cart that was drawn by a donkey practically shaking his hatred of mankind at us the way a dog shakes himself after comin' out of a river." Elizabeth chuckled and Dee took a breath through her nose to hold back her tears. "'Ye're one cantankerous beast so y'are! Ye've no right to wear the cross of our Lord Jesus!'" Elizabeth was stopped by this moment of memory, and Dee wiped away a tear. Elizabeth picked up the story, so alive in the force of recall that she sounded proud of the old woman berating the donkey. "'Ye've a mean nature and how you feel about your lot is the last thing botherin' my mind this minute!'"

Elizabeth yawned then, fighting it, hiding it behind her hand. Deirdre was about to suggest they leave the rest of the story till the next day but her mother shook herself, clearly wanting to carry on.

"At the railway station in Dublin, a sleeveen – one of the criminals went gathering up innocent country girls, wanting to turn them into prostitutes for Monto and the like – he tried to take my bag – an ould raffia bag with a little towel and soap and a clean pair o' drawers. I hit him such a wallop – and the next thing your father was there ready to do battle for me only it wasn't necessary, then he took me up on his sidecar and though you'd scarcely believe it, Dee, we were never apart from that day on until he went out heels first to his well-earned rest."

"I know – you were made for each other. But, speaking of rest," Dee stood up, "a bit of a sleep wouldn't hurt you one bit."

"You'd wonder why people are afraid of dying when sleep is such a lovely thing, wouldn't you, Dee?"

Deirdre embraced Elizabeth and kissed her. "I'll be in tomorrow. If you need anything Mary only has to call me on the telephone."

"We have everything we need and more, Dee. Mind

yourself till I see you tomorrow and look after your husband well, and give Kathleen a kiss from her granny and tell Eddie and Alfie I'll be down to see them for Christmas – you'll have me, won't you?"

Her mother's loss of memory startled Deirdre. She had brought the two boys and Sarah to see her mother just days earlier, and all three had promised to come back sometime next week.

"You have your rest now, Mammy. Love you." She kissed her mother's forehead.

"God love you, you dear girl. Never gave me a minute's trouble," Elizabeth found a weary chuckle, "though I can't say your father'd agree with that."

Dee found Mary in the kitchen kneading dough with the quiet intensity she seemed to apply to most things.

Mary smiled and said: "You used to be the envy of my heart one time, you know, how you dressed – you were the fashion plate I envied so much. Where did the change come from?"

Dee lit a cigarette. "How about a cup of tea? I'll make it." Mary nodded agreeably and Dee went to work as she answered her question. "It started to happen when I began cycling to Mountjoy Square. On the bike in the mornings I saw things about the city, like the poverty and the violence and the criminal deprivation that the poor endured every day of their life. That was when I realised how ridiculous it was, for me anyway, to be involved in dressing up."

Deirdre got home from Dublin in time to join Sam for

dinner on his return from London. She was feeling mellow after the time spent with her mother, and the short interlude with Mary over a cup of tea had been sisterly in a good sense.

Sam was hopeful that the Constance Brewer story would soon be at an end and they could just let it go into the past where it would be left alone for all time. He was also very full of how good it felt to have made his first tentative steps on the road to Awareness. He did not go into specifics with Dee but she was delighted to hear him so positive. In bed after a glass of port following the wine at dinner they were very close and made love for a long time. Sam was so aware of the old feeling between them, the words of love they offered each other as caring as they had always been.

As they finally snuggled down to sleep, Sam touched her face gently: "It should never be less that this between us. You know that, don't you?

"I do," she said sleepily, happily taking his hand – something she had not done for some weeks – and pressing it onto her breast that she might sleep the better.

Sam answered an early telephone call while Dee was pouring tea for them both. He stood quietly for a few moments – Dee turned to him and as though by osmosis knew what he had to tell her: "It's Mammy, isn't it?

Sam nodded and said, "Elizabeth passed away peacefully during the night." He put his arms around Dee.

"She was the best," she said quietly, "such a wonderful friend to me."

"And to me, Dee." He stood there waiting to be of service in whatever way she needed him to be.

"I'm going upstairs to pray for a little while."

"May I join you?"

"I'd love that, Sam," Dee sounded surprised.

As they were leaving the kitchen she said: "I don't know why I'm surprised – probably because of your talking about studying awareness." She found a wistful smile. "I wasn't sure about that and praying, side by side, like."

"I've got a long road ahead of me, so all the prayers in the world are welcome. No matter what I study, I'd want to give thanks to whatever deity gave us Lizzie." He had to sniff back tears as they climbed the stairs. "I was just sixteen years old the first time I saw her on Pat's sidecar."

Dee turned to look at him. "Are you all right, Sam?"

"I'm fine, Dee. Just remembering – Pat drove the sidecar at quite a lick up Dame Street and I thought 'I bet he's taking her home to his ma in Peter Street'."

"And he was," Dee said laughing through fresh tears.

"He was indeed." Sam was weeping openly. "He took her home to your Granny Doyle and old Bridie lashed spuds and bacon pieces into her. She had nothing, Dee. The shoes she wore were too small for her feet. But the great divine madness of her aunt, Molly Harney, it changed everything – with Bridie's prayers for a grandchild to be answered within the year – the arrival of you, dear heart. How lucky we have been."

"I'm sorry for –"

He pressed his fingers to her lips. "To me you need never explain, never apologise. I know your heart."

23

Autumn 1924

Sam did not get to meet with Gloria immediately
after her return from Turkey – she had to fulfil two
big engagements and would not be home at Cadogan
Square until later in the month. Having had her assurance
over the telephone that Mendel was in perfect health,
he also talked to the boy who had enjoyed the time of
his life. Sam decided for the moment not to say anything
about Jameson, the Head Gardener at Townley Castle
School. He did ask Gloria to call him on her return to
London – he needed to drop over and talk through
some stuff with her. All in all, he found his ex-wife more
than agreeable and he couldn't help wondering if she
had a man in her life, if she was in love. He was
surprised that the idea gave him some kind of pang,
shrugged it off without examining its cause, having
more important things to concern himself with at this
time.

Meanwhile, though he sincerely hoped Pack Rowan

could convince, even force, the old woman of Eaton Square to see reason and take the offer that was on the table, Sam continued coaching Kelly and Séamus Byrne and Angela on *The Story*.

All three had taken quickly and easily to the idea that what Gloria had written in her journals had never happened. The tale of the baby-swapping by Kelly and the other tales were created by Sam and Dee to help prevent Gloria from losing her mind. There was a great danger that this was actually happening because Gloria believed Eddie Brewer and her daughter Sarah were brother and sister due to her wild night of sex with Arthur all those years before. *The Story* claimed that Gloria's trauma was born of the fear that she had conceived a child by Arthur Brewer. This was her daughter, Sarah, who had even as a young girl, sworn that she would one day marry Eddie Brewer.

Sam also wrote up *The Story* for Deirdre to study. He had misgiving about this since he had no way of knowing whether Dee would react against the fact of committing perjury. He was uneasy too, about having to shelve his ongoing interest in Awareness, hoping to heaven that Pack Rowan's promise to make Constance accept the offer would manifest before they were all to be dragged through the Law Courts.

He nonetheless went on making time each day to read from Gopal's book, the overall proposition of which was that man did not have to do anything to become Self Realised.

Every great guru said the same thing – *You Are That, Therefore, You Don't Have to Become!*

Sam could hear this but it was just too abstract for him to grasp, willing though he was to believe it to be the truth of all truths. He felt he had years of study ahead of him but when the thought of going to India arose once more he smiled and remembered Gopal's message about Absolute Awareness being everywhere.

He remembered too an earlier protestation to the little Indian, "I need to read. I enjoy the studying. I want . . ." He was brought to a halt since Gopal was shaking his head ever so gently, a plea to stop, rather than an order to quit being so silly.

"One of the most powerful blocks between man and his own Self are those two words 'I want' – they have power to shut away Awareness as clouds have power to hide the sun from us. Dear Sam Sweet, for now simply put the question: 'Who Am I?' Let time come and go, you remain steadfast. And know that thoughts, dreams, and desires, the *wanting to become*, are the clouds that block the sun. Remember too that the sun never changes. It does not go away. It simply is."

Coming away from his meeting with Gloria who remained a stunningly beautiful woman, Sam felt a little easier about the nebulous connection between Mendel and the marker gardener, Joseph Jameson.

"I spoke to him just once, when our driver had a heart attack and died as we were being driven into Townley Castle. A big hairy Scot, he was more than willing to help us that day. That's all I can tell you, Sam."

As yet, Sam had kept Gloria well away from the

dilemma that her stolen journals had placed him and the others in. She was as highly strung as ever, working too hard, and he had no wish to provide her with ammunition to mentally beat herself up. She was a good mother to their son – she had her own special Cause, clearly longing for the day when she would have earned her place in Palestine, the singing for a Homeland's supper a thing of the past.

Dinner later with Prod McLoughlin was a catching-up session, the enquiry agent with his usual gusto polishing off his filet mignon and seven or eight potatoes with a selection of vegetables, before his report could be given. Sam ate about half of his portion, wondering to heaven how Prod remained so slight with such a dockworker's appetite.

Finally, Prod opened his contribution with a question: "Does the name Jem Riley mean anything to you, Sam?"

Sam was instantly captured by a rip of anger that triggered a pang of indigestion. He flamed for a moment or two before he gathered himself together. Down the years he had so often wondered what happened to the demon that had virtually murdered Rebecca, Gloria's mother.

He remembered how Riley had been about to rape Gloria in her pregnant mother's presence – the seventeen-year-old girl driven beyond dementia into some kind of demonic state where she found the will to kick him so hard that she might well have ended his life.

Gloria had passed out cold from her reaction to the blow her foot had delivered to Riley's temple. Regaining consciousness, the girl had raised her mother from the floor of the disgusting room, supporting and half-dragging Rebecca, who was miscarrying her lover's child after the kicking he had given her, from the King's Cross doss-house where the trio had been flopping for a couple of nights.

Somehow she had managed to get her mother to Euston Station and aboard the train to Holyhead and the ferryboat to Dublin, administering to her in every moment as best she could.

The thirty-seven-year-old Rebecca had, as a nineteen-year-old, walked from Lithuania pulling a cart with all her belongings on it, losing her father on the long walk west. The journey had given her time to get to know and come to love a man called Peter Stein who was on the run from the Russian authorities and whose hope to live in Ireland had become a dream for the couple who married in London.

While they were saving money to get them to Ireland with something to live on, Peter had been brutally murdered by people he worked alongside in a meat factory in London's East End, his life taken because he had discovered how a serious ongoing theft was being carried out, and as bookkeeper it was his duty to inform his employers. He could not have known that the manager of the factory, who treated him like a nephew, was the ringleader of the robbers – his brutal death by stabbing coming to him as a complete surprise. He died in the arms of his young, pregnant wife, Rebecca who would scribble into her journal: *'Were it not for the unborn child in my womb, I would now lie dead beside my husband. This black day is the 6th of September, 1888.'*

There was much more of the Rebecca-Gloria story that Sam remembered, the force of their suffering and deprivation burning each chapter into his mind. Many times he had tasted bitter almonds at the thought that Riley might have survived that kick that had left him unconscious, while mother and daughter escaped on the boat train to Ireland. But there was to be no reprieve from grief for the seventeen-year-old Gloria, her mother dying within sight of the promised land she and her husband had dreamed of.

"I know that name, Prod, from another time. What of it?"

Prod smiled self-effacingly, "The sister, Rose, she told me a little story. It seems that Rowan went to a deal of trouble to create terror in the life of this man Riley. Something of a power thing was how Walter Guildford saw it. Rose said he was sickened by the whole affair, though Rose felt he might have been putting it on a bit, pretending, in case she thought him a real shit. Guildford though was happy to see Rowan in good form. 'The millions he expects to receive have improved his mood no end,' – this is a quote from Walter to Rose – 'now that he has shown Constance Brewer who is the boss in their partnership'."

Sam's expression lightened and he made no bones about saying: "I'm bloody glad to hear that. But tell me, Pack. How and where did this terrorising of Riley take place? What's the connection between Pack Rowan and Riley? Did Rose give you any details of what they did to Riley? Tell me, anything she said and everything. My God, this is incredible, Riley showing up after all these years."

"Rose's telephone call was hurried, up to her ears in work. I told her to jot down every word Guildford said. She did say that Rowan's been staying at the house on Eaton Square, which sounds like feet under the table, wouldn't you say?"

"You're not suggesting that Rowan has taken Constance Brewer to bed, Pack! For God's sake, she's eighty years old or something. The mind cringes."

"Stranger things have happened, Sam. Personally, I find the image too bizarre, to say the least. But Rowan is a remarkable individual by any test and who knows? The appetites of history's greatest dowagers are legendary."

Sam grimaced. "In any case, him being there on the spot is a very powerful move to hurry up completion of the deal."

"I'm a bit surprised that it doesn't seem to bother you, the picture of Rowan walking away with many millions – have I got that right, Sam?"

Sam drew in smoke and savoured the taste of the tobacco on his tongue. "He and his woman May Murray did wrong from the start. The fact that they were willing to go to court along with Constance leaves them looking very black to my eyes. They didn't give a damn about the consequences of their blackmail attempt. Rowan, who claims to be Eddie's father, didn't give a damn what the revelation of his illegitimacy might do to the lad. All of that – and much, much more – Rowan proved heartless about all of it. For that, I regard him as an arch-enemy. The money doesn't matter a damn, but in my book he ought to pay – I feel he will pay – for the callous manipulation that could have destroyed the life of a really fine fellow like Eddie, not forgetting what the fall-out would do to Deirdre and the other children."

"And you, Sam?"

"Well yes, of course, but we're talking about people innocent to the savagery of the streets and the glare of public outrage. Nothing could prepare them for what would follow should Constance not have agreed to accept the deal." He smoked and ground out his cigarette. "So, in one way I am grateful to Rowan for being quick enough to see that millions on the table are much more tangible that all the pie-in-the-sky stuff Constance was going on with. That being said, I would deem it unlikely that he will walk away from this."

He looked at Prod McLoughlin and the enquiry agent felt relieved that Rowan, and not himself, was the object framed by Sam Sweet's antipathy.

"Rose didn't have the time to tell you anything more, Prod?"

"Guildford did tell her Rowan and company checked Riley out the morning after, following him as he drove to Townley Castle School in his van. Pretty frightening stuff, don't you think?" McLoughlin pulled a face. "Riley could be dead as a dodo this morning, but for the fact that Pack Rowan wants to have some fun first. I find both of them terrifying. Most men, being subjected to the terror tactics and humiliation that Riley suffered would have left Ramsgate by first light. But he goes to work at the usual time, the only apparent difference being that he has no beard, no monstrous head of hair to hide behind."

Sam nodded, his expression pensive. "Like Rowan

he must have ice in his veins. A man with that kind of built-in coldness, he'd be a very dangerous man to go up against. I suppose it's too much to hope for – that the pair of them could kill each other."

"Wouldn't that be *'an outcome devoutly to be wished'*?" Prod smiled at his witticism but Sam remained stone-faced as he wondered what sort of mayhem would be dumped on all their lives before this thing was over and done with.

"So what's your next move, Sam?"

"Where the deal is concerned, we simply have to wait. We wait for the papers to be ready and hope all goes well. Papers signed, sealed and delivered, we can say goodbye to Constance *et al*, celebrate the fact that we never have to talk to any of them again."

"What will you and Gloria do about Jameson-stroke-Riley in the meantime?" Prod moved his head to the left as a waiter poured coffee for him.

Sam waited until the man had left that table before he said, "I need to talk to Gloria. Really, I need to talk to Mendel but in the interest of ongoing harmony I have to have her with me when I do. If I learn anything of value from my son about the damned gardener, good. I need all the help I can get here. So, my ex and I will have to go to Townley Castle School together. If Jameson is Jem Riley, Gloria will not want our son anywhere near him. That goes for me too."

Kitty Daly tried to ignore the pounding on her front door, blot out the beseeching quality in Cormac's voice –

she tried to keep on working while he begged to be allowed in. Finally, unable to put up with it any longer she went to the window and pushed it open. Her heart moved when she saw the state of him – he was drunk and altogether a pathetic sight. She could see no sign of the man he had seemed to be when she had met him. Whatever he had been doing to himself for the past month or so, the price was too high.

"Please just go away!" she called down to him as quietly as she could. No need to advertise the fact that one of her men was outside her door behaving like a bloody lunatic. She knew she was fooling herself – several of the residents in the lane were out of their doors watching the scene unfold.

"Go find a police station and give yourself up. Maybe prison will be good for you, help you be a man again. I am not opening this door no matter how long you go on banging at it. You'd want to move on – somebody is bound to have telephoned the Flat Feet by now. Get going. Paddy left a sketch of you with details of what you look like in every house here last week. You've got no chance if you don't run."

Even as she spoke, two police cars drove into the mews, one passing Cormac at speed, stopping just beyond him, the second having halted close by the exit to Waterloo Road.

Paddy Doyle got out of the second car. Kitty saw right away that he had a revolver in his hand down by his right thigh. A uniformed officer wearing a protective jacket and armed with a rifle took up a position across the bonnet of the car.

Paddy Doyle walked down from the car, staying clear of the marksman's line of fire. He stopped and he looked up at Kitty, his face set in grim sadness, his eyes weighed down by his predicament.

"You'd be better off inside," he said in a flat, anonymous voice. Kitty shook her head and he gave her a 'suit yourself' kind of nod. Then he fixed his eyes on his younger brother.

Cormac was standing by the studio door, his revolver in his hand for all to see.

"Cormac!" Paddy called, his voice high and strong as he went on: "Throw down your weapon! Let us go from here so that we can get you the help you need."

Cormac said nothing. Paddy glanced toward the marksman. "Don't fire unless I tell you to," he said evenly.

The marksman nodded and Paddy turned back to face his brother. "I'm coming to you, Cormac, and I'm going to relieve you of the weapon and take you in. You'll get a fair trial, but first, I ask you to drop the weapon."

Cormac responded by raising the gun, aiming it at his brother who walked carefully down the mews toward him.

"Stay back, Paddy. Stay back. I'm not messing here – you come any closer and I'll shoot you down, I swear it."

Paddy stopped and said: "I'm giving you a chance to come out of this alive. Take the chance, Cormac. You will not be leaving here with that gun in your hand."

He walked another few paces. Cormac swung the gun upwards, going into the shooting stance, legs wide, the weapon steady as a rock between his two hands.

"Don't," Paddy said. "Don't force me to –"

Cormac took a deep breath, a sign that he was about to shoot. Paddy came on. His brother's finger tightened on the trigger.

The marksman waited no longer. He fired a single shot that took Cormac in his right chest, spinning him around so that he crashed against the door of Kitty Daly's mews house.

The word "No!" came from Paddy Doyle's lips as he ran the couple of yards to his brother, while the marksman used a handkerchief to wipe the sweat from his brow.

Paddy knelt and was saying an Act of Contrition over Cormac as Kitty's door was flung open. She stumbled over the corpse to fall on her knees beside Paddy who was now holding Cormac's head on his lap, his tears falling on the face of his younger brother.

Kitty sniffed back tears, angry with Cormac for throwing his life away. She wanted to say something but couldn't find a word. She made the Sign of the Cross on herself and began to say a silent prayer. Paddy lifted the revolver Cormac had trained on him, wondering to God whether his brother would have shot him. It was something about the weight of the gun that captured his attention. When he checked it for ammunition – there was none – the gun wasn't loaded, not even a round in the chamber.

Paddy looked at Kitty and she saw the horror in his eyes as he said: "He had no bullets here. He came here to die."

Kitty was weeping. "He couldn't put a gun in his mouth, because – he said it himself – he was such a fucked-up Catholic."

She rose and without another word went back into the house, leaving the door open behind her.

Later, when Paddy came up the stairs, he found her at the easel. She turned to face him and she saw the surprise in his face. She shrugged. "It's how I live, buy food and drink and cigarettes. Somebody paid for this in advance. He's coming to collect it first thing in the morning." She put the brush into a soft cloth and left it on the table. "Do you want a jar?"

Paddy shook his head. "I'm going to need a statement from you, Kitty. Would it be best if I came back in the morning, after you've delivered your painting?"

She heard the pain behind the control as he went about the job. "Come in the morning, if you would. I've got to get this finished tonight."

He nodded his head. "Okay so. I'll be here at half eleven."

She nodded and he turned and went down the stairs. By the time he shut the front door Kitty was back before the easel, smoking a cigarette that lodged on her lip, her beautiful brandy-snap eyes intent on what she was doing.

Sam made several efforts to contact Gloria before he left London, cursed himself for not giving her all his attention when she mentioned taking a health break after she left Mendel back at school. He remembered she had named some spa but for the life of him couldn't call it to mind. When he got back to Dunbla he went on trying to reach her – realising with a jolt that there was no obligation on her to let him know where she was likely to be at any given time. She did her duty by their son, Mendel, apart from which there was no need for her to contact Sam at all. He wrote a hasty note to his son asking him to contact his mother and have her telephone him at home in Ireland as soon as possible.

Needless to say he did not get a reply to his few lines – in truth, he hadn't expected any.

Soon afterward, he was surprised to find his picture in the *Irish Times*. This came about as Sotheby's announced the date for the auction of paintings by the late Victoria Brewer, a collection which, by all accounts, had the art world very excited indeed.

Sam wasn't sure how he felt about seeing his own picture in the paper. He got some kind of little boost from it, found he examined the likeness to see if his age was showing, wondered what others would think of it. That apart, he didn't think it was going to cause big changes in his life.

Kitty Daly saw the picture and smiled as she remembered him at Elizabeth Doyle's funeral some time before. She had not been a mourner, *per se* – going out of curiosity really, convinced that her ex-lover was wild enough, and sufficiently out of tune, to turn up for the burial of the woman he respected more than any other.

Kitty had come to the end of her time with Cormac – "I'll always love you, but I will not be sleeping with you any more," was how she had put it when it came to the moment. "You drain the very life out of me and I won't have it. I need my strength and my energy and my dreams to do what I do." He had threatened to take his own life but she knew this wouldn't happen. He had ranted too many times in drink that he was too much of a fucked-up Catholic to do that, and she had heard the sound, the truth in his voice even when he was three sheets to the wind.

Sam Sweet had interested her because he was clearly a man of means, he was good-looking, and there was about him the stamp of someone who had passion in his heart. Seeing him leave the cemetery, his arm supporting Deirdre, did nothing to dampen her interest. She saw Paddy Doyle following behind with his sister, Mary, so distressed that she was being half-carried by the big man. Kitty and Paddy weren't even friends any more – he had been unable to deal with the idea of sharing her with his brother.

At the funeral, Kitty decided that Sam Sweet was someone she had to meet. Seeing his picture in the *Irish Times*, she made up her mind that it would have to be sooner rather than later.

Deirdre was deeply saddened by her mother's passing but Sam knew she had been very fortunate to have had Lizzie (he held onto the name she used when he had first seen her on Pat Doyle's sidecar) in her life for so long. Not everyone lived to be almost seventy years old, though wives tended to outlive their husbands, or so it seemed to Sam. A lot of men died too young through working too hard without getting enough good food to keep them alive into old age.

"Mammy had so much kindness in her," Dee said, quite out of the blue, the evening of his return from London. She herself was on a three-day break from Cork Street, very glad to have him home again. "She never said a bad word about anybody in her lifetime," Dee found a wan smile, "unlike Granny Doyle who found it hard to find a good word about anybody. God, the times she told me again about the state of poor Mammy the evening Daddy brought her home for the first time!"

By the fire in the drawing room, Sam pressed a glass of cognac into Dee's hand and she smiled up at him. In the light from the oil lamp on a nearby table he could see that emerging spots of white were turning her hair grey, the laugh lines at her eyes emphasised by the sadness that would be about her heart for some time to come.

When he told Dee about the possibility that Jem Riley was somehow living on the fringe of Gloria's life, Dee was horrified. She knew all too well the story – his responsibility for the death of Rebecca who bled to death within sight of the Irish coastline.

"Sam, you must warn her right away."

"I don't know where she is. I've written to Mendel, asking him to tell her to telephone me when she calls him. There isn't much more I can do till I hear from her. Without labouring the point, her solicitor has instructions not to put me in touch unless Mendel becomes very ill, or has a serious accident."

"Perhaps you should go over and take Mendel out of the school until she returns to London. If that monstrous man knew he was her son, God knows what he might do to the boy." This thought fell easily from Dee's lips but Sam could see the impact it made on her as she realised exactly what she was implying.

"I have no legal right to do that, Dee. Mendel was so clearly glad to get away from me, so very committed to his mother, that I signed away all rights but those Gloria granted me for the boy's sake, rather than mine."

"Well, we must pray Gloria returns very soon." Dee was clearly appalled. "God knows what effect it will have on her when she hears this news." She leaned towards him where he sat facing her across the fireplace. "Sam, Gloria can't hear about this over the telephone. You must be with her when you give her this news."

Sam had never been so impressed in his life. He got out of his chair and came to kneel before his wife to kiss her fingers. "You are so fine. My God, thank you! Of course you're right – the shock could send her into trauma."

Dee leaned down and kissed his forehead. "We have to do everything we can. She will always be part of this family."

Standing, she drew Sam from his knees. They embraced and she kissed him lovingly.

He held her face in his hands: "The good and decent things that I find manifesting in my day-to-day behaviour, they have come to me through you."

Dee dismissed this with a nod of her head and a flick of her eyebrows. "You're a good man, Sam Sweet – I'm the lucky somebody in this relationship."

Sam moved to the drinks table, lifted the cognac bottle and held it out to her.

Dee pulled a tiny face and said: "I shouldn't. I'm getting far too fond of the old brandy." He waited, still holding the bottle as though it would not be on offer for much longer. He saw her smile emerge, her stiff-shouldered look drop away as she nodded and said with a sigh, "Oh go on so," sitting down then as she concluded, "but, it's got to stop so it has."

Sam poured cognac for them both. When he put the balloon into her hand, bringing his own near, there was that delightful little ping as fine glass kissed itself.

"Here's to temperance so!" said Sam, raising his glass jovially. "May we never die till a spider walks across our foreheads and kicks our brains out!"

When she had taken several tiny sips of the cognac Dee said quietly, "Paddy called on the telephone. There will be no enquiry into Cormac's death." She was close to tears. "It's good news out of a terrible situation. Poor Cormac, he was so driven."

"He had great qualities and when it was needed he found the courage to walk through fire." Sam was saddened but not in the least surprised her brother had got himself shot. Especially when he had planned his own execution, getting into a shoot-out situation without bullets in his revolver.

"Thank God Mammy didn't have to live through it. She had a very soft spot for our Cormac."

"And thank God Paddy didn't have to shoot his own brother," Sam said quietly.

Nodding in agreement, Dee said: "Amazing how we can, even in dire situations, find something for which to be grateful, isn't it?"

"That's the kind of bonus keeps us going when things get really rough. You're particularly blessed because it's like second nature to you."

"Sam," she said just moments later, "will you cancel the Sotheby auction for the moment anyway? Would you mind?"

Without hesitation he said: "Not at all, Dee."

"It needs a lot of thought – I'm feeling all right but I'm rent with grief – Mammy and Cormac being gone – I need time to find my sea-legs again."

"All I ask is," Sam said, his heart swelling with feeling for his wife, "let me be your support."

"You can't become what you are, Sam Sweet," she found a wan smile. "What you are, and have always been for me."

Part Three

24

Autumn 1924

When Pack Rowan telephoned him at the Ritz Hotel, Sam was more than glad he had gone and had words with May Murray at the Dunbla Tavern on the eve of his latest trip to London.

He had smiled as May feigned disinterest, a lack of understanding as he pressed her as to the urgency of his need to talk to her partner in crime. May was too cute to have given anything away – so to save time he mentioned money: "Tell Pack Rowan from me that he will earn ten thousand pounds if he will come to me at the Ritz hotel in London, any time after noon tomorrow."

He saw interest light up her blue eyes, then allowed her some seconds to digest it before he said: "I have several things to attend to in London. Pack should telephone the hotel before arriving there. I will meet him anywhere at any time, assure him of that."

As he heard Rowan's voice on the telephone he was pleased he had been so direct with the woman. It was time to force the hand of Constance Brewer and he was ready to do just about anything to get the matter resolved.

"I got a message from May Murray, Mister Sweet, and I like the sound of it. Tell me where you want to meet me and I'll be there on the dot."

"There's a pub called The Coachman's in St Martin's Lane."

They met by the bar of the fashionable alehouse, renowned as one of the most beautiful Victorian pubs in the West End. Being in the theatre district, it was frequented by artists and writers and, of course, no end of actors. This ambience made it an ideal place to meet, Sam accepting that he and the Irish tinker would be anonymous, if not invisible, in the company of so many performers.

Once they had drinks and had found a table at the back of the bar, Sam came straight to the point. "I know of your interest in a man called Jem Riley. If he is the same Jem Riley, he is the man who was intent on raping Gloria, the mother of my only son – he is responsible for the death of that lady's mother."

"Sorry to butt in, Mister Sweet – if Riley was intent on raping the lady, how come she got away?"

"His attention was diverted by the girl's mother, Rebecca. She was pregnant by Riley – as she tried to help her daughter he turned to choke the life out of the poor creature. In that moment Gloria kicked him in the head, and left him for dead in a King's Cross doss-house."

"Real pity she didn't finish him, Mister Sweet."

"Indeed," Sam heard himself say without regret.

"So how can I help you?" Rowan had got a cigarette going. "The money you mentioned to May Murray – you wouldn't be paying that to me to just introduce you to him, right?"

"I know only that I need your help. If you are prepared to commit to me, give me your word as a man that you will ensure that Jem Riley is well and truly neutralised for once and for all, I am prepared to visit my bank tomorrow and arrange a certified cheque made out to you in the amount stated." Sam now took a drink and, as he went about lighting a cigarette, ignored the nagging inner voice asking, 'Just what are you asking this man to do'?

"Are you asking me to kill him, Mister Sweet?"

Sam exhaled smoke and leaned closer across the small round table for two. "As I understand it, Mister Rowan, you have been searching him out for a long time. Through a contact of mine in the prison service, I know all about the rumour that was in circulation when your friend, The Vicar, was killed, murdered in Wormwood Scrubs. I know too, about your oath, how you swore to avenge that crime. May I take it that you remain in that frame of mind?"

Without missing a beat, Rowan said flatly: "As long as I have a breath left in this body, sir, you can take my word on that."

Sam said quietly: "I know that if I was facing Riley in a life-or-death situation, I would willingly kill him should I be able to manage it. So, to try and answer your question let me say this: as you are so intent on doing something that would seem to me just and right, if not strictly legal, I offer the sum already mentioned as an added incentive to you in the task you have chosen to carry out."

Pack Rowan smiled and indicated to a waitress to bring more drinks. "You can play with the words, Mister Sweet, I'll hand you that. Could have been a lawyer, I don't doubt. So if I offer you my hand here and now, promise you as a man that I will see to it Jem Riley never rapes another woman, you will pay me tomorrow by certified cheque, ten thousand pound. Have I got that right, sir?"

"You have," Sam assured him, "and here is my hand to prove it."

As they shook hands, Sam's inner sound was there, leaving him with a warning that he was in fact, shaking hands with the devil, and the voice insisted that sooner or later the devil would come-a-calling at payback time. 'There is nothing else I can do,' he reasoned, lifting the new drink for which Pack Rowan was already paying.

Sam's anxiety did not go unnoticed by Rowan as he saw him swallow the cognac, ordering another even before the waitress had taken the empty glasses from the table.

Rowan sipped his own drink, regarding Sam over the rim of the glass, nodding his head slowly, so that Sam felt obliged to ask what he was thinking. "I hand it to you, sir – you never looked down your nose like the rest of May's customers."

"I'm not one of them," Sam said frankly. "In many ways I am more like you." He savoured the taste of the tobacco from a fresh cigarette.

"You, more like me?" Rowan was surprised. "How

do you work that one out, sir, if you don't mind me asking? Like, I spent my life as a lad hauling a cart around the Irish countryside, never slept in a bed with sheets on it unless it was a house I burgled and went for a kip afterwards."

"My mother was one of more than two million Jews who had to leave their homeland." Sam tasted again the constancy of his admiration for Esther, the mother he had cherished to the end of her life. "My ex-wife Gloria was born to a mother who walked from Lithuania. Like your people, that the Irish call tinkers and knackers and other things besides, the Jews were not welcome in most places – and make no mistake, in this city of London, and in the city of Dublin right now, and in many another capital city throughout the world, the Jew is still looked down upon. The terms 'yid' and 'kike' did not grow like grass – those are words from the mouth of the anti-Jew. So, you and I – how are we so different from each other?"

"I never thought of it like that," Rowan conceded with an inclination of his head. "But, even so, I can't see a tinker getting to the place you reached in Irish society. I know you are a very well-off man, but that apart, you have been accepted all in all, in society. For a tinker, it could never happen, not in Ireland."

"It was an accident, well, an incident that came about accidentally, I suppose, is more accurate. I met a man, Arthur Brewer, through his sister – she and I had become friends – he helped me through doors I could never have opened for myself. The rest I earned – that is the reputation I have, anyway."

"I can't see the like of that happening for me." Pack Rowan threw the line out like an old and experienced fisherman, his eyes wily as he waited to see if he would get a bite.

Exhaling smoke, Sam returned the smile. "I come bearing a large cheque, Mister Rowan. I offer you an unorthodox business proposition – we have agreed on the deal – beyond that there can be nothing between us. I have all the people I need in my life – there is no more room at the inn."

Rowan nodded his acceptance as the waitress came to the table with Sam's fresh drink.

"So, as you are paying the piper, Mister Sweet, in what way do you want this thing to work out? I was going to end Riley's life anyway, but you get what you pay for, so you tell me how you want it to be."

"To begin with, I want you to have two men on him night and day. They are to watch him, never let him out of their sight – I don't expect them to watch him go to the lavatory – but everywhere else, I want their eyes on him."

"You want to make sure he never gets his hands on your ex-wife, am I right?"

Sam nodded and Pack Rowan accepted this. "I have the men to do the job. Anything specific you want to tell me?"

"As I understand it," Sam said, uneasy that his son and Riley were friendly, "Riley – known to my son Mendel as Jameson – has become friendly with him. Apparently, the boy looks up to him."

"I didn't know your son was at that school, Mister

Sweet." He shook his head as though bothered by this oversight. "You wouldn't want the lad to see what happens to Riley, have I got it?"

Sam was impressed. "Indeed you have, Mister Rowan. And when he and the boy are alone together, I want the surveillance as tight as it can be." Sam wanted to say more but was finding it difficult.

"You're afraid he might rape the boy, Mister Sweet."

Riley sounded caring enough that Sam didn't need to object to the overt language. He nodded his head.

Rowan said: "I wouldn't take your money if anything like that was likely to happen. Have no fear. I'll be in and around the situation as from tomorrow – I understand it'll be one more week before I get my cheque from the old witch. I'll guarantee the boy's safety."

Sam's gratitude powered his handshake but once again he was forced to ignore the inner voice that said: 'So Sam, lying down with dogs is all right when it concerns you and yours. To hell with what society thinks, damn the rules that people have agreed to live by, when your ship is under threat, blow the enemy out of the water making sure he won't be able to come back and create any more disturbance or aggravation. Neat, Sam, neat, if you can live with it, and always provided you won't beat your breast and weep salt tears when what you have sown has to be harvested.'

"I'd like you to call me here at the Ritz twice a day until this is all over. I am staying in England until Riley is no longer an issue."

Pack Rowan nodded agreeably: "The lads and I are going to Ramsgate tomorrow. We'll be there till it's over.

And I think you know enough about me to believe that I will deliver, or die in the attempt."

"Yes, Mister Rowan, I have every faith in you to carry out the job you have had in mind for so long." Sam stood up and Rowan followed: "If you would come to the Ritz tomorrow, I'll hand you the cheque. What time do you leave for Ramsgate?"

"I can be with you at noon, sir," Rowan said before the two men headed out into the night.

Sam would walk north along St Martin's Lane to turn left for Leicester Square and Piccadilly Circus, and a welcoming bed at the Ritz Hotel. Pack Rowan hailed a passing cab and asked for a pub in Chelsea where waited a woman who had told him the previous night that he was the mightiest lover alive.

Of their immediate circumstances, both men were fairly certain, Sam to sleep alone, Rowan to stay the night with a nymphomaniac calling herself Antoinette Le Touche.

Neither man found it necessary to anticipate the days ahead, days to bring their own stories to be lived through regardless of the demands they might make. They had agreed what was to be done. Neither felt the need to consider the law of uncertainty, master unto itself, proven by the fact that certain things were not always as they seemed to be.

The next day at three o'clock in the afternoon, Gloria arrived at Townley Castle School at Ramsgate. The visit was unplanned – she had been at a health clinic to recuperate after a demanding singing tour but left thirty-six hours after she had arrived. Back at her Cadogan Square flat in London, she had found a terse note from Mendel – not his normal form. His letters, few and far between, were always long and rambling – he allowed his thoughts to flow uninhibited, flattering to Gloria since he clearly trusted her to share all the things about himself he kept secret from the world, and his father.

His interest and belief in the notion of a Homeland for the Jews was something he discussed with her in his letters, already determined that when he was old enough he would be a part of the great new country the Jews would create in the wasteland that was currently called Palestine.

The note was terse – but Gloria felt grateful that her son was showing concern for the wellbeing of Sam: "Mother – Father called on the telephone – I did not get the call. He wrote me a note – I have no idea what he wanted, wants, but his sound suggests he is very worried. In fairness, I think you should contact him as soon as you get this. Mendel."

At Ramsgate station, she took a taxi to the school and was soon feeling reassured over a cup of tea with the Matron – her son was fit and well and relatively happy at the school. When Mendel walked into the Matron's room, she thought he seemed to have grown a couple of inches in no time at all. Gloria and he shared an embrace – his mother was the only person with whom this ever happened – and Matron could see exactly why his mother was besotted with him.

They walked the school grounds, Mendel linking Gloria's arm, as proud of his beautiful mother as he might have been had she been his affianced. They talked of Sam as from a distance. Neither of them had any wish to be any nearer to him in the emotional sense, but they agreed that he always meant well.

"I'll call him as soon as I get back to London," she decided. "If he is worried about something, we should try and help."

They walked past tennis courts and a rugby pitch, with running tracks along its sides. As they turned away from the manicured areas and rambled through knee-high dry grass – there had been no rain for days – they soon came to the perimeter fence of the market gardens.

This covered an area of two acres, enclosed with tightly wired fencing that actually did keep out rabbits and other small animals. They could hear hens and poultry keeping their din alive – Mendel pointing out the coops and barns at the far end of the gardens. A moment later he was telling Gloria they also kept a number of Jersey cows, so that the school was mainly self-sufficient, something that was considered quite radical.

Across the width of the largest area which was given over entirely to potatoes, Mendel saw Joseph Jameson at work drawing late spuds from the land which, due to its protective trees and fencing masked by hessian sacking, held the favoured spud in good health up to Christmas.

Mendel called "Hello, Mister Jameson!", receiving a

friendly wave in return though the man oddly kept his head down and didn't look in their direction. He was also wearing a wide-brimmed hat which Mendel remarked on as unusual.

"He's not in the mood for you today," Gloria said. "We all get days like that." In fact, she was surprised, but tried to hide this, anxious to salve her son's feelings. He had been writing her glowing epistles in relation to his friendship with the man. Mendel talked of Joseph Jameson as somebody who was both cultured and street-wise, and never too busy to give his time and his wisdom to the growing boy.

On the way back to the main building they were somewhat closer to Jameson. This time when the boy greeted him, the gardener raised his head for a second or two, again waving in a friendly greeting, but definitely intent – or so it seemed to Gloria – on not showing his face. She thought perhaps he had been in some kind of fight and was embarrassed, but then her son said in, something akin to amazement: "He has shaved off his beard, and his hair has been cut – it was hanging to his shoulders a few days ago."

The man called Jameson was badly shaken by the sight of the woman with the boy, Mendel. He knew she was the boy's mother – had seen her once before, but she had worn a veil over her face that day, and there had been a dead chauffeur to divert his attention from her stunning appearance. She wore no veil today, not that it would have made any difference. He had been pondering on her identity for some weeks, since the lad, before he had left for Turkey with his mother, had shown him a review of a performance given by Gloria Stein at the Wigmore Hall in aid of the Jew crowd that were claiming Palestine for their own homeland.

When he recovered from the shock, Jameson – real name Jem Riley – had been coming to terms with the fact that this woman was Gloria – daughter of Rebecca – the same kike bitch that almost killed him with a kick to the head while he was only doing what any man would do to his woman when she defied him.

The same brand of anger had surfaced as he remembered how close he had been to having his way with Gloria. He salivated at the memory of her dripping like a ripe swollen plum, her body begging for the blessing of a man to give meaning to her existence. The anger and fury sucked him back to those final moments in that room at King's Cross.

He remembered letting go of Gloria's luscious breasts, hating Rebecca for interfering in something that had to happen – he had exposed himself – ready and rampant he was to fire himself into the young cow and she aching for a ride on his handle . . .

The tortured reverie shattered as the violent intruder, the same surging cacophonic noise in his head, threw him backwards with its power so that he fell among the potato trays. His legs threshed, his arms flailed, as though his limbs were trying to get him out from under the waves of pain and torment. He heard again the hell-bent scream of a woman even as he was smashed into by a force that deprived him of everything he was.

He lay there in the market garden at Townley Castle School, beginning to breathe easier as he felt the attack diminish before it seemed to retreat to some hidden compartment in his mind. In moments he had recovered sufficiently to wipe away the froth at his lips with the sleeve of his working coat. The fearsome shakes and the violent noises in his head were gone for now but his breathing was a ragged threat in his throat. There was mucus running from his nose, tears that he had no memory of weeping drying on the skin of his face – a great weariness lingering all over his body as he swore that he would have his revenge for what the Jew cow had done to him – she had left him at death's door for weeks, half alive. He believed it had been anger, and only anger, that had helped him stay out of the grip of death. He had lain for weeks in the workhouse behind St Pancras, where he had seen a drunken old nurse smother more than one terminally ill patient during the nights there. He slept badly because of this, but remained steady about his need to get his strength back. He had to do that, get back to being the man he was, because he would need his energy, and a patient way, to help him find Gloria and Rebecca. Without having to give it one single thought, this quest had become his main reason for wanting to go on living the poxy life that had been dumped on him.

Rising from the potatoes he knew that the beautiful Jew cow was the Gloria he had been seeking all down the years. Her son who was also beautifully made – a lovely boy, in need of a man to love him, would be a prize he had not expected.

He was still breathing heavily, telling himself to be patient, take time, no need to rush, you're all right. He shrugged several times to release the tension in his neck and shoulders and sat down for a minute to smoke a cigarette. In moments he went from low to high, suddenly elated, uplifted, close to happy. This often happened after an attack, but this time it was different. This time the feeling of wellbeing was related to the stroke of luck that had brought Gloria into his life again. That she should come back, it was like an acknowledgement of his right to balance up their account. He had never lost hope even when it seemed she had slipped off the face of the earth. Many a night he had slithered into half-jarred sleep, many a night was his hand-driven orgasm powered by the sight of her in his mind as he ripped her clothes away and guzzled her breasts and her secret lips, his face safe from her claws since he had tied her wrists, all of her, every shade, ever pore of her available to his every need, all of the sensation enriched by the joy he knew in choking the life out of her, watching her struggling to breathe while he pumped himself in and out of her, having her at last as she gasped for her last breath.

And now he knew that she had been sent to him so that he could fulfil his need to get even, to take her life even as he took her. As he began to walk towards his old van, his lungs seemed to expand as the power of certainty surged through him like hot liquid filling his veins – his loins pulsating now, his tumescence so powerful that he thought of relieving himself in amongst the fruit bushes. He decided no, all the power, all the

414

juice and spunk was going to be kept for her. As sure as he could draw breath, he knew that he was going to shoot his power, fire the virulent essence of his lust for Gloria up into her like bullets from a rifle.

He watched Gloria and the boy as he made his way to his van and saw them get into a taxi. By the time they were heading into Ramsgate proper, he was driving behind them at a discreet distance. In the moment he decided that she must be behind the frighteners that had landed on him recently. Mendel and him being friends – the lad must have told her – she must have checked me out. You pay enough you can find anybody – he couldn't be sure, but she wasn't above paying somebody to hurt him, to set his beard and his hair on fire – to make him believe he was about to meet his Maker. No difficulty believing that she would do that – she had done far worse the day she kicked him to death's door and left him where he lay, to die like a dog in a kip house.

Well, all to the good, he vowed. You'll enjoy all the more taking her, poling her every way you want to, and then kill the Jew bitch. The boy would have to go too. He had nothing against young Mendel, loved him in his own way – he was beautiful. But while he attended to Gloria's last hours alive, the boy would have to be bound, and there was no going back from that, not once the youngster saw his mother strangled to death.

No, he has to go, much as I would love to keep him as my special companion – letting him live could send me to the hangman's noose.

When he saw the taxi stop, he pulled over and

watched Mendel and his mother enter the Grand Hotel. Leaving the van, he walked down the street and entered the foyer. He used a pillar as cover and saw Gloria sign the register at the reception desk, feeling very lucky that he had been able to witness this. Now that he knew exactly where she was, it made things simpler all around.

Leaving the hotel he walked back towards his van with a spring in his step. He stopped on the way and bought a fish and chip supper. He would eat before he got his brain going on the details of Gloria's destiny. After he had all that worked out, he would continue with his preparations to thwart a repeat of the ordeal he had lived through recently. Just in case he was wrong and it wasn't the Jew cow that had put the frighteners on him.

Those East End faces might be regarded as wide boys and very dangerous enemies. He accepted they probably would kill somebody as quick as look at him, once the money was right. This wasn't his business but staying alive was, and he knew how to do that, no matter how heavy the opposition believed itself to be. When they came back to the house, they could very well be in for a surprise or two.

Gloria still had that shape to her, the full hips and the glorious breasts swelling with life so that her jacket had to be tailored precisely to her curves and dimensions. He imagined himself kissing those beauties, sucking on them while she writhed and groaned – driving the van towards his house he exposed himself, his laugh a cruel cackle as he caressed his great erection. "You waited a long time, boy, and now she's going to get it every way a woman can."

When he got back to the house, he carried two large cans of petrol and locked them in the tool shed, going indoors then to pour himself a stiff whiskey while he worked out exactly how he was going to handle the situation. He knew the boy was the key to Gloria – once he had Mendel, no problem getting Gloria. He just had to get the details right first time.

Walter Guildford had agreed to drive down to Ramsgate since Pack Rowan was simply woeful behind the wheel of a car, and neither of the two heavies knew how to drive. He was not happy at having to go on the trip which sounded like curtains for Jem Riley but, having come this far, he was willing to put up with almost any inconvenience to get his hands on the money Pack had promised him.

Pack had assured him he intended to bring the Riley situation to a close rapidly – "It'll be an in-and-out situation and back to town, Walter, with me knowin' I did right by The Vicar, God rest his soul."

Since he knew that Pack could be fearsome when things turned physical, Walter was somewhat mollified – the last thing he wanted was to be in any way connected with murder, even if the victim was a rodent like Riley.

"With all that money coming your way, you don't need aggro of any kind," Walter said with care, trusting that he too would be the recipient of a substantial sum of the crispy folding. Then in an effort to lighten things up a tad, he asked casually, ."Are you likely to end up marrying your partner in Ireland?"

"The same lady was on my mind even as you spoke." Pack regarded Walter with an old-fashioned look: "You're not reading the crystal ball, are you?"

Walter got a cigarette going, leaving Pack to light his own, exhaling before he said: "She has to be a very bright person to have realised the possibilities that those journals presented, Pack. A woman worth the bother I'd say, and that can't be said about that many."

"No argument there," Pack conceded, thinking that May could prove troublesome when she heard that he was not going to marry her, nor anybody else for that matter. He exhaled smoke, deciding he had enough to think about – first get Riley out of the road – then collect from the Brewer bitch, and then cross the May Murray bridge.

Pack dozed worn out, so he had said at breakfast, by this nymphomaniac who could have serviced the Brigade of Guards and asked for more. Walter was happy to escape the usual blow-by-blow account of how the latest sexual encounter had worked out – he had never been interested in other people's sex lives – he'd had enough of that during a couple of short stays in the embrace of His Majesty's Prison Service – and, as the two heavies in the back seat never said a word unless they were asked a question, he was blissfully content to savour the sound of silence as they got closer to Ramsgate and an end to the life of Jem Riley.

He found himself thinking of Rose who was the

answer to so many of his needs. A good and kind woman who drank a bit and needed a fair bit of attention between the sheets, but so very useful when it came to getting the right information in a hurry, something that was very important in his line of work.

Pack shattered his reverie by snorting abruptly and waking to shake himself fiercely before returning to his slumber. Walter found himself smiling – say what you like – bloody Pack had touched for gold with this latest deal. Full marks for the way he had managed to get his foot in the door at Eaton Square. To get a signed deal with Constance Brewer that – Pack had revealed, jarred – he was to receive fifty per cent of all monies to come from the financial settlement that had been agreed between the parties concerned. Walter was taken by the size of the numbers, breathless as the images danced on a balance sheet behind his eyes – God almighty! Pack could be in line to earn up to ten million quid and even more than that. It made the mind stagger and Walter shook his head – his incomprehension strident – how such a fortune should land in the lap of an Irish tinker, an illiterate who learned his three R's from a queer clergyman in the Scrubs! He heard his own cackle of a laugh as he tasted the sheer fucking lunacy of life, shutting his eyes for a second to clear his head, set him free of the envy arising yet again.

In that precise moment, a tractor came out of a field on his left-hand side, no more than thirty yards in front of the car. Walter opened his eyes but he had neither the time nor the driving skill to avoid the collision that followed. He yelled in fear, bracing himself – it all seemed to be happening in slow motion – the car smashing into the tractor, the driver drinking from a bottle, his head thrown back – the bottle still in his hand as he went flying, the car breaking up before Walter's eyes before his chest impacted with the steering wheel and he knew no more.

25

Autumn 1924

Sam Sweet usually enjoyed train journeys. He loved the sound of the wheels, the chuh-chuh-chuh riding the tracks, the warning contained in the whistle's cacophony, the visual offering of town and landscapes flashing past as the iron horse ploughed through space and time. 'At speeds,' he often said to himself, 'our grandfathers could not have dreamed about.'

As the train slowed to a halt at Ramsgate station he realised he had seen nothing since leaving London, his mind being almost hypnotised by the power of his concern as to what was happening to Gloria and Mendel. He had concern too, that Pack Rowan would have done what he had to do by the time Sam got to the Grand to be with his ex-wife and his son.

As Rowan's name arose in his mind he ignored once more the sound of reason as it tapped at his awareness, asking him how he could have become involved with someone like the Irish tinker, a man prepared to destroy the life of Eddie and Deirdre.

Sam knew that by the book he hadn't a leg to stand on in terms of presenting a defence against possible charges of murder and God knew what else. He had made an uneasy choice, but he knew that he would give his life for Dee and the children.

He sat down on a bench on the station platform and lit a cigarette. Gloria's telephone call last night had brought him here first thing this morning. She had seemed pleased as she informed him: "Your son is worried about you, Sam. I thought you'd like to know that." This was in relation to the note he had written to Mendel asking that his mother get in touch as soon as possible.

Gloria's call had been made in a friendly mood and he was pleased that they could be easy with each other. They had been very close once, if not as close as he had believed. He let go of the pinpoint of angst – water under the bridge. Like everybody she did what she had to do in a given situation, and when he considered what he had got himself into in recent times, he was the very last person on earth entitled to throw stones.

The real problem during their conversation was his inability to tell her what he believed to be true about the gardener, Joseph Jameson. Sam knew he would have to tell her face to face – Dee had insisted it was the only way – hence his travelling to meet her at the Grand hotel in Ramsgate.

As the taxi took him towards the town and the hotel, Sam reminded himself to telephone Deirdre as soon as he found out what was going on. He had kept details of the present situation out of her reach – on a need-to-know basis, she did not need to hear that he had offered a serious financial inducement to Pack Rowan to avenge the murder of his mentor, The Vicar.

The morning ran chilly with rain working its way into the picture but Sam was sweating. Had he seen Gloria leave the Grand hotel in a desperate hurry – had he known the reason for her hasty departure, he would have been rather more than uncomfortably warm.

At her Eaton Square home, Constance Brewer was sitting in despair as Hector White pointed at various paintings around her drawing room, his men taking his silent instructions by removing them and taking them out of the house to his removal van. Constance had to sip brandy to stop herself from crying out in anguish. She shook inwardly with rage, vowing revenge on this creature when she got her hands on the money that was hers by right. She would willingly pay a lot to find somebody who would take White's life for what he had put her through in the last week. It began with a telephone call. He was the brute that Johnstone, her runaway butler, had hired to put paid to Pack Rowan for once and for all. Damn Johnstone for his duplicity – he had disappeared with her two thousand pounds, payment up-front for White to remove the dreaded Rowan from her life.

For his part, when White realised Johnstone had scarpered with his two grand, he had given the matter some thought before deciding the old girl might well be ripe for a good plucking.

"Oi'm sorry for your trabble, marm, realoise hah dissappoin'ed ya mast be wivvat devil Johnstone takin' orf wiv yer many loike vat."

Constance Brewer was not the first older lady that Hector White had talked out of her money. In this case, since there was no money, he charmed her on his first visit to the house at Eaton Square. He brought her roses, a magnum of Dom Perignon, apologising for the "ridiculous wy Oi speak buh it was ve best me ole mam could do for me, Gord be good to 'er."

He convinced her he would fulfil the contract she had paid for, that he would deal with the runaway butler in his own good time, and that the 'Oirish Poikey' would be dealt with in the only way he would understand. He had to explain that 'Pikey' was a pejorative term for gypsy or tinker, and clearly referred to Pack Rowan.

Within days, Hector White brought his team of labourers, big silent brutes that followed his every instruction to the letter, when it came to removing the valuables from the house on Eaton Square.

"For syfe keepin', moy lydy, in case vat veevin' little rat Johnstone returns wivvee intention of tykin' your valuables. They shall be returned syfe and sand as soon as my obligation to you 'as been fulfilled."

As she heard the van leave the terrace, she screamed aloud and had to down half a glass of brandy to stop her tearing at her face with her nails. Demented, she somehow managed to call her lawyer, with great difficulty finding the breath and the willpower to yell down the telephone: "Come now and bring that wretched paper for me to sign! Call the opposition and tell them I will

424

sign provided they give you a written guarantee that
the money will be transferred within three days. And
get it done now, now this minute, before I lose my
reason!" Constance fell back against her chair and let go
a breath that was like a release.

Suddenly she felt better. She lit a cigarette and drew
the smoke deep. She would leave this Hector White to
deal with Rowan, oh yes. But, as soon as that business
was over and done with, she would find a way to make
him pay. She would spend a million if she had to –
whatever it was going to take – she would pay it to
ensure that Mister White paid the ultimate penalty for
the way he had vandalised her home and her life.

As Sam checked into the Grand Hotel the desk clerk
handed him a note. Allowing a porter to take his
overnight bag he stood by the reception desk, opening
the envelope Gloria had left for him. *'Sam – the enclosed
note from Mr Jameson is self-explanatory. I'm taking a taxi
over to his house right now. Join me there as soon as you can.'*
Sam frantically opened the second sheet of notepaper
and read: *'Missus Stein – I met Mendel outside your hotel
– he was taking air, not feeling very well, and sooner than
disturb you, I have taken him back to my house – I live at 88
Thorn Crescent – any taxi driver will know where it is.*

Respectfully yours, James Jameson.'

Pack Rowan told the taxi driver to stop while he was
still a couple of minutes' walk from the house in which

he and his team had terrified Jem Riley. Paying the man off, he walked slowly up the winding street. He was not feeling the best – 'Bruised ribs'll do that to ye, Pack lad,' he chided himself, grateful he'd taken every precaution to ensure he was on his way to put out Riley's lights. He was also feeling lucky that he was still alive.

Poor old Walter, gone for his tea, chest crushed, and the other two gobshites with broken bones all over them. Lucky I was kipping so the doctor said. Lying like a sack of spuds you don't tense up which saves you when you hit something. Good reason for havin' a snooze, provided yer not the fella doin' the drivin'. An' the gobshite strawhead that caused the wreck pissed as a puddin' in a hedge so the copper told me, out of his mind on his own home-made scrumpy and not a bruise on him. No justice. He touched his ribs, grateful for the bandages, glad he was wearing the right gear, taking more aspirin wishing he had a drink to wash them down. Working the revolver around from where it was stashed in his belt at the middle of his back. Right by his hand for when he laid eyes on Jem Riley. No talk, no fight, no messin' – as many shots as it takes and out of there – find a pillow or a cushion first thing, muffle the sound a bit.

As he moved along the side of the house, his instinct told him there was nobody home. He was usually right when he trusted the gut but because this was such an important job, he moved very carefully – Riley was crafty enough to be quiet enough you'd think the place empty –he was one evil bastard but nobody could ever accuse him of bein' a gobshite.

In fact, Pack Rowan was right – there was nobody in the house as he went into the kitchen. In the garden shed immediately behind the house, Jem Riley stood over the bound and gagged figures of Gloria and her son, Mendel. He heard someone enter the kitchen, smiled, his left hand touching the abundance of hair, as black as pitch, piled high on Gloria's head. His fingers touched one of the bright baubles she wore in her hair as some kind of fashion thing he didn't understand.

She didn't move, not wanting to annoy him or make him do anything rash. If she had any chance of getting herself and Mendel out of this insane predicament, she had to stay calm. She felt Riley's fingers touch one of the four hairpins she wore, coloured bauble tops that relieved the blue-black mountain of hair that she now cherished as a generous gift from nature. Riley opened the door silently – Gloria glanced at Mendel who seemed stunned rather than frightened – she presented eyes of steel to him, willing him to be strong and to have trust in her to get them out of this.

She had already dealt with the pictures that recall had thrown onto her mind. No time for that, what happened back then – no time for tears or recriminations – she had wished for a moment that she had gone back that day in King's Cross and slit Riley's throat. Gloria knew she would have done just that had her mother not been almost totally helpless, needing all of her daughter's strength and will to get them out of there, away from the monster who now had her and her son in his power. Be brave – she willed the words to Mendel – we are in trouble, but things are not always as they seem.

Sam, having no luck with taxis, took some directions from a man who seemed to know his way around. He began walking rapidly, keeping his eye peeled for a cab. He tried to hold down his anxiety, hoping that Rowan would have done his work and that there was nothing for him to worry about where the safety of Gloria and Mendel was concerned.

Pack Rowan had found a stinking cushion against which he was pressing the revolver. Still under the impression that there was nobody but himself in the house, he pushed open a door and stepped into a disgusting ground-floor room with an unmade bed in it. As he stepped through, a bucket of cold water tumbled onto him and he stumbled in his efforts to get out from under. Banging himself on the edge of an old chest of drawers he was gasping for breath when Jem Riley, through the single window, blasted him with a shotgun.

Rowan was thrown backwards. and slammed against the edge of the open door. By the time he hit the floor, Riley was hurrying to the shed to fetch Gloria.

Riley's adrenalin was pumping and he felt elated that it was indeed his old enemy Kelly who had put the frighteners on him. When someone had sworn to kill you, it felt good to know he was lying dead inside in the room. His joyous relief was immense as he quivered in anticipation of all that he was going to do to Gloria.

Sam swore as another taxi passed him by. He pressed on in the direction he had been pointed, hoping to heaven that Rowan was earning the ten thousand he'd paid him to deal with Riley.

Gloria watched as Riley made Mendel more comfortable in the shed, wrapping him in an old tartan rug, so that though he was bound and gagged he would not get all that cold.

"I'll be back for you soon, lad," Riley said with a smile: "Have no fear. I'm still your friend."

In her mind Gloria was screaming 'You filthy liar!' grinding her teeth in her determination not to let anything show to this monster, who even now was untying the ankle bonds and pushing her out of the shed towards the house. She had heard the explosion a minute before and guessed that somebody had died. Riley had been expecting somebody to show up – once he had her and Mendel bound and gagged, he had finished his preparations against unwanted invasion. Now he was cock-a-hoop, shoving her roughly into the bedroom where somebody lay on the floor like a dead man.

Riley barely glanced at the body on the floor. When he was finished having this woman he had ached to mount down all the years, he would kill her and her son and lay them down alongside the tinker. Then he would use the two cans of petrol from the shed and start a fire that would burn up the bodies and reduce the house to a cinder.

He threw Gloria onto the bed and found a blanket to cover Rowan's body. Turning to her as he did so, he gave her a grin that made her stomach heave: "I wouldn't want the likes of him seein' what I'm goin' to do to you, my lady." He made a little bow from the waist and grabbed at his genitals, his cackling laugh to Gloria's mind that of a man gone mad: "I goin' to give you such a seeing to – down all the years I never stopped wanting you."

Gloria watched him, determined not to be in fear of him, wanting to face all the demons he had to offer. For the moment he didn't seem to notice that she was not fighting to break free.

She saw him step out of his trousers, watched him as he stroked his erection, nodding at her as though he was preparing something very special for her pleasure.

"You left me for dead, your dirty Jew whore. You left me without a thought that I saved you and your mother from certain death one night on a London street."

He was removing her shoes, close enough that she could see the saliva dripping from his mouth – he looked like a mongrel dog salivating and she steeled herself not to show any emotion to him. Clearly he was intent on terrifying her but she would not be his victim. She felt more than ever grateful for the self-defence courses she had been attending ever since she had decided that her life was bound up with the new homeland for the Jews in Palestine.

His hands on her legs after he had ripped off her skirt – she had a memory flash from the room at Kings Cross some twenty years before – his hands up under her vest on her breasts, the girl almost fainting in revulsion – his angry grip then as he fingered her vagina as though she was his slave. 'All in the past, Gloria, he can do what he may. He will not touch a part of you that matters – soap and hot water will wash away those things that once made you want to die – to be touched in that way – not now, not now, Riley – and may God help you should I find one moment . . .'

He ripped away her knickers, stopping her mind for a moment. He was stooping, bending down to lick at her below. Not satisfied, he pulled a knife from his belt and held it under her nose.

"Be sure I'm going to have my way with you, Gloria. I am going to ride you to hell and back. I am going to have you every way a man can have a woman – I have this knife and I will slit your throat if you try to interfere with what I am going to do. I dreamed, screamed for this chance, the time when I would get even for what you did to me in that kip-house in King's Cross. If you try to thwart me, you will pay dearly. I'll cut you up into little strips. So open your legs now and don't dare defy me."

Gloria opened her legs without allowing him to stare her down. She saw him roll up a heavy bedcover and moved as he shoved her so that he could raise her bottom off the bed. He probed her with a finger and she stifled her breath of disgust before it became audible. She would give him nothing, not even that.

He tore off his long-sleeved vest and untied his boots and kicked them and his trousers away from him, his erection powerful as he straightened up. She bit her lip and used all the techniques she had been taught – she would not to show him anything. He undid the cloth around her mouth and she breathed a sigh of relief. He stood over her, handling himself, drawing the foreskin back and forth over the puce knob. She stared at him, giving him no sign that she was afraid.

Quickly he leaned down and ripped away her silk blouse and her brassiere and she saw his eyes glow before he leaned over, the knife against her throat and began to suck her nipples, first one then the other.

She closed her eyes briefly and thought how brave her son had been in the moment when he realised that something wasn't right about Mister Jameson. Riley biting her nipple brought her back to the moment and the stinking room and the erection that now hovered by her mouth. "You know what you're going to do now, don't you, Gloria?" She remained silent and he said in a hoarse, sex-laden whisper. "Open your mouth or I'll slice off your ear." She looked up at him, ignored his words, and made up her mind that she would go through with this because as long as he got what he wanted in the moment, she might yet get the precious seconds she needed to turn things around.

Sam finally found a taxi and discovered he had been walking in the wrong direction. He bit down on his frustration and asked the driver to go as quickly as possible.

Riley sat looking at her, smoking a cigarette and smiling little secret smiles that only he could savour – Gloria more than ever convinced he had lost a major part of his mind, would willingly have smoked a cigarette to help her lose the taste of him. Above all, she was determined to hold on, wait and pray that her time would come. He killed the cigarette and stood up, again handling himself, cackling delightedly as he found another erection mounting in the palm of his hand.

"This time I'm going to mount you missionary style. Later, we'll do a few variations, Gloria. But this time, I am going to kiss you, suck your mouth, eat your tongue and you are going to give me what I give you or I will cut out your tongue. Do you hear me? Do you understand what I'm saying to you? 'Cos if you don't and you don't do what I want, you will choke on your own blood, woman. Do you hear me and do you understand?"

His manic sound stopped only as he had to gasp for breath. It seemed to Gloria that his mind had run away on him, that he could not stop it from tumbling over itself in his effort to impress upon her how helpless she was.

"I'll kiss you, Jem. I'll do whatever you want. I'll be your woman, anything, but just don't hurt my son Mendel! He thinks you are his friend." Gloria said the words passionately, wanting him to believe her.

He stopped as though he had been slapped in the face and he gave her all his attention for some moments. "I'm going to cut the rope away from your wrists. While I'm stuck up you, I will be holding your wrists alongside your head. The knife will be by my right hand. If you play fair, give me what you just said you will we might be able to work something out. If you defy me, if you try to take advantage of me, you'll pay with your life."

"I won't, Jem. I won't. Oh come and do it. Do it to me. Let me show you I won't defy you!" Gloria put all her acting skill into her voice and her eyes and she saw him begin to allow for the possibility that she was being straight with him.

He moved the rolled-up bed cover further under her bottom and he prised her legs further apart. She felt the rope cut at her wrists and, following his order, she placed her hands up alongside her head.

'Halfway there,' she thought, keeping her eyes on him all the time. It was his eyes that told her he was about to plough into her and she braced herself for the pain this would cause. For a moment her mind went numb and then he was driving in and out of her, his hands holding her wrists, his chest heaving as he fought for breath.

"Oh, oh God," Gloria almost vomited on the lie as it shot out of her mouth: "Oh God, you are making me come. Oh God!" On the words she began to buck underneath him, meeting his thrusts with all her strength, needing to gather some pinpoint of power over him if she was to survive this day. She saw the surprise in his eyes as she met his every move, watched his mouth open further as he fought for more air, then she felt his hands move from her wrists, going down her sides to take her buttocks as he blundered towards his own orgasm.

In the very moment when she was about to take his life, he grabbed her wrists again because he had to take a breather from the power of his thrusting. At the same time, Gloria wondered was she imagining things as she saw the man come up off the floor unleashing a terrifying yell of fury as he aimed to grab Riley with both hands.

Riley let go of Gloria's wrists and turned in the instant to smash the back of his right fist against the temple of Pack Rowan. The tinker fell to the floor unconscious, Riley yelling in triumph: "I'll cut your bastard heart out, Rowan, when I'm done with this whore!"

He turned back to Gloria, his eyes opening in terror as he saw the weapon in her hand. Stunned for that single moment, he allowed her the time to make her one killing move, and she plunged the steel pin into his temple with such venom that the red bauble handle lodged on his skin as the switchboard of nerves underneath it was shattered, putting an end to the life of Jem Riley.

Sam was coming into the room with Mendel in tow as Gloria pulled the pin from Riley's temple and kicked him in the groin even as he fell sideways onto the foul floor.

Mendel's eyes stood out like organ stops, his breathing distorted as he watched his mother use a piece of her torn blouse to wipe Riley's blood from the hairpin of reinforced steel, introduced into her life by her personal instructor who was preparing those women who would be among the first to go to Palestine.

Realising that Mendel was gaping at her naked breasts she covered herself and got off the bed to find her skirt. There was nothing she could do – Mendel could see she had killed Riley – she was half-naked – clearly she had been raped – he would have to deal with it himself – he might turn to his father which would be no bad thing.

Right now, she had to get to a tap, get some water and soap and hope against hope that the monster now lying dead on the floor had not made her pregnant.

"I'm so sorry, Gloria." Sam remained by his son, his hand on the boy's shoulder. "I couldn't get a taxi."

"It's all right," she said, not looking at her son.

"Did he?"

"He raped me. I'm going into the kitchen. I need a few minutes' privacy to clean myself up. Take Mendel out of here. I won't keep you waiting long."

As she started to leave, Sam said, in back of a weary sigh: "I couldn't tell you Jameson was Jem Riley. I couldn't just say that on the telephone – been better if I had."

"You're right there," Gloria said frankly. "But you wanted to be with me when you told me that, right?"

Sam nodded: "Of course."

"Thanks for that."

Before leaving the wretched house, Sam left Mendel with Gloria while he went to take a look at the corpse of Pack Rowan. Coming in from the outside it took a moment or two for his eyes to become accustomed to the gloom. Riley lay naked on his back, his eyes wide open as though he would be surprised for eternity. Sam went and pulled back the faded drape over the front window and to his surprise found no trace of Pack Rowan. His foot knocked against something and when he picked it up he was holding a bullet-proof vest that weighed a ton. Sam could not but smile, his questionable admiration for the tinker overcoming his reservations.

Throwing the vest into a corner he threw a foul-smelling blanket over the corpse. Then he left the house.

Having started Riley's vehicle, he left Gloria and Mendel for a minute and went to the shed at the rear of the house. Finding what he wanted, he took the twin cans of petrol back inside and sprayed their contents all over the body of Jem Riley. This done he sprinkled the remainder liberally about the foul room. Stepping outside of the room he put a match to the torch he had fashioned from newspaper and throwing it inside he pulled the door shut. Within a minute he saw flames rising through the window and backed Riley's van out onto the street – to drive away towards Ramsgate without glancing back.

The following day, Constance Brewer ignored the reaction of dismay from Sir Albert Whimby as he viewed the virtually empty walls of her private study. He saw her mouth go tight as a rat-trap but he wasn't to be denied his protest. "Good God, old thing, you have been consumed, eaten up by bloody roulette!"

"Oh shut up, Albee, and show me where to sign this damned paper."

"You'll just shoo it all down the drain, anyway, but as you're so fond of telling me, it's not any of my damn business."

"Precisely, you old fart. The first cheque I shall write will be to you, after that I will bid you goodbye, have no further truck with you as a lawyer – you're far too impertinent."

Without a word, Sir Albert went to the drinks table and poured two very large measures from a pot-bellied bottle of Napoleon V.S.O.P. He came forward then and presented a balloon to Constance.

"And what is this for, may I ask?"

"I want to toast your threat of a few moments ago – to the end of a tortuous professional relationship!" He raised his glass and Constance, with genuinely mixed feelings, did the same.

Then the old woman found a whimsical smile. "Of course, should you learn some table manners I may extend to you the occasional dinner invitation."

She emptied her glass with a flourish and Whimby, having done likewise, brought the agreement between Constance and the Brewer Estate to her desk.

"Before you write your signature, old girl, Samuel Sweet *et al*, they have to be here. Sweet has to sign the agreement too."

Constance, who seemed to have forgotten this caveat, blanched at the very idea. Whimby waved the paper and she nodded her head.

"Get on with it, Albee."

Alex Gibbon represented the Estate – there had been no need of a defence barrister since they were still some way from going to court when the old lady finally accepted the offer.

Sam Sweet stood alongside Alex as he and Sir Alfred checked out both sets of papers on the desk. A nod between them signified that all was in order. All that was needed now was the old lady's signature followed by that of Sam Sweet with Alex Gibbon as his witness.

Constance didn't address a word to Alex Gibbon or Sam Sweet. She allowed Sir Albert to help her from her chair and over to the great mahogany desk. It took her some moments to sit comfortably and she indicated to Whimby to pour her another drink. As the ageing barrister scurried to obey her silent command, the old woman picked up the pen and dipped it into the inkwell before her.

"May I ask you, Mister Sweet, if you have heard anything of Pack Rowan?"

"I have heard that he seems to have disappeared, ma'am." Sam smiled inwardly at her duplicity. She wanted to know something so it was politic to be civil to the Jew.

"Do you regard your information as reliable, may I ask?"

Sam looked at her and said matter-of-factly, "I wouldn't stake my life on it."

Constance sniffed and lifted the balloon glass Whimby had placed by her hand. She put down the pen and sniffed the cognac before she put the glass to her head and gulped down what was rather a large drink.

Reacting to the power of the amber nectar as it found its mark, she exhaled a breath and picked up the pen. She adjusted her reading spectacles and set herself to write her name where indicated.

At that moment, something happened inside the old woman and she seemed to go rigid for several moments. Then she started to shake a little. This led to her emitting a short gasp that might have been caused by an aggressive proctologist ramming his finger fiercely into that spot where the sun never shines.

Her hand clasped the pen tightly, at which point she seemed to set like cement.

Nobody moved, least of all Constance Brewer.

The three men looked at each other and Sam said softly: "Looks to me like she's had a stroke."

Sir Alfred Whimby tottered slightly, recovered sufficiently to nod his head in agreement, "Typical bloody Constance," he mumbled in an aggrieved voice: "She couldn't have waited a few more minutes."

As he moved to the desk, Sam and Alex broke into large smiles, giving each other thumbs up – the stroke of good fortune put an end to the agreement since Constance had not signed it.

Whimby touched Constance Brewer on the shoulder. "It's Albee, old thing. Are you all right?"

He got no answer and Constance did not stir. The old man now bent over and looked up at the face of the old woman. He let her be then, and turning to face the others, he said in resignation, "Upon my word, her eyes are still working. There's life there. However, Madam is not at home!"

"And forgive me being hysterical, Dee," Sam choked on his laughter as he related the moment when Sir Alfred Whimby uttered the verdict that condemned Constance Brewer to a living death for as long as her natural deterioration needed to take its course. The dowager had indeed had a stroke, which had left her almost totally paralysed – but it seemed that a part of her mind had been spared.

"And she has to live with that," Sam said and began to laugh again. "God, I have to stop talking about it – these bad jokes just keep on coming."

Dee rose from her chair facing him across the fireplace in her drawing room. As she poured him a cognac, she smiled, and when she brought it to him she kissed his head, leaving her lips there at his hair for almost a minute.

"I accept that I was hard, Sam, in relation to the whole business involving Constance and that man Rowan, and the woman running the public house." Dee sat down and sipped her white wine: "You were wonderful. You went after justice with all your magnificence, and, in the end, that's how it seems to have worked out."

Sam exhaled smoke and sipped his brandy. "It's only in the trenches you can find out what you're prepared to do when the going gets tough. I have to admit, Dee, I was shocked at times by how far I was willing to go – I know it was with the view of saving you and Eddie above all, but there was Séamus, Angela, Kelly, and of course, me, to be considered, too. We all had to be saved from God knows what. But, my thoughts, my willingness at times to ignore the voice of reason – frightened me more than I can tell."

"Is it likely to give you trouble in the future? Can you not just put it behind you, now that we have been relieved of Constance with her sadness and her madness?"

Sam knew she was concerned for his health and his wellbeing. "I don't think it works like that, Dee. What I am sure about is that I intend devoting much of my time to the search for truth. I wanted badly to win against Constance, for the safety, the future of all of us. But it became something else. I just got caught by *the wanting*, and when it was at its most demanding, I felt pretty wretched. Wouldn't have mattered who it was that bought into the Rowan/Murray deal – anybody willing to stoop so low, they were beneath contempt – but the point I'm making is that *I wanted* so badly to win that it made me bad, in that I felt bad from the inside. The chronic *wanting* created spaces in me for anger and resentment and indeed, fear that I might not get what I wanted. With Constance bringing in Pack Rowan and God knows who else, I felt entitled to do the same – I worked with Rowan in an attempt to get Constance to quit. Quite unconsciously, I told him we were alike. I offered him the notion of 'The Tinker and the Jew,' in the Irish context – both outsiders, that kind of thing. It was only afterwards I realised we were alike in another way too – both of us – we were ready to do almost anything to get what we wanted. And that frightened me greatly. I don't want to ever feel like that again. I know that I would not be willing to live like that, no matter what the cost to me personally."

Dee rose and came to him. She embraced his head gently, pressing him against her body. "I pray to live long enough to be there when you find all that you are. You are a magnificent man, yet, like the rest of us, you are just the tip of your own iceberg."

She drew him up from the chair. She kissed him and let him know she was in a demanding mood. "We've seen so little of each other lately, I want you now and I want us to make love more often than we have been doing of late."

"You're preaching to the converted," Sam smiled and tucked his hand under her arm.

"Then take charge of that end of things, Sam. You know I have never had a headache since we have been together." She grinned at him and he lifted her up as though she was a feather.

"I'm going to be an unmerciful lover tonight," he said as he carried her up the stairs.

"I can relax so," Deirdre said, laughing happily, "you being a man of your word."

26

Pack Rowan whose real name was Eddie Kelly, and James Jameson whose real name was James Riley, seemed to disappear from the face of the earth at about the same time. It is a fact that the old house in which Jameson had rented for three years burned to ashes during the autumn of 1924.

A woman named May Murray who claimed to be the fiancée of Pack Rowan, turned up in London and spent time and money trying to trace the last movements of the man she had been going to marry. To this end she hired a private enquiry agent, Prod McLoughlin, who charged her much less than his usual rate for his services, finally having to tell her that this was a case of a resourceful man who did not want to be found.

May Murray returned to the Dunbla Tavern just before Christmas, 1924, where she continued to serve drink and food to the same customers who had patronised her house from the day she first opened for business. During the year that followed, May was seen to be drinking heavily, and on several occasions she left the bar while customers were still on the premises and wandered off into the darkness of the countryside. It was said of her that she was drinking herself to death over her lost love, but none dared suggest in her presence that they had Pack Rowan in mind for that particular role.

On the day of the Autumn equinox in 1925 – May turned up at the end of the wedding ceremony of Séamus Byrne and his life partner, Angela Keegan, who declared as they left the church: "I have finally made an honest man of my own Kerryman."

It was clear to all in the little chapel by Killiney that May was under the weather but nobody commented, and there was no suggestion that she was anything but welcome to look on like some others who were not in the wedding party.

In the wedding group, as pictures were being taken by a professional photographer, Sam Sweet and his pregnant wife, Deirdre, were to the front of the group. They had filled the roles of Best Man and Matron of Honour to Séamus and Angela.

It was a fine day but cold and everybody wanted the pictures over and done with so that the wedding party could repair to Dunbla House where a sit-down meal and all the trimmings would be provided by Bray's best hotel – and served by people hired for the day.

As the Wedding Party dispersed to various motor cars, Séamus and Angela were already in the Rolls

Royce, while Sam held Dee's hand, his intention being to help her into the car with their friends. Deirdre was four months pregnant with the couple's second child – their small daughter Kathleen was at home in the nursery of Dunbla House with her nanny.

As Sam prepared to give Dee a little help getting into the car, May Murray's voice called loudly: "Sam Sweet!"

Sam turned to find the blonde woman standing not six feet away, pointing a revolver at him. Dee attempted to get between them. Sam held her with a stiff arm so that she was to one side of where he stood.

"What can I do for you, Miss Murray?" Sam kept his eyes on the gun, saying to Dee from the side of his mouth: "Stay calm, love, don't worry."

"You can tell me what you did with Pack Rowan. Tell me where you buried him after you killed him." May was unsteady but there was a manic glint in her eyes that suggested she knew what she was doing, and felt herself capable of doing it.

"I have no idea where Mister Rowan is, and I'm not sure I understand this talk of killing. I hardly knew the man."

"You killed him. The money you promised if he met you at the Ritz Hotel, that was just bait to get him over to England where you could get rid of him, kill him so that he wouldn't be there to help the old woman take you pair for a fortune."

"I'm sorry for your trouble, Miss Murray, I really am, but I have no idea where this nonsense came from – now, you'll have to excuse me, I have a wedding reception to attend."

Sam moved to help Dee into the Rolls. It was then that May Murray started shooting. The first bullet hit Deirdre who cried out and would have fallen to the ground had Sam not scooped her up and into the car. Closing the door he turned to confront May Murray even as she was turning the gun on herself.

Before he could reach her she shot herself in the chest, falling backwards against people running to get clear of danger. Somebody ran back into the church to use the telephone to call the police.

As the equinox ended at midnight Sam sat by Deirdre's bed in the Mater Hospital. He had been there since she had come back from surgery at six o'clock. A nurse brought him tea and he nodded a silent thanks. As he sipped the brew he saw a flutter of Deirdre's eyelashes and he put the cup and saucer to one side. Then he sat holding his breath while he waited to see if she was going to wake up.

Moments later, Dee came around, finding a wisp of a smile and giving his hand a squeeze. "I knew you'd be there when I woke up." A tear rolled down her cheek: "Always there, always there for me, my Sam Sweet."

"The medical men say you'll be back to normal within a few weeks."

She nodded her head slightly, and sniffed back on other tears. "I won't be the same though. You know that, don't you?"

Sam nodded, finding it impossible to speak.

"We didn't just lose our baby today. We won't be

having any more 'childer'. Are you all right with that, Sam?"

"Is there no use in me talking to you?" he said, like he was playing with her. "I'm in deadly earnest, Dee. I have you and Kathleen and our lovely brood of teenagers – I ask for no more. So put your mind at rest and know that had you been killed on me today, I do not know how I would have survived the hours till now."

"Asham Gopal wouldn't approve of that kind of talk, would he?" She found a tired, wan smile for him, touching his hand.

"It's all right," he said chuckling: "I've a long way to go before I get to *perfect*.

Dee slowly raised her hand to touch his face. "I know you forever and you've always been perfect to me."

"Does that mean I can ask a special favour?"

"Ask me anything you want, rascal!"

"Would you be agreeable to us having Robin to stay with us for two years or so?"

Dee tried to sit up but in the instant her condition put paid to that idea. Taking a few moments to regain her breathing, she said with relish: "Are you serious, Sam? I'd love that." Her eyes were wide in anticipation even though bearing the remnants of her recent sedation. "How can such a great thing happen to us?"

"Gloria's going to Palestine for a couple of years and perhaps for longer. She can't take Robin with her. It's simple, Dee. She needs us to mind her daughter."

"Tell her *with a heart and a half*."

"I will so," he said, starting to rise as he saw the Ward Sister approaching with a look in her eye.

"I'm on my way, Sister."

She responded to his smile while turning to Dee. "This wonderful man has been sitting here for six hours. Where on earth did you find him, Missus Sweet?"

Dee smiled and let go of his hand. "No good asking me that, Sister. They broke the mould when they made Sam."

"Correction, Sister. They broke the mould and then they made me anyway."

The woman laughed and Deirdre said: "That's what Vicky used to say about you, you old cheat!"

As the nurse was taking her pulse, Dee said: "The truth is he found me in Long Lane when I was four or five years old and I was never the same again."

"Time for you to rest now." The Sister tucked Dee in: "We'll give you a little draught to help you sleep." With a nod to Sam she moved away, warmed by the incorrigibility of a woman who had nearly died today, and the kind of husband that was a new experience in her book.

"I know you won't be sitting here all night, but," Dee tapped her heart, "you'll be in here wrapped up in me."

He nodded, gave her a tiny wave, hearing her say: "I love you."

"I love you, Dee, and the more I get to know you, the more I like you." He moved away, seeing her start to drift off to sleep. Stepping outside the ward he stopped and let the tears come. For several minutes he allowed the burst of emotion he had been sitting on since Deirdre had been shot. He was quite drained by the time he was able to walk down the stairs. On the way to the street, he importuned the Sister that he might use the telephone to tell the family the good news that their mother was as comfortable as could be expected.

"Wonderful, Daddy!" His daughter Sarah's voice rang musical in her relief and her joy. "We'll surely still be up when you come home. There'll be no sleep on us tonight after this wonderful news."

"I'll stay in Merrion Square tonight, darling. I want to nip in and see Dee first thing in the morning."

Duty done, Sam made his way out onto the street. He was thinking about Robin, the girl conceived by Gloria as Jem Riley had raped her. She was a beautiful child, 'a rubbing of her mother', and he was happy that she would be coming to stay.

When Gloria had first let him know that she was pregnant, he had been appalled – who would want to have a child by a monster like Riley? She however saw it differently. "The longer I live, Sam," Gloria had said with a quiet acceptance, "the more I realise that things are rarely as they seem to be. I want to have this child. This innocent, untarnished life inside me deserves to be born."

He stepped out of the Mater where John waited with the car. Sam gave him the good news about Dee and was about to step into the Rolls when a tall, very beautiful woman with hair the colour of brandy under the lamplight, stopped and said: "Forgive me being so bold, but aren't you Mister Sam Sweet?"

Always happy to talk to a lovely woman, Sam admitted, "A rather tired, ageing sort of Sam Sweet – that's me all right."

She held out her hand: "Mister Sweet, I'm Kitty Daly.
I'm a sometime actress and a full-time painter, and ever
since I saw your photo in the *Irish Times*, I've been
trying to find a way to meet you."

Sam was genuinely curious. "May I ask why?"

"I want to paint you," she said frankly. "From the
moment I saw the photo, and let's be honest – pictures
in newspapers don't do justice to anybody."

"So, having seen me in the flesh, have you had a
radical change of mind?"

"Good God! No! I'm even more consumed by the
need to have you sit for me. Would you? Would that be
possible?"

Sam heard himself saying: "What are you doing on
the streets at this time of night?"

"I was doing the coats in Old Time Hall – that's a
dance hall, Céilidhe and Old Time. The pay is small but
y'know. Just finished there, and I'm on my way to the
chipper to get a late dinner."

"I'd be very happy to give you a lift, join you in the
chipper, or, if you'd rather, I could take you for dinner
somewhere else. Interested?"

"If I choose 'somewhere else', will you let me try
and talk you into sitting for me in my studio?"

Sam pointed at the back seat of the Rolls. "If I fall
asleep over my soup, you mustn't take it personally. My
wife was shot today and for a while there it was touch
and go." He raised his hand to reassure her: "Deirdre's
going to be fine though we lost a baby. Now, do you still
want to go to dinner?"

She nodded, sniffing back her tears and got into the

car. John closed the door behind Sam before getting in behind the wheel.

"You're a very beautiful woman, Kitty Daly," Sam said honestly.

"I know," Kitty said wiping her eyes with a white linen hankie "I've always been, so you get used to it. And you know what, Mister Sweet?"

"Call me Sam," he said.

"You know what, Sam? Beauty is all very well, but when you need a packet of cigarettes you have to put money to all this beauty stuff or you go without a smoke."

Sam chuckled. "Have you always been this forth-right?"

Kitty laughed shortly: "Only since I discovered that men love it." She laughed louder and he felt she was relieved. "I'm only joking, Sam," she said, wondering if he could tell she was lying.

Dee was thinking yet again about losing the baby. The loss was a thing of real sadness but, ever since the night when she had bargained with God, offering her return to the fold as a symbol of her sincerity, she had been waiting for something to happen.

To her mind it was inevitable that she would be punished for daring to make arrangements with God, a deity in whom – despite her willingness and the endless rivers of wishing – she found it hard to believe. Because she saw the loss of her baby as a punishment she had to allow that there was some power that balanced the books in the day-to-day life. Then she considered, for the first time, that all of it was just that, the day-to-day life happening, the good, the bad and the unwanted all part of the same tapestry.

She had prayed for Mary Kearney that night in the laneway by the clinic – her plea seemed to have helped Mary deliver a twelve-pound baby boy. After that Dee had continued praying – the words learned in childhood bringing comfort at times. She went on *acting as if* in the hope that in acting she would be relieved of her agnosticism.

Before long, Sam's generosity enabled her to provide Mary, the twenty-three-year-old Civil War widow and mother of three small children, with a home at his house on Leinster Road. Mary was installed as housekeeper, earning a wage and a home as she became carer to the transients passing through the Lying-in Clinic, that were desperately in need of a temporary home. The fact that Mary's life was so much better than before added to the guilt Deirdre felt over her inability to believe in the God of her growing-pain days. Because of her mother's total belief she had early wanted to embrace the entire Roman Catholic lexicon that Aunt Molly Harney had introduced into Elizabeth's life.

Failing, Dee had hidden her disbelief. Going to college, exposed to the predictable student discontent with all things adult, facilitated her need to become a Free Thinker which, now that she was no longer hiding her truth, was how she expected to be for whatever time was left to her in the land of the living.

Lying in the bed in the Mater Hospital, she could not deny that alongside her sense of loss ran a stream of relief. With a gentle sigh, as deep sleep claimed her, she let go, believing she was back on level terms, her integrity intact as she allowed the gods their space, while claiming the same privilege for herself.

EPILOGUE

Christmas Day 1924

The morning was uncommonly mild for the time of year and Sam felt grateful for the space and the silence about him as he climbed the path by the Pets' Cemetery. He smiled at the thought that it seemed steeper these days, putting it down, just like the twinge in the hip, to oncoming age.

Looking down from the summit he was not that surprised to see a couple of people bathing in the surf while he sat down on his favourite rock and reached into the huge pocket of his greatcoat for the very last of the unopened Christmas cards. He smiled as he looked again at the unfamiliar handwriting, wondering why he had not just read it in his study with the others.

The postmark read Wellington, New Zealand – he knew nobody living there – had this simple fact intrigued him? Could that be why it had been given its own private opening? He chuckled at his desire to adorn the morning's garment with a hem of mystery. "Open the bloody thing, Sam, and stop the song and dance!" Had he actually yelled the words aloud before he ripped open the envelope?

And found himself looking at a Christmas card with a lone man, a Maori warrior, hurling a spear under the umbrella of the words *Happy Christmas*.

None the wiser as to the sender's identity, Sam opened the card. The penmanship in black ink was bold, forceful enough to suggest to his romantic nature that the words wanted to fly from the page.

"*Hello Sam Sweet,*" he read. "*This is the first Christmas card I have ever written. I am making money here in Wellington, some of it (a little bit anyway) legitimately.*

This warrior caught my eye, reminding me of myself and reminding me of you, for like us both he is an outsider, regardless of the fact that he was here before Them.

I wish you a good life. I doubt that we shall ever meet again. But life seems to happen at the behest of some power that has never felt any need to ask my permission as to where the next step will take me. So, who knows!"

There was no signature, not that Sam needed to see one to identify the writer. He put the card into his inside pocket, knowing he would keep it.

By the end of January 1925 he had learned through the good offices of the enquiry agent, Prod McLoughlin, that the account at the Westminster Bank at Hammersmith in London had been cleared of the ten thousand pounds he had paid to Pack Rowan. But, Prod had written: "*Five hundred pounds has been left on deposit in that name which might suggest to some that our friend intends to some day revisit these shores.*"

THE END

Direct to your home!

If you enjoyed this book why not visit our website:

www.poolbeg.com

and get another book delivered straight to your home or to a friend's home!

www.poolbeg.com

All orders are despatched within 24 hours.

Published by Poolbeg.com

Dancers
OF
Fortune

LEE DUNNE

It's 1902, and Sam Sweet from Dublin's Little Jerusalem dives into the Liffey after a street arab who has stolen his wallet. But little does Sam know that this one crazy act will change the course of his life forever.

When the beautiful Miss Victoria Brewer witnesses the heroics of a dashingly exotic man risking life and limb in the capital's raging river, she is struck by an immediate attraction. The unlikely pair recognise something in each other and become passionate lovers. Sam is an ambitious building contractor and Victoria heiress to her family's brewing fortune. Victoria's twin Arthur becomes Sam's firm friend and together they prosper in business. Sam will stop short of nothing on his road to prosperity, but when he meets and falls for the beautiful and devout Jewish actress Gloria he realises how far away from his Jewish faith and life he has come.

As the years pass and the Irish Republican Brotherhood exposes the discontent of the Irish people, Sam and Arthur come to realise their complicity in the system which keeps Irish people poor. By Easter 1916 both men and Arthur's wife Deirdre are heavily involved in the cause, with Sam becoming one of Michael Collins' right-hand men and taking danger and risk in his stride.

ISBN 1-84223-214-2

Published by Poolbeg.com

Goodbye to the Hill

LEE DUNNE

"The Hill was a scab, a sort of dry sore on the face
Dublin. By the age of ten you knew all about puddi
clubs and doses of the pox and you smiled sardonicall
even though you didn't know that that's what you we
doing, whenever anybody talked about Santy Cla
and the Stork and all that rubbish. That was how it w
on the Hill, you learned fast whether you wanted to
not."

When *Goodbye to the Hill* first appeared it was
controversial bestseller. Forty years later, L
Dunne's bitingly honest novel about life
Dublin's slumland is still
potent. It is rich in humou
truth and honesty and its her
the loveable Paddy Magui
who nurses a burnin
ambition to get off the Hill,
one of the most memorab
characters in fiction.

40th Anniversary Edition

ISBN 1-84223-251-7

Published by Poolbeg.com

Barleycorn Blues

LEE DUNNE

Set in New York and Dublin, *Barleycorn Blues* explodes into life when alcoholic writer Joe Collins collides with hopeless drunk photographer Telly Sampras outside an AA meeting in New York.

The two men decide to join forces to beat their addiction, but their willpower is severely tested when they encounter two captivating women with weaknesses of their own.

In no time Joe and Telly find themselves entangled with political corruption, hit men, and a ménage a trois and start breaking their own rules. Can they keep on the straight and narrow?

ISBN 1-84223-212-6